MASTEF
REICH

A Joe Brennan Spy Thriller

By IAN LOOME

This story uses U.S spellings of common words.

PROLOGUE

1.

ISLA QUIRIQUINA, CHILE
Off the Coast of the City of Concepcion,
August 23, 1915

The searchlight swept the beach in a long, slow arc, the swirling, angry Pacific Ocean spraying the beam with white droplets of mist. It slid meticulously across the sand from side to side, meeting midway and crossing paths with a beam from another tower, a half-kilometer to the south.

German Intelligence Officer Wilhelm Canaris ducked down behind the overturned wooden fishing boat. It wasn't much cover, just a twelve-foot-long skiff encrusted with old barnacles, years after it was wrecked on rocks, washed up and left on the beach as driftwood.

At just a few inches past five feet tall, the German officer was accustomed to his stature being a disadvantage. But it helped in the moment, the thatch of dark shadows behind the boat affording ample refuge.

He wore his blonde hair in a crewcut, his blue eyes stern and intense at all times, as if always deep in thought.

Sirens began to wail, a prolonged, terrible drone.

They had discovered his escape from the British internment camp. If he were fortunate and they followed typical behavior, they would head for the bay and the docks. Fishermen from the nearby town of Concepcion were allowed use of the harbor during the day, to drop materials off and to load new provisions. When weather was rough, they would let them anchor in the harbor overnight.

It was such a night. The air was cool and windy, the sea choppy, white-capped peaks slapping the shoreline. If anyone had a boat available to take a man to the mainland, that was where they would be, and that was where they would expect him to go.

The British were loud, coarse and crass when dealing with their German opponents. But they had been careful about being too forceful with the local population. They made it clear they knew they were guests, and that if no one aided or abetted their enemies, they would try to keep life as normal as possible. As normal as possible during a war, anyway, one that had grown from a minor dispute over regional politics into an international conflagration with seemingly no end in sight.

Canaris shifted his feet in place, the sand slipping under the soles of his sandals. He knew there would be no help for him at the docks. No one would risk a bullet so that one twenty-eight-year-old officer could escape. He was there anonymously, travelling under the false identity of a businessman named "Reed Rosas". No one cared whether he could rejoin a war begun thousands of miles away, between two countries with few legal claims in the region.

It was not for lack of familiarity, however. Many Germans had moved to Chile and the Andes in particular since the nation's call for immigrants a century earlier, seeking opportunities to rekindle the land-owning legacy of the Junkers in Prussia and the southern states.

The Junkers' riches had been founded on battle, knights conquering lands and establishing feudal kingdoms on the backs of impoverished serfs. South America afforded equally cheap labor, which many supplemented with their own considerable sweat equity. Ranches began to dot vast tracts of empty land. Breweries, bakeries, and butchers opened in the cities. All told, there were several thousand former German families in the region by the time the Great War erupted.

Some would help, he had no doubt. But their ranks did not generally include fishermen and most of them were in Santiago, Osorno or over the mountains in the disputed region of Patagonia, which fell along the border with Argentina.

The spotlights swept the beach once more, the sirens continuing to wail. There would be, at most, one man in each tower, Canaris knew. The naval harbor was on the island's east side, where the Bay of Concepcion waters were calmer than those of the ocean, light ripples set against the silhouetted shoreline palm trees. It was pragmatic for men who came and went regularly to drop off supplies or catch.

The west side's beaches ran the length of the island and each secluded segment featured at least one such watch tower. They would not expect him to push off from there, however. Finding a boat would be difficult, if not impossible, and going without one would be suicide. The island was more than a mile from Tumbes, the nearest mainland village. The water was less than sixty degrees Fahrenheit in late August; exposure, alone, would numb his senses, rob his limbs of their strength to go on, long before he reached shore – as if making it past the sheer roughness of the waves was not challenging enough.

But Canaris knew something the British did not: for weeks, smugglers had been taking contraband liquor, tobacco, and toiletries to the prisoners on the island, among them the crew of the Dresden, Canaris's assignment. It had been scuttled nearly a year earlier, facing imminent capture.

The smugglers saw opportunity amidst the conflict. But they weren't welcome on the island's east side. Instead, they were landing at a small cove just above the island's southwestern tip.

Between his hiding spot and the cove lay a mile of dense woods, running from the tops of the sand dunes to the cleared land on the east side, where the navy base and prison were situated. Within a half-hour of the siren, the woods would be crawling with men looking for him. But the British only had a crew of perhaps two dozen. If he was exceedingly careful, he knew – as well as lucky – he could hide near the cove until one of the smugglers' eighteen-foot, one-mast wooden boats appeared.

Then he would either convince them of the potential rewards that lay in helping the Empire… or he would force the issue, as sometimes was the cost of war.

A gap in the trees had forced him to risk traversing the dunes and hiding behind the boat. Canaris lifted his knees out of the sand and raised himself to his haunches. In a few moments, both beams of light would swing back, rapidly, to the other ends of the beach. A gap of perhaps fifty meters sat between him and the start of another copse of overgrowth.

He would have to be quick. The men in the towers might have missed him before the sirens began to wail, he knew, but now would be on high alert. Though they would be too far away to shoot him, word would go out quickly. They would begin closing the area down, cordoning him in with men.

The spotlights swung back to their starting point and Canaris sprinted for the woods, his sandals coming off halfway, caught in the sand. He reached the edge of the tree line and dived into cover, just as the spotlights swung around to his position once more.

Had they seen him? His breath was heavy, his chest tight, waiting for the whistles to sound, voices to call out. If they found him, he knew, they might shoot him rather than risk another escape attempt. The information he'd gathered and memorized on British holdings in Argentina, their plans for the Falklands, their plans to militarize the Tierra Del Fuego region... all of it would be lost.

But he knew he would have to allow himself to be taken. Even if he had the means to fight back – and Canaris was by no means or any measure a coward – it would make no tactical sense to do so. It meant certain death; at least with capture, the possibility of evading a firing squad and escaping once more still existed. The war was far from lost, and Canaris believed – knew – he could yet help bring glory to a greater Germany.

In the distance, from the north and the route he'd just taken, he heard the faint sounds of whistles and voices, men calling out.

The hunt had begun.

2.

Hassan Al Saad braced his bare feet against the gunwale of his one-man fishing boat, *Abundancia*, pushing off as he tugged with all his might at the black line of the drift net.

Its loops had become snarled in shallow waters, just off the southern tip of Quiriquina, likely caught on rocks or debris. The boat jostled and bobbed but he was experienced, used to standing in choppy water.

He had had luck there before, gill netting red snapper and turtles, even though local officials frowned on the practise close to the British-occupied base. The British were usually tactful with locals, but on occasion they could be violent, ill-tempered. They'd gotten drunk at a tavern in his family's area of town just days earlier and smashed up people's property, celebrating some victory over the Germans.

As long as his livelihood was not affected, Hassan tried to take their sudden incursion into Concepcion in stride. For now, he had bigger problems. The nets were only of any use close to shore and that came with complications. He left it there eighteen hours earlier, third in a line along the island's west side. Hassan hoped he would return to find it brimming with catch. Instead, with just two hours left until dawn, he still had two nets to retrieve and one causing him nothing but grief.

Later, he knew, he would sit down over a strong cup of tea and discuss the matter with his wife, Sophia. They had been living in Concepcion for two years, since taking a discharge from their merchant marine vessel, the Italy-registered steamer *Citta Di Napoli*, and beginning life anew in South America. That, in turn, came after five years together in Malta, where both had found an adopted home.

A Moroccan by descent, his father had impressed upon him that, to his knowledge, after thousands of years, the desert continued to offer little but sand and war. And so, he had taken to Europe, in search of a new life. He intended to find a wife willing to convert to Islam, and a career at sea as a merchant marine. Instead, a beautiful young Italian woman convinced him to convert to Catholicism and move to Chile to fish red snapper.

It was about as far from the desert as he could have possibly imagined.

Now, he faced the latest blow to their meagre finances. Already, he was beginning to doubt his own optimism, the face he presented to his wife whenever she raised the notion of returning to Italy, and whether he was happy with their decision.

He wanted to avoid cutting the net loose, the hours of splicing it would take to make the woolen links strong and useable again. It was the third that autumn, and the second had been irretrievable.

"Shake free, you accursed piece of..." he barked at the net in Arabic, restraining himself from outright blasphemy. "I swear by all that is mine, you will not cost me another..."

His yanking finally bore fruit, albeit somewhat bitter. The net tore, the young Arabic man's own efforts pushing him across the bottom of the boat, his head slamming into the opposite wall. The boat tossed furiously from the momentum. Hassan lay on its floor with a torn piece of black wool between his fingers.

"Cursed!" he declared. He pushed himself up so that he was sitting on his backside. "I am cursed by incompetent net makers and an indifferent God."

He rose and took a seat at the stern of the vessel. He reached into the small black bag of personal affects that he usually brought along. His snack was long-eaten and Hassan instead withdrew a packet of Gold Flake cigarettes. He pulled a smoke from it and lit it with a wooden match, struck against the boat's hull. It sparked brightly in the darkness before dawn, his vision momentarily reduced to shadows.

The water slapped gently against the hull, black caps barely lit by the moon.

The fisherman blew out a vast cloud of thick smoke. "Just remind yourself that compared to life and death... it's not a problem," he said out loud, the breeze catching the smoke contrails, twisting and turning. "Your father said it first and best, Hassan: "most of the time, it's not a problem.""

Their little girl, Maria, had never met her grandfather. He hoped that would change one day, although the old man probably didn't have many left.

He exhaled smoke again, thinking back to Malta, just after she was born, five years earlier.

But before he could extend the thought to his family and friends so far away, Hassan frowned.

The shore was less than fifty yards away, but the man running along the tree line seemed tiny, almost ant-like. The fisherman's gaze drifted slowly to the left. A few hundred yards behind the lone figure, torches flickered in odd spots, flames dancing in the breeze, their bearers obscured by distance and shadow.

His view flitted back to the lone figure. The man was perhaps a mile from the cove. He would get there well before them. Were they chasing him, or simply headed in the same direction? Either seemed odd, given the fact that the only people on the west side of Quiriquina were usually smugglers or fishermen. The naval types stayed on the other side of the island. That hadn't changed since the British took over the facility.

Up the beach, perhaps a mile or two past the torchlight, he could see the faint glow of two spotlights flitting around.

They were looking for someone. That meant the man was probably being hunted. What had Esteban the sponge vendor said? That the British had prisoners there now, men from a German ship?

He felt a nervous tug in the pit of his stomach. If the man was an escapee, he might try to flee the island. That would mean patrol boats, perhaps even a gunship. His tiny skiff wouldn't stand a chance. Hassan stared at the bow of the craft. With a diesel vessel or steamboat, a heavy wake alone could probably sink it.

But he wanted those other two nets. If he left them, they might still be recoverable after another day. Or, they might drift too far, be pulled out by the tidal currents. They wouldn't have to go far before the square area around them required for an effective search became a matter of bad timing – and in the wrong place for good measure.

Hassan lifted anchor, hauling it up hand-over-hand via its long link of chain. He stored it under the rear seat then moved ahead to the sail, unfastening the broad sheet of grey-white cotton and unfurling it, ready to find the wind. Even if one of the men on shore noticed him, by the time they sent a ship over from the other side of the island, he would at least have had a chance to bring the nets in.

Abundancia was a swift little vessel, and he had great faith in her ability to outrun trouble.

3.

The boat had covered less than a quarter-mile of coast when the light began to flash from shore. It was a small object being used to bounce reflection, possibly a vanity mirror, or the smooth casing of a pocket watch.

Hassan knew he should ignore it. The person was alternating the object's angle of deflection, the light strobing on and off. Was it…?

Morse code? He'd taken it as a merchant marine. It seemed to be an attempt at an S-O-S, with three short flashes, then three longer, then three short.

This is not your business, his inner monologue suggested. *You leave this matter to the authorities. Whatever they are upset for, it has nothing to do with you.*

The skiff continued on, the choppy water bringing the bow up into the air and back down to the hard surface of the ocean in short, hard thumps. He glanced back up the beach. The torches were getting closer, perhaps a mile from the cove. There was no point turning around to help the man, he told himself. Even with a good tack and wind behind him, he would be lucky to get there before the mob. Whatever the man had done, being pursued by torchlight suggested he was in for a difficult night.

That was a reality Hassan understood all too well.

It had been four years since he'd been caught out after curfew in Valletta and thrashed within an inch of his life by the police, set upon with truncheons in a darkened alley, beaten like a frothing dog. They'd chased him for blocks, falsely believing him a serial robber of drunken bar patrons in the Maltese city. The ache he still felt on cold nights from his poorly-knit ankle ligaments stood as a more visceral reminder that Arabs were expected, in many places, to know their place – particularly when the British were ahead of them.

The man had given up signalling a minute ago. But it began to flash again, the same insistent pattern. Whoever it was must have been hoping to find a vessel, someone to give him a ride. Hassan didn't know any Germans, just that there were supposed to be more than a hundred of them in the camp. He'd heard at church that Germans had helped build the cathedral in Osorno, and fund the home for orphans. And there were usually smugglers operating in the area.

On a whim, he made his decision.

He tied the rudder down momentarily so that he could tack, swinging the sail's boom mast over to the other side of the boat, then retaking the rudder to steer it in a broad, arcing curve towards the shore. A few moments later, he had the wind behind him and was heading back the way he'd just travelled, towards the cove.

What are you doing? You have a wife, a daughter. This man is probably a soldier, a war criminal or spy. The British will arrest you if you help him, have you shot. Who will provide for Maria if you are shot?

He knew the risks but felt compelled to intervene, nonetheless. Hassan wasn't sure why. Perhaps it was because he wished someone had helped him when it would have mattered more. Perhaps if someone had called out, said something... even just drawn the streetgoing public's attention. Perhaps his ankle would not ache nightly, and he would not awaken from nightmares regularly.

Perhaps if they had, you would not have fled Malta, and you would not be pursuing this fool's errand.

He looked back along the beach. They were no more than a mile away and closing, the torches bright enough to count five... six... seven men. Their shadows betrayed the rifles each man carried or slung from his back.

The boat passed over the shelf a hundred yards from shore, the water becoming shallower. If he took the *Abundancia* any closer, he knew, she risked becoming beached, her keel caught up in the soft sand. Hassan turned hard to starboard, angling the nose of the boat slightly away from the island. He drew down the sail momentarily, letting it billow loosely. He reached into his pocket for his matchbox and withdrew another match, snapping it against the mast to charge the flame, before lighting the small oil lantern that hung there.

Then he retreated to the stern of the vessel and cupped his hands together to yell toward the beach, twenty-five yards away.

"DEBES VENIR A MI!" *You have to come to me!* he yelled in Spanish, trying to be heard over the crash of the tide. "DEBES VENIR..."

The man had gotten the message and was sprinting towards the water. He seemed to slow suddenly and duck, hands cradling the top of his head like a man fearing a low-hanging object. Hassan heard the rifle's retort a moment later, a light crack, followed by another, then another, one echo rippling into the next.

His would-be passenger began running again, hitting the water and continuing to run until it reached his knees, when he was forced to slow down, wading as quickly as he could. The boat had no more than two feet of water under the keel, Hassan estimated. As long as the man was near six feet tall, he would have no problem…

The man began to swim.

So… not a tall individual, then.

He reached the side of the boat. He was young, in his twenties, with ice-blue eyes, his blonde crewcut hair beginning to lengthen out, a five o'clock shadow beginning to turn into a beard. He stopped swimming, able to stand though the water was up to his chest.

"Please! Help me!"

Hassan reached over the gunwales and grasped the man by either arm, pushing off as he had with the net earlier, bracing his toes against the boat. It allowed the man to cling onto the edge and pull himself up partially, though the weight of the water meant he seemed to weigh a ton. Hassan shifted his grip to under the man's armpits and leaned back with all of his weight, pushing hard. The man slumped over the rail and thudded onto the bottom of the boat.

They would be at the beach at any moment. The young fisherman put out the boat's small oil lantern, plunging them into darkness. He moved to the midship seat and found the oars stored above the ballast tanks on each side, then fitted them into their oarlocks on each side's riggers. He began to pull the oars back, then push them forward, rowing in smooth, long strokes. If they were lucky, he knew, by the time the men on the beach were parallel to the man's point of escape, their vessel would be a hundred yards from shore, barely visible in the three o'clock darkness, even if they knew where to look.

His guest continued to lie on his back, panting. After several minutes, he pushed himself up onto his backside, then rolled to one side to find the strength to rise. He made his way shakily to the rear seat. "Thank you!" the young man called out in Spanish. The bay remained choppy, the moonlit, roiling waters loud enough to make shouting necessary even from just ten feet away. "Why did you help me?"

The accent was unmistakably German or Austrian, Hassan knew. Perhaps the story of the German prisoners was true. "The British were chasing you?" he asked.

The man nodded. Then he rose from the woven seat and ventured just far enough ahead to reach out and quickly shake Hassan's hand. "I do not wish to interrupt your fine rowing stroke, but I needed to do that," he yelled, returning to his seat. "And... yes, that is the case. I am pleased to make your acquaintance, sir. My name is Reed Rosas, and I am a businessman from Santiago..."

"You are a spy from Germany," Hassan yelled back, matter-of-factly. "Or you would not be interned on a naval base controlled by your enemy."

"I assure you, good sir..."

"Assure me that you will speak truth and I shall not judge you. But I deserve such deference. I have possibly just saved you from a beating, or a firing squad or worse. Can you grant me that?" Hassan replied in fluent German. He had always had a gift for languages, and those with a Latin base seemed particularly easy for him.

The man's surprise was evident, his eyes widening. The notion that a grubby fisherman from Chile might speak his language seemed to truly shock him. The water's chop had lessened, the creaking of the wooden oars against each brass couplet louder.

"But... you speak German? This is fantastic!"

"I would not view our present circumstance in quite such laudable terms," Hassan offered sourly. "But... yes, I speak German. And Italian, and Maltese, and French, and even English when forced to do so."

The man smiled, his gaze narrowing. "You do not like the English, Mr....?"

"I am Hassan Al Saad. Why do the English seek you out, Mr. Rosas? Or... whatever your real name is, as that sounds remarkably like some sort of falsehood."

A smile at that. "I require some tact in this area," Canaris admitted. "They believe I might have information useful to the war effort. Or, they merely wish it known that they do not condone escape attempts. Either way, if you had not picked me up, I would most assuredly have been executed."

"And is there a reward for your capture?" Hassan asked. He did not believe in insincerity or guile. If he decided to turn the man in, he would be honest about it.

"Possibly. It would not be very much, I imagine, as I am just a ship's intelligence officer. And the ship in question, the *SS Dresden*..."

Hassan's eyebrows were raised. "The ship upon which Mr. Rudolf Diesel is rumoured to have died."

"Before the war, yes, when it was a regular passenger vessel between England and the continent. Now, it sits at the bottom of the ocean floor…"

"You were sunk."

"Scuttled, rather than be captured… although, in truth, it seems a terrible waste of a good vessel. English arrogance would have prevented them repurposing her as anything more than transport. Hassan…"

"Yes, Mr. Rosas…"

"Please: call me Reed."

"All right. Reed…"

"Why did you help me? You did not answer when I first came aboard. Is it a facet of your Muslim faith?"

No, and I'm Catholic. It's because you're worth nothing to me dead. That was the answer Hassan supposed he should give. He pulled on the oars, his shoulders getting tight and tired. Those two nets were going to cost him his profits for weeks. If he had any sense, he knew, he would take whatever pittance the authorities offered for the man.

Instead, he replied, "I have been in your position, more or less and in another time and place. The English think they own the world…"

"And much of it, they do…"

"But they do not own my boat."

They were far enough from shore to put up the sail. Canaris helped, steadying the boom while Hassan pulled it taut. If luck favored them, the Arab knew, they would be back in Concepcion before daybreak, and before the British began combing every harbor from there to Santiago. If luck favored them… he would have a guest in their home, a man with problems who offered nothing in return save a salve for old wounds.

Bismillah! And that is the best-case scenario.

4.

Sophia was livid, but was managing to restrain herself, nonetheless. The man sitting in their humble house's main room was short, bedraggled, and wearing what appeared to be a prison uniform.

He was drinking a pint of milk from the bottle, guzzling it as if he'd been in a desert without water for days. She held her nightgown tight and looked around the large room, conscious the living area was messier than she would like. Maria's toys littered the floor around the long occasional table, and the dishes, though washed, were stacked beside the sink on the other side of the room, not put away.

Maria, aged five, was sleeping in the only other room.

Her husband, who had always seemed a sensible and trustworthy man, was sitting by the wood stove, drying off his clothes. "I understand the part about him needing help, Hassan. I do not understand the part where you decided to be the one to do so. If he is a prisoner then he has probably done something very wrong..."

She was not a large woman, about the same height as the blond man on the stool. But she knew she could impose her will when required. She crossed her arms officiously and gave her husband an exceedingly dirty look. She loved him dearly, but he was prone to dangerous curiosity. His beating in Malta had come from venturing into a neighborhood where they were not welcome. And helping this man? Well, she could scarcely imagine the problems he might have attracted.

Hassan was trying to appear non-plussed, as if the worries of a woman were not his concern. He wasn't fooling her. "If I choose to make a decision, as a man, then it is to be respected..."

"I respect your right to make choices," she said, staring him down. "That does not mean I must respect the choices made. We should tell him to leave, at once, before he brings our daughter into harm's way. Before you do the same."

That prompted a frown from the damp fisherman. He knew his wife to be generous of spirit. "He is not a criminal, he is German. They are at war with the English, and the English control the coastline right now…"

"You should have talked to me first, your wife!" she admonished.

"There was no time! He was fleeing armed men, on the island. I was right there. It was a matter of doing the right thing…"

She hung her head. When the British in Malta had tried to force a confession from her husband to a series of robberies, they had made it clear that the flogging he was about to take would be the sole punishment, that it would all be over that much more quickly if he admitted the crime.

Three days later, he had been dropped at their home in Malta, dumped in a bloody mess on their doorstep, the skin practically flayed from his back, his arm, nose and cheekbone broken. And all because he had stood on his principles and refused to confess to something he had not done.

If he had done it any differently, he would not be the man you married. "Then… now what? What do we do with him? The English will enlist local police and soldiers. They will hunt for him."

"They may assume him lost at sea," Hassan suggested. He said it as earnestly as possible, eyes wide. "They may think it good fortune, to have one less mouth to keep."

She sucked on her tongue skeptically. "Uh huh, certainly. They will throw a parade in your honour… and at the end maybe hang you both as a reward. You realize they will have men at every port, every harbor, jetty and dock."

"They will expect me to flee by boat, to rejoin the effort as quickly as possible," Canaris said. "Madam, I do not wish…"

"Shhh!" Sophia held up a finger. "Be quiet! You have gotten us into this mess, you do not get to determine how we get out."

"Let him speak, Sophia! It is his neck first and foremost that stands to be chopped, after all."

She frowned at Hassan. But Sophia had never been arrogant. "Fine. Say what it is that you have to say."

"They will not be expecting me to flee across land," Canaris said. "I have a friend in Osorno who has offered to help me. But I must get there first, and the roads will be closely watched.

"There is a train," Sophia said. "It runs twice per day. You could attempt to gain passage."

"They will be looking at the station," her husband advised.

"They will," she said. "But there are always hundreds of people there and onboard. They will not have the resources to check closely, which makes the chance of it working much higher than trying to sneak aboard one of perhaps a handful of boats. Are you a religious man, Mr. Rosas?"

He shook his head. "Not especially, though I do look to the Lord, as do all good men, when the need arises."

That brought a small, assured smile to her face. "Then we shall pray on the answer. And this evening, when it is dark once more, we shall place our faith in the night train to Osorno."

5.

The train had been travelling for two hours, making steady time along the coast, then turning inwards, cutting through woodlands, tracks arcing up and over the slopes of the Andes foothills.

Canaris watched the scenery pass through the car's window. He was sharing the bench with strangers, a young couple canoodling next to him, lost in each other's eyes, an older woman and her husband on the wooden bench across from them.

He could not have wished for better fortune, the intelligence officer knew, than to have met Sophia and Hassan. As frightened as the woman had been, her decency demanded they not condemn him to his pursuers.

Though the war raged in some fashion or another across the globe, from the western front to the jungles of Siam, its presence in South America had been largely a matter of naval engagements, as if they were not quite actually involved. And so the train trip felt surreal, as if the war was over and he was sharing a car with tourists or commuters, people on their way to holidays in Brighton or Konstanz.

The mood changed as the train approached Valdivia, a port town north of their eventual destination, the city of Osorno. Canaris had anticipated that, if the authorities were to stop the train, Valdivia was a potential location. There was little he could do about it. He had no papers, no identification of any sort.

Just the ruse created by Sophia Al Saad. And it was a clever one, at that. Canaris was uncertain it would work, but it had been worth a try even though it was "blasphemous beyond all belief," in the diminutive Italian's words.

Across from him, an aging man in a grey-brown three-piece suit leaned forward with a package of John Player cigarettes. "Father? Do you smoke, by any chance?"

The priest's collarino was just a backward dress shirt under a black sweater. But taken with the silver cross and ornate Book of Common Prayer they'd given him, and which he'd kept clasped in hand throughout the trip, the image was complete. "Thank you, my son, most generous of you. It is not the most clean or Godly of pursuits... but it does help calm the soul."

His companion smiled at that, satisfied to have scored some points toward the afterlife.

The train shuddered, the brakes squealing as it slowed its approach to the platform at Valdivia. The conductor opened their cabin door and leaned in. "Please stay seated during the wait," he said. "The authorities wish to board and inspect the train and wish for it to be as orderly as possible."

He departed; the door slid shut behind him.

"What could they possibly want?" the aging man's wife asked. "We have taken this trip so many times over the years..."

Her husband puffed on his cigarette before flicking the ash into a turnaround ashtray built into the cabin's wall. "It's a war, my dear. A great many strange things happen during wars."

Canaris felt his nerves twitch, his stomach gurgling from anxiety. It wouldn't be long, he imagined. They would be looking for someone matching his description. The canoa hat, a wide-brimmed black lifesaver for those who ministered in hot countries, helped disguise him somewhat by covering his blonde hair. He'd left it on when aboard, despite the polite tradition, hoping it would be seen by the faithful as part of his official garb.

He heard a rattle from the hallway, the sound of the folding doors being pushed open. His anxiety grew, nerves fluttering his stomach, the stifling mugginess in the cabin suddenly apparent.

There were two sharp knocks on the door before it slid open.

The policemen were both local, unaccompanied by any foreigners. The officer in charge was a small man, of similar stature to Canaris but with a clipped black moustache and dark wavy hair under his hat.

"Tickets and identity papers, please!" the man announced pleasantly. "We are just having a little check, ladies and gentlemen." He saw Canaris's garb and cross. "Father, my apologies for the inconvenience."

Canaris nodded and smiled as sublimely as possible. His Spanish was fluent but his accent decidedly Westphalian.

The policeman returned the smile but fixed his gaze upon the priest while his partner received the documents. When he'd gone through them all, the second officer said, "this last ticket without the papers... I assume this is yours, father?"

He nodded once again and raised a palm, laughing gently at the notion of a priest needing papers.

"You are not carrying any form of identification, Father?" the first officer asked. Was he suspicious? Canaris couldn't be certain from the inscrutable stare.

"Most unfortunate," Canaris explained, trying to flatten his Germanic brogue. "I appear to have left them in Osorno this morning..."

"I see." The policeman nodded several times, as if agreeing. He tilted his head and studied the passenger. "Your... accent. You are not from Chile originally, I take it?"

It was a test, of that there was no doubt. "Ah!" Canaris offered, as if delighted. "You noticed! I have been here for so many years now that I came to believe you could not hear the Danish tone..."

The policeman nodded. "Denmark? Then... you must know Father Hansen well. He has been in Osorno for... what, thirty years now?"

It was clearly a trap, but Canaris knew he was caught in it. His chances were down to a coin toss, it seemed.

"Ah!" the second policeman said, gesturing towards the priest. "You were at the commissioning!"

He was staring at the jewelled bookbinding, the thin metal holder for the prayer book inscribed and inlaid with art in ten-carat gold. Canaris took a chance. "An amazing building," he replied. "It truly glorifies God." If the man had been talking about a statue or vessel, Canaris knew, he was done for.

The second officer looked put off. "This hardly makes sense…" he muttered.

Canaris felt his stomach turn.

"… to describe a Cathedral so grandiose and regal in such banalities!"

His fellow policeman smiled and nodded. "It is always as such from a man of the cloth," he said. "While we are impressed, they are humbled. Father, make sure to carry your papers, eh? There is a war on, after all."

The second officer handed him back his ticket. "Go with God, my sons," Canaris offered, crossing the air in front of him.

The cabin door slid closed, and the spy let out a sigh of relief. The couple next to him went back to the conversation, the woman across to her knitting. Only the older man kept his eye on Canaris, the look knowing. "Another cigarette, 'father'," he said, the tone exactly as intended.

Canaris thought he recognized something in the man's voice. The passport he'd handed over had been Chilean. But there was a slight hint of an accent. Possibly German. "I wouldn't turn it down for the world," the spy replied in Spanish, because it was war time, and one could never be sure.

Canaris lit the cigarette with a proffered match, which he deposited into the turn-around ashtray under the window. He stared through the glass, watching the ocean in the distance. Then he felt the coldness of the metal book holder under his thumb. He flicked it open to the first few pages.

There was a note written on a small square of paper, tucked into the blank page right after the thin leather cover.

"Rosas, or whatever your name is: know that we are grateful to been able to help and wish you well. Take this book and find the peace in it that I have. I am an Arab, my wife a white from Italy. Like the English and the Germans, we are different. And yet we are the same, two people, no more or less important in God's eyes than any other. We love one another, and we extend that love where possible to all who would allow us into their hearts. Perhaps when the time comes, and you must make a difficult decision despite the potential cost, you will feel the same joy we do to have helped, rather than hurt. For in such moments, we are all redeemed. Good luck, and may God be with you."

He closed the book, a feeling of guilt and shame settling in. But Canaris pushed it away. He had dedicated his life to naval service, to strengthening a greater Germany. He knew there would be times when his difficult choices might be the wrong ones, might cost his country. But he also knew that when the time came to make them, the stakes would be too high for sober reflection and humanism.

Perhaps, though, there was something in the man's message that, for an impractical wish, nonetheless bore consideration. Where was there strength without decency, the kind the fisherman had offered him? What was the purpose without an end acceptable to others, and not just himself?

When he arrived in Osorno, he supposed, the German network there would find a place for him to lie low until his intelligence reports were complete. Then they would spirit him across the border via San Carlos De Bariloche, in the mountains, a small Argentine village founded by German settlers. From there, it would be on to the big cities, Buenos Aires or Montevideo, for a slow boat back to Europe and friendly territory.

He felt the weight of the Book of Common Prayer in his hand. Canaris hoped the act of generosity by the kindly Arab fisherman and his wife would bring them no harm.

In a world consumed by madness and fire, kindness seemed more valuable, even, than victory.

PART ONE

6.

LONDON, ENGLAND
Oct. 15, 2020

Joshua Brennan stared down the Queen's Guard, the tip of his twelve-year-old nose just a few inches from the soldier's.

As advertised, the Buckingham Palace sentry was unmoving, practically unblinking.

He stood sternly at attention in his pillbox guard house, the brass buttons and medals on his red serge uniform glinting in the light of a partly sunny day. His bearskin hat made him seven feet tall.

In fact, he was about six-two, the same as Joshua's father.

"Really… we're completely sorry about this," Joe Brennan offered, holding the boy aloft at the waist, his five-foot-five frame eye-to-eye with the grown man. "It's juvenile, and disrespectful, and in no way reflects the great respect we have for the British military."

The guard flashed the smallest, quickest smile – but not even; more a twitch of the upper lip. It was barely perceptible but might as well have been a shout. It said, 'we enjoy your parental suffering.'

"Did he blink, dad?" Josh asked. "I blinked a couple of times, so I might have missed it. How do I tell if I've won if I have to blink too?"

His son had gotten the notion of staring down a Queen's Guard into his head before they'd crossed the ocean for the two-week vacation. They'd decided to get it out of the way quickly, on day two.

"So?" the boy asked. "Did we win?"

His sister Jessica was standing ten feet away, chewing gum, her hands clasping her phone, eyes lifted for just long enough to acknowledge the scene. "Yeah... we're all winners here," she said dryly.

Carolyn looked on joylessly. She was a stickler for schedules and productive time use. Fun with the kids was great, but they had an agenda to maintain, and they were supposed to be at Harrods by ten-thirty. "Are we about ready to go, Joe?" she asked, putting the onus on Joe to speed things up. He'd spent so much of his career on the road, she feared, he'd begun overcompensating with the kids, allowing them too much leeway. She wondered sometimes if he was trying to make her look bad, less caring by comparison.

That was how Jessica acted these days, she thought, like she was the enemy. Josh had always favored his father, which was only natural. But Josh was a twelve-year-old boy, a raging hormone on a daily path of destruction. He seemed so hyperactive she'd tried to get Joe to talk to Dr. Simons again about whether ADHD was an issue. He'd reminded her they'd already talked to the man, the doctor was the expert, that ADHD was a serious developmental disorder and not just an 'attention thing.' He'd gotten flustered, as if there was something wrong with her showing concern when the problem hadn't really been dealt with. As if there wasn't really a problem at all.

Joe lowered Josh to the ground. "I think we're going to call it a draw, son," he suggested.

Josh looked up at the sentry. He could swore he gave him a wink, just before he'd completely turned his head... "Dad! Dad, I think he broke character!"

Joe looked over his shoulder but the guardsman was as stoic as ever. "Yeah. I get a sense that guy is trouble around the poker table." He thought he caught another tiny flex of the mouth muscles, a twitch of smirk. "Come on: your mom's getting impatient, and the big store is next."

"Chocolate!" Josh declared, one fist quickly thrust aloft as if calling down lightning. "I call upon the power of Kuru-Rah, the unholy one..."

Jessie sighed loudly. "Mom... Josh's doing Dungeons & Dragons again..."

"Josh, you know that drives your sister crazy. Save it for later," Carolyn said. "Joe, I think this is our Uber..."

The hire car took them along South Carriage Drive towards the Kensington Road turnoff. Joe sat between the kids on the back seat; but he kept an eye on Carolyn as best he could. It was their first vacation together in nearly a decade. Her doctor had insisted upon it, that she take proper time off of her career, put work behind her and decompress. Her blood pressure, never a problem in her family, had been forty points too high.

She'd hated the idea, even though her latest project at the National Security Council saw her advising a joint taskforce on foreign debt acquisition that included Joe's morally ambiguous boss, Jonah Tarrant. Joe figured working for Jonah would drive anyone's stress through the roof and that she'd welcome the break. It was also the first time they'd had a chance to take real time off with the kids in years.

Instead, she'd been tense for the first two days, harping about schedules and cramming her nose into the London guidebook, trying to ensure the kids saw as many historical and culturally significant sites as possible. The 'family' vacation rapidly felt like it was turning into a guided school trip.

It had been terse between them for a while, he knew. Nothing these days seemed to change that, or her general irritation with him. Since the Chinese sleeper incident two years earlier and his return to "unofficial" blacklist status, he had effectively been a house husband. Having him home with the kids was supposed to make her life easier; instead, it just seemed to add to her tension. Then they'd finally let him retire, and it had become tense every day.

At the department store, amidst crowds of tourists and well-heeled Londoners, Josh had been in his element, running from section to section of the massive toy display. He wrestled with a life-sized stuffed tiger, he tried diving out of a plane in virtual reality, and he screamed loudly enough for the other floors to hear him. He was going great guns until he tried to climb behind the wheel of a miniature Lamborghini Countach despite the 'do not touch' sign prominently displayed on the door. A navy-suited arm came seemingly from nowhere and yanked him away at the last moment, then gently pushed him towards his father.

"He seems to be having a rather fun time, sir," the elegantly dressed sales associate said. "But we try to keep them away from that one."

"Ah. World's most expensive pedal bike; am I right?"

"It is, in fact, a real vehicle sir, miniaturized and working off a much smaller, battery operated engine, but capable of top speeds in excess of twenty miles per hour and in every way a piece of refined Lamborghini machinery. And, as sir surmised, it would cost a very great deal to replace."

Joe didn't ask. It was the kind of place where if you had to, you couldn't afford it. Carolyn and Jessica sidled up next to him. "I'm nervous that after this," she said, "a football ground is going to seem tame."

That drew a smile. She'd never been to a match in England. "Oh, I wouldn't worry too much," he suggested. "Martin's club is very popular, and it tends to be… boisterous."

That gave her pause. "Boisterous?"

"Boisterous."

7.

There was a hush through the crowd, a moment of sublime silence as the ball arced through the air, a banana curve struck from just by the corner flag that flew, fast and true, off the instep of a white Nike boot. It blipped past the stark white of the near goalpost, a half-dozen players leaving the ground in tempo, heads tossed towards the leather sphere, one finding it.

The ball rebounded at an acute angle towards the far top corner of the goal, the keeper's neon-yellow gloved hand reaching out at full stretch, fingertips just so near but not near enough, knotted twine bulging as it settled into the net.

And then the roar hit like a close-call jet engine, sixty thousand souls standing in unison, arms raised in howls of joy. Josh was compelled to jump to his twelve-year-old feet with everyone else as the Gunners buried the first goal of the match, eyes wide, wonderstruck.

Martin Weiss turned to Joe and grasped him by both shoulders as if to administer the kiss of death. Instead, he shook his American friend like a frightened parent grasping a child who does something foolhardy. "GET IN SON! Get in! Yeeeeessssss!"

Joe laughed even as Martin treated him like a stubborn pinata. The Englishman turned the other way and hugged Carolyn effusively, her face registering shock and disbelief. She hadn't really been paying attention, engrossed in her phone.

After the noise had calmed a bit and the players had paraded back up the pitch to the center circle, Josh looked past their host to his father. "Dad…. Why isn't it like this at games in D.C.?"

"Well, soccer is a new thing in America, relatively speaking. And it is, sometimes, we just haven't gone yet."

"Why's that, Dad?"

Because I'm a lousy father. "Because … it just hadn't come up yet. But we will. I'm home now all the time…"

"He means football," Martin politely interjected. "Here, we call it football. You can tell what it is, you see, by the fact that the players have to use their feet."

Josh frowned. "What do you call … you know, 'Football' football?"

"We call it American football, because for the most part, America is the only place that plays it. We call Australian Rules Football… Australian Rules Football. The only other type is Rugby Football, but we just call that Rugby, most of the time anyway."

"That seems…" the boy began to respond.

"Like your way of doing things," Carolyn interrupted. "We have our own way of doing things, and in America, this isn't football."

We're not in America, Joe thought. *So why make an issue out of it?*

Martin smiled politely. He'd never liked Joe's wife and his impression hadn't improved with their prolonged visit. They'd only met twice before, when he was seconded by MI6 to the embassy in Washington for a period a decade earlier. She'd seemed defensive then, too, but softer around the edges. Not that it mattered now, not with his team leading. She couldn't sour the mood.

"We're not very good right now," he said instead. "We'd become something of a powerhouse a few years ago, but then a lot of new money came into the league and some other teams got better. But we're still the greatest club ever."

Josh nodded enthusiastically, one hand gripping the loose ends of the Arsenal scarf Martin had bought him. He and the boy were the same height at five-foot six. It was oddly comforting to talk to someone at eye level, and Joe's son seemed marvellous: happy, confident, enthusiastic, bright. Whatever her issues, she'd done well there, he surmised.

Now, the boy was a fan for life. "And what ARE you doing in London, exactly, Joe?" Martin asked casually, keeping his voice down. "I can't see you scheduling something like this trip unless you have an ulterior assignment..."

Brennan gently shook his head. "My friend, I am being one hundred percent honest-to-goodness straight with you: I'm retired. I'm out of the Agency entirely, my papers were accepted, my pension is secure. I'll be doing some freelance security training with a friend who ... will be available next year." *When he gets early release for his co-operation in a federal conspiracy case. But he doesn't need to know that part.*

"And..."

"And this is exactly what I said we were planning: a family vacation."

Martin smiled and took a sip of beer from the overpriced plastic cup. His friend's protestations meant nothing, he knew. It was entirely possibly he was lying, because that was just part of the business. A big part. Weiss had been with the Metropolitan Police for sixteen years and had retired two years earlier. He was long out of the military intelligence game, and publicly quite happy about it.

But Brennan had been a lifer, as far as he was concerned, the kind of dedicated covert operative who could take on any role from blunt instrument to subtle influencer ... as long as it was somewhere overseas, near the action.

Retirement? In his early forties? He didn't believe it for a second. "Right. Then, you're going to offer... what? Weekend security courses to bored executive retreats? That doesn't sound like you."

Brennan wasn't surprised his old friend was unconvinced. Martin had served in The Troubles in Northern Ireland and in Malta before joining MI6 as a liaison to the Army. He'd moved on in the latter half of his career to the Metropolitan Police.

Prior to his relatively sedate role as a commercial crime specialist with the Met, he'd spent more than two decades surrounded by duplicity, by smooth-talking conmen and women of the highest order: spies and politicians.

Brennan wouldn't have been surprised if Martin was still in the trade somehow. "Why are you asking?" the American posed. "If I didn't know better, I'd say it sounded like professional curiosity..."

The two men stared at each other without speaking for a few seconds, as if each was waiting for the other to break an unspoken tension... and then the crowd roared once more, rising in unison as the ball pinged around the box, a striker -- who seemed tiny next to the defenders -- putting his laces through it, the ball zooming towards the lower corner... before banging off the outside of the post, and out.

A collective groan of despair went around the grounds. Josh clutched the top of his own head with both hands. "SOOO close!" he moaned.

Brennan gestured towards the boy and gave his old friend a smile. "See what you've done? You've turned him into a true believer."

"Yes, well, the apple and the tree and not falling far, and all that…"

Brennan was glad he'd called him. It would always feel a little like business with Martin, but that was okay, too. That was in the past.

His phone buzzed. He withdrew it from his jacket's side pocket and checked the number. He allowed his head to slump for just one moment, just long enough for Martin to notice it. "You have got to be kidding me," Brennan said to no one in particular. He looked at the name and number again… then turned off the phone and put it back into his pocket.

8.

They were back at the hotel, taking a break in their rooms before going out for dinner, when Carolyn's phone rang. She looked at the number and answered immediately.

"Jonah! Good to hear from you."

Brennan felt his sense of irritation rise immediately. No matter how practised a stoic he could be outwardly, the mention of his former boss's name gave him a visceral sense of revulsion.

"Yes! Very happy with it, sir. It's a great posting. Of course!" She sounded like they were talking about her new role. She'd be talking to Jonah just about every day of the week, a notion he liked even less.

Then she looked his way. "Joe?" she replied to the caller. "Sure. This... isn't work related, I take it?"

Joe was pleasantly surprised she'd asked. After years of demanding he spend more time at home, she'd reacted strangely when he'd finally been taken off the freeze list and allowed to retire. The notion of him being home most days with the kids while she was at work in D.C., half an hour from their Maryland home, had seemed to unnerve her.

"Oh," she said. "Sure. He's right here." She walked over and handed him the phone. "Don't worry, he says it's nothing official."

Joe tried to keep his expression unconcerned, just two former colleagues catching up. "Brennan."

"Joe! Good to talk to you. How's London?"

"It's English," he noted bluntly. "What's up?"

"I have a referral for your new business, a freelance job."

That... was a new approach. But Jonah had always been good at working with the details on hand to create the narrative he wanted. "Really? So soon? I've been retired for less than a month."

"Yes. Well... this came across my desk and knowing what a self-motivated guy you can be, I thought you'd probably jump at it. There's a big payoff, I suspect."

"Who's the employer?"

"The Defense Department, Division of Historical Records and Archives. They're trying to get their hands on some documentation from the Second World War, stuff from the Berlin Airlift, some stuff that Immigration and Naturalization wants."

It seemed tame, the kind of thing any field agent could handle. What was Jonah up to? "Why me? I'm an ex-spook, not a records guy. I wouldn't know authentic time period stuff from the Antiques Roadshow."

"The material is... challenging to obtain," Jonah suggested. "It's not exactly freely available."

Joe could feel another shoe about to drop. "And it's held…"

"In the vault of a corporation. You might have heard of their American brands, Rightway…"

Like most people, Brennan thought of Rightway as a pyramid scam, a grocery and home supply company that sold its products wholesale to "multi-level marketing partners", individual members who were then expected to resell the items at a profit.

However, to make any real money, they had to recruit new members below them and get a cut of their supply line purchases, as the generic products were hard to move. People ended up spending all of their time recruiting "downstream consultants" who would kick up to them. He'd seen enough mob prosecutions by federal colleagues to know the Mafia's structure wasn't much different.

"You want me to break into Rightway?!"

"In a manner of speaking."

"In D.C.? Or… where are they based, anyway?"

"The American Branch is out of Traverse City, Michigan. But the information in question is in the vault of the U.K. branch, where they're known as RightBuy. They have a broader array of holdings there: a payday lending company, a discount airline, a sporting goods company, an array of branded pubs."

Brennan wasn't sure what to think. "I've been out of the service for weeks, and you're asking me to commit industrial espionage on behalf of a U.S. government department…"

"There's a unique opportunity tomorrow, so the window of time to talk to you about this was limited."

"Opportunity?"

"RightBuy is having its annual corporate retreat at an estate in England's Lake District. Its archivist will be presenting the documents to the board as a key acquisition in their online data harvesting model. They intend to release it via a select group of ancestry websites. When the current generation of users link themselves to the people in the European emigration records, they will create trackable patterns of wealth, gain and loss in families. That, in turn, will tell them exactly where to target their products in America."

"And that's a problem, because...?"

"The government could care less about how companies decide their approach to market," Jonah said. "But it does care that a private corporation has historically important documents obtained in dubious purchases that should belong to the American people."

Who was he kidding? America had been part of the ECHELON/Five Eyes program of international surveillance since the war, partnering with other countries to spy on one another's citizens, getting around domestic surveillance restrictions. All of the nations, including the United Kingdom, had shared personal data without so much as a second thought, sometimes for ludicrously trivial, political reasons.

"Jonah, I trust you less than I trust siding salesmen. Why should I be so much as gracing you with five seconds of my time, let alone..."

"The pay is enormous."

Well... that is more interesting. But only a little. Years of being on the government's payroll had never been lucrative. It had never been about the money. Now?

"Have you ever heard me say I wanted to get rich..."

"It's enough to pay for one of your kids' college education. At a good school."

At a… These days, that was a six-figure sum. He looked at Carolyn out of the corner of his eye. She was watching him intently, one forefinger pursed against her lip, clearly aware some sort of bargaining was going on.

The problem with Jonah, he knew, was that a person could never tell where honest began and duplicity ended. If he wanted a 'relatively simple' job done and was willing to pay six figures, it could be as much about getting Brennan on the hook, willing to work black again, off the books.

"Okay. Just of curiosity," Brennan suggested, "and I do mean 'just out of curiosity', I'm committing to nothing… what did the Defense Department have in mind?"

9.

Oct. 15, 2020

WINDERMERE, England.

Naomi Grainger walked into the village pub brimming with confidence, her sleek and sexy black evening dress highlighting the body she'd worked on for two hours a day, four days a week for more than a year.

The locals were underwhelmed. A few heads raised from a few pints, a couple of likely lads at the back of the room paying too much attention. But for the most part, it was indifference, the house public address piping through old acapella songs by The Spinners from the late Fifties, a steady stream of conversation pattering over it.

"Well? What were you expecting?" her friend Clarissa suggested, from off her left shoulder. "There's plenty of money in the Lake District, darling, but it's hardly cosmopolitan, wouldn't you say?"

They found stools at the bar and sat down. "Well, pooh!" Naomi commented. "My mother went to school near here, when the boarding school was still called St. Anne's. She always painted it as rather exciting."

The barman approached. "What can I get you?"

"Pint of shandy, please," Naomi said.

Clarissa sighed. "We'll each have a glass of white wine. Save the shandy or lime 'n lager or whatever provincial nonsense you enjoy for when you're visiting your parents in Otley. This village is absolutely stuffed with young corporate executives right now and you don't want to seem uncouth, darling."

She said it with a mockingly upper crust tone, so that Naomi would know she wasn't completely serious. Completely.

"I hear the man himself is going to make an appearance," Naomi said, wanting to change the subject, away from Clarissa's typical voracious husband hunt.

"Yes, I understand that's why they're holding the retreat here in the first place. He has a big house on the lake. He calls it his 'cottage' but apparently it's the size of a smallish Spanish province."

"A reporter asked him a few years ago about it. It was marvellously uncomfortable," Naomi recalled as the barman returned with their drinks. "Thank you."

"Thank you darling," Clarissa told the burly, middle-aged server. Naomi gave her a stern look as the man walked away. "Well, he is beefy and stubbly and rather lovely in a weather-beaten sort of way…"

"He's old enough to be your father…"

"…Except that he's within five hundred miles of me, so that couldn't possibly be daddy. You were talking about Michael Wolf, darling…"

"What? Oh... yes!" Naomi remembered. "The reporter. He asked Wolf about his cabin and said something like, 'Is it because the Island nearby is where they filmed the classic family film "*Swallows and Amazons*?" and Wolf looked at him like the man was completely deranged. "Of course not, don't be silly," he said in his typically austere Austrian accent. "The land was priced well given the likely future increase in value. And I like the water."

Clarissa giggled at her imitation then blanched, her eyes widening. "Ohmigod... he's right behind you."

Naomi's eyes shot wide open. She turned, her body rigid with fear... to see the next spot at the bar empty. "You're awful," she said turning back to her laughing friend.

"Well, I wouldn't say awful," a man passing said. "I mean... no one's lived a perfect life." He was older than them, in his late thirties or early forties, handsome, a slight layer of stubble suggesting he'd missed a couple of days shaving. And he looked genuinely offended.

"Oh!" Naomi raised her hand to her mouth, as if shushing herseif a few seconds too late. "I'm so sorry, I was turning and I didn't see you..."

"Oh!" He looked awkward, realizing she hadn't been addressing him.

"Yeah, my friend was trying to be funny...."

"And I was succeeding quite marvellously, darling," Clarissa insisted. She held out the top of her hand in a dainty shake motion. The American gripped it awkwardly and gave it a gentle shake. Naomi saw his awkwardness and felt a surge of warmth. It was endearing, seeing someone embarrassed by Clarissa's aggression. She laughed and held up a fist for him to bump. "Come on, lay one on me," she said.

The American fist-bumped her, his momentary discomfort giving way to a sly smile at her bailout. Naomi's eyes flitted down to his hands for a moment to check for a wedding ring. Then she kicked herself for listening to her friend's constant PR job. For someone who claimed a successful husband was at the top of her 'to do' list, Clarissa didn't seem in a rush to settle down herself.

"You're here for the annual retreat?" Naomi asked.

He nodded his head. "Well, tangentially anyway. The company I work for has a supply contract with the district for computer server maintenance. Pretty exciting stuff if you're heavily into script."

She nodded but said "Not even a little bit," and that elicited a smile. He was rather handsome... but definitely too old to flirt with.

"You're here for the RightBuy event?" the man asked. "He extended his hand to shake. "I'm Jerry."

Naomi shook. "Nice to meet you. Do you have time for a drink?"

He did, and before long, it had turned into two drinks, then three. He was funny and nice, and sexy, but also just unexceptional enough to be forgettable – which was exactly what he was going for.

A few hours later, Brennan rolled out of the hotel double-bed in the early-morning dark and began to get dressed.

The champagne bucket and two glasses were still on the round breakfast table, adjacent to the steamer trunk she'd brought along for the event. The woman from the bar had taken twenty minutes to fall asleep once she'd drunk the spiked bubbly. He'd barely managed to keep her occupied, to avoid cheating on Carolyn. He'd never been the type of operative who'd favor sex as a means to an end and wasn't about to start now that he was working for himself.

He looked back at Clarissa. Given the choice, he'd have spent the night chatting up the nice, polite one. But the vamp was the corporate archivist, and by the time she awoke, the steamer trunk would be missing one of the massive binders within.

She would notice immediately, as she was as fastidious as sexually aggressive. She would feel violated and betrayed. But she would fear the corporate response and cover it up, rationalizing that one binder of documents out of two dozen would only be missed if she allowed anyone to notice. They were historical, essentially valueless for anything but preservation, after all.

He didn't pause in the darkened lobby of the small hotel and walked straight out to his rented car, not pausing to call Jonah and confirm until he'd stopped to refuel, a half-hour outside Windermere.

When he hung up on the call, he checked the phone's map tool and prepared to drive back to London and the hotel.

He felt dirty, even without any sex being involved. He had no sense that he'd done right or wrong, just that stealing something from a drugged civilian felt like the latter.

He tried to focus on what it would mean for Jessica and Josh to go to college. Brennan pulled the rented white compact back onto the road and headed towards the city.

10.

Oct. 17, 2020

NUEVA ESPERANZA, ARGENTINA

An Experimental Community, South of
San Carlos de Bariloche, Patagonia

Gurchuran Das squeezed out of the gap between the steel bleacher seating, the roar of the three-hundred strong crowd making it clear no one was looking backwards or paying any attention.

He'd had to hold his tote bag in front of him to make it through the narrow passage. He slung it back over his shoulder.

The bleachers were just ten yards from the colony's north wall and, as per his habit, the armed guard who usually manned the corner watchtower was taking a break for a cigarette. He'd leaned his rifle against the guard box and was sitting on its edge, his back to the long stretch of wall as he clicked open a steel Zippo lighter and the cigarette flared.

Now. Das bolted towards the wall. He'd taken his chances with the colony's security being lax by tying the short length of rope to the lamp standard a day earlier. It was just three feet of rope with a few knots, but gave him enough to grasp that he could pull himself up to the top of the wall and over it. There was no barbed wire or glass to worry about; no one was really expecting anyone to break out, after all. The guards were there to prevent unwanted intruders, in the knowledge that Dr. Gabriel Verde's research would be ground-breaking and valuable.

Das knew much more. He'd worked on the genetic recombination portion of the project for two years. Its implications were staggering, the potential consequences to humanity vast and world-changing.

That made it valuable, indeed.

Unbeknownst to his employers, Das had money problems. There was the gambling habit, credit cards run up by tens of thousands of dollars. There was the mistress in London, with her expensive shopping habits. There was his wife and two young children at home in Hull. Then there was the extended family in India to whom he was expected to mail monthly assistance.

It added up to more than he could make, even at the above-average pay Verde International doled out monthly. It was a constant anchor of worry around his neck.

He dropped over the wall. The parking lot was just a hundred yards away. But he'd have to walk right under the tower to get there, then around to the front of the compound. From there, he'd have to cross fifty yards on foot, in the low light of early evening, but with two guards at the front gate able to spot him and ask questions.

Das edged cautiously along the wall, looking up, waiting for the guard to lean over the rail and start shooting. That wasn't how it would go down, he was sure, as they'd be more cautious; they wouldn't want a lawsuit from accidentally shooting a nosy local kid. But if they spotted him, alarms would sound quickly and he'd have a team on his tail. He saw a gun barrel poke past the edge of the railing…

And then it slid away and disappeared.

Das kept moving.

At the corner, he chanced a glance and saw that the parking lot was full of vehicles, but clear of people.

Verde's announcement and speech was being broadcast by a handful of news outlets, by special invitation, and no one had permission to leave the compound for the night.

When he'd signed up, he'd understood having employees agree to limit their movements until the project was done. The work was game-changing in the field of genetics. The sacrifice of a few months' privacy was worth it, he'd insisted to his brother Adrees.

Two years later, he felt trapped. He had information to sell but no way to sell it. He could not transmit data from anywhere within a mile of the compound without the signal being picked up; he couldn't get into Bariloche by legitimate means, as they were sequestered without vehicles, the array of food and entertainment on site designed to suffice.

But Das was a keen observer. He'd befriended one of the dayshift guards at the gate. He'd visited him frequently, enduring seemingly endless conversations about Argentine football. After about thirty such conversations, the guard said something meaningful. He said the same bus went by the northeast corner of the property every night on the way from the airport to the city. It stopped at the intersection with the road to Bariloche. It was stupid, the guard noted, because nobody from the compound ever got aboard. And yet, every night, despite few homes within miles, the bus made the designated stop.

He'd looked up average bus speeds, done the calculations. It would take ten minutes to get to town, another five to drop him off at the depot. The speech would go on for another ten minutes, minimum, after which a group of the staff had a rock band that was going to headline a live show and dance. It was all very communal.

Das began walking towards the lot, peripheral vision flitting to his left shoulder to see if the guards were paying attention. They finished talking about something and one turned in his direction. He felt himself freezing instinctively. But he covered the move, bending down to tie his shoelace. By the time he got up and continued, the guard had turned back to his friend's conversation.

The bus was on time, pulling up in front of the parking lot as he crossed its asphalt. He walked towards it at pace, not wanting to break into a run and give himself away but feeling the urge, nonetheless. He was afraid the driver would be so accustomed to no one boarding that he would just drive away, without noticing the approaching passenger.

He heard the squeal of the bus's retarder brake, the engine picking up, its wheels beginning to turn as it began to pull away from the curb without him. Das broke into a trot, still wary of onlookers, the overhead streetlamps in the parking lot seeming like the brightest floodlights in the circumstances.

The bus squealed to a halt. A moment later, the bifold door flipped open. The man behind the wheel was older, deeply tanned with bright white hair and a moustache. His smile suggested it was a nice change of pace. "I almost missed you!" he said in Spanish as Das climbed aboard. "The town council says this is an important stop on the route, in case the domestic staff who work security out here and such need it for work. But we have never gotten anyone in the two years I've been driving."

Das paid the fare in loose change. There was a woman seated at the back in a plain dress, carrying a wheeled shopping bag. Das sat halfway up, by the side doors. Verde had plenty of pull in the community, he recognized. Getting the bus stopped by the police or Army and having him removed would not be hard. Then there would be questions, lawsuits. And there were rumors about the legendary researcher – or, more specifically, about his cryptic personal assistant, Peter Bruner, a dour, middle-aged Swiss former army colonel who had been with Verde for decades. Some of the staff suggested Bruner would do anything to protect his employer, right up to and including making problems disappear permanently.

Not that Das believed it. The nature of the work had some sinister overtones – it was a genetic engineering project, after all, and that could put a scare into the public. But Verde's record for devising treatments, remedies, vaccines … he was beloved by the international scientific and business communities, even if it had not resulted in mass public acclaim.

But the people who funded him? No one on the project outside of Verde and Bruner seemed to know where his money came from. Assuredly, he'd made a fortune – millions upon millions of dollars – from prior patents and inventions. But Nova Esperanza was the size of a small town. It cost as much in a single year just to run the place and pay everyone. That meant the millions being spent were coming from other sources, people likely far less inclined to magnanimity.

The bus rolled through the darkness along the mountain road. Bariloche's sloped streets had been partly founded by German settlers more than a hundred years prior and its architecture of spires and arches and old wood resembled a quaint Bavarian village. Even the grandiose homes that ringed the nearby lake were in the style, the properties passed down between members of German, Swiss and Danish families, rarely sold on. He could barely make them out in the dark, just a few twinkling lights, beyond reach, as the bus trundled its way towards the glow of the small city.

Five minutes later, it was on Paseo Drive, surrounded by two and three-story buildings, home to clothiers, chocolatiers, music stores and craft shops. Das watched a police car zip by the bus as it waited at a light, the police light flashing and siren wailing. He felt his nerves take hold, his stomach rumbling, body trembling slightly. Were they rushing to beat the bus to its depot? Were they there to arrest him?

He looked up at the driver, then back through the window to the road ahead and the curve around which the flashing lights had just disappeared.

Das made the decision in the moment. There were hotels all around the downtown area that had free wifi. All he needed was a few minutes. He stood up quickly and tugged the bell to signal he wanted to get off. The driver looked into his gigantic rectangular rear-view mirror, saw it was the man he'd talk to earlier, and put on the bus's turn signal, pulling it as far to the curb as he could without hitting parked cars.

Das gave him a small wave of thanks as he climbed off. He looked both ways down the sidewalk. Even at night, the tourism base of the town, which was just minutes from several ski hills, meant plenty of people were out and about. His eyes flitted between neon and backlit signs until he saw it. 'Hotel El Capital, Wifi, televisión por cable.'

He looked both ways and waited for traffic to slow then jogged across the street. He checked the street again as he walked through the hotel bar entrance, waiting for someone to say something. But it seemed quiet.

It wouldn't take long if the connection was good. He'd managed to warn his brother a week earlier that he'd be sending something sooner than later. Adrees worked in the British Department of Defense as an analyst. He had access to the kind of information, and the kind of people who would be extremely interested in what Das had to offer.

The café was nearly empty, just a young couple canoodling across a booth table by the far window, the barrista behind the counter, an old man in the corner reading a newspaper at one of the raised round tables.

He walked to the counter and ordered a black coffee and an hour of online time.

The barrista prepared it and he carried the white porcelain cup and saucer to the back corner table and a computer terminal.

Das waited until the staff member's back was turned, the man's attention on cleaning the coffee thermos. He took the USB stick out of his pocket and plugged it into the port on the front of the tower.

Das brought up a command line window and checked the computer's connection to the internet. He brought up a new connection and pinged an address in the United Kingdom. A few moments later, a code prompt asked him for a password and he entered the string he'd stolen from his brother on his last visit home.

A confirmation string appeared and he copied the USB data folder to the foreign FTP server. It began replicating and sending each file, compressed and encrypted. There were twelve gigabytes but at least half of that, he supposed, was Verde's arcane encryption and file management system. The connection was okay, the time to copy all of the data just a few minutes.

He glanced up at the picture window facing the sidewalk outside. The man was at the far edge, leaning just far enough past the edge of its frame to keep an eye on him but remain surreptitious. He was older, with a roundish, heavy face and grey-silver hair. He wore a pair of square, steel-framed sunglasses. The man pulled back slightly.

Is he... watching me? He looked older than the average rental muscle Verde had at the compound. He'd gone back to watching the street. *Perhaps he was just curious about the businesss. You need to calm down.*

He checked the file. Three minutes, thirty-four seconds to go.

His eyes wandered the width of the picture window. On the other side of the street was a bus stop. An older woman in a mink fur coat was reading a newspaper, an old man seated next to her. A bus pulled up, blocking Das's view of them. A moment later it pulled away. The old man and woman were gone, replaced by a tall, thin man with a bony face and a navy-blue peacoat. He wore sunglasses and he stared straight across the street at the café. The sun would be shining on the windows outside, the glare restricting their view. Neither man likely knew he was there, Das realized.

They were waiting for someone to walk out.

A car pulled up to the man by the bus stop. Another two men climbed out, younger, one with a blond buzzcut, the other shorter, a brown mop top. They looked like prep school students, their dark blazers and ties matching. They began talking to the peacoat passenger.

Das checked the file. Two minutes, nineteen.

Who had tipped them? Someone who saw him enter the building, or… someone in the café? He stared around the room. The young couple were still giggling. If they were working for Verde they were Oscar-caliber actors. The barista hadn't taken his eyes off the machines he was cleaning. He glanced over to the old man with the paper.

The senior raised it suddenly, trying not to make the motion look jerky as he lifted the top edge of the paper above eye level to hide his face.

The scientist checked the window again. The three men were crossing the street, jaywalking, waiting midpoint for a car to pass then heading towards the front door. He looked down at the transfer.

One minute, four seconds.

Most of the files had gone already, he knew. He had seconds to decide. If he waited for the whole thing they'd be on him. Getting the data sent off was of no use if he was arrested and charged with industrial espionage. *Damn Verde's file system.* He was worried if he yanked the drive early it might corrupt the whole thing, make the effort wasted. He saw the right-front door begin to swing inwards.

Das grabbed the drive and ran, heading for the front counter. He ignored the server's protestations and vaulted over the counter, then ran into the kitchen area. As he'd expected, they had a rear exit. He jogged past the central prep station and the shocked short order cook. He burst out the back door, the sound of shouting behind him. There was an alley behind the hotel, nearly blocked up with staff cars from the surrounding businesses. He skittered between them, then down the narrow exit between the backs of two buildings.

At the street exit a block south, he looked both ways for a cab. He was sweating, obviously nervous, attracting attention from pedestrians. If he was lucky, he could find a cab and it could get to the airport before anyone called ahead. He could get out of Argentina before Verde used his pull to sick the local police on him. Or worse, before Brunner set his security guard thugs upon him.

That could end badly, Das knew. There were rumors that locals who'd broken into the compound had wound up in Bariloche's hospital, and only left breathing to send a message to anyone else who interrupted the sanctity of the research colony. Would they do worse to an accomplished scientist, even one with his personal problems? Probably not. If he'd thought they were that crazy, he wouldn't have risked the theft in the first place.

He saw a cab pass two blocks to the west, then a few moments later another. *A stand. There's a cab stand nearby.* It was probably outside one of the bigger hotels. It made more sense to head that way and try to flag someone down, if possible, on route than to wait in vain. And they would be right behind him at any moment.

Das began to jog west.

'Hey!"

He heard a yell a block behind and glanced over his shoulder. Three men were running hard, trying to reach him. He almost knocked down a mother and child, staggering to avoid them. He sprinted diagonally across the street, cutting down an alley and between houses, trying to limit their view of him.

A few inches from his head, a leaf disintegrated to a 'thwipp' sound, a split second before he heard the rifle crack. *Is... Did... Is someone shooting at me??!*

Das began to sprint for his life, his feet pounding the pavement as he headed for the next corner, looking down the street to the next block, his eyes searching for the hotel cab stand. He heard another yell, voices not far back. He rounded the corner and sprinted across the street. There was a Lutheran church on the corner, old concrete and rebar with a cross atop the spire. He ran up the steps. Nobody would risk trying to hurt him in church, Das reasoned.

He sprinted into the nave, the long walkway between the double rows of pews. The church was cavernous, creosote-soaked wood beams holding up the cathedral ceiling forty feet above. Ten-foot tall stained-glass windows featuring the twelve apostles surrounded the room, scattered beams of light cutting through, alighting the altar at the head of the room.

The priest approached him with a stern expression. He was wizened, with half-spectacles and a crown of dark grey hair. "What is the matter, my son?" he asked as Das walked toward him.

"Father, I…" Das began to say, the words caught in his mouth as the priest's hand came up quickly from his side, the stiletto blade sliding out even as he drove it into Das's belly. The old man jerked the blade upwards, his face a stoic grimace as he held the knife there, forcing it home with all his strength. The scientist grasped at the other man's shoulders as the shock and pain overwhelmed him, ruptured organs failing, eyes wide in surprise, his strength waning as his blood spilled out onto the church's stone floor.

He slumped to the ground, unconscious, life ebbing from him. The priest looked down dispassionately, then reached down to wipe the blade on Das's clothing. He retracted the blade just as the church doors were flung open, the café watchers running inside.

The priest nodded towards the prone man's corpse. "He won't be any more trouble," he said in Spanish, his accent tinged by his European roots.

"Go on, take him! Don't make me do your jobs any longer than necessary. Yes, good? You better hope he didn't manage to send a message, or we'll all be answering difficult questions. Just keep in mind how much is at stake here."

11.

LONDON

Oct. 17, 2020, 10:45 PM

The girl with the fake pearl earrings was fascinated. She reached out with her index finger from her position in the passenger seat of Charlie Rich's decrepit Vauxhall Omega. Its tip traced the screen of the laptop as code flew by.

"What's it doing, Charlie?" she asked in a hushed tone, like a child who thinks she's seen a fairy. "It's going so fast…"

It was dusk and they were two blocks from the Defense Department on Whitehall Place. He hadn't been able to resist showing off his latest find, a new series of wireless access hubs the department had introduced with faulty encryption and an admin backdoor.

"See those little dots?"

"The groups of them?"

"Yeah… those are called packets. And what my piece of software here does is it intercepts them when they pass through the modem going from one place to another."

She paused and considered that, unsure. "What's in them, then?"

"Information. Data that I can sell."

"You mean government secrets, like? Hang about, love… this in't illegal like, innit?"

He'd met her at a Greek restaurant in Bexley while driving through, a night earlier. She was a lovely lass, slightly plump and with big blue eyes.

What was her name again? Jenny? Genevieve?

Gemma.

"Not to worry, Gemma, love," he said, flashing his pearly whites. "I wouldn't want to get either of us into trouble, would I?"

She'd said he reminded her of Jack Whitehall, which was somehow both flattering and emasculating. *But she'd also wanted to go into the loo and shish your kebab, my son. So… patience.*

She leaned into him, snuggling into his armpit as they watched the glow of the government buildings. "You aren't half smart."

"And you are absolutely lovely."

"Aw…" She pantomimed dabbing at her lash extensions. "Go on then… make me all emosh."

"So… would you like to get to know Charlie Jr. a little better?" he asked, moving her hand to his thigh.

"Gah!" She smacked his leg with an open palm. "You men are all the bloody same. You know me from nowt on five minutes and you think I'm going to rip me knickers off…"

"I really didn't mean anything by it, really…"

"Oh? You really didn't? Well you can really take me home, you really enormous twat!"

"Gemma, darling…"

She crossed her arms. "Don't you 'darling' me, Charlie… I mean… Shu'up! I don't even know your last name, you cheeky bastard. Go on then! Start the car. Take me home."

Charlie sighed and did as requested, the thirty-two-year-old Vauxhall spluttering a few times as its aging fuel pump did the trick, before the motor finally kicked in. It wasn't ever going to be mistaken for a flash ride, but he'd managed to keep it on the road for years, using the tips his father had taught him.

He frowned as he pulled out onto the road and switched off the indicator. He hadn't thought about his father in months. Robert Rich had died at eighty-four, a year earlier. He'd been a strangely wise man, more boisterous than your average Englishman but also prone to periods of long privacy and reflection. A former Army Engineer, he'd gone on to work for a land surveying company for many years before being unceremoniously laid off, a victim of his ethics and his concern over how the company was treating clients.

That deep morality had seemingly done nothing but cost his father, throughout his life. Being decent wasn't respected, Charlie had learned. It was just seen as weakness. He believed in his father's ethic, his lessons. But he knew better than to make any of his fights public. The world had changed that way, and his father had never accepted that. He'd spent the last twenty years of his working life as a day laborer, happy to do a solid day's work building houses or roads in exchange for a fair wage, nothing owed to either party but mutual, quiet respect.

Losing his profession hadn't made him a lesser man. If anything, it had brought his strengths of character to the fore. He still went to his local pub two nights a week and drank with his mates, stopped in every now and then during the week. He still watched football with Charlie's stepmom, the boy's mother having died when he was just eight, a victim of staggering bipolar depression and, despite her husband's best efforts, a suicide statistic.

They'd never been rich, but they'd always been decent and thoughtful, respectful of critical thinking and intellectual humility, of constant learning.

Charlie figured he'd be a terrible disappointment to both of them.

"Should I worry about any of that computer stuff?" Gemma asked out of the blue, after five quiet minutes of negotiating London's night traffic, no better really than much of the day.

She took her cigarettes from her purse and lit one, blowing out a plume of smoke, then noticing his quick, uncomfortable frown in her periphery. She rolled down the window. "Sorry."

"I'm fine," he replied. "And, no, you shouldn't. Technically, what I just did isn't illegal. The packets were unencumbered, which is to say, they were in open air, unencrypted, between a router hub and modem. As long as I don't actually open them..."

"Oh... sort of like driving behind a mail lorry and picking up packages that fall off then?"

He smiled. She seemed like a homespun Eastender, the kind of girl others prejudged as vacuous, and if he was being honest with himself, she hadn't shown great complexity in the two days of pawing each other. But that was his own snobbery, Charlie realized. He hadn't tried to find out if she had anything going on between her ears. She'd simply shown, on occasion, a quickness and cleverness with the unfamiliar.

It was a shame it wasn't going to go anywhere.

Sonya would be back in a few days. She'd take him back, as she did every time she packed off to her mum's house in Brittany in a huff. She'd rant about why he hadn't proposed yet, even though they were both two years clear of university. She'd whinge about his lack of career motivation and why he didn't take his obvious skill with code to a big company. She'd remind him of how much she was sacrificing for them, how hard she was working at the public relations house.

And then she'd let him move back into their apartment, the same apartment on the third floor from which, arms spread wide, she had tossed the majority of his clothing and possessions a week earlier.

Things would get back to normal.

"Love?" Gemma said.

He'd zoned out, Charlie realized, his eyes taking in the road and obstacles but his brain thinking about Sonya. "Hmm? Absolutely, my dear."

"And if you don't open the prezzies, you don't get nicked?"

"Quite. There's no information to suggest ownership and, unlike a solid object, I can't 'turn them in' to be claimed as they're technically exact duplicates of the packages the person originally sent. My software intercepts and 'clones' the package, then lets it go along its merry way, to its recipient."

She turned his way quickly, shifting her bum in the passenger seat. "So you're literally, actually a hacker... literally, actually... like in the movies?"

Charlie hated the term, as did most of his mates. "That's not really a thing. It's like professional hitmen or western quickdraw gunfights, darling: an exaggeration for entertaining effect."

It took thirty minutes to get her home. He pulled the car up to the curb and put it into park, leaving the engine running. After the fiasco at the Defense Department, turning it off and asking if he could come up for a coffee seemed unwise, at best. A slightly bigger girl, Gemma was no wilting flower, and he rather suspected she'd punch him in the nose if he even raised it.

Instead, she turned his way again. "Give me your phone," she demanded.

He did as requested. She entered her number. "Text me if you want to get together again some time, but bring your manners," she said.

Traffic was lighter on the way back towards Central London. It was nearly ten-thirty but there was still time to stop in at the pub for a pint with Aubrey and Tim.

He heard the faint strains of a police siren, the klaxon alarm shrieking through the city night. Charlie checked the rearview mirror. The flashing blue glow was a few hundred meters back, closing quickly. He felt a surge of nerves, an electric shake across the skin.

His stomach turned. He hadn't been entirely honest with young Gemma. He'd used an administrator password, an accidental backdoor, to tap into the router in the first place. Given that it was a government building, it broke at least a half dozen rather serious laws.

But there was no way anyone could have flagged him. He was running off network, just using his own modem and software to connect directly through the hub. Even if they'd gotten around his security and tossed malware into the intercepted packets, there was nothing native for them to execute; the laptop was running off his own script, its BIOS protected by yet more security, well beyond the average government coder. Its signals, when transmitting, were further disguised with both redirection and cloned IP addresses.

The squad car drew nearer quickly, the lights brightening, the Vauxhall's rearview mirror filling up, the siren blaring above its relatively quiet dashboard radio.

A hundred meters back now, still closing.

12.

A corner was coming up quickly but the light was red. Charlie knew he'd have to at least slow the car down for it. But if they were after him, it would present a moment to make a decision: whether to step on the accelerator full force and try to lose them, or whether to pull over and take the consequences.

After running a magnet over the laptop first, of course.

The latter seemed more sensible.

Or… perhaps you're just being paranoid, my son. Perhaps it makes more sense to just pull over to the shoulder. He flicked on the indicator and spun the wheel.

The squad car zoomed by in a streak of white, still accelerating. Charlie let out an enormous sigh. Behind him, a Mini from the inside lane had also pulled over. Its driver honked the horn, to prompt him to get moving. Charlie raised a hand, hopefully visible through the rear window even in the gloom, before putting the car back into drive.

Three minutes later, he was safely parked around the corner from the Southampton Arms, just off Highgate. Aubrey Fitzhugh had managed to turn a four-person table into a sort of storyteller's dais, a lectern that came with convenient wooden seats and pints of Hallets cider, a small crowd listening to his Irish brogue as he regaled them with drinking adventures past.

"Charlie, my boy!" Aubrey broke away from his tale to greet the smaller man. "Ladies, gentlemen, this is the esteemed Mr. Charles Ruddiger Rich, heir to the Ruddiger's Baby Formula Fortune and, it is rumored far and wide, the penis model for Mark Wahlberg's prosthetic in 'Boogie Nights!'"

There was a smattering of applause. "Thank you, thank you," Charlie bowed. "I was, in fact, merely Mr. Wahlberg's naked body double for the sex scenes…"

There was a smattering of boos and laughs. He pulled out the remaining chair on the far side of the elevated table. "Oh… bugger off, the lot of you. No one appreciates the true me."

A server sidled up to the table. "Pint of Smithwicks, Charlie?"

He nodded. "Thank you, Jan."

"You've got forty-five minutes. We're packing it in at eleven thirty tonight."

"Thank you, Jan."

"Don't be cheeky. I knew your father, young man…"

"Thank you, Jan."

She shook her head and retreated towards the bar, her expression somewhere between annoyance and concern. Charlie had been coming to the pub for more than a decade, since he was old enough for his father to sneak him a shandy.

"Where've you been, then?" Aubrey asked. "The lasses you scared off have been marveling at my bard-like balladry and my homespun Irish wit. I was going to take them all home with me, I was…"

"And doubtless fall asleep from the nine pints before you managed to get your shoes off, let alone theirs."

Aubrey tilted his head and thought about it. "Huh. 'Tis true, I suppose." Then he frowned. "Why're you so late, anyhow?"

Charlie grimaced playfully.

Aubrey's frown shifted to a suspicious glare down his nose. "What've you been up to now?"

"You remember that vulnerability I mentioned this morning…"

"You didn't."

"I…"

"You did not, because that would be really bloody stupid, now, wouldn't it? Compromising a top-secret facility just to prove to yourself how smart you are…"

"It's what I do…."

"… when you know you couldn't sell anything you got…"

"Well now, technically…"

Aubrey shook his head vociferously. "No. No, no, no, no, no…"

"I mean, technically I could physically sell it and take money. It wouldn't necessarily be the wisest use of my time…"

"Tell me you haven't taken anything yet."

It sounded like 'any ting' in his brogue. Charlie smugly pursed his lips, trying to not grin broadly at precisely the wrong time, but enjoying his friend's discomfort.

"Nobody's being hurt here... I was just poking around, having a little fun. I wanted to impress this smashing bird from Bexley..."

"A sentence one does not hear every day..."

"Anyway, I showed her the vulnerability and she got nervous, so we left."

"And that is how it should stay," Aubrey suggested. He downed the last of his pint and then craned his head around looking for Jan the server. "Now, she knew I only had a half left but she buggered off before I could order another, deliberately. I swear, that woman doesn't want customers, she wants custody rights."

"She's worried about your liver. She shouldn't be... it's tougher than the rest of you, or you wouldn't be alive."

"Don't try to change the subject," Aubrey said as he caught Jan's eye and waved for another pint, the room busy and the din of conversation making the approach practical. "We were talking about your immense problems, not my relatively petty issue with the drink...."

"Petty...?"

"Ah! Subject changing! I said 'none of that now!', my lad. You're going to agree not to go back there and try that hub again, aren't you? Aren't you?" He put a hand on Charlie's shoulder and gripped it stridently. "Because to be frank, any financial outlay that I might previously have had available to bail you out has, unfortunately, been spent on alcohol."

"No worries, my son, no worries."

"Ah. Hah! No one's gotten hurt yet, so keep it that way. Sooner or later, we have to make the decent decisions. The arc of history favors civility." He turned and looked over his shoulder. "JAN!" he yelled over the din. "WHERE ARE YOU WOMAN! It's almost eleven-fifteen and I don't have a pint!"

The odds favored Aubrey's suggestion, Charlie knew. But that was the point, wasn't it? If it wasn't risky, it wouldn't be fun. It would be just another job, acquiring data and selling it. He might as well have been dying slowly in an office.

It was easy for Aubrey, whom he'd spent four years ganging up with in school; Aubrey had a four-book publishing deal, appearances on panel shows. One studio was paying him just to think up ideas for shows that might never even be made, a 'holding' arrangement or something.

Charlie knew his world would never be one of privilege and easy money. He'd always have to fight and claw for what he got, like his father.

He thought about the router again and the information that it might be so poorly protecting. Surely there was material worth a lot more than a few trade secrets about plans for a video game or whether someone launched a site off borrowed code. A few relatively harmless patent discoveries sold to the right Silicon Valley firm or Russian oligarch, and he could start shopping for a nice little flat of his own, give Sonya the notion he might actually have a mature, respectable bone in his body.

An hour later, the noise and bustle of the pub long behind him and quiet beginning to command the night, Charlie sat in his car across from the Department of Defense Research and Development Complex. He was in the shadows, out of view, the streetlamp just far enough ahead of his car to prevent attention falling upon it. His laptop rested on the passenger seat but he hadn't booted it, not yet.

Aubrey had him thinking.

MASTER OF THE REICH

The admin backdoor was the real problem, Charlie decided. The fact that it still had a generic "admin" login and password was, however, something he could use if caught, the kind of thing any curious young technophile might punch in for fun, just to see if it worked. He could plead ignorance... right up until they seized the laptop and asked why he also had wardriving software to capture packets.

He looked over at the building. It was so quiet, no one about. There was a guard at the front door, but he looked bored, the hour approaching one o'clock, most people settled in bed for the night. He glanced at the laptop, then back at the building. He knew Aubrey was right, technically. He knew there was risk, real risk of trouble.

But it's so tempting. Just... just a quick look. Just to see if it's still unguarded. Wardriving gave him a sense of control, like he could make sense of the world on his terms for a few minutes.

His hand hesitated over the power button for a moment. Then he pressed it firmly and quickly, the screen flashing to life, the computer booting. He used the trackball to highlight the grabber software and clicked it, then typed in the hub's IP. A screen prompted him for his login and password. He entered 'admin' for both.

The software's graph showed packets entering and leaving via the hub. Charlie watched them for a few seconds, looking for traffic that looked out of place, anything that might indicate a security protocol. A packet of data five times larger than others flitted onto the left of the flow-through graph. Charlie clicked it and the app began recording its data into a separate packet. The original continued on its way... and then dropped, disappearing from the graph.

He felt a flutter of nerves in his stomach. He knew he shouldn't have recorded anything, that it was theft as soon as he'd breached the access point. He reached down and slammed the laptop shut. Then he started the car.

In for a penny, in for a pound, Charlie my son...

Sonya would have him back soon, Charlie decided, as his aging vehicle negotiated the light traffic. He drove back to the residential hotel near Tottenham Court Road. The grimy third-floor room wasn't much, but it was cheap, and he could steal a decent wi-fi signal off a nearby restaurant. It was time to get some sleep.

In the morning, he reasoned, he could see if the risk had been worth it... or just another cheap thrill.

13.

Oct. 18, 2020

LONDON

The diminutive man striding the hallways of The SIS Building at Vauxhall Crossing was clearly irritated. His hands were thrust into the side pockets of the tan raincoat he wore over his tweed suit and he scowled as he stared straight through the marble floor.

He passed a woman in a business suit and another colleague, both pausing for the barest moment to acknowledge a senior department man... then thinking better of it when he didn't break stride. Peter Chappell, OBE, CMG, twice deputy head of the service and its newly appointed head of reorganization, was not a man who suffered time wasters gladly.

Today, someone was wasting his time.

The briefing memo had arrived on his phone thirty minutes earlier, a vague reference to a security breach that had prompted an immediate encrypted call to C, the head of the service.

The only man with more power in the building had found it mildly humorous that less than two days after Chappell's reorganization memo had gone out agency wide, demanding secure personal data and electronic devices, someone had breached the network at the Defense Department's research division, a day-to-day partner with the Secret Intelligence Service's own scientists.

"Apparently, they didn't get the memo, Peter," C had suggested.

"You can always count on the helpful military types to act with tact and subtlety. Get everyone together, find out what's going on, would you? I have lunch with the PM tomorrow. It would be rather nice to tell him something positive."

At the end of the hall a police guard stood outside double wooden doors. The 'war room' was reserved for meetings of the executive council, the body comprised of division leaders. The policeman pushed the door open as Chappell approached, not pausing for a moment to look at identification or consider the individual, whose reputation preceded him.

Four men and one woman sat around the table, all middle aged or beyond, suits perfunctory, expressions dour from the distraction. "Peter," Tony Hardcastle offered. The foreign operations chief was the largest person in the building by some measure at six-foot-six and three hundred pounds. "I suppose from your expression this isn't some silly drill dreamt up by..."

"No, it is not," Chappell said, not slowing as he rounded the table, tossing his binders down on the horseshoe desk with a loud slap. "We have a breach of the Defense Department's covert operations FTP server. Due to the changes at the department and the recent renovations, they'd brought in some new equipment and missed a wireless 'hub' router that had not been properly encrypted or protected."

Hardcastle's eyebrows rose. "And how long was this..."

"Three days, at most. Sara, is there something you should be telling me?"

At the far end of the table, Sara Hannigan looked up from her briefing notes, surprised to have been called on and not really paying attention. "Sorry…?"

Chappell exhaled loudly through flared nostrils but left his annoyance at that.

"You're our liaison to the Security Service. Surely if we had constant foreign surveillance on our most important defense facility in the heart of London, we would know about it. And yet that's what the window of opportunity suggests."

He didn't need to elaborate. Hannigan knew the chances of the Russians or Chinese picking that exact window of days was slim to none. That meant MI5 and the local police had missed something. "Whatever they missed," she said, "it won't be due to a lack of co-operation on our part. We've been diligent."

"Apparently not," Chappell said dryly. "The systems analysts say there was data sent to the FTP from an address in Argentina's Patagonia region last night, just before oh-one-hundred GMT. Someone intercepted the data. Subsequently, the same file was resent to the server two hours later using the same login and password; but its contents were gibberish and overwrote the earlier data. Tony…?"

Hardcastle shook his head. "We've already heard from all of the foreign desks, we have nothing covert or long-term that would have been sent from that region. Whoever sent it, it wasn't a spook. And it clearly wasn't DND…"

"There is another possibility."

The voice surprised him. Hardcastle had forgotten their adviser was present. It came from the back of the room, where two aging, corduroy-draped olive armchairs sat in sharp contrast against the red-orange wall by the bathroom door. The man seated on the right-hand chair was elderly, with a bushy moustache and thick glasses.

"Archie?"

The table turned as a whole. Archibald Grimes was a retired spymaster, a long-time field agent, then case officer and bureau head, eventually foreign service director. He'd been forced out for political reasons during the last bloodless management coup. But he'd been given a courtesy services contract at the minister's request, a reward for advice given when the politician was just a young man in law school.

Neither C nor Chappell liked having him around. Archie was a stickler for the rules, for playing it straight. He'd never shown a hint of ambition, beyond a desire to win in the field, for England. He had no vices, save a love of chess and feeding the pigeons in the park, near the two-bedroom house in Kingston-on-Thames that he'd owned since the early Nineteen Fifties.

He was eighty-five years old, and even in his youngest days with the service, right out of the army, he'd never given a single damn what anyone thought of him. That did not mean that he lacked tact. Indeed, Chappell had long concluded, there was no more even-tempered a man in London than Archie Grimes. It merely meant that when it came time to find something to hold over him, matters of pride, legacy and ego had been no more helpful than compromising vices.

"It could just have been unlucky," Grimes said. "I did some reading on the way over here…"

Hardcastle's stomach turned. Whenever Archie had "done some reading" it meant the rest of them had missed something.

"It turns out there's a rather common practice in London call 'war driving'," Archie said. "The youths use mobile tracking software to send 'pings' of data that find compromised wireless hubs. It seems far more likely that someone was just fooling about, given that there are probably dozens of them doing it on any given night. And government buildings make marvelous targets, one would think."

Chappell scoffed at the notion. "Really, Archie! You'd have us believe a complete coincidence on the one occasion that there's a breach?"

"I highly doubt there's only been one occasion, for one," Archie said. "I'm sure if we put our minds to it, we could think of a few occasions when both intelligence services and the defense department have had... issues."

Hardcastle jumped in to defend Chappell. He needed the reorganization to affirm his position. It had been a lean year. And Archie didn't really carry weight, not anymore. Not outside the odd invitation to lunch with someone immensely powerful and distracted. "That's really not the issue now, is it?" Hardcastle intoned. "Let's give Peter his due on this one, Archie, it would be a real wiz banger of a coincidence."

"I suppose. I would not, however, rule it out."

"We have strong contacts in the local computer coding community," Hardcastle said. "Inquiries?"

"Right away," said Chappell. "The sooner we clear this up, the better.

The morning had been a graceful affair. Jonah Tarrant sat next to his counterpart from MI6's operations branch at one end of the long restaurant table, as the man waffled on about the changes he'd seen in forty years of service. If he hadn't known better, he'd have expected a stiff breeze to come along and the man to turn to dust.

"Of course, in the post-Cold War era — which is to say the post-Soviet era — things have changed drastically, from issues of dominating a war space to dominating economic models..."

He pronounced "issue" as "ih-s'you." It was doubtless some upper crust affectation, Jonah thought. A server leaned over his shoulder. 'More scrambled eggs, sir?"

Jonah waved the waiter off. The food was all heavy here, too, at least when eating with the local bureaucrats. They all wanted beef: Wellington, Au jus, in the form of thick steaks and knobby sirloins. He'd been in town for two full days before he'd seen someone just enjoying a salad, a girl in the restaurant at Joe and Carolyn Brennan's hotel.

"... and of course, once Putin had his hand firmly in the corporate acquisitions sector, there was no chance of turning back..."

Jonah nodded politely. The get-together was a once yearly tradition, the London Chief and his CIA boss meeting with their MI6 counterparts for a cordial lunch and off-the-record note comparison. The timing had been fortunate with respect to the missing immigration files and Joe's vacation.

Well... the former, anyway. The vacation timing had been a quiet request to Carolyn. They'd grown close in their time working together and she was still eager to please him, to make it known she was senior management material now that she was back, seconded from the NSA.

Brennan didn't need to know that. He didn't take kindly to being manipulated. After fifteen years in covert ops, Jonah thought, he should've gotten accustomed.

He felt a tug on his sleeve and checked to his right, expecting the waiter to once again be trying to get his attention. Instead, it was Reeves, a twenty-something new recruit and the local office's babysitter.

"Sir, we need to make polite excuses and head to the office. We have an emerging situation..."

"... Not that we minded in West Berlin, if I'm being completely honest," the MI6 man was droning on. "We had enough to worry about with so many former Stasi chaps out of work and looking for the first lifeline they could find."

His opposite number was publicly identified only as 'C', though in the era of modern accountability, Sir Cedric Campbell-Jones's appointment had required legislative assent. He was well into retirement, in reality, the heavy lifting left to those below him.

Jonah turned his way and affixed the man with a serious stare, then interrupted him, accompanied by the lightest touch on the forearm. "Sir Cedric, you've absolutely spoiled me with your time this morning, but I've been called away..."

"Oh! Anything I should know about, old boy?"

"Nothing serious, just a political request. You know how that can be..." Jonah clapped the man on the back as he rose. "Hopefully, next year we can get you to come over and visit us in the Colonies, take in D.C."

He was on the phone to his number two, Adrienne Hayes, as soon as he hit the back seat of the limousine. "Talk to me."

"I'd like to be able to tell you it's something massive, because it probably is..."

"But...?"

"But we don't know what's going on. What we do know is that our embassy listening stations are getting all sorts of traffic about a data leak from the Brits and multiple interested parties from the Continent."

"Such as?"

"The Germans, the Austrians, The Russians, The Israelis..."

If she'd been in the car, Hayes would've seen his surprise. Instead, Jonah asked, "Anything specific at all?"

"Not to the item. But the package may be a local amateur, and the contents are something that would've been of interest to the Defense Department's 'r and d' people. It was lifted off an insecure wireless point..."

If she was fishing for cheap shots involving the Brits, Jonah wasn't biting. Adrienne was tactically brilliant and even more ruthless than he; but as a consequence, she was also ambitious, and he shared as little genuine sentiment with her as possible.

"And the local?"

"Sounds like an educated guess that paid off," she suggested. "They started looking and made enough noise to attract the other services."

"Hmmm. Throw chum in the water and you get sharks," Jonah suggested. "Any idea how close they are to a target suspect?"

"Hours," Hayes said. "I know one thing for certain: if it is just some amateur, I'd hate to be that guy."

14.

Oct. 18, 2020

LONDON

Charlie woke early, his head throbbing slightly from the pints of Smithwicks and the late night. Normally, he wouldn't have been roused by anything short of a bursting bladder for eight solid hours, and he knew instinctively as his eyes fluttered open that something was off.

There was a hum, a buzzing sound in the background.

He turned his head from the sofa bed and caught a glimpse of the old wooden chair he'd been using as a bedside table. His phone was vibrating, its black plastic case rattling slightly on the hard surface.

Charlie stared at it, willing it to stop. After another fifteen seconds of trying to win his attentions, it complied.

"Hmmm. Good."

The phone began to buzz again. Charlie sighed and turned fully toward it, glaring at it as if his eyes might produce lasers with sufficient annoyance. "Stop. Ringing."

He paused to think about his aching skull.

The pub.

The girl. The access point.

He remembered how his nerves had fluttered when the police car blared past on Tottenham Court Road. Charlie grabbed for the phone, knocking it onto the floor in the process. He saw the announcement on its screen as soon as his fingerprint had unlocked it: 13 messages.

The phone buzzed again, this time to signal a text. He switched apps. It was from Tim, Aubrey Fitzhugh's younger brother and a decent coder in his own right.

He'd already sent several, it appeared, beginning an hour earlier. Charlie opened the latest.

"GET. OUT. NOW."

Charlie rolled out of bed. His feet found the hardwood and he moved quickly, grabbing the jeans and shirt he'd worn the night before from the floor nearby. He dressed and put on his tennis shoes before grabbing his duffel bag and throwing his laptop into it. He left the room door unlocked. If the police were coming, they were going to turn it over anyway, finding only clothes.

He turned to walk the length of the hallway to the front stairs but stopped as soon as he heard the boots coming up them. He backtracked to the other end of the hallway and the rear flight. He pushed the stairwell door open... and immediately heard more boots from below.

The fire escape. He could barely make it out through the smudged glass of the stairwell window. The building was already decrepit; he doubted the old emergency stairs were any better. He moved over to the window and pulled up hard on both handles.

It didn't budge.

The boots were right below him now, clomping across the fourth-floor landing. He shoved on the frame with both palms, but it wouldn't move, either painted shut or swollen tight from years of moisture and neglect.

On the half-stairwell below a helmeted tactical officer craned his neck to look up and saw Charlie's frantic efforts. "Police!" He yelled. "Charles Rich, you are under arrest. Put the bag down and..."

Charlie ignored him, turning to sprint up the roof stairs, two at a time. At the top, the old wooden door was locked. "Damn it, not now!" He muttered. The officers turned the corner to his stairwell, pistols raised. "Down! Down on the ground, now!"

He flung himself at the door, crashing shoulder first into it, the lock hasp breaking. Charlie staggered out onto the roof, boots pounding up the stairs. He sprinted for the far side and looked down.

The fire escape only went to the fourth floor. The drop to its rusty iron grating floor was probably only fifteen feet, but it looked like a half mile in the moment. He looked over his shoulder to see the officers coming through the door. One of them chambered a pistol round.

Oh God, don't miss. Don'tmissdon'tmissdon't...

Charlie jumped.

His tennis shoes slammed into the metal grate, body bouncing off the safety rail. He let go of the duffel bag and it tumbled to the edge of the fire escape, hanging half over the edge. Charlie grasped for it frantically but only managed to further its momentum, the duffel bag slipping over. He stretched as it fell, his arm suspended above the backstreet, fingers barely finding the canvas shoulder strap.

The data was all he had, his only way out. He needed to find out what it was, he knew, or get rid of it so thoroughly that even a hard drive trace analysis wouldn't be able to recover it.

The former idea seemed sounder; if they already knew who he was, they had to have evidence of his intrusion, some sort of digital fingerprint.

Above him, the senior tactical officer was looking down from the roof, pistol outstretched. "You've nowhere to go..."

Charlie looked down at the street below. He had a well-honed distrust of authority and as far as he could tell, there was no one stationed behind the building. He scampered to the ladder release and threw the handle. It rattled downwards just as a trio of rappelling ropes dropped from the roof.

He followed it, climbing through the square hole in the grate and down the rungs. Boots echoed off the grate above him as the officers descended. The young hacker moved as quickly as he could, not worrying about the possible fall.

And then his feet went out from under him. He grasped the rung he'd just released with his left hand, barely holding on, the ladder having ended a floor early. Charlie pulled as hard as he could, stretching up with his knee, searching for the step with his right foot and finding it.

The first officer was just ten feet above him. He had no choice. He climbed to the bottom rung and let go.

The ground rushed towards him and his feet slammed into the asphalt, Charlie rolling sideways to reduce the impact. He sprinted for the end of the lane, losing himself amongst the morning foot traffic.

15.

Jonah Tarrant waited as the three screens flickered to life.

"Jonah, my boy, good to see you as always." CIA Director Nicholas Wilkie was wearing his Navy dress uniform. He'd taken to calling upon it for public events more and more often as he approached the end of his tenure.

The director was retiring in six months, just out of his latest hospital stint and expected to name Jonah as his successor; the younger man had been acting director for most of the prior two years, due to Wilkie's ill health.

Jonah hated video conferencing and had made the point repeatedly. But as a member of the National Security Council's Foreign Intelligence Subcommittee, he was accustomed to sharing airtime with his counterparts from the National Security Agency and Homeland Security.

"Bill, Mike," Jonah greeted their colleagues. "It's a strange one, to be sure."

"Is there a chance the Brits end up with egg on their faces over this?" Homeland's Michael Niven was shrewdly political and always looking for the leverage angle.

He always seemed to have a scrap of paper in hand and his ballpoint, forever scribbling old-fashioned reminders instead of just using a phone. He was anachronistic, maintaining his crown of grey hair in an era when most balding men just shaved it off. "We still owe them over that whole mess with Lord Abbott."

Trust him to bring that up. "We haven't forgotten, believe me," Jonah said. "As for their exposure? We're not sure. The interest from the continent seems excessive for generic, undefined intel. So perhaps they stand to lose more than reputation. But it's early days."

"Who do we have in play over there right now?" the NSA's Bill Wheeler asked. He was leaning back slightly, fingers arched ahead of him like a Disney villain. He had that look, Jonah thought, the pinched face and lifeless, dark eyes. "We need to firm up the value of the package before we can rule out a threat. If it's nothing major and they're just fishing, we need to steer clear."

"Of course," Wilkie agreed. "But that's a big if. Jonah? Do we have a suitable asset in London?"

"Nobody. Well... one freelancer. But nobody we'd want involved with anything sensitive."

"How long to get someone in play?" Wilkie asked, giving him the benefit of the doubt.

But Niven wasn't done, smelling blood in the water. "Hang on just a second there, Nicholas... Jonah, you mentioned a freelancer?"

"A former clandestine ops specialist. But he's retired; we threw him a bone on something small a few days ago, so technically we already owe him some money, but..."

"Ah! Now, let's not rule him out just like that," Niven asked. "Who is he?"

Jonah held in what would have been a loud sigh. "Joe Brennan." He didn't elaborate. He knew it wasn't necessary.

"Well now he'd be ideal, wouldn't he?" Wilkie asked. He was one of Brennan's biggest admirers but had an arm's length, senior management knowledge of the man and his methods. "Brennan has come through for us on multiple occasions."

"That's what I've heard," Niven contributed. Jonah could see the barest of smirks on the older man's face. Everyone in the service knew of his falling out with Brennan, the man who'd saved his career five years earlier during a 'false flag' nuclear incident in upstate New York.

"Understandable approach, gentlemen," Jonah suggested. "But our budget for freelancers right now…"

"Oh, come now, my boy!" Wilkie waved a hand towards the camera. "We always have that kind of money in contingency. How much could he cost?"

"These days? You'd be surprised. We just guaranteed him six figures for a data acquisition…"

"Like the director said," Niven interjected. "Petty cash for the mighty Central Intelligence Agency. We need to get this done, Nicholas…"

"I'm inclined to agree," Wheeler added.

"Sir…" Jonah began.

But Wilkie cut him off. "Then it's settled. Get him moving, Jonah. We can worry about the fine details later."

16.

BARILOCHE, ARGENTINA

The hotel dining room was old-fashioned, staid, unchanged in decades save for a new coat of paint on the eggshell white walls.

The carpet was dark green in a false Persian pattern, and the curtains swept down from twenty feet above to cover the double floor-to-ceiling windows that ran along one wall.

The room was divided up by long dining tables covered by white linen tablecloths, one at the head of them running horizontal to the far wall. It was bisected by a dais.

A short, paunchy man with thinning blonde hair stood at it and surveyed the roomful of guests. They were in evening gowns and tuxedos, Italian suits and Gucci bags.

He smiled at the sight, everyone having fun. He had a small handle-less gavel in one hand and appeared to be waiting for the opportune moment to use it.

At the head table, Gabriel Verde sat and listened as his seating partner droned on about tourism and infrastructure funding for the small city, one of Argentina's prime tourism destinations and a growing economic influencer. It was dreary, bureaucratic fare but he smiled and nodded politely. To his left sat his valet and bodyguard, Manuel.

Verde was a large man, with strong features and wavy brown hair that seemed to defy his rapidly advancing years. He had been to events like this seemingly hundreds of times and was successful enough that he no longer worried what most onlookers thought of him, his body language in the dinner chair so relaxed as to be almost slouching.

In a few moments, he knew, he'd be called upon to address the assembled diners. But until then, he told himself, it would be rude to ignore the man.

"... by the time the ski season is at its low ebb. But with the new investment that Nueva Esperanza is bound to bring in, none of those issues are likely to continue for too long! We really can't thank you enough, Doctor."

"Of course, Alderman Martinez, of course. It's never my intent to involve myself deeply in the economic matters of the communities in which my facilities operate, however I take some pride in the notion that we have been of assistance. Now..." Verde gestured to the dais just as the gavel was raised and lowered with a decisive thump.

The speaker repeated the action twice, the room quieting.

"Gentlemen, ladies, please! If everyone could cast their attention upon the head table for just a few moments... yes, I know, not the best view in these parts! Ladies and gentlemen, we are here tonight for the singular honor of naming San Carlos de Bariloche's Man of the Year for 2020. It is, of course, no surprise, having been leaked to the local press several weeks ago. And in truth, with the imminent completion of his grand project, Nueva Esperanza, just days away, no one would have assumed otherwise.

"His experimental community, funded by some of the world's wealthiest family trusts and his own considerable list of patents and inventions, may soon change humanity's fortunes with respect to death and disease, bringing the world into a new and prosperous era. And so I introduce to you tonight our Guest of Honor, and your Man of the Year... Dr. Gabriel Verde!"

The room erupted in applause, three hundred diners standing in near unison, a wall of elegance, silk and Saville Row, the cream of the local community. Verde stood slowly and raised a hand, his eyes lowered, his expression one of pure humility. Had it been spontaneously possible, he would have been certain to blush. He wanted them to realize how much the award meant to him.

Verde moved to the Dais, the deputy mayor shaking his hand and presenting him with a small glass-and-wood statuette. Verde was over six feet tall, any intimidation presented by his stature muted somewhat by the tan linen suit and simple blue dress shirt. He raised the microphone by bending its flexible line. He set the glass statuette down. He raised his hand again but they kept applauding. Five more seconds passed, and he motioned with his downward palms for quiet. "Please... Thank you! Thank you, ladies and gentlemen, thank you... If we could continue... Again, thank you..."

The crowd settled down. "Ladies and gentlemen, I won't talk long. As most of you know, I prefer to spend my time in my laboratory, working with my staff on their immense contributions to life-changing drugs and technology. When our long experiment goes live next week, however, I want you to be assured that I will look forward to a year in seclusion, secure in the knowledge that it will eventually be over, and I will be able to rejoin you in this wonderful community."

The crowd erupted into applause again. Verde momentarily wondered if Bruner had seeded the audience with well-wishers. He pushed the notion aside. "In the meantime... Thank you... Thank you, everybody... Please... In the meantime, I know Stefan and the boys have put together a wonderful night of dining, drinks and fireworks overlooking the lake. Let's enjoy it together, and raise our glasses in a toast. To a new world, and to those of us who would, in humility, propel it forward!"

Glasses clinked as they were elevated room-wide. Wine and beer were downed in equal measure. "Thank you again, everyone. I look forward to speaking with each of you individually as the evening proceeds." He stepped away from the dais and returned to his chair to another round of applause. The deputy mayor egged them on, pointing his way with both hands, calling his name again.

A beefy man in a dark suit sidled up to him and crouched next to his chair. It was Verde's bodyguard, who was never far away. "Sir, a quick word...."

"What is it Manuel?"

"We've had to let one of the scientists go, from the genetics team. It seems he'd been having some money problems and was attempting to use his systems access to break into the department's records."

"Oh dear! Which one was it?"

"Gurcharan Singh Das, sir. The young gentleman from Hull in England..."

Damn it. Das was talented, despite his obvious maturity issues. "It could not be helped, I take it?"

"Not at all sir. We actually gave him a chance to confess but ultimately termination was the only way to drive the point home."

Verde maintained a stoic facade. He didn't want to upset anyone on such an auspicious night, even if the news was as disappointing as he'd heard in some time. Such was the nature of business, he told himself.

Onward and upward. Whoever replaces him will be even better, I'm sure.

"And sir..."

"There's something else, Manuel?"

"Yes sir. Mr. Bruner called. The investors from Europe are quite keen on a face-to-face before you seal the time lock on Nueva Esperanza. They've expressed... some trepidation, it seems, over the roll out."

That was a delay he didn't need, a wrinkle worth avoiding. "Tell him to stall them," he said. "They have their grand designs and I have mine. Of the two, my track record is a lot better."

But he knew they wouldn't like it. Soon, they would come knocking on the community's door.

17.

LONDON

Aubrey sucked on the cigarette with considered intent, watching the cherry ember creep south as his lungs filled up, before blowing a plume of white smoke out that bounced off the windshield and ran down into the crannies of the old Jaguar's dashboard.

"When you think about it, I have commented, off and on, for many a year now that I should get my head examined," Aubrey suggested. "This, then, would stand as proof positive."

Charlie was slumped low in the passenger seat, just able to see over the dash and across the road to the car park where most of the Defense Department's research team left their vehicles daily. "Just make sure you get a picture of each person who comes out. And you remember the profile I showed you?"

"Yes, yes, calm down! I think I can manage to identify younger males. I was one once myself, you know, until you showed up and accelerated my aging process."

"The sloppier looking, the better. I want an unlikely lad, someone who couldn't get a date if he paid for it."

"Cruel, but I shall comply if it will get us out of here and over to the pub for a pint."

"Absolutely."

"So you'll be joining us?"

"Absolutely not. If they found me living in that flophouse, they can find me anywhere I show my face. Until further notice, I shall instead be hanging out in your basement with the Collective."

The Collective was the hacker group run by Aubrey's younger brother, Tim. They'd all had brushes with the law, some severe, and none were fans. They also hated the term "hackers."

"Fine."

Another twenty minutes passed, Aubrey listening to the BBC while Charlie used a ghosted IP address to log onto a local restaurant's wifi. He used a search app that included usenet groups and dark web mentions. Given how many unauthorized sites were streaming police bands or communications directly, it seemed the best bet to intercept any serious traffic.

But after a day, so far, he'd heard nothing new. Aubrey had gone over to Sonya's agency to see if she'd heard anything, only to find the place crawling with police and plain clothes officers of some kind.

"Hang on a mo...." Aubrey suggested. "Who's this then? He's quite the dour looking fella, he is."

Charlie shielded his eyes from the windscreen glare. An overweight young man was guiding a too-small moped out of the building. "He's perfect. Snap some pictures and let's get after him."

"Again," Aubrey said as he started the car and put it into drive, "for the sake of posterity I feel inclined to mention my concern that this is, in fact, insane."

But it was his only real option, Charlie had already decided. He needed to find out what he'd stumbled across. The easiest way to figure that out was to find out, first, who the recipient was. But to do that, he needed to gain access to an everyday department email account.

"We're not going to even meet the man, Aubrey. Stop worrying, my son. He's never even going to know we were part of his life."

"Isn't there some more technical way of achieving this? Something that involves less following around of people in your friend's borrowed classic car?"

"What? You mean like 'hacking' into the department's server code, like in the movies? Maybe while some clock is counting down my inevitable detection by cyberpunk guardians?"

"Right. Very funny, you are. Once again, popular culture is a complete bloody let down. And how, o wise computer god, do you intend on getting him to help us?"

"Depends."

"Upon?"

"His taste in junk food."

"Eh?"

"By my reckoning, Aubrey, that is a man who does not dress to impress, a man of steady habits, most likely involving a computer game, an impressive array of artery-clogging snacks and a favorite junk food. And that, my son, is where we come in."

"Oh good. Well, I'll be certain to stay terrified and in place until then, shall I?"

Charlie gestured ahead. "He's taking the A40."

"Wonderful. A drive to the Chiltern Hills. Marvelous. Hopefully, nobody recognizes me on the way there."

"But that's all the better. They'll never believe a famous satirist is involved in anything untoward."

"I was with you until you used the expression 'Famous Satirist.' Unless you're referring to the kind of spreadable-cheese-eating denizens of Channel Four and Dave who watch my shows, you might be surprised by just how unknown a famous person I am."

Behind them, a police siren blared, distant but coming up quickly. "Oh dear. Oh dear, oh dear, oh deary me," Aubrey intoned. "I knew it. I knew this was a terrible, terrible..."

The police car sped by them. Aubrey glanced at Charlie, who looked unimpressed. "I'll just shut up until we get where we're going, then...."

18.

Oct. 18, 2020

Jonah had hoped meeting Brennan in Hyde Park would mute any negative reaction, keep things tactful and cordial.

He'd evidently been wrong.

Brennan arrived at the bench and took one look at who was waiting for him, then scowled.

"You must be off your nut," Brennan muttered. He took in the tranquil surroundings, the handful of other people around, joggers, new mothers sitting with their strollers. "If we're doing this here, away from Carolyn and the kids, it's got to be something significant. And if it's something significant, I'm out. You know that. ARE YOU OUT OF YOUR DAMN MIND, JONAH!? He half yelled the last line, his frustration spilling over.

Jonah looked both ways guiltily over the noise then held both hands wide, an acceptance of what was. "Don't you think it's embarrassing for me to be here, cap in hand? We're one of the most powerful spy agencies in the world, and yet I'm reduced to imploring you to consider the big picture..."

Brennan took one hard stride forward, toward the smaller man. Jonah must've been forty-five, but he looked like he was right out of college, and he flinched backwards into the bench at the hint of menace.

Brennan wanted to pop him in the mouth; just one, quick, hard, shot, a wake up. *Like a cold glass of water, only with a fist attached.* He took a deep breath. *Take it down; Jesus, you're a professional*, he told himself. "I should punch you in the goddamned mouth right now..."

"I know."

"You left me stranded in China, you laid the blame for New York on Daisy Lee and that poor, deluded kid..."

"You know how much of that had to be off the books, Joe. Look, hate me if you want..."

"Done and done..."

"But at least hear me out. I'm not sending you into Moscow or Beijing. It's just another local job, but also important. And thanks to Lord Abbott, we have no one in London and no one sympathetic left inside MI6."

"You assholes made that bed. Now you get to lie in it," Brennan suggested.

"All we need you to do is track someone down and hang onto them for a day or two. It's nobody, a hacker. You'll be done with it in a few days."

"Yeah... I'm sure it's that easy. That's why you're here to wave... what, another six figures under my nose? Because there's no risk or issue of exposure. Jonah, I have two teenagers. I'm closing on forty-five-years old, but I have joints like I'm sixty. I have enough scar tissue on my body to build another person. So... no, Jonah. No to whatever this is."

"There are others in play already. The target is, we believe, innocent to the danger."

Damn you, Jonah. Don't bring outsiders into this... "Whatever they did, it must've been bad to bring around international attention..."

"Not really. It's a kid, sticking his nose where it didn't belong. I mean, I'm sure this is thrilling for him, but our analysts give him a less than five percent chance of getting out of the city. The numbers for him making it alive aren't great, either."

"Jonah..."

"He's some mother's son, Joe, some poor kid who just...."

"You're one goddamned piece of work, you know that."

Jonah tilted his head just slightly in acknowledgement of the truth. "We do what we have to, Joe. You know how it is."

"You don't give a shit about some British kid…"

"I won't lie and tell you his fate keeps me up at night, no. But I know your conscience, and the possibility that you'd be leaving him to his fate. Like I said…you know how it is."

"Rarely. Rarely do I know what you're actually up to. Are you going to tell me where he is, or what?"

19.

Aubrey was down to his last three cigarettes and was as bored as he'd been in quite some time.

"You know I had a chance to do 'QI' this week, right? I could've been trading bon mots with Sandy Toksvig. Instead, I'm sitting in a McDonald's in West Ealing listening to the…" He looked over his shoulder towards the restaurant's glass-enclosed central play area, where young children were squealing. '… What is that thing again?"

"The ball pit, I believe they call it. Just… be patient."

"We've been watching this less-than-engaging fellow's apartment for two days…."

Charlie glanced through the restaurant's front windows to the apartment block across the road.

"And we'll wait two more if… Hang on, hang on!" Charlie's phone buzzed and he stared at the screen for a moment. "We're in!"

"Explain how this works again? You sent him lunch and somehow…?"

"I sent him a coupon by email, a bar code purporting to offer him a second meal free at his favorite chicken restaurant. He just clicked on it, and in doing so downloaded a Trojan to his hard drive."

"Why do I suspect you are referring to neither a small rubber prophylactic nor a large Greek soldier?"

"Same idea, though. The file sits quietly, like the Trojan soldiers in the giant horse, until he reboots the machine. Then it runs a program in the background that records every keystroke on the machine and sorts out the repeats...."

"Giving you his passwords. I take it back, that is..."

"Pure genius?"

"Incredibly creepy, I was going to say. But if it'll get us out of here and to the pub, then by all means, it's practically the theory of relativity."

Charlie tapped rapidly with both thumbs. "He has his work email paired with his home, silly boy. Let's see what the Defense Department has been talking about for the last two days, shall we?"

And there it was. A memo outlining a security breach, followed by one a day later announcing the two-day suspension of Adrees Das, late of the department's mechanical engineering department. He pulled open a dark web browser and found the last postal address for ....

Charlie sighed.

"What?"

"There are thirteen Adrees Das's in London."

It was Aubrey's turn to sound melancholy. "I'm not getting that pint any time soon, am I?"

20.

Oct. 19, 2020

LONDON

Charlie kept his hands in his pockets and hugged the shadows inside the entrance to the block of flats.

The alcove was perfectly positioned, due southwest of the condominium building, far enough away that he could just make out each person coming and going through the front door and still maintain anonymity.

Aubrey had begged off, with Charlie's encouragement. He'd already put his neck much too far out. One fewer set of eyes came with risks, not the least of which was being spotted by the Met.

Charlie got up after just four hours of sleep, at six in the morning. He'd been in position by seven.

If he was lucky, Charlie thought, Adrees Das would lead him straight to the research building, just a half-dozen blocks away... confirming he was the right Adrees Das.

He would return to the block of flats that night and begin another phishing campaign and hopefully uncover a few more answers. Failing that, Tim's friends would crack the packet encryption and they could just read it for themselves, find out exactly how deep a hole he'd dug.

His vantage point was just off a three-way intersection, providing at least one distinct disadvantage: he couldn't see if someone was closing from behind and keep his eyes on the doors to the apartment building. The alcove was the equalizer, Charlie hoped, providing just enough cover to prevent detection.

Just before eight, the doors swung open.

It was Das.

He was pushing a racing bike, clips on the cuffs of his trousers. *Damn it. Damn it, if he climbs aboard that...* But Charlie knew he would. He already had the helmet on.

Das pushed the bicycle beside him along the pavement for a few seconds then looked both ways and hopped aboard. He began to peddle east.

Charlie knew if he didn't make good time, he would quickly lose him. He skipped out of the alcove and onto the sidewalk. It was littered with pedestrians, people walking to work or the shops, middle aged wives with shopping bags in one hand, phone in the other, kids engrossed in same, the odd older man looking slightly surprised by it all. He cut in and out of the other bodies.

There was no time for caution. As long as he didn't knock anyone over, there was no reason to think he'd attract attention.

The city was busy at the start of the workday, with bigger matters. He ran as hard as he could, slowing just enough after a few blocks to elevate himself to his tiptoes and spot the rider.

He resumed his sprint, passing Maxwell's on King Street.

And then he slowed to a walk, a satisfied look on his face as Das rolled the bike up to a parking ramp, before hopping off to guide it down by hand.

The Defense Department's Covent Garden research and development office. We've found our guy.

He wouldn't have noticed the limousine crawling along the street in the other direction had it not been for a glint of light off the chrome wing mirror. It drew Charlie's attention for just long enough to also notice the man on the opposite side of the road.

Dark glasses, earpiece... and he ducked out of sight as soon as I turned...

He switched his gaze quickly to the street and pavement behind him. A man in a round-collar leather jacket was reading a newspaper and he turned the page immediately, switching his attention to the far page. Charlie let his field of view swing to his right. Across the street and fifty meters back, two men were sitting in a plain sedan.

Am I... being watched? That's not possible is it? No one could know I'd be here...

The man across the street buttoned his suit jacket and smoothed it as he turned nonchalantly to cross the street in Charlie's direction. Charlie looked back to see the man with the newspaper close it, eyes ahead, as he began striding towards the young hacker. The sedan occupants got out of the car, their eyes on the newspaper man.

Time to make yourself scarce, my son.

He looked ahead, then checked his shoulder again. *Nothing for it but to put space between us...* Charlie quickened his pace to a fast walk, then a trot, then a run, cutting in and out of the foot traffic, almost tripping over a woman with a baby stroller, the sound of his pursuers shoving others aside behind him.

He heard a pistol being cocked, the breach opened then snapped into place as a round was chambered. Charlie's heart pounded in his chest, his skin vibrating from nervous fear as he waited for the sound of the gunshot, knowing he'd feel it before then...

To his left, the limousine had been keeping pace. But as he began to run, it accelerated. A spot opened in traffic and its driver swung the big Lincoln Town Car in a u-turn, squealing to a halt next to him. The left rear door swung open into Charlie's path and he almost slammed into it. Before he could negotiate his way back to a run, another man leaped from the rear seat onto the sidewalk.

21.

The limousine door swung open and Brennan threw himself toward the target. Twenty yards back, he saw a tall man trying to get a bead on them with a pistol, deciding against it in a crowd.

His target was young, early twenties according to the profile but he looked barely even that. The young man's eyes widened in terror when he saw Brennan hurtle towards him, and he raised both arms, as if blocking a runaway cart.

Brennan ignored the reaction and grabbed Charlie's jacket collar, taking a vice-like grip upon the coat and shirt underneath. He pivoted on his inside heel, using his body weight to yank the young man towards the open limousine cabin, then throwing himself shoulder first after him, the momentum carrying them both crashing to the seat and floor.

"Go!" Brennan screamed. The driver complied, flooring the limousine, pulling around the car ahead and into the opposing lane, ignoring oncoming traffic as if it wasn't there, a semi truck heading right for them.

Charlie looked up for just long enough to see it fill the windscreen and threw up his arms defensively again, closing his eyes as if it might help them avoid the impact...

The driver yanked the wheel left at the last moment, pulling them back into their lane, clear for a block ahead. Brennan righted himself onto the seat next to the young man then checked the rear window. Their pursuers were in the road, probably trying to get as many last details as possible before they disappeared.

The limousine turned left, the driver putting as much distance between them and the scene as possible. Ahead, a grey sedan accelerated out of an alley then stopped abruptly, blocking the lane. The limousine driver swerved, not seeing the second car pull away from the curb and block the other lane, the gap too narrow for the elongated Lincoln to navigate.

"Out!" Brennan barked. He grasped for the car door handle and yanked, using his shoulder to push it open as they clambered free of the backseat. A pistol shot chipped stone somewhere nearby.

The driver ran for the door of a nearby office building. Brennan grabbed Charlie's collar again and flung him towards the opposite alley. "Cover, go, now!" It looked narrow enough to dissuade either of the cars from backing up to follow, which put their immediate threat down to those already pursuing on foot and anyone joining them.

Charlie ran down the alley, Brennan behind him. He drew the .45 Smith & Wesson provided by the local office and chambered a round. The alley turned left at the end, a ninety-degree bend. They rounded the corner. "Go, go!" Brennan urged the young man on.

Ahead, one of the sedans pulled across the end of the alley to block it.

Charlie skittered to a halt.

Brennan gestured behind them. "Back!" he ordered. They ran back down the alley. They rounded the corner; the fist came from seemingly nowhere, hammering Charlie in the jaw, his legs turning to rubber as he crashed to the alley floor.

Brennan reacted immediately, kicking a stray wooden pallet just ahead of him with all his force, the half-crate slamming into the two men running their way even as he spun his torso the attacker's way, a second punch whistling by him.

Charlie was groaning, trying to pick himself up off the ground. Their attacker was fast, a blur in a black suit and white shirt, turning from his missed punch, his fist coming away from his body gripping a nine-millimeter pistol. Before he could complete the move, Brennan hammered down upon his forearm with a right elbow, the man dropping the gun.

The American moved behind him, wrapping him in a half-Nelson. His friends had risen and one took a bead on Brennan, squeezing off a round even as he turned, holding the first man as a shield, the slug burying deep in his torso.

Brennan shoved the wounded man forward and ran behind him, cutting off their angle as both men tried to find him in pistol sights.

He shot the first through the forehead, ducking low to turn and shoot the second in the groin.

The two men from the sedans behind them wheeled around the corner directly into the fray, the American standing between them.

He threw an elbow back, catching the first man as he stepped in, staggering him. He dropped his pistol and it clattered to the concrete near Charlie.

Brennan spun left on his heels, continuing the motion into a straight punch, the second man firing a wild shot as Brennan's right cross caught him flush, dropping him to his knees.

Before he could follow it with a kick, he heard the slide on the pistol behind. He threw himself backwards, the man's gun arm extending past his shoulder as he crashed into the attacker, sending them both down. Brennan lost the grip on the pistol and it skittered away as they slammed into the ground.

His partner scrambled for his gun. Charlie saw it lying on the cement as he raised his head. It rested for a bare few moments, equidistant between them. Both men looked at each other, then pounced towards its handle. Charlie's hand found the pistol grip and swung it around hard, the side of the gun clunking into the other man's temple, dazing him.

He scrambled to his feet in time to see his rescuer rise at the same time as the third man, who still had his pistol. The American's eyes were hunting the ground as he looked for his pistol. The third man raised his gun, so that it was pointed directly at the back of his rescuer's head. But the man moved with sudden speed, ducking low, swinging his right leg out and around in a sweeping motion. The kick caught the shooter at ankle height, his legs coming out from under him.

His gun clattered to the ground. As he tried to right himself, the American scooped up the gun and slammed him across the side of the jaw, the third man joining his unconscious friends.

At the opening to the alley, the newspaper carrier had joined them, rounding the corner cautiously, a pistol gripped in both hand. He saw them and yelled, "Police! Charles Rich, stay where you are..."

Charlie froze. The man was forty yards away, and Brennan weighed their options, then shoved the young man in the other direction.

"Run! Now!" he bellowed.

22.

They ran back towards the two sedans blocking the other route. Charlie could hear sirens nearby, from multiple directions, the sound echoing off the high alley walls.

Brennan pushed him towards the front car, its doors open and its engine still running. "In, now!" he yelled.

Charlie complied, jumping into the passenger seat while the other man ran around the bonnet to the driver's seat. He slammed the door and threw the car into drive.

"Where are we going? Where are... Who ARE you?" Charlie demanded.

"A friend who'd like to see you avoid jail or worse. We have to get to a safe location. My associates have a place. But we need to ditch this vehicle quickly."

"I don't..." It was all happening too quickly and Charlie had lost his focus. "Ditch..."

"It could be tracked; it belongs to the people chasing you, and that alley was likely monitored by city cameras. There could be public descriptions and photos of us out on the news within hours, or in the hands of MI5 at the very least."

Charlie sat up straight and composed himself. "I think I'm in a lot of trouble."

Brennan threw him a quick glance. "You think?" He threw the wheel hard left, swinging the sedan around a corner too quickly, cursing internally for not concentrating, letting his adrenaline take over. *Drive normally, idiot. You're in traffic.*

He spotted the car park and slowed the car, turning off the road. "What are you doing?" Charlie asked.

"Shopping for wheels. Keep your head down. The security cameras in dark garages aren't usually good enough to identify faces well but it's better not to take chances." He drove the car ten feet into the garage and double parked it behind other vehicles rather than waiting to find a spot. "We do it on foot. The cameras will be angled to pick up drivers and passengers, not people standing and looking at their shoes. Let's go."

He opened the door and climbed out. Charlie followed, hesitantly. "Stay behind me at all times, do exactly what I say and you'll make it," Brennan ordered. "Diverge from that and you might as well be wearing a red Star Trek shirt. Got it?"

Charlie's head bobbed vigorously. Brennan turned and began to follow the row of cars, scoping out each model. They walked past ten, then twenty, thirty cars before reaching the next level.

"Is there something specific...?"

"Shh. We need quiet," Joe said. "Safety issue."

Charlie felt his apprehension build. He looked back briefly, wondering if he should flee. The man had defended him in the alley... but for all Charlie knew, the men chasing him might have offered a deal as well, or aid of some sort. He had no idea who this person was, what he wanted in return.

Brennan sensed his unease. "Just keep cool for a few minutes, okay? If I was a threat to you, I've had plenty of opportunities to prove it already." He reached back and put a hand on Charlie's chest, halting their progress. "This one."

Brennan rounded the older model Ford and jimmied the passenger door. "The driver's side lock on these can be popped with a pocketknife," he said quietly. "And it's from before they put engine arrest on as standard, to prevent hotwiring. And..." He gazed through the driver's side window. "No security system."

He opened the door and got in. Brennan reached across the passenger seat and unlocked the other door. Charlie climbed into the cabin. "I have a normal life. Sort of. A girlfriend. Again... sort of."

"I know this is all throwing you for a loop, kid, but just bear with me until we go black, okay?"

"Go..."

"Beat the pursuit and get off the grid."

"Ah."

Brennan backed the car out and turned it towards the car park exit. Jonah would be waiting at the safe house, expecting them to be there by now if the analysts had called the hacker's intentions correctly. He considered using the burner phone to check in then opted against it. A random signal pickup from an unencrypted device would be a stupid way to go down.

He had a secondary problem now; he'd entered England on his real passport, with his real identity and picture, a picture that would be picked out of the national security database by facial recognition once police had a street camera image.

Whatever that kid downloaded better be important, he thought. *And Jonah better have a way to get me out of here.*

He turned the wheel and steered the car back onto the street.

23.

WASHINGTON, D.C.

Matthew Misner stood in front of the Intensive Care Unit observation window and watched his political mentor as he lay passively, the ventilator mask covering his face.

Jed Bryant was a legend in the Beltway, a five-time Senator and his party's best hope of retaking the White House in November.

Misner barely moved. People passing in the ICU corridor might have compared his stoic outward appearance with his clean-cut reputation and thought him dispassionate.

But inside, his guts were churning, his life about to be flooded with too many choices, too many important decisions.

Bryant had been leading the President by twenty points in the polls when the stroke had felled him. To the public, it was just a mild episode related to his diabetes, no big deal. He'd be back and out on the campaign trail in no time.

The reality? The reality was far different, and Misner knew it. In a few hours he was to meet with the national committee. They'd either be thumbs up or down, and that was it. For all of the pretense of state delegates getting to pick a candidate, the 'Super Delegate' voting system allowed trusted insiders to overrule them, in effect. And the national committee controlled enough Super Delegates to ensure it got what it wanted.

A lifetime, he thought as he gazed at Bryant. A lifetime of serving the people and that close to the most powerful role in public life on the planet. And it comes down to one faulty blood vessel.

He was only fifty-two and he knew the committee was divided. His age wasn't the big factor; Kennedy, Teddy Roosevelt, Lincoln... they were all relatively young when they won the presidency. The question was whether they would accept an agnostic.

His head told him they should. His gut told him they wouldn't. What had his adviser said? "A man who doesn't believe in God will never sit in the Oval Office." And then the man had quit, calling Misner's admission 'political suicide."

Of course, it hadn't been. He'd been re-elected as mayor of Tucson for a second term and the city's massive improvements had led to his political legend growing. They wanted someone young as a vice-presidential candidate, they'd lost out on their first choice now that she was running for governor of South Carolina. And he had heat, buzz, media attention.

As a VP candidate he was perfect. Someone had wisely figured out, early on in the campaign, that agnostics and atheists actually represented a larger voting demographic than any subgroup other than Caucasians and Latinos. The polls suggested the VP's stature was significantly below that of the Presidents with Evangelical and orthodox voters, which meant he could actually help the president's numbers.

And then Bryan had collapsed at a rally in Iowa, and everything had changed.

That was ten days ago, and the minutes had flown by, Misner thrown into the public eye as the de facto face of the campaign until Jed was back up and about. But now, they were being told that was unlikely. In fact, the doctors weren't confident in a recovery.

But the hands of the clock didn't care. They kept ticking away. Misner felt trapped; he didn't want to usurp his mentor's role. He just wanted Jed to recover. But that didn't appear likely to happen. It was like being told he'd won the lottery, when he was really trying to cash in a friend's ticket.

"What are you going to tell them?" The reflection that had sidled up to his in the window glass belonged to Stuart Chiasson, his longtime friend and adviser. They'd worked campaigns together going back to high school.

"What option do I have? I tell them the truth. I tell them that my personal views are already out there for the world to see, that if they want to go ahead, it will be with the knowledge that my views will be a matter of public debate."

"I know you think their minds are made up..."

"Come on, Stu... Let's be realistic here. These guys had a social democrat candidate lined up who was crushing the President — I mean crushing him — in the polls long before this year's domestic troubles did the job for us. Even his most hardcore adherents weren't going to put up with a crumbling economy and a spate of scandals..."

"It's about winning..."

"If this was just about winning, they'd have taken that option in the last cycle. No, this is about maintaining their ideological brand, as well. And that brand has a lot of money coming from 'moderate' religions."

Chiasson put a hand on the shoulder of his friend's dark grey suit. "Have a little faith. I know it's not your strong suit, but..."

And that made Misner smile a little. If they dropped him, his national political career was probably over. If they elevated him to Presidential candidate, he was an immediate underdog.

The night was long, and full of terrors.

But it wasn't over yet.

24.

LONDON

Brennan pulled the car to the side of the road two blocks from the safe house.

"Why are we stopping?" Charlie asked.

The American nodded to a row of parked cars across the road. "Third from the front, the Green mini." He nodded to their side, further up the pavement. "The couple looking in that shop window."

He flicked a fingertip in the direction of the upper floor flats, above the opposite side shops.

"The third curtain along is being held back by a hand, as if someone is waiting to see something. Normal use would see it tied back. Or, alternately, something already going on in the street ahead, something worth staring at."

Charlie felt his mouth loll open slightly as his surprise registered. "You saw all of that in the..." He checked his shoulder. "Ten seconds since we rounded the last bend?"

"Consider yourself lucky it's not part of your skill set. Threat assessment isn't needed by most people, with good reason."

"Which is?"

"It's why they pay people like me."

"And... now what? I assume our destination is one of the buildings on this street..."

"And this street is crawling with MI5 and police. So... we need other options." Chances were good the safe house had been blown by domestic intelligence a long time ago, then sat on until it was relevant, he knew. That meant Jonah would be in there, likely unaware a trap had been set for Charlie Rich.

And that meant they had to leave. "We need to find somewhere else."

Charlie shrugged. "I know a place."

Brennan peered at him cautiously. "A place?"

"Some friends. They run a sort of... electronic gatherers' collective."

"They're hackers."

"I mean..." He nodded his head nervously. "Don't use that term there, okay? Most of them think it's pretty stupid because of the social definition..."

"Yeah... Whatever. Where and how?"

"It's a basement warehouse conversion in Shepherd's Bush, totally off the grid, unmarked, anonymous. They park blocks away and get in through a sewer access door like something out of *The Third Man*..."

"The what?"

"*The Third Man*? Orson Welles , Joseph Cotton. Murder mystery in post-war Vienna?"

"A what?!?"

"A movie. It was a movie..."

"Oh," Brennan said sullenly. "I don't get a lot of time for that kind of thing."

Charlie just nodded but kept an eye on the man as he drove. He had the sense that...

"Just a sec... I've just realized I have no idea who you are. Do I at least get a name?"

"It's Joe."

"Okay. Okay, then, that's something. I'm Charlie."

Brennan gave him a withering look. "I know. Where are we going, Charlie?"

"Joe, you and I are about to visit geek Heaven; Nerd-vana, if you will. Prepare yourself."

25.

Peter Chappell sat in his office and spooned a forkful of cold flat noodles into his mouth. He was expecting an update on the hunt for their hacker as well as the recovery of the lost email.

If they didn't make some progress on either, the report to the minister would be bleak, indeed.

There was a knock on his office door. A head popped in before he could respond. "Got a minute, Peter?" It was Ken Loach, their senior systems analyst.

He gestured with his forkful to the office chair across from his desk. "Don't mind my eating while you talk, all right? In and out these days."

"Quite, quite..." Loach stammered. "We've managed to recoup a copy of the partial data file that was overwritten on the FTP server. Turns out there was a backup image of the server made right before the second transmission, so we have it in its entirety. Which, I should say, is just a portion of what we suspect should be there."

"And what is it?"

Loach played with his earlobe, a nervous habit, and he shuffled his left foot slightly, like a bashful child. He was a nice man. Chappell had always felt he was unsuited to the dirty world of espionage and national security. "Yes... well... that is another matter entirely. We're not really sure. One of the chaps at R and D — a top egghead of some such — believes it may be a form of DNA mutation that has been mapped."

"Important because...."

"That's just it, sir. We're really not sure. We've engaged a specialist to take a closer look."

"And the hacker?"

"Well... as far as I can tell we've had no luck so far, although we picked up a pair of Austrians who may have engaged the target."

"Austrians? Why the bloody hell are they getting involved?"

"Also, the Russians and Israelis."

"We're checking other cases for any crossing paths?"

"Yes sir, and liaison officers are running it by SIS and the Met."

"Good, good. Keep me abridged, there's a good man."

What on Earth was going on? In a year of international political and economic turmoil, anything seemed possible. It seemed impossibly unlucky that a member of the public had stumbled into whatever game was afoot. If he had, Chappell realized, they still needed to know what else he had, what else he knew.

The man being sent the file, the scientist; what was his name again? Das. Adrees Das. Their debrief had uncovered a brother he thought was working in Buenos Aires, putting him at least within reasonable distance to be the source. He didn't know the nature of the work, but his brother, Gurcharan, was a geneticist of 'great potential.'

They'd taken that to mean personal problems; that was usually what it meant, and that was often useful, for leverage if nothing else.

The Americans. We haven't heard from them yet. Why not? They had to be in play; when an item was receiving international attention, they always wanted to be first though the door. What was the name of the deputy, the one meeting with Sir Colin?

Jonah Tarrant.

He took out his phone and scrolled through the numbers, then made a call.

The sewer tunnel was claustrophobic and smelled about as he'd expected. They were twenty yards from the sewer access tunnel door when Brennan put a hand on Charlie's shoulder. He'd been leading the way for the five minutes it had taken to get there since going underground.

"Camera," Brennan said, pointing to the cove of the wall and ceiling across the viaduct.

Charlie grinned. "It shows a twenty-four-seven static photo of the area ahead of it from, I believe, twelve years ago? Something like that."

"Your friends are resourceful."

The younger man chuckled as he resumed walking. "You don't know the half of it, my son."

At the door, he flipped open a metal junction box. There was a number pad behind the cover. He blocked it with his body and punched in a code. The door lock clicked open. Charlie pulled the door clear and they walked into a small antechamber, empty aside from the metal floor and another door on the other wall. He pulled the door closed.

There was a camera in an upper corner. "The first door just gets you where they can see you," Charlie explained.

"Yeah... I get the drift. "

They waited a few more seconds before the lock on the second door also clicked open.

Charlie led them into a long concrete corridor with a tall ceiling, one wall split horizontally by electrical conduit lines. They passed a pair of boarded over doors. The final door on the right led into a large room, probably storage at one point, with stone pillars supporting the roof above. Desks were strewn about, and natural lighting streamed through a reflecting skylight, using the same principle of paired mirrors as a periscope.

Each desk was draped in a carpet of mess: computer monitors, partial-build PCs, wiring, bags of chips, candy wrappers, junk food boxes.

"This place is..." Brennan began to say.

"Eclectic," the man walking towards them said. He was tall and gangly, younger, with beard stubble and the last vestiges of his teenage acne. He held out a hand for Joe to shake. "Tim. Charlie...?"

"Yes, Tim?"

"Could you please explain to me why you've brought this individual into our Fortress of Solitude?"

"He saved my life. And he didn't really give me a choice. I'm hedging my bets."

'Tim' did not look happy, Brennan thought. "If it's any consolation, I'm one of the good guys," he offered.

Tim leaned in slightly, his voice soft and low. "Everybody thinks they're the good guy. Charlie..."

"I'm in trouble," the younger hacker said. "I was war driving, at that unprotected hub I told you about..."

Tim's eyes closed gently, and he took a deep breath. "Go on, then! You could not possibly have been that daft. You silly bugger! What did you get?"

"Are you sure you want to know that?" Brennan asked. "Because we don't, not yet. But Charlie figures maybe one of your guys can suss it out."

Tim crossed his arms. "Okay: now you've got me curious. Show me what you've got, Charlie."

26.

Brennan borrowed a phone from Tim and found a quiet corner. He dialed the hotel and asked for their room.

"Hello?" Carolyn answered on the first ring.

"Hey."

"Where are you?!? Jonah called with some vague bullshit..."

"Need to know," he said. She'd been in the management end of the trade long enough not to question it.

"How serious? I thought this was another quick job. Jonah said you'd be escorting someone and that was it."

"Yeah. That went south quickly. We're off the grid for the time being."

"Joe, we still have six vacation days left. The kids..."

"I didn't create the situation, hon."

"But whatever it is, Jonah wants you to resolve it."

"Not as such. We haven't even gotten back to him yet. When we do... I'd be surprised if he doesn't have a whole lot of questions."

"Tell him that wasn't the deal."

She was probably right, he knew. He didn't know Charlie or his data from Adam. There was no reason to feel responsible for the kid's safety.

He gazed over at the horseshoe of desks, where Charlie was standing next to Tim, both behind a seated giant with red hair and a wispy beard, tapping furiously on the keyboard.

"I'll do what I can," he said.

"Six days, Joe."

"I'll see you soon."

"Be careful."

He ended the call and joined Charlie. "Anything?"

Charlie gestured to the red-headed giant. "They're through the first level of encryption and have the contents. Now they need to try and make some sense of it."

The man at the keyboard turned slightly in his rotating desk chair. "It's weird as hell, whatever it is. I've got a PhD in computer engineering, but my first master's was in biology. If I had to guess, given how the decrypted notations refer to the interplay between whatever this produces and the human genome, it's either a virus or the cure to one."

"Ah...bugger me sideways," Charlie muttered.

"If it's a bioweapon, the government will assume you could be a threat," Brennan said. "And the foreign players will think it's an asset... and that makes you a threat."

Tim clapped Charlie on the back. "You are absolutely buggered, my young friend." Then he turned to Joe. "You're American. I assume some sort of intelligence operative?"

"Apparently, they're trying to help," Charlie said dryly.

Joe shrugged. "Most of the time, on this kind of thing? Yeah. Sometimes... not so much. It's a difficult line to walk."

"Why should we trust you with this?" Tim asked. "How does this get Charlie out of trouble?"

It was a fair question, one Brennan knew he couldn't answer. "I'm not a lawyer," he said. "But my boss is. And his budget, his ability to help... it's not insubstantial."

"Adding espionage to the charges?" Tim said.

"Unlikely," Brennan said matter-of-factly. "We have a 'five eyes' data sharing agreement with the UK. Anything I get will go right back to your government, along with our strongly worded request that you be given a pat on the back for helping and sent on your way."

"And that will work?" Charlie sounded hopeful.

"Probably not. They'll probably still charge you with something just to put a scare into you. But it won't be major. And who knows? Maybe you'll catch a break and they'll listen to us for a change."

A younger man ran into the room from a door in the far wall. "Tim, we've got visitors."

They followed him back to the adjacent room. Another man was sitting into front of a bank of monitors. "Six officers, two at your brother's front door, four more in a pair of cars out front."

"Tim's brother Aubrey owns the converted warehouse above," Charlie explained. "We're mates, so it's not surprising they're visiting."

"They won't find us," Tim said. "There's no exit via the building, walled off years ago." He nodded towards the screen. "It looks like Aubrey's having a good chinwag with them, then."

On the screen, the two officers were laughing along with the TV personality. "Why are they being so nice?" Brennan asked. "Is your brother famous or something?"

"Semi famous would be more like it," Tim said. "He's more popular back home in Ireland but he does the odd panel show on the BBC or radio bit and the like..." He crossed his arms and rocked on his heels, the subject obviously a sore one. "Not exactly a towering intellectual challenge, but he enjoys it."

Brennan refrained from the comment that popped into his head, deferring to tact. No one really wants to be reminded when their job isn't legal, he supposed.

"We need to get going as soon as this pair is done," he said instead. "Odds are good they'll leave the other two units behind to watch the place. The longer we're here, the more chance they find something showing the car in the neighborhood or us on a camera and start looking more closely."

"But... where can we go? Your safehouse is blown."

"I have an idea," Brennan said. "I've got an old friend in town who has some background in law enforcement. And he insists he owes me a few favors."

27.

Martin Weiss's feet hurt. It was a familiar sensation; he'd been an infantryman for six years, military intelligence for fifteen more, and a policeman for sixteen years after that. He'd suffered fallen arches since his mid-thirties.

He sat in front of the fireplace in his favorite armchair, opposite that of his best friend, his late wife, Anne.

He always missed her, every day. But sometimes, when he was just sitting reading, drinking his tea, he'd feel her there. He wouldn't look up, as he didn't want to spoil the company.

He'd spent four hours with his grandson, Lou, at the kiddie restaurant, the park, shopping. Now, he just wanted a nice cup of tea, to watch the news and read his book. The boy was tiring, devoid of an off switch.

He took a sip from his mug, then reached for the digestive on the side plate that rested on the coffee table. He took a bite, enjoying the crumbling sensation of the dry biscuit.

The doorbell rang.

His eyes closed momentarily. *Preserve me. What now?*

Martin rose and trudged through the living room, along the main hallway to the front door. They'd lived in the semi-detached two-bedroom since the Seventies. Visitors were infrequent in their later years, which meant it was probably someone selling something.

He opened the door without the chain, despite years of The Met counselling Londoners to do otherwise. *If they get me now, at my front door, it would have to be fate.*

"Hello, Martin." Joe Brennan looked stern. He had a smaller, younger man standing just behind him.

"Joe." Martin looked over at the kitchen clock in the adjacent room. "Little late for a surprise visit. May I presume something is, as they say, up?"

"Can we...?" Brennan gestured past him.

"Of course, of course, come in."

They entered the house. Brennan looked around, absorbing the decor, the older wicker chair by the telephone table, the antique coatrack. It was about how he'd expect Martin's place to look, English and old-fashioned, whitewashed walls and throw rugs.

"Are you expecting any company for the next few days?" Brennan asked.

Martin closed the door behind them. "Not that I know of. My daughter stops by from time to time but she's always polite about calling first. Please..." He gestured towards the door to the living room. "Tea?"

"That would hit the spot right about now," Brennan said.

"Please," Charlie confirmed.

He disappeared into the kitchen while they sat down on his puffy cream-and-black checkered sofa. He returned a minute later and took the wingback armchair on the far side of the fireplace. "Right, kettle's on. Explanation time."

Joe was anxious, Martin noted.

That was never a good sign.

He'd known the American, off and on, for more than twenty years, since Joe was a young man, freshly out of the U.S. Navy SEALS and working overseas officially for the first time. He'd always liked him for his obvious conscience, his humility.

"This is Charlie Rich," Brennan said.

Charlie raised one hand in a limp greeting. "Yeah... Hi."

"Charlie is a genius hacker type. In more pragmatic terms, he's a freaking idiot of monumental proportions."

Charlie crossed one leg over the other and grasped his knee like a man clinging to an ocean-slicked rock for dear life. "Yes. Also true."

"Charlie downloaded something he wasn't supposed to, a data file that was being sent to the Defense Department."

"Ours or yours?"

"Yours. Some kind of mutagenic virus or bioweapon."

"Christ." The kettle whistle began to sound, a low tone at first, the pitch rising with the steam pressure. "Hang on, won't be a jiff." He got up and headed back to the kitchen. He reappeared after another two minutes. "Tea's steeping." Martin sat back down. "I take it you've somehow scooped him off the street and that the wrong kinds of people want him."

Brennan nodded. "If it were just your authorities, I'd have just turned him over," he said. "But there's a fair cross-section of nations trying to get their hands on that data, which mean we have an interest, too."

His host frowned. "You've probably told me too much already. Fortunately, the kettle was whistling so loudly that I didn't hear anything implicating anyone in espionage against Britain. Right?"

"Oh, absolutely," Brennan nodded, straight-faced.

"I know you well enough to know you'll try to resolve this in a way that looks out for the public. I don't know anyone else involved, and it's best it stays that way," Martin said. "Are we clear, Charlie?"

"Hmm? Oh, yes, certainly. Absolutely."

"I need you to sit on him for a few days," Brennan said. "I know it's a lot to ask..."

Martin shrugged. "As I said, a friend of an old friend needs a place to stay. Age old story."

"Thank you. I'll try and get this all sorted out as quickly as I can..."

"What are you going to do now?"

Brennan looked circumspect. "I'm not sure. It's not really up to me. I'll let Jonah know what's going on and he'll demand the code Charlie's friends have already cracked."

"And you," Martin said, "having promised not to involve me in anything that might have the whiff of espionage, will stall him until you've fetched Charlie here and taken him in."

"You will remain uninvolved, officially and otherwise," Brennan promised.

"Then... I just stay here?" Charlie worried. "That feels passive, like I could be doing more..."

"Oh... I think you've done quite enough already, there, chief," Brennan offered. "Keep your head down. It's probably the best way to insure it remains attached to your neck."

28.

Brennan took a taxi back to the hotel. On the seventh floor, Carolyn hugged him at their room door. "That was a little unnerving," she said.

"The kids...?"

"They're playing on their phones, next door." They'd gotten the kids their own room, a matter of considerable pride.

"Any inquiries..."

She shook her head. Then she frowned. "You were expecting trouble to follow you here?"

He knew she needed placating. "No, hon, that's not it. Not that type. Officials: police, MI5, anyone wanting to have a little chat, as the locals put it."

She shook her head. "But Jonah called a half-hour ago. He has a war room set up at the embassy. He suggested if I heard from you that I should send you his way. Joe..."

"I know, hon. I'm trying. But there's a kid involved..."

"Really? A child!?"

"Well... no. A man child, unfortunately. But an innocent player, nonetheless. The guys trying to take him today were carrying, and they were from multiple teams."

"What are...?" She saw the grim expression he put on whenever he couldn't talk about it. "Never mind."

"The truth is, right now, we're not really sure."

"But... it had to be you?"

"It was timing. But I'm not handing the kid to Jonah until I'm sure he can vouch for his safety. We're not even on our own turf here..."

"He won't like that."

"I can explain around it. I'm using a personal asset to stash him..."

Her gaze narrowed. They knew a few people in London. It was probably best not to know which was helping.

"And if he wants you to follow this through..."

"The money will be significant... and nobody else gets dragged into it to start over from square one."

The truth was, something about the kid had made him anxious. He wasn't serious enough; he wasn't invested in the problem that would probably, as a consequence, end his life.

He needed protecting.

Brennan took another taxi to the American embassy. He checked in at the security gate and was ushered through the office area to a large conference room at the back of the main floor.

Jonah was sitting with a small group of staff around the conference table. They had a mugshot of Charlie up on the digital projector's screen. Jonah stood up and greeted him, his hand moving towards a shake, only for him to limply withdraw it when Joe ignored the motion.

"Joe. Where's our boy? When you didn't show..."

"I've stashed him. The safe house was blown."

"Excuse me? I was there."

"I counted three separate teams there at the same time, Jonah, and they weren't going to play nicely. I figure with the traffic you've already mentioned, they were all from different countries, and they all think a bioweapon of some sort is on the loose."

"Is it? You're the only person here who's seen any of the code contained in the data packet..."

"His hacker friends weren't sure. It was something to do with genetic recombination, combining DNA types or breaking them down. So it could be medicine... or it could be a bioweapon, sure."

Jonah ignored the matter of Brennan's caution with the kid. "I'm sure you're handling him as you see best. What I care about is the data," he said.

Brennan reached into his pocket and took out the thumb drive and handed it over. "This is the segment he downloaded. Whether there was more there or not, he couldn't say."

"The team you ran into in the alley..."

"Austrians, I think," Brennan suggested.

"But not the Austrian secret service," Jonah said. "One of the two vehicles' drivers was caught on a city security camera and we obtained a copy of the image from Chappell at MI6. Janet?"

At the other end of the table, a young woman clicked a remote and another image supplanted Charlie's mugshot on the screen. It was a multi-stage zoom on a man's hand, the image so enlarged as to be blurry and pixelated. He was carrying what appeared to be a rectangular fob on his key chain. "We did an enhancement using some of the agency's latest software. It can't replace what isn't there but it can fill in detail based on a next guess, using the existing shapes, shades, contours and colors in the image, then comparing the overall image with millions in our database."

She clicked the button again and a sharper image of the hand came up, still blocky and poor. But the detail on the keychain had been filled in. "You'll notice in the lower right corner of the plastic there are the fine lines of an embossed image."

She clicked the remote once more and another zoom in showed the fine, pale scratching of the molding lines, and the image of a stylized wolf's head.

Brennan looked at Jonah. "Any hits on the source?"

Jonah nodded. "You remember the company that purchased that archive? The one you... liberated for us from the Lake District?"

"Rightway? The multi-level marketer?"

"The very same. Its principal shareholder is an Austrian industrialist, Michael Wolf. Rightway has a subsidiary, Lupus Plastics, based in the Czech Republic. It produced the thumb drive, according to the logo. But they don't offer them via retail outlets, as far as we can tell."

"So... who's their customer? And how does this relate to the archive?"

"We're not certain yet on either front," Jonah said. "Wolf is a long-time supporter of authoritarian causes, the European hard right. He hasn't gone as far as giving money to out-and-out fascists, but he puts considerable money into a quasi-religious group called The International Family."

"Never heard of them," Brennan said.

"That's not surprising. They are, however, massive. Initially, they were dozens of diverse, separate lobby and political groups, although all supporting the same causes: anti-democracy, opposed to freedom of choice and believers in a staunchly orthodox form of Christianity having a daily role in governance."

"So... fascists, basically."

"In essence, but without the stated intent. They claim to work entirely within the law, and their membership includes many other wealthy old families, along with up-and-coming hard-right politicians from around the globe."

"You think there's more to them?"

"We do. They've been funneling money for years into South American governments and companies. If this originated in Argentina, as appears to be the case, there may be a more direct relationship."

"What's the play?" Brennan asked.

"We want you to go to Curacao, the Island off Venezuela. Wolf is attending an IF conference this coming weekend, a rare public appearance for him. Find a way into his camp, find out what he's up to. See if he's inquiring about the code."

"Carolyn and the kids are still at the hotel."

"We'll pay for a first-class upgrade to fly them home."

"She's going to kill me," Brennan said. "This had better be worth it, Jonah. And how do you expect me to get out of England, exactly? My face, or a close approximation, was caught by the downtown cameras…"

Jonah reached into the side pocket of his suit jacket and produced a small brown envelope, which he passed to the agent. "A diplomatic passport in a new name, your tickets, cash."

"Great. Won't help with the wife."

He ignored the comment. "What about the kid? Are you going to hand him over to us or the Brits before you go?"

Charlie had nothing else that could help them. But they'd make his life hell. "Work on getting him a pass on any criminal charges and we'll talk," Joe said. "And my ticket to Curacao better be first class as well. I need some goddamned sleep."

29.

The REGENCY HOTEL
ISLAND of CURACAO

Peter Bruner waited on the massive wrap-around balcony of his host's penthouse apartment, looking out over the pale blue water off the South American island's coast.

The glass of Cinzano Bianco was keeping him cool and the view was nice. But he was nervous. He'd never met Michael Wolf in person; he'd been in the same room with the man several times, but never the one doing the heavy lifting of trying to impress him.

But Gabriel Verde relied upon Wolf's money. And that meant keeping the Austrian industrialist happy. The International Family conference was the closest he'd be to Argentina any time soon, and Wolf was a star amongst the IF's many wealthy supporters, a "self-made" billionaire.

Of course, by 'self-made' they were referring to the growth in his family business, one begun by his great-grandfather and already worth tens of millions of dollars when he'd taken it over in the Nineteen Eighties.

Verde was one of his rare apolitical projects, as far as Bruner could tell. As far as Wolf and his cronies were concerned, Dr. Verde was spending their millions on revolutions in cloning.

Some even believed they might gain a sort of immortality eventually, growing new bodies to replace the old as they withered and died. And they had a somewhat more diabolical long view of how the technology could be used.

It was, of course, complete nonsense, the kind of fantastic wishful thinking that only the most fervent would believe possible. The money was going to a far more pragmatic use. But they didn't need to know that until the time was right.

For now, he just needed to keep Wolf at bay.

"Ah, Mr. Bruner!"

He turned back to the open-fronted apartment. Wolf had just stepped out of the private elevator.

"It's a shame Dr. Verde couldn't make it but I'm well aware you have his full confidence." The industrialist was flanked by two bodyguards in suits and dark glasses as he approached.

Bruner held out his hand and the men shook. "Mr. Wolf. I'm honored, sir."

"I'm sure you are. I'll take it as a commitment to be completely straightforward with me." A butler appeared from the general direction of the kitchen. Wolf held up a crooked finger. "Ah... Perrier with lime, extra ice."

The man scurried off. Wolf was an infamous teetotaler but his man had made a point of offering Bruner a drink from the small bar on the patio before the meeting. He wondered absently if it was a challenge of sorts, to see if he met Wolf's standards of sobriety.

Wolf strode over to the edge of the balcony and looked out at the beach and coastline. "Paradise, isn't it, Mr. Bruner? Most of the men attending this conference are hardened to aesthetic considerations. I have tried, however, never to let the work get in the way of appreciating this world and all in it."

Bruner smiled politely. Wolf was not known for being a gentle advocate for nature. His plastics and drug companies polluted on a global scale.

"But I would enjoy this event a great deal more if I could tell my fellow members of the International Family Council that the two-hundred-and-forty-two-million we've invested is about to bear fruit. Will we see working evidence of human cloning by the time Dr. Verde's time lock shuts them all in for a year? His sustainable community project, while doubtless fascinating to many, stands to cost us a year of time if we do not see something..."

Bruner nodded reassuringly. "Dr. Verde has authorized me to tell you that he thinks you're going to be marvelously surprised at the official kick off. He has made some amazing strides in the last few months, truly groundbreaking."

That was what Wolf wanted to hear. He beamed with appreciation. "That's fantastic news, Bruner, fantastic! I can't be there personally for the event but I will attempt to get away from the meetings for a few words..."

"Dr. Verde expected such," Bruner said.

"Well... listen, I mustn't keep you," Wolf suggested. "I must prepare for the executive council dinner and I'm sure you are busy."

It was his cue to depart. Bruner gave him a short, perfunctory bow. "I am most pleased to have finally met you, sir," he said, clicking his heels.

Bruner turned to leave, the butler escorting him to the door.

Wolf took a sip from the cold glass of mineral water and watched a cruise ship a mile off coast. The news was wonderful, the penultimate stage of a grand design.

In America, the other pieces were already falling into place. The day of ascension was approaching, at long last.

He walked over to the far end of the balcony and looked north, towards the private airstrip and helicopter pad that adjoined the hotel. A private jet was taxiing to take off and Wolf wondered what it had been like back when everything began, back when they were about to lose everything.

Back before they began to rewrite history.

PART TWO

THEN

30.

NOVEMBER 17, 1944
OVER THE ATLANTIC OCEAN

The four-engine Dornier long-range bomber hung just above the clouds, the blue sky and bright sun above belying the tension inside its bullet-riddled airframe and tiny cockpit.

Luftwaffe Lt. Helmut Marks gripped the yoke of the aircraft like it was the last rung on a ladder to nowhere, his gloved fingers trying to hold her as steady as possible. His face was sweaty, etched with anxiety and nerves, his jaw set solidly in a muscular grimace. His blue eyes flitted to the fuel gauge, even though it already read 'empty' and it wasn't going to rise on its own.

The bomber was descending. In a few moments, it would drop through the obscurity of the cloud cover. He hoped beyond hope to see land.

He held his breath as the view ahead cleared.

But the horizon offered just endless blue-black water, the Atlantic Ocean merciless and cold below. White caps suggested it was as choppy as one might expect so far from land. He didn't know how much fuel was actually in the tank, but he knew it was going to be close... assuming he was on course.

His co-pilot lay dead in the other cockpit seat, as were the three men who'd volunteered to man the gun turrets for the suicide mission. An American P52 Mustang fighter, itself off course from a carrier steaming towards Europe, had strafed them multiple times halfway through the crossing. It was possible they'd hit the American, as he hadn't returned to finish them. Or perhaps that was wishful thinking. Perhaps he'd just been low on fuel and had to return to his ship.

Either way, Lt. Marks was alone. He knew the trip was a one-way mission, that he was expected to crash the bomber into a populated area as soon as he dropped its payload. But his instruments had been damaged in the aerial assault. He was no longer sure he was on course. He'd expected to see land, and there was none.

If things had gone smoothly, the retrofitted bomber would've come out of the clouds to the sight of New York City on the horizon. He glanced back over his shoulder as he considered his payload. If the mission briefing was to be believed, the bomb was powerful enough to destroy much of the city, using a new technology called "fission".

He heard the sputtering sound to his left and checked the window. One of the engines had just shut down. Was that damage, from a bullet? Or was there so little fuel left that it had stalled or become air locked?

He crossed himself and said a silent prayer to God and the Fuehrer. His own life was unimportant, he knew. The Glory of the Fatherland, the turning of the tides of war? That was everything.

Soon, the Americans would regret taking sides.

They would regret underestimating Germany, as everyone had since the signing of the Treaty of Versailles. They would regret helping the English, who dropped bombs on his country and underwrote the evil of the perfidious Communist and the scheming Jew.

He saw the ripple in the water and the submarine surfacing miles before he reached it. If they'd sent an escort, it would've taken days to get there. He would've known before taking off.

That meant it was almost certainly a Russian or American sub. Had the trip been smoother, he might've ordered his men to engage, bomb the oblivious sailors while they were surfaced and vulnerable.

But he was alone, and they had no spare space for bombs other than the one, gigantic payload, a rugby-ball-shaped explosive. It bore the name "Gherecter Streik", or "Righteous Strike", painted on one side, a swastika-and-eagle on the other in the same white paint.

It had taken several weeks of prying information from his commander to learn that they weren't certain the device would work. It had never been tested, due to the Reich's demands that both the program and the heavy water supply in the Sudeten Mountains of Silesia remain secret.

The boat would have spotted him already on radar, likely called it in by radio to shore. But if an American squadron were close enough to easily find him, he would already be close enough to shore that it might not matter, Marks knew.

He maintained his altitude. If the fuel gauge was working, he could decide whether it was safe to go in on two engines, save the fuel from the third. But he had no idea if there were gallons left, or droplets.

He had to stay below two thousand feet. They'd been clear that, if the time came and either pilot had to become a makeshift bombardier, they were to drop the device from as low an altitude as possible. It meant the submarine's top-mounted machine gun was technically in range, and he could see the barest flashes from its muzzle as the plane soared over head. But from that range, their accuracy was poor at best.

A bullet passed through the right wing, the superstructure making a sharp, cracking noise. He checked the ailerons and made sure they were still functioning. It only took a few more moments before he was out of the submarine's range.

He peered at the horizon. How far off course had he gone? Marks thought about his wife, Helga, in Düsseldorf. He was glad, in the moment, that he had not impregnated her. She would find someone new, he told himself. And he would be a hero of the Fatherland.

The pilot strained his eyes, searching the horizon for any sign of...

Land. The slightest darkening, a thickened spot on the horizon due northeast. It was jutting out, tiny, a spit of coastline. Long Island, maybe?

No. He cast his mind back to the coastal images he'd absorbed trying to get positions correct in case of such an occurrence. But the shape didn't appear familiar.

"God damn you!" he exclaimed. He smacked the altimeter with the flat of his palm, twice. "Work damn you! Work!"

He heard a second sputtering trail and looked over at the left wing. The second inboard engine had quit, the prop slowing.

Then it's the fuel. We're out of fuel. He searched the horizon again frantically, more dark patches filling in, the barest sign that he was nearly at the continental United States.

"But where!" His mission wouldn't amount to much if he dropped the bomb over an underpopulated area, he knew. And the damage was to be counted in more than lives: Hitler felt humiliated by Roosevelt's involvement and he wanted an American symbol to be destroyed, using a power so vast that no one would stand against them.

He punched the altimeter one last time. His death would pave the way for...

The altimeter ball began to roll freely again. It bobbled around for a few seconds before coming to rest on his latitude and longitude.

Marks' mouth fell open. He was multiple map degrees too far north.

Ahead, on the horizon, land came clearly into view, the dark swatches suggesting acres of forests. By his estimates, he was just off the coast of the State of Maine.

"God damn it!" He screamed and punched the dash one more time, breaking the little finger in his hand.

To his right, he heard another long, sputtering sound. He turned his head slowly, not wanting to look as the third of four engines quit and the propeller spun down.

He tried to guess how far it was to land. But heavy bombers, loaded with weight, did not make good gliders.

Too far.

The fourth engine was not enough to keep their airspeed up, to push enough air up and over — and under — the wing to provide lift. Their airspeed was dropping precipitously, the nose beginning to dip. He would crash off the coast, he knew, and on a mission so secret, there was a chance no one would ever find his body.

31.

January 26, 1945

LONDON, ENGLAND

It was a rare moment of respite from his twenty-hour days of responsibility, and Prime Minister Winston Churchill shuffled into the private study beneath the Treasury building at Westminster.

His bodyguard closed the oak door behind Churchill. The politician shuffled over towards the rosewood sideboard and the silver serving tray containing a selection of cognac and sherry. He poured himself a glass of Remy Martin and breathed in deeply, clearing away the tension of the day.

"Sir, would you like a situational update?"

He turned to his right. The young man at the wall chart held a long stick used to manipulate the map tokens. Normally, it would be groups of British and German planes. But the young man, whom he'd forgotten about in looking for somewhere private, had a unique task: receiving radio updates on a lone English Lancaster Bomber.

"My apologies, young man. I found myself preoccupied with the fate of the nation and forgot you are part of it."

"Yes sir. I mean… I should say… I'm most honored to serve, sir…"

Churchill nodded grimly but didn't answer right away. The light caught the decanter of cognac. "I'm sure you have considerable courage already, but perhaps another ounce would make the task at hand more enjoyable…"

The young man looked nervous, clearly unsure of how to respond. "It's quite all right, lad," Churchill reassured. "Your devotion is admirable. Where is she now?"

With a range of more than four thousand kilometers, the Lancaster could stay airborne for more than thirteen hours. At the end of every twelve hours, the plane would veer away from its circular pattern and another would take its place.

"She's north of the mountain, sir. Hitler has been at The Berghof for three days. Our spies in the village nearby suggest he's apoplectic with rage." The young man smiled broadly, hopefully at the idea of Der Fuehrer venting against the blue skies that surrounded him.

"One rather suspects he feels violated," the Prime Minister suggested with a confident, wry smile. "It might give him an inkling of how the rest of Europe feels... but I rather doubt it. He seems to have almost child-like emotional self-control. Vicious little rotter."

He saw the boy smiling from the corner of his eye as he studied the board. "Any sign of opposition?" The Lancasters were fully crewed, armed to the teeth and each carrying just one device: a heavy-yield bomb that would explode on contact with the ground, ensuring that shooting down either plane would yield the same results.

Inside the bomb was a new chemical, Diphenylaminechloarorsine, a toxin so strong it had the potential to kill thousands within miles of impact. Beyond the obvious risk to himself and his consort, Eva Braun, Hitler had to worry about the region of his beloved Bavaria becoming a toxic wasteland.

It was an illegal weapon, according to every accord signed after Versailles. But it was, Churchill and the Chiefs of staff had jointly agreed, the only counter to the rumored nuclear fission device the Germans had developed.

Their intelligence reports suggested two bombs: one complete, but lost in a foolish attempt to bomb New York City, months earlier. The other, incomplete but near potential use. For all of the vagaries and horrors of war that fell outside the rules of engagement, the nuclear payload, their American allies insisted, made chemical weapons look like sparklers.

Word had been passed through to the Waffen SS and Hitler's inner circle that Britain had a device of its own: not a nuclear device, but one so horrific that its impact would be felt for generations. And if a Heinkel or Dornier bomber was spotted headed towards Great Britain, the Lancasters would drop their payload.

It was as close to detente as they could muster, Churchill knew, possibly until after the ground war was concluded – which looked increasingly like it might come in months. Germany was already in retreat on all fronts after six months of being pounded by the Allies in France and their failure to hold the eastern front against the Soviets. It was the time for desperate maneuvers, and he did not trust Hitler, as mad a man as they came, to not try for one final, insane grab for power.

Churchill swilled the brown liquor and sipped some back.

"Would you like me to give you a few minutes peace, sir? It's unlikely to really matter..." the young man suggested.

Churchill shook his head. "Perhaps it's fitting. For the job is not yet done."

32.

January 7, 1945
BERCHTESGADEN, GERMANY

Adolf Hitler, Chancellor of Germany and leader of the Third Reich, stared out from the stone balcony of his private mountainside retreat, The Berghof, down towards the valley surrounding the town of Berchtesgaden. In the distance, he could see a bare pinprick of shadow against the horizon, the silhouette of an airplane.

It seemed so far away. In reality, the Lancaster Bomber was just ten miles from his home.

Churchill, that swine. He's taunting me. He knows all is lost in the war, that nothing can turn things around now. He's telling me that he can hold me here, captive. That I cannot strike back.

"My dear? Are you all right?"

He turned and gave his consort, Eva Braun, a perfunctory nod. "Of course? Did I say otherwise? I am always all right, eventually. And eventually..."

"The Luftwaffe seems convinced the English bombers are essentially untouchable."

He scoffed at that, scowling. "The ignorant English pig thinks I am worried about some peasants and farmers, the dullard offspring of Junkers. As if I will not unleash Hell upon London as soon as the device is ready."

"But... we are within range..."

"Fool!" He bellowed. "My god damn!" Hitler slammed his closed fist down upon the balcony's stone bannister, immediately regretting it. "Aieeh!" He shook his bruised hand. "God damn the English! Where is Doctor Morell? I need my pills. I need my medication, right now!"

"I shall find him, my darling, don't fret!" she enthused. "I shan't let you down."

"We are within their range NOW," he continued. "Soon, we shall depart this valley of abject failure."

"We... We're leaving?" Braun asked. She looked unsure.

"Just for a short while," he lied. "We'll return to Berlin for a short while, then move onto the next phase of our plans."

She looked curious and puzzled. "The war... everyone says it's going so badly..."

Hitler nodded once, a bleak acknowledgement. "It is already lost. But we make plans, we prepare for the long fight to come. The Third Reich is immortal, as I promised."

"You... have a plan, my darling?"

"A young man, a protege of Gehlen, the intelligence boss. He has a shrewd idea. It is... not my preferred method of battle. I prefer the old ways, to look a man in the eye before I kill him...but it has a certain resiliency, which will serve us well."

"And... Berlin will stay in German control?" She sounded so hopeful. She was such a little idiot. He felt a momentary temptation to hurl her off the edge of the stone balcony, to watch her body be dashed against the rocks below. But it was unseemly, and he was the Chancellor of Germany.

"Of course, my love," he promised. "You must know, after all this time that your Fuehrer is here for you. But..."

She frowned. "But..."

"I need you to be brave, darling. When you first return to Berlin, I will remain here to direct the war effort."

"But... for how long?"

"It's is almost the end of the month. Based on our brave boys' efforts in the field of valor... as late as May, my darling. But Horst will be there..."

She rolled her eyes. Hitler's double was a near perfect physical replica, thanks to both extensive facial and dental surgery. But he was a bore, terrified of his employer becoming upset and dispatching him, as had been the fate of at least a half-dozen predecessors. That she knew of.

"If I must," she said. At least it would spare her his rages, when the 'medication' his doctor provided ramped his energy up to manic, violent proportions.

Hitler gazed back out across the valley again, turning counterclockwise in place until he finally caught view of the bomber. Soon, he would depart his humbled adopted homeland, and a new reign would begin.

33.

TRONDHEIM, NORWAY
Jan. 30, 1945

The Junkers twin-engine passenger plane taxied down the runway towards the hangars and small terminal. An open-topped Mercedes sedan waited for it, a driver in an SS uniform accompanied by a young officer, his boots shined to perfection.

Otto Skorzeny felt a tremble of nerves, a rare event. Even under fire while assisting Franco's fascists in Spain and hunted in Italy while freeing Mussolini, he'd maintained a steady hand. But he'd only met Hitler once before, during a group event in which he was shuffled to the back of a group, receiving a perfunctory nod but nothing else from their leader.

He revered what Hitler had accomplished, his fight for a warrior social class, his desire to lift Germany to world domination. At his heart, Skorzeny was a warrior, though he'd learned as a young man that he could accomplish more with guile and influence than at the point of a pistol.

"My nerves, colonel..." the young driver suggested. "I have never even been close to the Fuehrer before..."

Skorzeny gave him a chin-up motion with a small wave of his fist. "It is a proud moment for you then! Do not worry. We must deliver him to the submarine base, and then you will be sent about your duties."

In fact, the young man would be shot in the head as soon as Hitler had departed. There was to be no record of the trip, no attention paid to the two U-boats leaving that afternoon. A refugee ship sailing from Danzig had been tipped to the Allies as containing Nazi officers. By the time the Allies realized most of the thousands on board were merely poor and indigent, hours would've been wasted first in the attack and then the relief effort.

The plane slowed to a stop. After a few moments, the cabin door opened. Twenty yards away, two airport workers hurriedly pushed the rolling staircase over to the doors. Though their exposure would be mere seconds long, they would join the boy. Skorzeny considered himself a refined espionage officer and, though he had little conscience of which to speak, considered killing witnesses a crude method of handling things. But in the speed of events, it was their sole option.

Hitler appeared at the top of the steps. He looked older, frailer than Skorzeny recalled, his black leather coat with the fur-lined collar fairly hanging off him. The woman, Eva Braun, was not with him. He'd arranged for her to spend the remainder of the war in Berlin. When the Allies closed on the city, they would feed her and his double the cyanide capsules. Any doubts about the double's superb dental forgeries would be papered over by the absolute certainty of Braun's demise.

For good measure, they would poison the dog, too.

He sauntered over to the base of the steps as Hitler reached them. Behind the chancellor, his bodyguard and a nurse followed closely. Both would also be executed, although the nurse was with them until Argentina.

"Heil Hitler!" He snapped a fascist salute. "Mein Fuhrer!" Skorzeny saluted vociferously. An emotionally even and stoic man, he surprised himself with his excitement.

"Sieg Heil!" Hitler responded with a short, curt salute in return. "Lt.-General Gehlen speaks very highly of you, Skorzeny. We put the future of the Reich in your hands; you realize the responsibility you bear, yes?"

"Yes, my Fuhrer."

"Good. You should be very proud, Skorzeny. The solution you've found to our temporary setbacks in the war mirrors very closely what I had already been discussing with the party leadership."

If he believed the statement, Skorzeny kept it to himself. He gestured towards the Mercedes parked not far away. "If you would proceed to the vehicle, my Fuhrer, the submarine awaits."

"And Richter, he is already aboard?"

"He is. The device is on the first submarine, of course, due to the radiation exposure."

"It is quite high?"

"It is."

"So the sailors on board...."

"Will all die eventually, yes. But in the service of the greatest of needs."

The Mercedes carried them across the property and main road to the submarine base, still under construction despite Germany's failing status. At the main gate, the guard had a shocked look on his face.

Skorzeny realized he was staring at Hitler. "He's an actor, a double designed to deceive Allied spies," he explained. "Thus the lack of ceremony."

Ah! The young guard nodded knowingly but his expression suggested he wasn't certain. Skorzeny smiled warmly at the boy. He would be dead within the hour.

The Mercedes followed the new concrete road down a slope that led to the covered docks. It followed the rectangular two-story building, larger than a football stadium, for sixty yards, parking a few dozen yards from where the facility emptied out into the North Sea. Skorzeny held Hitler's passenger door open as the German leader and his bodyguard debarked. He led the two men to the sliding-door side entrance to the facility, pulling it back.

Inside, long concourses surrounded the building, running around the perimeter and between each of the recessed docks. Only two were complete and functional and the tower of a German U-boat poked above each.

They walked the twenty yards to the first gangway.

"Here we are sir, ready to go," Skorzeny said. "Soon you will rule from a new land, and can prepare for the next wave of our glorious destiny."

His zeal brought a glint of energetic happiness to Hitler's eyes. "And we shall prevail!" he insisted. "There will be no more failures brought on by the weakness of subordinates! We will crush Churchill, and Roosevelt, and the insidious Jews who underwrite both men."

The sub's top hatch opened and its commander climbed out. He saw Hitler and his face blanched. He sprung to attention and saluted. "Heil Hitler!"

"At ease, commander," Hitler ordered. "We are going to be in each other's presence for several days. It would do you well to become accustomed to the notion."

And when they landed in Argentina, the captain and entire crew would be executed, Skorzeny knew, the U-boats scuttled once unloaded. They were not ready for Hitler's escape to become known, not by a long shot. Until they had a guarantee of military or political superiority, Hitler would remain officially very much dead.

The German leader boarded. He gave a final wave before disappearing down the ladder, then a straight-armed salute. "A new beginning!" he declared.

The captain followed, pulling the hatch closed behind them.

Skorzeny returned to the car outside. The driver started its big engine and the Mercedes pulled away from the U-boat station, towards the road.

Near the gates, another man was getting out of a similar car, a 1935 Daimler. He was smaller than Skorzeny and older, with balding brown hair and a Gallic, beak-nosed profile. Hitler's Chief of Intelligence, Reinhard Gehlen, had devised the plot with Skorzeny.

Skorzeny tapped the driver on the shoulder. "Slow down, I want to talk to him."

Skorzeny waited until the Mercedes had stopped adjacent to the other vehicle. Both men climbed out of their respective cars.

"Lieutenant-General," Skorzeny saluted and Gehlen returned it.

"Then it's done?" Gehlen asked.

"It is."

"And the decoy vessels? The refugee boats?"

"Filled to the brim and departed from all cities. A cable from our man in London confirms the High Command plan to attack at least two of the vessels for harboring fugitives."

Gehlen smiled shrewdly. "Good. That mistake alone will take them years to remedy and investigate. The ensuing chaos will cover any hint of his departure."

Skorzeny looked back at the U-boat station. He appeared puzzled, however. "I still do not understand why you don't go..."

"I told you, the path to freedom for senior officers has already been secured. The intelligence community around the world is salivating at obtaining our expertise, just as the Americans and Russians want the scientists who worked on the project. In the aftermath of a war, information remains far more valuable than life itself."

Behind them, the alarm sounded, and the red light flashed as the giant bay doors that led out to sea slid open across the face of the building. The U-boat taxied out of the dock and towards open water.

"And what of him?" Skorzeny said. "What becomes of the man who began all of this?"

"What of him?" Gehlen shrugged. "He will be the figurehead leader he has been for years; as long as we have competent men handling things and he is fully supplied with his drug regimen and the odd chambermaid to molest, he is content."

"Then he will never truly lead again?"

"No! God, no. And thank goodness," Gehlen said. "He believes his own bullshit, and supreme confidence can make any man inspiring. But he was never competent."

"It seems like such an ignoble end."

"It was never about him. Not really. The money that supported him was old, the ideas older. The right of nobility and conquest," Gehlen insisted. "The right of man's strongest to lead."

"And now? What now?"

"You will move on to Spain and work from there. Globke has talked to Francois Genoud to arrange the funds. If you should encounter any issues, I will speak with the Americans. I have associates to visit before I return and officially surrender."

Skorzeny didn't like Genoud, a Catholic fascist and racist who worked out of Geneva. But the man was incredibly effective at wearing the public face of upper-crust supremacism, so that his wealthy and more famous benefactors like Coco Chanel, William Randolph Hearst, Hugo Boss and a panoply of American and French business executives could remain in the shadows, donating to and supporting the war, and profiting from it.

"The Americans are expecting you?"

"They are being most gracious and polite; quite amenable. They're easy to manipulate when all of their senior men want glory."

34.

Jan. 31, 1945

The SS *Inez Marie* shuddered and listed slightly to each side, towering Atlantic Ocean waves slapping against the giant hull of the ship. Its upper deck, open to the elements, was nonetheless packed with people, crammed in like storage crates, sleeping, eating and defecating where they lay at night. Ocean spray showered them with moisture regularly.

In the shadow of the main cabins and the bridge, Jacob Grech and his young wife Maria huddled against a steel wall, Maria clutching their infant son Mark tight to her body. The ship was a converted cruise liner, their passage assured by a generous Italian patron of Jacob's trade as a cobbler

The wind howled and the sea drenched everyone. They had one blanket to share. Maria had managed to smuggle a small paper bag of food under her coat.

The voyage across the ocean would take seven days. Already, just a day in, two men had died from heart attacks and a boy had been swept overboard. They shared only one element of their simple life with their patron: both had most of their family murdered by Communists, advancing on Mussolini's failing regime.

But Jacob was determined not to let his family down. To give his son a better life in America. They knew the trip would be perilous, with the possibility of attack by vessels from both sides.

"Cigarette?"

He wasn't sure when the man next to him had sidled up.

The man had a rain slicker, as if prepared for the conditions. Jacob accepted the smoke gratefully and took a light. He took two puffs then passed it to Maria, who followed suit.

"Thank you!" He had to raise his voice to be heard over the ocean's roar.

The man extended a hand. "I am Luigi," he said. "Luigi de Cesare."

Jacob shook. "Jacob Grech."

"Grech? You are not Italian..." the other man observed.

"From Malta. But we had been living in Naples for several months. I... do not know what we are going to do."

The Italian put a hand on his shoulder, a comforting weight. "What you will do is what we all must do in these most desperate times: survive, so that your wife and child can survive also."

Jacob nodded and smiled. He took the proffered cigarette back from his wife and took a deep puff. They were strong. He rolled the cigarette between his fingers, trying to establish its brand in the rain-slicked half-darkness of the deck.

"They're Lucky Strikes, American cigarettes," Luigi offered. "I have family in America already, in a town called Chester. Near Philadelphia. Many jobs. Many opportunities. A great place to raise a family."

Jacob exhaled. "I have begun to wonder if anywhere on Earth can offer peace and quiet," he muttered.

"In Pennsylvania," Luigi affirmed. "You'll see. I will help you adjust, Jacob. The Communists are behind us. You have nothing more to fear."

NOW

35.

Oct. 20, 2020

WASHINGTON, D.C.

The restaurant was trendy, the kind that only people with expense accounts or personal fortunes could afford. Alex Malone downed the last of her double scotch as the bathroom door swung open and her lunchmate emerged.

He was a handful. For one, the man had been inside the Central Intelligence Agency for more than a decade. For another, his acceptance of a free lunch had been begrudging, annoyed as he was at Malone for using off-the-record material.

But she needed him, she knew. She'd burned a lot of bridges in a decade of reporting on Capitol Hill. The Korean nuke incident had been the last straw, and she'd spent the three years since covering an increasingly dismal series of policy stories, her editor no longer trusting her with anything salacious.

It wasn't that she got the story, he'd told her. It was how she'd gotten it — by, among other things, blackmailing diplomats and shutting out her reporter colleagues.

The intelligence officer sat down again across from her and retrieved the fork from next to his steak. "Christ, even the johns in this place are nicer than my apartment," he offered.

"If they're going to charge you fifty bucks for a steak, the facilities for getting rid of it after the fact better be nice."

He chuckled a little at that. "I always liked you, Alex. Even when the department said you were off-limits completely, I figured you do your job for the right reasons..."

"Sure."

"But I can't help you this time."

Damn it. It wasn't like she was asking for much. She knew there was an operation in the UK that had buzz, and it had something to do with South America. And that was it.

What she wanted was a confirmation that Joe Brennan was involved. That was all she really needed, that and a location. She'd let her relationship with the clandestine operations officer lapse. Then she'd heard about his late, unofficial save of the Chinese premier at an event in New York, a story that no one landed and officially never happened.

The truth was, she knew, she needed a hit. She'd burned so many sources and annoyed so many editors that nobody really wanted her copy anymore. It was only temporary, she knew; freelancers tended to be as popular as their most recent scoop. If she landed a big enough story, she'd be back in the limelight, back to accepting decent assignments instead of dry, policy-heavy think pieces that hardly paid.

"I'm not looking for hard details..."

"I can't help, period," he said.

"Then who can? Surely there's someone..."

"Are you on speaking terms with Jonah Tarrant?"

The acting director of the agency? *Sure. I'll just ring him up on our private line.* "Not really. We've met, during the big one..."

"Sure." She didn't really need to elaborate. Everyone in Washington's media establishment had been crushed by her exclusive into the North Korean incident.

She'd come to believe at least a small part of her industry exile was rank resentment, jealousy that she'd gotten the story of a lifetime without any of their help. "Well... that's who you need to work on. Because he's the one who made you off limits."

Tarrant only worked strategically. It was never personal. In a way, Alex knew, it was a sign of respect, the notion that she might be so effective as to get in the way of an operation.

It didn't help in the moment. A waiter arrived table-side to remove their plates. She gave him a game smile. But her mind was elsewhere.

Where are you, Joe Brennan? And what the Hell are you up to?

36.

Oct. 21, 2020

CURACAO

The beefy blonde man in the blue shorts and striped golf shirt had a short, efficient backswing. He swung the driver with whip speed, its smooth-faced club head finding the dimpled ball flush, power propelled through it, the shot soaring in a dramatic arc over the fairway.

He watched in a frozen position at the end of his backswing until the ball bounced softly on the short-mown grass, rolling parallel to the palm trees that surrounded the hole. "Now that's a drive, right there!" Brett Steel exclaimed. His accent was straight-up 'trawna' — a Torontonian by way of Calgary, taking a break from the Canadian fall on the Dutch island, North of Venezuela. "Beat that, my English friend!"

Brennan had tailed Steel to a bar in the Sheraton Hotel, away from his own high-priced resort room. Steel drank away from other International Family conference members, suggesting he either liked his privacy or, perhaps, was uncomfortable in social gatherings where most spoke French, Spanish or German.

Not that there weren't Americans and other Canadians attending; but Steel didn't really fit the mold. He had plenty of money, to be sure, from the sale of an oil field supply company in Alberta. But he was no captain of industry or ambitious political force. Instead, he seemed to be along for the ride.

Brennan lined up his tee shot and smacked it down the fairway, opening up his body at the last second of his swing to deliberately slice the ball slightly. It flew straight and true for about thirty yards before beginning to veer to the right.

It settled on the edge of the fairway, near the rough and forty yards behind the other man's shot.

"Ha!" the big Canadian declared. "That one's mine." They had a five-dollar bet on who could hit the longest drive on each hole, along with bets on the number of putts and overall score.

Brennan handed his club to one of the two young men standing to one side of the tee box, caddying their bags for them. He gave the kid a wink and the boy smiled sheepishly.

From the corner of his eye, he saw Steel's smarmy grin. "He's cute," Brennan said. "But... a little on the mature side, if you know what I'm saying."

Steel smirked. "You've got that right," he said.

The caddy couldn't have been much more than eighteen. But the agency's file on Steel suggested he liked his boys much younger — as infants, if possible. A pedophile of the worst magnitude, his money and ability to travel to find his victims had insulated him from prosecution.

He made Joe's blood boil. Every second in his presence required conscious disconnection from his emotions, because if he didn't, he thought he might kill the guy. Steel's file had been complete.

They walked down the fairway, the caddies following ten yards behind. "I'm having a little party tonight," Brennan suggested casually. "After the big dinner. Just a few friends over for some fun."

Steel nodded knowingly. "Fun's fun. I could go for that. Are we talking...?"

"There are a surprising number of poor people for such a lovely island," Brennan said. "Mothers who are desperate for money and don't mind having us... babysit for the evening."

Steel's gaze lingered as they walked. "Really? That's..."

"Exciting, I know," Brennan said. He told himself there were only four holes left to play. *Four holes and you can go break something, then take a shower.*

The details had already been arranged by his Washington handler, an officious weasel named Murray Peacock whose sole concern seemed to be how Jonah Tarrant would react. The boys at the party would look underage but be technically legal. The photographic evidence of Steel's behavior would be thorough and convincing.

Brett Steel was about to have a very bad week indeed.

Brennan tried not to think about what it would mean to cut the man loose, for the Agency to hold onto him as a compromised source rather than ensuring he wound up in a prison cell, where he belonged.

Or maybe a hospital intensive care unit.

37.

LONDON

The phone was on its fifth or sixth ring by the time Charlie realized Martin hadn't moved from his armchair. Instead, the retired former policeman was staring at the ringing receiver intently.

"Are you going to...?" Charlie asked.

Martin shook his head. "If it was family, they'd use my cell phone. That means it's either my former work, or someone else. Neither should be calling in the middle of a weekday morning, as I am retired."

"Which means...."

"Which means it's probably someone probing for information, someone who knows that I have a personal relationship with Joe Brennan and that he's operational."

"Ah. But you don't..."

"... Want to know who? Certainly. But better to be patient. If I let them hang up, we'll know from how quickly they try again whether they're serious."

Charlie wondered how Martin remained so calm. Perhaps it was the nature of policemen and retired policemen. He'd only ever gotten to know them while fleeing.

The phone stopped ringing. They remained silent for a few seconds. Then Charlie said, "Well, I suppose that means it's nothing...."

The phone began to ring again. Martin gave him a knowing look as he rose and crossed the living room to answer it. "Martin Weiss."

"Martin! It's Nick Temple! We haven't talked in a while..."

"Nick Temple. As I live and breathe. It's been, what..."

"Ten years?" the caller suggested. "You were working on the Met's homicide squad and I was at Justice..."

"Of course, of course. Is your brother still a serving member?" It was all very congenial, Martin thought wryly, just old mates catching up.

"He's a consultant now in Edinburgh, cybercrimes and such. Anyway, I was in town working on something and I thought I'd give you a quick call."

"Oh? You're not based in London, then?"

"No, I'm in Washington, D.C. these days, of all things. Security job, typical hush hush government nonsense, I'm afraid. Listen... while I've got you, I thought I'd check on the Joe Brennan thing, just see if you needed a hand with anything."

Martin had been a policeman for far too long to walk into a false confirmation. "The what?" he asked.

"You know, the thing with the young man. That which cannot be mentioned."

"Nick... I genuinely have absolutely no idea what you're talking about," he lied smoothly. "Joe Brennan? The American agent?"

"One and the same. You and he..."

"Go back quite some way, yes. He used to visit me down in Brighton when he was briefly stationed in England. But that was twenty years ago, Nick. I really don't know the man very well. Why? Do you need to get in touch with him or something?"

"Could you?"

Now he was just feeling him out, trying to gauge if the retiree was lying. "Probably not," Martin said. "I mean, I suppose I have a number for him in Washington somewhere. If you really need it, I could begin looking, but... I suppose I could make some calls, see if anyone has it at hand."

"Hmmm. No... that's quite all right. But... listen, if you do hear from him, would you very much mind giving me a ring? Him or the young man."

"I will do that, of course," Martin said. Then he caught himself. "Sorry... the 'young man'?" Temple had almost caught him out, the oldest trick in the book.

"It's a long story," the other man suggested. 'Can I leave you my number...?"

After he'd hung up, Martin stood by the phone pensively for a few minutes.

"Who...?" Charlie asked.

"An old associate, looking for you and Joe, as I'd suspected." He gestured to the door. "Come on, pack your things. We need to move. They won't be satisfied with a phone check if they're still coming up empty a few hours from now."

38.

Oct. 22, 2020

CURAÇAO

Joe sat at the patio breakfast table and picked at his ham and eggs. He didn't have much appetite after the night prior.

First, he'd had to explain to Steel that he couldn't provide him with prepubescent children to assault; then he'd offered him the compromise: a gigolo who looked so alarmingly juvenile that using him to blackmail the Canadian wouldn't be difficult. There was no need for two-way glass or hidden rooms or any of the excesses of the past; modern technology allowed them to film Steel's performance with four tiny fiber optic cameras, broadcasting to a laptop in the next room.

Peacock had insisted on staying up and reviewing the footage, cutting it into the most salacious form possible. Joe had waited until it was confirmed they were recording and gotten out of there, spending the rest of the night at the bar in the lobby. Peacock had gathered the footage together and put it on a memory stick, which was included along with the agency's existing file on Steel.

The wood-and-glass door to the patio opened, a waitress in white-and-black holding it for Steel as he tromped out and over to Joe's table. He had a thick Manila envelope under one arm, and he tossed it onto the tablecloth with a dramatic thud.

"What the Hell is this?" the Canadian spat.

Joe leaned back slightly in his dining chair, pushing away from the table with his elbows and arching his fingers together. This part, by comparison, was going to be way too enjoyable. "Oh... we both know what that is." He smiled as he said it. He wanted Steel impotently angry. It wouldn't make up for who he was or what he'd done, but it was a start on the road there.

Steel sat down and leaned in towards the American. "You realize what will happen to you if any of this..."

"That's irrelevant, isn't it?" Joe said. "I mean, if I was worried, I suppose it wouldn't be irrelevant to me. But it's certainly irrelevant to you. If that gets out, what happens to me is going to be the last thing you're thinking about, I imagine."

"I have powerful friends..." Steel began.

"Oh please. My employers don't give a crap what you think of me, Mr. Steel. I'm just the errand boy, the one delivering the message and your instructions."

"My what?"

"Instructions. The things that you're going to do for us to ensure that file remains private. And let me reassure you: should you fail to comply or act up in any way, they are going to take the greatest of pleasure in delivering all of that to the police in every major nation on the planet... and a few newspapers and television stations, also."

Steel's face drained of color. He'd come to the meeting angry, hot headed and expecting to bully Brennan. But he'd been in business long enough to know when he was in over his head.

"What do you want?"

"The group you've joined, The International Family, has a series of high-level meetings coming up in Argentina. We want a location, and we want to know what they're about. We also want you to inform the IF that you've been called home due to the sudden illness of your stepmother. I'll replace you, under the name Mark Kruger."

Steel stared at the tablecloth sullenly. "They'll kill me if they find out I've talked to you. I'm probably dead already and it's just a matter of time."

"The meeting: where is it, and what's its purpose?"

Steel looked around the patio for potential eavesdroppers. It was nearly empty, just an older couple in the far corner. "It's in a town called San Carlos de Bariloche, in the mountains. They've got a bunch of properties there, lake chalets and junk. It's like Banff, only with smaller mountains, I guess..."

"Whose property, specifically?"

"I don't know. We weren't going to be told until we checked in at a hotel in the city."

"And the meeting? What's the subject?"

"They have a project, something they're financing. But it's hush hush crap, high-level stuff."

"Not good enough. We need details: is it a political project, or business? Scientific?"

"I don't know, I'm telling you..."

"Maybe. Or maybe we should just release everything to the media and see what shakes loose..."

"OKAY! Okay..." Steel simmered down for a moment. "Jesus H, you sonsofbitches better never let me find out who you are..."

"Your worries would multiply exponentially if you did."

"It's... it's some kind of science project. There's a bunch of stuff based out of there, but the big one is some research grant."

"To whom?"

"Whom! 'To whom,' he asks. The balls on you..."

"Steel..."

"Dr. Gabriel Verde."

Brennan was trained to hide his emotions, but it wasn't easy. Verde's world-renowned research had made the scientist immensely wealthy and produced a score of commendations from dozens of nations, his vaccines helping to save the lives of millions. It was widely believed he would eventually be awarded a Nobel Prize. He'd been nominated twice.

"You're full of shit."

Steel held up both palms wide. "Hey... I know what you've got on me. You think I'm risking that? That's who's getting the lion's share of the money. I know: they hit all of us up for an extra ten thousand in the last quarter, minimum donation."

Brennan wanted to punch the pedophile from across the table. He made his skin crawl. He wasn't going to bother asking the man why he'd support a fascist organization; birds of a sick feather tended to flock together. It was the kind of movement that didn't care where the money came from or about the truth, as long as its members were perceived as powerful.

The American rose from the table. "You better make some travel arrangements. Once we know you're heading home, we'll know you're behaving yourself. But if you decide to play hero to the movement..."

"I told you, I don't want to go to jail."

"Jail?" Brennan scoffed. "Double cross us and I'll put a bullet in your head myself... and relish the opportunity."

He turned and walked back into the hotel.

39.

LONDON

It was a chilly morning. Peter Chappell followed the banks of the Thames with his wife's Corgi, Bosephus, at the end of a short leash. He didn't mind the morning walks, which gave him a chance to clear his head before going to the office.

They were also anonymous, twenty minutes from the heart of the city and surrounded by enough greenery to become part of the scenery. He found the bench where they'd met so many times in the past and sat down.

Archie Grimes was already there, tossing bird seed from a small bag to the magpies ten feet away. "You're late. Anything the matter?" he asked Chappell, without looking up.

"No, just getting Bosephus to eat his food... she got him something new, you see, and they're creatures of habit. I have to wait a half-hour to walk him after he eats or it's bad for his heart, or tummy or something."

"You're meeting with Norris today?"

"This morning, yes."

"Then he's the last."

"Ken Loach, this afternoon."

"Ah."

"I rather suspect it will take a while for anything to filter back to us."

Chappell had followed Grimes's instructions precisely after the last meeting. He'd let slip a different piece of information about the International Family to each of the attendees, in their offices, in private. If they were correct, the IF would act on the leak, attend a location, identify the leaker in the process.

"What about South America?" Grimes asked. "Are we sending anyone to find out what they're up to?"

Chappell shook his head. "The Americans have decided to climb all over that one. Good luck to them, I suppose. I rather suspect they have a larger political stake in the outcome."

Grimes turned his head quickly, intently. "Why? What have you heard?" The American election was in just a few weeks. "Are you suggesting...?"

"Oh... I'm sure they're exerting political influence, through sympathetic foreign leaders in Russia and Italy, among others. And they're spending money. But... nothing more than that so far, no."

Chappell knew Grimes as the only man at the heart of the agency who was unimpeachably trustworthy. But they weren't sure yet what the IF was up to in the United States, or Argentina. Better to remain undecided than to jump in and get it wrong.

"One other question," Grimes proposed. "The Israelis: how on Earth did they get involved in this? The Russians and the Austrians I can understand; both countries have core leadership that is IF affiliated. "But the Israelis?"

Chappell shook his head. "We don't know. From everything to date, it seems the young man was just a hacker trying to steal something and make a few quick bob. The fact that it was connected to Argentina and all of this... well, that was really just terrible bad luck for him. But the Israelis? That's worrisome. We have no idea what they know or how they know it."

"Then it seems we have another mole to root out, Peter. Doesn't it?"

40.

PEACEHAVEN, Sussex

Martin Weiss's ex-partner on the Metropolitan Police was a copper-haired woman with a broad, wide nose and a fleshy, pale face. Ruby Downey had retired a year earlier — five years after Martin — but was young enough to have started a second career as a security consultant.

Her husband had died of cancer while she was still a serving member, but she'd kept their little bungalow on the quiet street in Peacehaven, just west of Brighton, a community of mostly retirees and middle-class families.

She listened in the sunroom they'd built on to the back of the house as Martin went over the days prior. Her frown and look of anxious concern grew throughout. Eventually, she said, "So... you thought it would be a nice idea to drop in on me instead..."

"Ruby, I'm really sorry, love, honestly," Martin offered. He really meant it; they'd always cared about each other, beyond the job even. If he hadn't been married, he'd sometimes told himself... Well. That was in the past, of course. "If I knew anyone more anonymous to the people looking for the boy, I'd have called them."

"I haven't heard from you in four years, Martin. Do you think it's just possible that I have a right to be upset that you're here now, asking for a favor? Whatever happened to 'a place by the sea? You'll never get rid of me'!"

Martin hung his head. "I know. After my wife died, I stopped talking and going out as much..."

That made Ruby frown, too, but it was a look of concern, not anger. "I know what that's like. You know Gary and I did everything together. We'd be out golfing right now, if he was still alive..."

Charlie felt the mood heading south. He sipped awkwardly on the tea she'd brought them. "Well, I'm very glad you're here now and that you two are having a chance to see each other again. At least there's that," he offered optimistically.

Martin nodded his way. "See? He's a good lad, he's just a right twat when it comes to decisions."

"Is this from your military intelligence days?" Ruby asked him. "I can't see you having made too many spy friends at the Met."

"Yeah, an American who helped train us when I did some work in Cyprus. We won't be any bother..."

She looked quizzical. "So... you were thinking more than just the night, then?"

Martin looked embarrassed, which suited Ruby just fine. She'd always had a bit of a crush on her ex-partner, even though he was fifteen years older than her. He didn't want to encourage it, now that they were both single. He was older, and he missed Anne every day.

Ruby knew all of that. But her expression suggested he should have called.

41.

NUEVA ESPERANZA, Argentina

In a vast concrete square in the center of the shopping-mall-sized compound, surrounded by two-story offices, rows of young men and women exercised.

Their movements were coordinated as they dipped and stretched and sat up and jogged. In one corner, above the arched walkways that surrounded the community square, a loudspeaker offered a healthy dose of Mozart and Handel to keep their moods boisterous.

Dr. Gabriel Verde paced the perimeter and watched. A dozen yards away, by a wall, sat Manuel, his valet and bodyguard.

All forty-two of the subjects were eighteen years old. They looked so healthy, Verde thought, so full of purpose. They came from communities across the globe, all selected for the purity of their ancestral line: all good Aryans, with families who were once powerful, and noble, and rich. In some cases, they still were. All filled by idealism and hope and conviction that it was their lot in life to make a difference.

To a man and woman, they were divorced from the beliefs and political affiliations of their ancestors. If any were aware of who was funding the entire venture, he had no doubt they would walk out en masse.

Or try to. He glanced at the four guard towers on each corner of the property. The men looked alert, rifles at the ready.

"Everything is on schedule?"

He turned. Bruner had returned from Buenos Aires. "Peter! That was a short trip..."

The older man looked mildly irritated. "I wouldn't have flown down if it was just banking matters," he said. "I thought Lopez and a few of the other local contributors wanted some face time. But they're coming up for the IF meeting in a few days, so they begged off, knowing I'd be here."

The meeting. Verde hadn't thought about it in several days. "They still demand an audience, I take it?"

"Of course. They've invested $250 million into this venture over the last thirty years, and many of their families contributed for years before that. I rather suspect they want more than an audience this time; they want tangible proof of results, or they'll pull the plug."

And he did not have tangible proof, at least not of what the International Family expected. For three decades, it had funded his magnum opus, his most impressive genetic engineering goal.

But throughout, the fascist organization had imagined a far different end than Verde's real objective.

"When they find out what I've actually been working on..."

"It will be too late, assuming they don't act before the launch," Bruner said. "And after that, nothing else will matter."

Verde looked back over at the exercising youth. "If I get this wrong, the consequences will be devastating beyond compare."

Bruner shrugged. "Depending on your perspective, they will be anyway. You can't wipe out most of the population of the planet, after all, without breaking a few eggs."

42.

Oct. 22, 2020

CURAÇAO

Murray Peacock sat with the digital recorder propped on the table in front of him, perched on a white linen tablecloth. Across the table, Brett Steel had sat for an hour, answering in-depth questions about his membership in the International Family.

"I'm telling you: I have to go to the meetings. They won't buy the family excuse. I've already felt them out."

Brennan was certain the man couldn't be trusted. But he was their only person on the inside. "If you tip anyone there that I'm not with you, or that there's a problem, they'll just send someone to take my place. And that person will kill you. Do you understand?"

Steel nodded.

"I don't see an alternative," Peacock suggested. "We don't know what kind of time constraints we're working under…"

Brennan had paced throughout, throwing down questions of his own. Steel's face had reddened the entire time, until he looked like an over-stewed tomato that was about to collapse.

"You keep telling us to trust you, Mr. Steel. But you're a criminal and a pederast. And you expect me to follow you into this meeting without any kind of confirmation phrase or pass code...

"I keep telling you," he insisted. "The only confirmation code is the handshake. It's complicated enough. They think it's funny or ironic, because they stole the idea from the Freemasons, who they can't stand."

"Show it to me again," Peacock insisted. "Then Brennan."

He went through the elaborate rigmarole one more time, the two men slapping palms, then the backs of their hands, then hooking their top two fingers together, twisting them, then bringing them to their temple for a split-second salute.

Brennan stifled a sigh. It looked like something out of the Bull Moose Lodge on the Flintstones.

Fucking Fascists: even their hand signals are dumb beyond belief.

He'd had to listen to Steel drool over the IF's international influence for more than an hour, for the second time in less than two days. How they'd worked closely with the Russian premier to cement his power base, how they'd helped finance elections in the United Kingdom, Brazil, Italy, Indonesia and Western Canada.

Their supporters included billionaires, right-wing politicians; a retired Canadian prime minister, a former Austrian chancellor, a media tycoon. It amounted to a lot of wealthy, avaricious, sociopathic individuals who believed they had a God-given right to rule, Brennan supposed.

After they were done and Steel had slunk off to his own room, Peacock went back over a few of the recording's more salacious suggestions. "Is that it with that guy?" Brennan asked. "Because he makes my skin crawl."

"For now, we need him," Peacock said sternly. The two men had never worked together before and were getting along like oil and water. Peacock struck him as a young, brash, privileged type, probably from a Beltway family, a graduate of Yale's Skull and Bones or something similar.

Peacock sensed his unease. "The end objective in all of this, whatever it may be, is decidedly more important than your natural distaste for people of Steel's ilk."

Sure, Brennan thought. *Just like last year, and the year before that and the year before that. There's always some lunatic with too much money and the wrong intentions.* "Now what?"

"Now, you go to San Carlos de Bariloche, you follow him, and find out what has Steel's fellow club members so anxious."

"And when I find it?"

"You report back to me. And that is all you do, Mr. Brennan. Are we clear on that? I know you were with the agency for a long time..."

"Sure felt it."

"Yes, well... things have changed. We have a new era of accountability because of the increasingly politically charged national mood in America. The last thing we need is some well-intentioned individual throwing fuel on that fire during an election campaign by creating an international incident."

"I can't figure Jonah Tarrant wants to cough up a six-figure payment for me to just gather intel."

"Probably not. But that's not your decision to make, is it? And it can't be made until we know more. So... pack your bags, Mr. Brennan. You're going to Patagonia."

"Whoop-de-freakin' do."

43.

LANGLEY, Virginia

Jonah Tarrant took the video call on the secure line in Adrienne Hayes' office, the CIA officer waiting a few moments for the channel to unscramble, a wavy pattern of blotched color and botched audio suddenly clearing up, Peter Chappell's ever-serious face appearing.

"Good morning, Peter, good to see you again," Jonah suggested.

"Good morning, Jonah. I take it as it's been nearly a week, you've got something to update from South America?"

Jonah knew he had to play the British carefully. They were conducting their own investigations, spurred on by both the theft from their military and the sudden interest of other nations. "As long as you've got something to tell me about your end, of course."

"Naturally," Chappell said.

"Do you have the young man who hacked your system in custody?" Adrienne interjected. She had a habit of skipping to the point before people were comfortable, Jonah had noted, although she sometimes managed to turn it to her advantage.

"We are extremely close, I can assure you," Chappell said. His expression betrayed no doubt that the question was sincere, or that they might know where Charlie Rich was hiding. "And your man in Argentina?"

Jonah smiled. They hadn't even discussed a location yet, so the Brit was trying 'backwards confirm' something he thought he already knew. Still, the acting CIA director couldn't see any harm in it. "He's arriving in Bariloche today. It's a small city..."

"Yes, we've been aware of it for quite some time, due to Priebke."

Erich Priebke was a former SS officer who had used the same "rat line" as thousands of other Nazis to escape justice in Europe after the Second World War. He'd settled in Bariloche and both intelligence agencies knew dozens of other Nazis followed suit.

Bariloche was founded by Germans nearly a century earlier, and there had been great sympathy for the Nazis.

"You think it's a coincidence they're meeting there, in particular?" Jonah asked.

"Of course not. They're up to something. This is the most public they've been in years, outside of sending the odd envoy to a hostile meeting, like Bilderberg or the Geneva summits. The symbolism of it being there..."

"You know, there's a rumor that floated around the agencies for a long time after the war...." Jonah began.

"Ah! Please... let's not get into foolish speculation," Chappell advised. "The dental records from his bunker in Berlin were pretty definitive."

"True enough," Jonah said. They both knew, of course, that almost any post-mortem condition could be faked, altered, doctored. Not that it would matter so many decades later.

Adolf Hitler was long dead, his movement with him.

Jonah hung up the phone. They'd be calling soon for the multi-party National Security Agency briefing on the election campaign. The number of lunatic fringe conspiracy groups had skyrocketed over the prior four years, and many of them seemed to be targeting newly minted Presidential candidate Matthew Misner as a 'savior', even though he was the underdog, a suddenly controversial figure due to his agnosticism.

It was the one trait a candidate had, in the past, had to deny no matter what. Americans would elect someone homosexual, or a visible minority, or even someone with legal troubles. But the accepted reality was that they would never elect someone who didn't believe in God.

Misner was challenging that. Many of his supporters described themselves as avid Christians and Muslims who believed his promise that he had no interest in curbing anyone's faith, just acting evenly on behalf of all Americans.

The message that Misner was a man of change was being amplified online... but often by bad actors, foreign powers who saw him as a divisive figure, perhaps one that could be influenced to work against the nation's best interests.

Jonah didn't see it; he'd been through the man's file and every speck of information the agency could find on him and, if anything, he seemed like the kind of man the country needed, someone looking at the big picture instead of protecting ideological turf.

So something was off; something was wrong in the informational picture, the puzzle that was Matthew Misner.

He wondered how it tied to the archives he'd had Brennan recover from Rightway; the agency knew post-war immigration records were being used to target voters online, using location-specific advertising on social media groups. Former residents of countries wrested from Nazi control by the Soviets had poured out of Europe at the end of the Second World War, with thousands moving to middle-class and small cities across America.

Many of them saw the Nazis as the lesser of two evils, preferring authoritarians that were predictable to communists who seemed to want to purge the Earth of anyone with whom they disagreed. That deference to authority made them easy to frighten, through misinformation, a cultural belief that no leader would ever represent them, tailored media messages and the online practice of "siloing", people only visiting "safe space" -- news websites that agreed with their existing perception of the world.

But Misner? An open atheist with European and Arab ancestry who was also loved by the political center, and even some left-wingers?

It made little sense.

And the hours to election day were running short.

44.

Oct. 22, 2020

BARILOCHE, Argentina

The taxi rolled up the hill towards the small city and Brennan almost did a double-take.

He looked over at Peacock, who was sitting quietly on the other end of the rear bench seat. "You're kidding right?"

"No. It is exactly what it looks like."

What it looked like was a town in Europe's Alps, right down to the old German and Swiss architecture; dark rich wooden beams, tiled, spired roofs, colorful plaster exteriors in pink, yellow and white, brick and concrete structures; a towering church steeple that could have come straight out of Augsburg or Munich.

The sidewalks were busy with pedestrians. Most were dressed normally, casually in jeans and t-shirts or attire suitable for work. But they were a minute into town when a man walked by in full lederhosen.

"Probably caters to the tourists," Peacock suggested, before Brennan could even ask. "They actually called the place 'Little Switzerland' affectionately for years. Half the land around the lake is owned by old European families."

Given the backdrop, it wasn't hard to see why Nazis like Priebke and Reinhard Kopps had settled there, Brennan thought.

Once again, Peacock was a step ahead of him as the taxi neared the hotel. "Before you even ask, the agency is aware of at least a hundred former SS officers of significant rank who resettled either in Bariloche or Osorno, Chile. There are likely many more. There are concrete signs -- from hidden rooms containing weapons caches to safehouses documented in recovered records – that they felt quite seriously about re-establishing a "Fourth Reich" in South America. But time passed them by, it seems. They're all dead now."

"And their families? Their kids?"

"That's... a sensitive matter," Peacock said. "State doesn't want us levelling accusations that tar people with the sins of their fathers. There are thousands of them, after all. When it comes to legacies of distrust, we have enough of that to worry about at home, already. And besides, it may not be what you want to hear, Brennan, but there are a hundred thousand people in Bariloche; the vast majority have no connection, family or otherwise, to any of that. I grew up in Savannah, Georgia. Does that make me a Dixiecrat?"

The taxi slowed to pull up in front of their hotel, a squared off building in mustard-colored plaster. "Yeah, point taken. I mean... I get that," Brennan said. "But the 'vast majority' aren't really the ones I'm worried about."

The cabbie unloaded their bags and they carried them inside.

The hotel was a boutique facility, with just a dozen rooms spread throughout a converted walkup apartment building. It had a central courtyard with a pool for people to relax, and a small lobby stuffed with cowhide furniture.

Brennan had wondered about the selection, and Peacock had noted that Steel and several of his IF associates were staying there.

A jovial, red-faced senior was manning the counter. He had a lapel button that said "Franz". They checked in separately to avoid any appearance of working together.

"You're here for skiing?" he inquired in Spanish-accented English, as he took their information. "Mr.... Kruger? You book from Canada? You've got relatives here?"

"No, but some folks back home have recommended it," he said. "Just here for business, just for a few days. But it looks swell."

The man tipped his head slightly to one side. "I... would normally recommend May or June, as the lake water is very warm and I prefer to swim. But that is just me."

"I shall have to keep that in mind," Brennan smiled back, accepting the proffered room key.

"Ah! We do not have an elevator, but if you need help with your bag..."

"I'm good," Brennan said. "Thank you."

"If you need anything, don't hesitate to ring the desk. We have someone here until three o'clock in the morning and back again at six."

The manager waited until Brennan had found the stairs then held up a hand, stopping Peacock in his tracks as he approached the counter. The man hurried to the small office behind the counter and picked up the old, corded handset, quickly dialing a familiar number. "Yes... it's Weber. You wanted any and all American or British... Yes, that's right. What about Canadian? Sure. Last name Kruger, first name Mark. Hometown is listed as Calgary, Alberta, Canada."

The elderly hotelier hung up the phone and went back to the counter to check in the next guest. "Welcome to the Sunrise Inn! How may I help you?"

After Peacock had checked in, he joined Brennan in his room. The handler passed him a thick file. "This is everything we have on Gabriel Verde's compound, Nueva Esperanza, south of Bariloche. He's been there, mostly full time, for the better part of ten years now, although there is some evidence that he was visiting the city decades ago."

"And he's how old?" Brennan flipped open the file. A photograph of Verde was clipped to the top of the pile of photocopied documents. "He looks reasonably preserved."

"He's seventy-two."

"So it's possible he could've crossed paths with some of the local Nazi contingent even as an adult?"

Peacock's brow furrowed deeply. "Are you going to keep on that angle, Brennan? As your handler, I think perhaps I should advise you that the IF…"

"Is a fascist organization that supports the right of rule by nobility and force, that has massive old fascist money flowing into it, right up to and including old royal lines from a smattering of European countries. If anyone is likely to be continuing the work…"

"To what end?" Peacock demanded. "Most of its supporters are wealthy capitalists and industrialists; they don't want to be ruled…"

"Krupp and Bayern and Mercedes didn't seem to mind during the Second World War," Brennan said. "The only deference dictators tend to respect is when money is involved. IBM made punch cards for the Nazis. The vice-president of General Motors wrote a book extolling the virtues of Hitler's fascism…"

"And it was more than half a century ago. Times have changed."

"People haven't," Brennan muttered.

"Just… stick to the matter at hand. The IF meeting and their support for Verde. That's what we care about, not digging up the ghosts of the past," Peacock insisted. "If this is anything nefarious at all, it's most likely industrial espionage of national secrets. Anyway, go over the file. From what we can tell, he's been hiring geneticists and microbiologists at a heightened pace for the last decade. In that time, his company has put out several vaccines and pioneered new methods in more accurate DNA recombination. He's been on the short list…

"For a Nobel, I know. That's why I'm having a hard time seeing him being a fascist stooge."

"Find out what that meeting's about, and why here, and perhaps we can eliminate that as a possibility. After all, the various IF members have built their public personas as much on political sway and public altruism as through pure acquisition of wealth. If we know why they're here, that connection will come."

They needed the Canadian to come through. "Maybe I should apply some more pressure to Steel..." Brennan suggested.

Peacock shook his head. "He's perilously close to breaking already. If we push him any further, he'll run to the other side telling tales. Wait for him to contact us. He promised he'd update us by nine tonight."

45.

WASHINGTON, D.C.

Alex Malone read a magazine as she sat at one of the diner's window-side tables, casting occasional glances at the parking lot, the D.C. skyline looming to the southwest.

The reporter hadn't expected Carolyn Brennan to agree to meet her; Joe's wife was a senior NSA staffer seconded to the CIA, and that meant seriously top-secret clearance.

She also had no public profile, no time in the limelight to suggest she had media training or would be the type of senior officer they'd want talking.

And yet she'd agreed.

It was either curiosity, Alex decided, a chance to finally meet the woman who helped her husband save New York... or a chance to scope her out as a possible mistress. Or maybe...

Alex shook her head. She was being paranoid, she knew. Even Jonah Tarrant wasn't so worried about her that he'd let staff have confidential chats just to find out what Alex was working on.

Would he? She sipped her coffee and thought about it, then admitted to herself she wasn't sure. He was the most devious man she'd ever met, and that was in spite of liking him; after all, Jonah had saved her life.

A car door slammed, catching her attention, which she reverted to the parking lot, through the floor-to-ceiling front windows. Carolyn had cut her formerly long blonde hair short; Alex had seen a picture and she looked as elegant and sculpted as she had five years earlier.

Carolyn pushed open the diner door and walked in tentatively, tilting her head slightly, searching for her lunch date. She saw Alex and lifted her chin in recognition, seemingly happy to see her, before making her way past the rows of tables to Alex's perch.

She removed her coat and hung it on the back of the chair, then sat down. "I can't believe it's taken this long for us to finally talk," Carolyn proposed.

"Thank you for this," Alex said. "I've been out of the loop for so long, I just lost track of everyone who was involved in New York. And of course, Joe was never officially…"

"Of course," Carolyn said.

A waitress sidled over to the table. "Would you like…"

"A Caesar's salad with a chicken breast, light on the dressing," Carolyn said before the woman could finish her sentence. "And a glass of water."

The waitress turned to Alex. "And for…"

"Cobb salad, extra boiled egg, light on the dressing. And another coffee."

The waitress noted it down. "Well… okay then."

She sauntered off.

"Joe and Jonah spoke so highly of you that I assumed we'd meet at some point, what with you still being active in the Beltway..." Carolyn let the question hang there.

"Yeah," Alex grimaced. "Yeah, about that... I sort of got blacklisted. A lot of editors and assignment editors looked pretty stupid for missing a near nuclear incident under their noses. Barring a story being so good they can't turn it down, my name is mud in this town."

She didn't mention the fact that her ruthless tactics had caused half the alienation. The last thing she needed was to make Carolyn nervous.

"I'm sorry to hear that."

"But, the good news is... I've got something." Alex let it dangle there, the notion of the unknown. Carolyn's rep in the intelligence community was good. That meant she was intellectually curious, disciplined but still likely to probe for more.

Even though there was no more. She didn't need Carolyn to know that, either. She just needed one piece of information.

"What?" Carolyn asked. "You can't just hang that out there without expanding on it."

Alex looked exasperated, trying not to oversell it. "I... want to tell you, but I can't. The problem I have right now is that there's an element of danger involved, and I'm afraid one of the people they might go after is Joe."

It was a complete lie, and she knew she'd feel lousy about it. But Alex was desperate.

Carolyn's furrowed brow spoke volumes. "Joe's in danger?"

"I mean... possibly, but not certainly. But there's enough there that he'd want to know and to look into it, when he can," Alex said. "Maybe I can meet up with him..."

The older woman shook her head. "No, he's on a freelance assignment right now of some sort. I can't really get into it. You know..."

"Oh! Oh, yeah, of course. If I gave you a package of info…" Then Alex stopped herself and frowned again. "No… no, this stuff is kryptonite to agency people. I can't do that…"

"I wish I could help," Carolyn said. "Maybe the threat assessment could go to our people without names or details attached, just a general description, and then we could worry about…"

Alex shook her head vehemently. "No! No, my sources will freak if this goes to Langley. I need to get it to him in person. Shit… How long…?"

"No way of knowing. He's not even in the country," Carolyn said.

Alex snapped her finger as if the thought had just come to her, wide-eyed. "You can't tell me what his assignment is or his mission parameters… but you could point me to a location where I can cross paths, or at least give him what I've gathered. That way I can't compromise whatever he's up to, and I can still give him a heads up."

Carolyn thought about it. She looked doubtful. "I mean, he doesn't have any restriction on his whereabouts being revealed as he's technically freelancing and not even on a specific assignment, just investigating. But I don't think he'd approve, not without knowing more…"

Alex looked her squarely in the eyes. And she lied again. "Carolyn, you know what happened at the nuclear plant. And you know I went into that warehouse to save his keister, with a small army inside. I almost died. I'm not going to fuck him over now. But I have a short window, maybe three days, to confirm some things and wrap this story up. Then my source disappears."

The time crunch was the last piece of the puzzle, the pressure of sentiment on the clock. Carolyn took a deep breath and was clearly thinking hard, trying to figure out if Alex had an ulterior motive. But the truth was, the woman hadn't worked with Joe in nearly five years. Whatever she had, it had to be important; that was her work, by reputation.

Carolyn picked up the white paper napkin from the table. She scribbled a word on it.

The waitress reappeared with their salads. Carolyn rose and grabbed her coat. "I'll get mine to go... I suspect my friend has some arrangements to make."

"Okay then," the waitress said, resigned to her fate. She led Carolyn to the other end of the lunch counter, by the register, to repack her food.

Alex looked down at the single word on the paper napkin: BARILOCHE.

46.

WASHINGTON, D.C.

Oct. 23, 2020

Matthew Misner and Stuart Chiasson sat in the first two of a row of aluminum-framed chairs, outside an office, in a low-rise near the White House. Both men looked slightly ill-at-ease, like school children waiting to be called before the principal and punished.

It wasn't that they felt threatened. It was just that the National Security Council's domestic terrorism briefings kept referencing Misner's campaign for president, and that made them nervous.

Misner, famously, did not get nervous. A former Army 'sapper' – a bomb disposal expert – assigned to Baghdad during the worst of the Iraq war, he'd also championed minority and gay rights while touting his atheism as being as much a freedom of religious choice as any other.

But this new issue felt beyond both of them, a sudden upsurge in support from fringe groups: conspiracy theorists, militia organizations, even some groups that seemed authoritarian and against the core principles upon which he campaigned.

"They're making us wait on purpose," Stu said. "They set this meeting up four days ago, and yet we're already at a quarter-past the hour. They know we're sitting out here..."

"Relax, okay? They've got a lot of responsibility, a lot more than just their own agenda to consider."

The door to the office opened. A pleasant woman with short brown hair and glasses leaned out. "They'll see you now, gentlemen," she suggested.

The four representatives of the NSC subcommittee on domestic terrorism sat at the far end of the conference room table. Misner recognized men from the NSA and Jonah Tarrant, the still-unconfirmed acting director of the CIA. He assumed the other two were FBI and Homeland Security, but no one moved to introduce themselves as the pair sat down.

"Jonah?" a colleague prompted.

"Gentlemen, as you know, I'm Jonah Tarrant, with the Central Intelligence Agency. My colleagues and I wanted to meet with you discretely today, well in advance of the vote in November, because as you're no doubt aware, we have serious concerns about your campaign's impact on the domestic security scene. I'm here because a significant portion of that threat seems to originate with bad actors overseas…"

Misner was shaking his head in what could have been disbelief or consternation. Either, Jonah supposed, would have been appropriate. "Thank you for the background, acting director. But, as I said to my longtime friend Stuart here just yesterday, we're the prohibitive underdog in this race since Jed Bryant's illness. Everybody knows it. We aren't taking big corporate donations, we don't have a huge war chest, and our policy book is the most liberal in the history of a U.S. election campaign. So… you can see my dilemma. I can't see any reason why half of these people would even know my name. I mean… I was a two-term Mayor of Tucson, Arizona, not a celebrity."

He appeared genuinely flummoxed, Jonah thought, although telling a man's state of mind from his outward appearance was always fraught with room for error or duplicity. "Much of it seems to stem from a series of Political Action Committees that became active as soon as your mentor went down with the stroke…"

"Jed's a good man," Misner stressed.

"Lobbyists?" Chiasson asked. "For a campaign that doesn't take corporate money…"

"Nevertheless, it's groups like "Americans for Closed Borders", "The Human Race", and "America First Always," that are spending the most money using social media ads to influence and deceive voters. They're going hard after you. Can you give us any idea why?"

Stu shook his head.

"Nothing," Misner confirmed.

But... there was one potential avenue that could explain it, Misner knew. A conversation long in the past, when he was young enough that its full meaning had been lost on him. He hadn't thought about it for an exceedingly long time. It was deeply personal, and nothing that related to an election campaign... just to his late father.

It was also none of Jonah Tarrant's business. "What would you suggest we do?" Misner said, changing the subject, trying to move the conversation along. "We have no control over Super PACs that are registered independently. We can turn down their money... but it's not coming to us directly, it's being funneled into ads praising us and attacking my opponent."

"For now, keep us in the loop," Jonah suggested. "You can contact all of the agencies through the committee secretary, Wendy Tupper..."

The brown-haired woman had been sitting silently taking notes on a table to one side of the room. She raised her hand in a quick wave.

"She'll make sure one of us gets back to you quickly. But any contact or offers, any proposals that seem too good to be true or just weird... we'd like to know about that. And if either of you can think of any reason – any promise made in the past, any compromising material after the fact – that would make a political entity see you as malleable or easily influenced..."

Misner shook his head again. "I have no idea what they're up to," he insisted. "It's just darn strange."

Jonah nodded, but he'd seen a flicker in the man's eye, a moment of indecision, as if a memory had given him pause. That was worth pursuing. Maybe by the time he'd convinced Misner to reveal his train of thought, Brennan would have found something in Bariloche.

Under the table, Jonah crossed his fingers.

47.

LONDON

The knock upon Peter Chappell's office door was tentative. Ken Loach, the senior systems analyst, stood nervously in the doorframe, his head almost bumping it. Loach was six-feet-four inches tall but milder mannered than anyone else in executive.

"You wanted to see me, Peter?"

Chappell gestured to the chair ahead of his desk. "Have a seat for a moment, if you would, Ken."

Loach sat down. "Am I in trouble?" he asked nervously.

"No, no. Nothing like that. I just wanted to see how your work schedule is right now; we're expecting to recover a laptop shortly from the hacker…"

"Oh! You've found him."

They hadn't. But the idea was to feed out useless information that would still get the International Family's attention. If Loach was the leak, it was a prime morsel. "We think he might be staying with a former police officer in Brighton," he said.

It wasn't true, but the American, Joe Brennan, had a former police colleague whose partner lived there. Since they'd already ruled out Martin Weiss as an accomplice, directing them to Weiss' ex-partner would come up empty.

But Loach was the only one who would get the tip, other than Chappell and Grimes. If anyone showed up sniffing around Ruby Downey, they would know instantly that Loach was the leak.

Not that Chappell expected it. Of anyone on the fifth floor, Loach seemed the least ambitious, the least interested in personal gain.

Checking out Weiss had been Grimes' idea. He knew the man from his Military Intelligence days, knew he'd been quickly vetted by an old colleague. Now it was a matter of seeing what Loach did next.

"Then an arrest might be immediate?" Loach asked. "I have a lot on the go from the reorganization..."

He certainly didn't seem interested, just flustered. He wasn't a trained field officer, just senior support staff.

It would probably go nowhere, Chappell thought.

"In a day or so at most," Chappell said. They were monitoring desk and official mobile phones for all five men in the inner circle. Michael Wolf's people had descended upon the hacker, Charlie Rich, like they'd been invited weeks earlier.

Someone had helped them. Assuming whoever leaked their operation to the IF was still embedded at Whitehall or the SIS Building, he didn't like the young man's chances of surviving the week.

48.

BARILOCHE

Alex took the local bus into the city from the airport. She'd done some research before leaving D.C., but even so, the quaint Alpine architecture surprised her.

It was an odd place for Brennan to be. As far as she could tell from her library visit, Bariloche was famous for just two things: skiing and Nazis. The former didn't seem like Brennan's style. The latter was more his speed, but about a half-century past due.

Her D.C. contacts had been exhausted. The best she'd managed to determine was that Jonah Tarrant had met with British counterparts over the two weeks prior. It was frustrating, working in the dark, but she was determined.

Brennan owed her. Alex had agreed to avoid mass panic by holding back some of the story from the New York incident. She'd softened the story for them. They'd promised her their support, but she'd had little help from Tarrant, and none from Joe. No big leaks, no scoops. At first it had been galling, then just another cynical reminder not to trust people in authority.

Now it was motivation. Whatever he was up to, it had to be something less pressing than the nuclear threat had been. But it would still be a story, something she could use to rebuild demand in her work.

She climbed off the bus a block from her hotel. She'd almost reached its double front doors when she noticed the chocolate shop, two doors down. Alex's reporter instincts were kicking in. The hotel staff might be able to help her, to give her the lay of the local land, but it would be the commercial version, the story they told tourists keen on immersing themselves. A local businessperson, someone who ran their own non-franchise shop, would be a lifelong resident, someone to whom the reality of living there was second nature.

The door to the chocolate shop jingled merrily as she walked in. The customer area was small, a dining-room-sized square with shelves along each wall, covered in boxes of handmade delights. The front counter topped a glass case, displaying the store's best efforts, row-on-row of light and dark-brown sweets in varied shapes and sizes.

The man behind the counter was elderly, with giant white whiskers that connected to his sideburns. He would've made a picture-perfect Santa Claus, Alex thought. "Bienvenidos!" he offered. "Welcome!'

Alex put her bag down by her feet and clapped both hands together. "Now... THIS... this is perfect. This says 'old Germany' to me."

The man spread both hands and tilted his head slightly, a gesture of mild disagreement. "In my family's case it would be Switzerland, but we are all Argentines now. You are American, yes?"

She nodded and approached the counter. "My! They all look delicious! What would you recommend?" People liked to be professionally appreciated above most other things, Alex had long ago realized.

The old man beamed. "My life's work. The top row are our limited edition 'flavors of the world', each refined carefully over decades to melt in your mouth and to excite your senses."

"I'll take a half-pound..."

"We have a pre-boxed three-hundred-gram collection..."

"Perfect!" She took out her purse.

"That's twenty-two-fifty." He clasped his hands ahead of himself tersely, as if quoting a price embarrassed him.

Alex handed over twenty-five hundred pesos. He retrieved her change from his register, along with a receipt.

"You are in Bariloche for vacation, si?"

She nodded. "In a manner of speaking. I write for a magazine and they had an opportunity for a travel piece. I think it's one of those deals where the tourism board picks up the expense, or something."

"They will have many good recommendations for you, I'm sure," the shopkeeper said, handing over the ribbon-wrapped box.

"I'm sure they will." She let it hang there for an extra moment, the slight note of dissatisfaction. "They'll have their promotional priorities. Do you mind if I ask...?"

"Anything, please."

"How would you approach a week in Bariloche? The skiing is obvious. They've got me in a boutique hotel...'"

The old man didn't seem to approve of that. "Tcch! This? This is not ideal. There are many families who have lived here for a hundred years or more, and they offer bed and breakfast, guest rooms, this sort of thing. Or, if you do not mind to spend a little extra, one of the cattle ranches just outside the city."

"I see. The guest houses..."

"Are very reasonable, yes. They have a website, you see. They know everything there is to do for fun in the community. Most of the ladies who run them are local widows or have large families. Sometimes, I think they know more about my business than I do, from what gets back to me. But, I keep them happy by making chocolate they love."

"I suppose they have a grapevine, too..."

He looked puzzled. "Que? I don't know this term..."

"A grapevine. Gossip."

"Oh! Oh yes, of course. Bariloche is not so large that everyone avoids everyone else's business."

"Then they'll know enough to help me fill my article."

The old man reached under the counter and withdrew a page from a printer. "Here: a list of numbers and names. The ones on the lake are, of course, quite a bit more expensive."

Alex thanked the man and left the shop, heading up the sidewalk, busy with pedestrians and visitors even late in the year. She wanted to get to her hotel room, get some rest before she plotted her next move. She had no intention of staying in a bed and breakfast; but the old man's list gave her a local network to begin tapping for information. As he'd said, it wasn't a big city; Brennan would show up eventually.

49.

Oct. 24, 2020

PEACEHAVEN, Sussex

Martin had walked the two kilometers to the Sainsbury's and back, a double-bag of groceries suspended from each arm. He'd gotten used to walking in the mornings in London, to keep his fitness up now that he didn't get out as much as when Anne was still alive.

His hips hurt, grinding a little with each step, and his arches began to ache after a half-kilometer. When he was a constable, the Met hadn't talked much about the toll walking a beat took on your feet. When he'd become a detective, being on the go had seemed the entirety of the job. Now, on the downside of sixty, the years had begun to take their toll.

Ruby's neighbors, Mike and Jonathan, were tending their front flower garden. Mike gave a small, cupped hand wave. They'd only been staying with her for a few days, but it seemed everyone around Cissbury Avenue knew Ruby, and seemed friendly by extension.

Martin opened the thigh-high wrought-iron gate built into the brick-façade front wall. The bungalow was identical to four others in a row next to it, and to a few dozen more in the surrounding blocks. It was a supremely quiet suburb, far enough away from Brighton to appeal to retirees, although it had also become a less-judgmental haven, from the eighties on, for the city's large gay community. Most people seemed to keep to themselves, but those who did not were friendly and helpful.

He opened the front door with the spare key Ruby had cut for him a day earlier. Martin reminded himself of how lucky he was to have an ex-partner who'd cared about him so much. She'd been a giving, concerned policewoman, the type of character the force had been lucky to have. The type of person the law needed.

"I'm back!" he called out as he put his keys down on the telephone table and closed the front door. "They had a sale on Mr. Kipling's, so I bought an extra box."

He heard a thump from the bedroom. "I couldn't find the Ribena though, so you're out of luck on that front." Martin carried the bags to the kitchen. He put them down on the counter. On the stove, a teapot was boiling furiously, the water beginning to splash the stovetop. He reached over and turned it down. "You're boiling over here, Ruby D…"

He began to unpack the grocery bag. His hackles stood up. He hadn't heard a word from either of them since entering the house. Martin made his way out of the kitchen cautiously, following the runner carpet down the hall to the two bedrooms. "Ruby?" he called out softly. He looked around the corner of the bedroom doorway.

Ruby was lying on the queen-sized bed, her throat cut, blood beginning to pool around her, her gaze lifeless. Beside the bed, a man was pinning Charlie down. The young man was struggling for all his worth, but the attacker's carving knife was inching ever closer to Charlie's windpipe.

Martin moved on instinct, bounding the two steps that put him right behind Charlie's attacker. Before the man could look back in puzzlement, Martin grasped him around the chin with both hands from behind, even as he drove his kneecap firmly into the back of the man's neck and snapped his head back. The man's neck broke and he went limp, slumping over sideways.

Charlie crawled out from under him, his face white, a picture of terror. "He came in through the back patio door… caught us both by surprise. You… you killed him…"

Martin felt his anger well up over Ruby, followed by an intense flush of despair. But he knew they didn't have time to commiserate. "We have to get moving. Get your bags."

"We can't just leave her here…"

"There's nothing we can do for her now, lad. I can alert the authorities anonymously. But where there was one, there will be more."

"Where will we go?"

"I only have one option, but it will have to make do. Come on: we need to get to the city, before his friends check on him."

50.

BARILOCHE

Brennan rapped on the hotel door with two knuckles. "Steel? Are you in there?"

He hadn't contacted them by dinner time, as he'd promised, and three more hours had passed before Peacock had agreed Brennan should check on him. They hadn't wanted to contact him openly, but the man wasn't answering his room phone or his cell.

"Go away!"

"Steel, open the damn door or I'll have to bust it in, and you'll have to explain it to the hotel. The hotel will probably call the cops…"

"I'm not coming out."

"But I am coming in, if you don't open the door within the next twenty seconds."

Brennan began a silent countdown. The door opened before he'd reached 'ten', Steel standing to one side. "Get in, quickly," the IF member hissed.

He closed the door behind them. "I know what you're going to say, but I'm not doing it. I'm not going to the meeting," Steel started in, before Brennan could comment. "They know. I don't know how, but they know I'm talking to someone."

"You're just getting cold feet. Chill out. You know what happens if we're unhappy."

"How do I know that if I help you, you're not going to throw me to the cops anyway?"

"You don't." In fact, Brennan was relishing the opportunity. "But as long as you're here, working for us, you're not in jail somewhere else. That can change really quickly, though."

Steel gave him a venomous stare. "You're as bad as they are."

"Oh, my heart bleeds for the child molester. Shut up and do your job. Where's the meeting?"

"There are two. There's a general session at a private home across the lake, in Villa Campanario, tomorrow night. Then there's a meeting between the IF board and Gabriel Verde at his compound in three days, right before he announces his big experiment, his project."

"Then you know what you have to do."

"If I'm right, they'll kill me."

"Yeah... I don't care. If they're onto you, just don't buy any attempt to offer you a deal or be nice..."

"I know who I'm dealing with," the Canadian said. "Do you?"

"They recruited you, didn't they?" Brennan spat. "So yeah... I've got a pretty good idea."

"Then you should know, they'll kill you, too. They're powerful and they've been around for a long time."

"I don't trade in sympathy for the devil. And whatever you think of them, I guarantee you, we're bigger and tougher." Brennan headed for the door. "Tomorrow night. I expect a full report the second that meeting ends. Or, as close as not getting your head blown off will allow."

51.

BRIGHTON

Charlie had cried in the car over Ruby's death. He hardly knew her but she'd seemed lovely, and the image of her violent end seemed imprinted on his memory, impossible to shake.

It took them fifteen minutes to get to Brighton and Martin's escape plan. He parked the car a few blocks away due to street restrictions and they set out down the busy pavement of Middle Street, hands jammed into pockets, furtive glances cast about for rapid movement, signs of obvious pursuit.

By the time they got to the building, Charlie's tears had dried up. Martin clapped him on the back once. "She was lovely. She didn't have family, so she'd have been happy someone cared about her at the end," he offered. "And we'll get the bastards, Charlie. I promise you that."

Charlie gave him a half-hearted nod. He looked up at the enormous pale-brick building, its arched frame roof forty feet above them. It was fronted by great columns in faded ochre and two floors of ornate bay windows. The giant wooden door was set back slightly from the road.

"Very impressive," he said. "But I'm not sure how going to a museum is an ideal way to deal with our current dilemma."

Martin sighed a little. The young man seemed a good soul, but he was irritatingly glib sometimes. In this case, it was probably a defense mechanism to what he'd just experienced, he decided. "It's not a museum. It's a synagogue. Come on: we're going around the back."

Martin opened a small wrought-iron gate and led him down the side of the building to the backdoor. "It's a nationally significant building but it's closed most of the time to protect it," he said.

"And you've chosen this rather strange and terrifying opportunity to show it to me because…"

"Because, more than anything, we need to be off the street right now and away from prying eyes."

He rang the back doorbell, then waited.

After about ten seconds, Charlie offered, "Perhaps no one's home?"

"Patience lad, it's a huge place inside."

Sure enough, another twenty seconds went by before the door finally creaked open. The man who opened it was aged, his face heavily wrinkled from more than eighty years on Earth, short and stocky, with silver-grey hair under a yarmulka. He glanced around the corner of the door. "We're closed right..." Then he saw Martin's face and his own lit up. "Martin!" He stepped outside and gave the bigger man a firm hug. "It's been so long!" Then he took stock of Charlie. "And who's this? Is he your..."

"No! No, we never did have a boy."

"I didn't think so, but I was assuming maybe a nephew or..."

"A friend. Charlie, this is Rabbi Barak. Look, would you mind if we went inside to talk? We're in need of some help."

The Rabbi frowned gravely. "Your kind of trouble is usually pretty serious."

"And it is."

He gestured for them to follow him. "Then come, come! I'll make you both a nice cup of tea..."

They followed him inside. There was a small office area immediately to their right and Rabbi Eli directed them towards it. But Charlie didn't notice, his breath taken away by the synagogue's interior. The ceiling towered dozens of feet above, rows of pews to either side of the hall set on two levels behind arches, like boxes in an opera house. Gold railings and gilt ornaments glinted from sun that streamed through the upper windows, the light playing off the ornate relief carvings set into the joints of the roof.

"This is...."

"One of the most important historical buildings in the country," the Rabbi said. "Unfortunately, to run it full-time and maintain it costs more than we have. We try to rent the rear outbuildings for income when possible, but we rely on generous donations to keep her in this kind of shape. But please... come, sit and drink some tea with me and explain what's going on."

He walked behind his desk and they took the two chairs that fronted it. The Rabbi poured them each a cup of tea from a serving tray resting on the radiator behind him. "Now, my old friend, you have to tell me what's so important that you needed to use the back door?"

"Ruby's dead," Martin said. "The men who killed her are looking for this one." He jerked his head towards Charlie. "He seems to have pissed off some old friends of yours."

The Rabbi's eyed widened. "You don't mean..."

"I do. They're back, as promised."

Charlie feared losing the thread in all the ambiguity. "WHO is back? And who promised what? I'm sorry..."

"It's all right, and stop apologizing," Martin said bluntly. "The Rabbi has some history fighting fascists."

It was Charlie's turn for surprise. "Fascists? As in..."

"Fascists, yes," Rabbi Barak said. "As with the Nazis and Mussolini and a few places since, too. They never go away, my boy. They represent the power men take over the weak in lieu of offering society something more. That always exists, and there are always damaged men who cannot develop authority of expertise or social acceptance, men who grasp for power and intimidation as the alternative."

Charlie noticed the Rabbi's half-full ashtray on one corner of his desk. "Do you mind if I...?" he asked, gesturing that way.

The Rabbi studied Martin's face for a split-second in case of opposition. When none came, he waved a hand Charlie's way. "Yes, yes, of course. It's terrible, and you're too young to be this stupid about habits, but if you must..."

Charlie lit a cigarette and noticed his hands were trembling. His nerves had been on edge for two days. Focusing on whatever was directly in front of him was keeping him sane. "You're telling me the people who killed Ruby, the people trying to kill me... are Nazis?"

"They don't call themselves that, of course," Rabbi Barak explained. "It's a damaged brand, you see. But in effect, yes. The Nazis were one strain of fascist, if you will, of the German variety. But they exist and have existed in many other countries. They are a product of inequality, of economic disturbance, of people's needs not being met and no better alternative being offered. Their ethos exists whether they are organized or not. That is what they realized after losing the war: that as long as someone existed to fund their activities, they would always find support among those lacking empathy, those willing to become the bully... and sometime, sadly, the bullied themselves, striving for any power or legitimacy they can obtain."

"But... why me?" Charlie asked. "What does data from the defense ministry have to do with fascists?"

"From what our American friend described," Martin suggested, "my suspicion is that they're using historical American immigration data, somehow. He said he'd retrieved records from the same Austrian company that has men after you."

The Rabbi nodded, pensive, considering the moment. "The question is, what can I do for you both? Whatever it is, my door is open."

"We need to stay here for a few days," Martin suggested. "There will be people looking for us all over the city..."

"But it is highly unlikely they will venture inside a synagogue, or even think of it." The Rabbi finished his thought for him. "So: you'll need food, some changes of clothes, some bedding... I will need to make some arrangements. But ... I don't think any of that will be a problem. How long...?"

Martin shrugged. "Not sure. Our American friend is working on some matters overseas, trying to answer the same question about some data our friend Charlie hacked..."

Charlie held up a plan. "Please... not that term. I didn't 'hack' anything; it was substantially more elegant and complex than just..."

"Be that as it may," Martin cut him off, "the fact is you took data from the government. Until we know it's purpose and why the International Family wants you dead, we're stuck here."

52.

Oct. 25, 2020

LANGLEY, Virginia

On the far wall of the fourth-floor conference room, a digital projector cast an image of two maps of the United States. Both were covered in digitized push pins.

"Map one is the data that was seized from Wolf's archives, the historical final places of residence of the wave of European immigrants after the Second World War," a bony-faced analyst with square, frameless glasses explained.

At the head of the table, Jonah Tarrant took a sip of water. He had another meeting with the campaign managers for the Presidential candidates in just a few hours. The data was his immediate priority, however, because it could explain why Matthew Misner – a fiscal conservative and social Liberal – was getting money and support from companies either directly tied to Michael Wolf or who supported the same causes.

"Map two is a data set of all of the locations in which pro-Misner rallies became violent last weekend. In all, there were forty-two rallies and nine incidents of felony violence, along with another twenty involving looting or damage. Now, the media spin on this – pushed heavily by Wolf's own network – is that these were intolerant people attacking Misner supporters because he is an agnostic. However, our own investigation suggests the rioting was pushed almost entirely by this new group, which calls itself "The Human Race, or 'THR'." It's stated goal is that "race doesn't matter," which is compelling for people who already consider themselves open-minded to Misner's position on faith."

"But?" Jonah asked.

"But the reality is that THR has many of the same organizers and financial backers as white supremacist groups who supported southern separatist candidates in years past. They are subverting the culture and message of their political enemies, arguing equal rights for all as a way to clamp down on improving the rights of the marginalized. Groups who can prove they've been treated unfairly under the law and by society are depicted as trying to gain "an advantage" when in fact they're already far behind. It's a divide-and-conquer strategy."

Jonah studied the map. There must have been more than a hundred pins on the one board, fifty on the second. "So they're using existing hatred of the political "left" by lumping all of it in with communism, then seeding the notion that it is trying to push a white majority into servility. That's..."

"Diabolical," Adrienne Hayes offered.

Jonah couldn't help notice the slight smirk she bore as she said it. "Clever though."

"Oh, sure," she said. "I mean, when the average person can't parse fact from fiction, the Internet makes demonizing other people pretty easy."

"It goes further," the analyst said. "By pushing all of these divisive messages via social media groups that people already trust, a lot of relatively naïve people are left with the impression that these were their own ideas, that they just "shared" the notion with these new "reporting" outlets. In fact, they've been slowly seeded with this broad conspiracy for over a decade, via much less obvious methods: memes, shared personal pictures, famous quotes that are misconstrued, doctored images – you may have seen a famous one suggesting the Canadian Prime Minister is actually Fidel Castro's son. Most don't look up a separate picture of Castro or the prime minister, and never realize it's the two images blended, to make them look more similar. By the time whoever is behind this began feeding them those kinds of misleading news stories, they already believed what the 'media' was telling them."

"And finding out later that they're false...?" Jonah began to ask. "That doesn't shake their confidence."

"It does… but only in public information sources. They don't have the critical thinking skills, generally, to see that they continue to trust the outlets that actually presented the misinformation: the social media groups, the political conspiracy groups. They stick with the group and the perceived "strength of numbers" over the news entity which – although far more likely to be balanced and accurate than their own 'sources' – is nevertheless unfamiliar to them. These people were not, for the most part, big consumers of mainstream news BEFORE this all started. So afterwards, they place far less faith in it."

The analyst clicked a button and the second map slid sideways, over the top of the first.

"We can see when we compare them directly that the protest locations exactly match the communities and states where the majority of the Eastern European diaspora relocated. In other words, they found the communities where people were already most willing to hate the political 'left' in any form… because these are places where two generations ago, everyone fled the Soviets when they displaced the Nazis and their puppet regimes."

Hayes tapped a pen on her notepad anxiously. "This is what you expected, Jonah. But the scope of this is…"

"A real problem." Jonah finished the thought for her. "The bigger question is: why this guy? Why Matthew Misner, a man who, if it wasn't for his views on religion, would appear cut out of a "Mom, Dad and Apple Pie" magazine? He's a veteran, he's socially progressive but he worked for a Fortune 500 investment firm out of college. He's no communist, and he's no fascist."

"Then the question," Hayes proposed, "is what is he? Who is Matthew Misner, and why do so many bad actors want him to be the next President?"

53.

LONDON

The elevator to the Fifth Floor of Secret Intelligence Service Headquarters was notoriously slow and busy, but after three decades in the Vauxhall building, Archibald Grimes had become accustomed to it. He stood with his newspaper under one arm, his umbrella in his other hand.

The doors pinged. A second later, they slid open. Peter Chappell strode out smartly, a small entourage with him.

"Peter! You're going out? I thought we could meet for a quick update…"

"It would have to be very quick indeed. We're off to Essex to pick up Ken Loach."

Grimes eyebrows rose. "Loach? You're not suggesting…"

"It appears our hacker was in Brighton. Or, Peacehaven to be more exact. Unfortunately, the woman who was sheltering him was murdered yesterday. We believe one of her killers, a man we've been unable to identify, was then taken out."

"But… that was supposed to be a false flag. That was just a rumor to flush a mole. We weren't even monitoring the location yet." Grimes' shock was obvious.

"And in brilliant MI6 fashion, we chose his actual bolt hole."

"Then… he's being hidden by the American's associate, the ex-policeman…"

"Martin Weiss, yes. We suspect he subdued the victim's killer before fleeing with the hacker."

"That makes our next step somewhat easier to decide upon," Grimes said. "If we can find him, we'll find young Mr. Rich. They're probably still in Brighton somewhere."

"We're already checking all known associates in Sussex. Weiss has been in law enforcement for a long time, and he was Army Intelligence before that. He knows a great number of people."

Grimes stroked his moustache pensively. "It would help if we knew what the IF wanted with the boy. When you have Loach brought in, I'd like a chance to interrogate him."

Chappell nodded. "Of course, Archie. Now we best be off. We've got MI5 and the Army helping with this one and they'll be anxious to plan the arrest."

Grimes gave him a nod. "Good luck to you, then."

After they'd left, he went back to the elevator and pushed the button. The doors pinged and slid open.

At the Fifth floor, he gave a small wave to the executive receptionist before finding his way to Chappell's office. The door was left open, as usual, with other directors rarely away from their own fiefdoms down the hall.

He checked his surroundings to be sure, then entered the office. He used his handkerchief to pick up Chappell's telephone and dialed a number.

It was answered on two rings. "Hello?"

He lowered his voice to a monotone bass. "An MI5 hit squad is about to try to assassinate you. They'll door knock and pretend it's something innocuous. You have been warned."

He hung up the phone. Chappell was predictable. Loach was a pleasant, slightly nervous man but he'd also been with the service a long time. He would consider trying to flee; but ultimately, he would bunker in, telling himself it was a misunderstanding, something that could be worked out. But he would be armed.

And they would door knock politely, exactly as Grimes predicted. If things went well, Loach would go out in a blaze of paranoid glory. Whether he did or not, his reaction would be flighty enough to convince Chappell that the murder in Brighton was on Loach's head – at a location that had been Grimes' proposal, a seemingly innocuous mistake that allowed his assassin to act with impunity.

He had been the International Family's man within MI6 for more than a half-century. He wasn't going to let a juvenile delinquent's computer hobby ruin decades of preparation. If Loach made it back to him in one piece, he would lead the interrogation, as he'd had Chappell promise… and further muddy the waters.

54.

Oct. 26, 2020

BARILOCHE

The stately three-bedroom home on Santa Cruz Avenue could've been a picturesque rural Bavarian inn, with flower boxes under the windows and dark-wooden lattice work crisscrossing the structure. The woman who greeted Alex at the door, however, had a cocoa complexion and dark, almond eyes, an obvious nod to South American indigenous heritage.

"Ms. Malone? Please, come in! Welcome, welcome!" She held the front door open. It had a glass insert; a gold, scrolling typeface across it read "Gastehaus Schmidt". "We got your message on the website, of course! Please…"

Alex smiled nervously as she entered the home. "Thank you so much for having me," she suggested. "I really didn't want my trip to follow the same old tourists guides and suggestions…"

"Then you have selected the right place, for certain."

The front door met a long, carpeted corridor that went by a pair of rooms to the left and the stairs to the right. Above, a giant crystal chandelier lit the red-carpeted cloakroom from an eighteen-foot tray ceiling. "The home was built by a German architect, Friederich Stabler, in 1894," Mrs. Schmidt intoned with a familiarity that suggested she gave each visitor the same speech. "Along with this fabulous crystal chandelier designed by Rene Lalique in 1899, there is a stained-glass ceiling in the ballroom created by Louis Comfort Tiffany in 1913, and each room upstairs has its own balcony with the most fabulous views of the lake and mountains."

Alex looked around, trying to seem reverent and awe inspired. She had no real interest in the home's provenance; but it was clear from the local historical society's websites and the families connected to it that the Schmidts had political clout. More importantly, two of them had worked directly with Priebke, the ex-Nazi who'd run a local school for years: one as an advisor and the other as a board member for the school.

She was still banking on the Nazi connection having something to do with why Brennan was there. She doubted they had any real presence anymore, but the locals had family and historical ties. And anything involving powerful local German families usually involved Anna Maria Schmidt's husband and his brothers, or other cousins.

"Let me show you to your room," Schmidt offered, lifting the hem of her gray formal dress as she began to climb the stairs.

Alex followed her. "I noticed you do a great deal of work with the historical society," she said. "You're from here yourself originally?"

"I am from Osorno, in Chile," Schmidt explained. "But I have lived her for thirty-two years, ever since marrying my husband Rolf." She paused at the top of the steps. "Family is extremely important in Bariloche. It also makes it such a good place for families to visit."

She turned back to the hallway and led Alex to the last room. "Each of our rooms is named after a great composer. This is our Beethoven Suite. It is more like a room at home than a hotel, but we find people prefer that warmth to something austere."

"The old German stereotype is to be avoided, I take it."

The older woman smiled a little at that. "Of course. Germans adore humor, which you would know right away if you ever watched my husband attempt to cook. Here we are..." She opened the room door, which featured a silhouetted bust of the composer. "There is a double bed, a place to plug in your laptop or tablet and a television... although we have so much to do here, I doubt you will use it."

Alex put her case down on the bed. She'd kept her room at the hotel and left her other bag there, just in case she needed a safe bolt hole. But for a day or two, probing Anna Maria for information was bound to yield something. "I was thinking of focusing on the lake and everything there is to do there," she said casually. "Perhaps looking at some of the big estates down there." She planned to follow the money; whenever someone attracted the CIA's attention, it always cost money.

Schmidt frowned. "Given how late in the year it is, the water is quite cool now. We are gearing up for the busiest part of ski season, after all. And the homeowners there are quite private. The roads are public, of course, but they have high fences and most are wealthy, so they don't entertain soliciting of any sort."

"I'm sure you could get me an introduction though, for my article?" Alex suggested.

"I don't think this is – how you say? -- such a 'great idea'," Schmidt suggested, her English good but heavily accented from Argentine Spanish. "Better to talk to some of the legends of our local skiing and outdoors community, yes?"

"Absolutely," Alex confirmed with a smile. The moment she had a chance, she decided then and there, she was visiting those homes on the lake. An invitation to stay away was usually all the motivation she needed.

55.

Brennan's pay-as-you-go 'burner' phone rang just after four in the afternoon. They'd been waiting in his hotel room for an update from Jonah, some notion of what they might be looking for, when Steel called in.

"I can't talk long," he said as soon as Brennan hit the answer button. "I'm being watched. But this is big, bigger than you thought. It's huge."

"What is? Why was the IF meeting?"

"You have to come here and see this for yourself. I'm at a house in Villa Campanario, on the lake. 431 Paseo Antumalal."

"Don't be stupid, Steel. Just come back here and fill me in yourself."

"I can't. And I can't explain right now... just... Look, if you want this information, you'll have to come see for yourself."

He hung up.

Brennan stared at the phone with suspicion. "He gave me an address and hung up."

Murray Peacock took a deep breath. The handler was sitting on the edge of Brennan's hotel room bed. "Meaning..."

"He said I have to meet him there, some home in a village on the lake."

"Well... I mean, it screams of a trap."

Brennan sucked on his tongue for a moment to keep himself from saying something sarcastic. Peacock was a young handler, probably in his early thirties at most, and he had developed an annoying knack for stating the obvious as if it were the profound.

"Clearly he's up to something," Brennan conceded. "But it doesn't really matter. I still have to go and get him, see if he has anything we can use. You're tracking his phone?"

Peacock nodded. He checked his own phone for a moment. "The app has him at 431 Paseo Antumalal, as advertised."

"Yeah... not much point in moving the bait."

"I should go with you, given the circumstances..."

Brennan shook his head. "I appreciate your skill as a handler, Murray, but you're not field qualified and this has the potential to get messy. So... no, you'll stay right here. But don't worry... I'm a big boy. I can take care of myself."

56.

PHOENIX, Arizona

The sky was grey and spitting rain. Cemeteries always seemed solemn, but the weather and the times made Matthew Misner's visit feel that much more morose. He stood in front of the headstone with his hands tucked into the pockets of his wool overcoat.

The headstone was inscribed "Christopher Maurice Delph, Loving Father and Husband, June 3, 1949 to September 12, 2012."

It wasn't much of a description or epitaph for someone so important to him, Misner had often thought.

Delph hadn't been a public figure. He hadn't sought office or leadership, and he hadn't chased fame and fortune. He'd been a college professor for most of his adult life, a distinguished fellow in Neuroscience at the University of Phoenix, then later at Georgetown University in D.C.

He'd become Misner's guardian after his father had died, when he was twelve.

"I wonder what you'd think of me now. Not impressed, I bet," Misner said aloud. He came to talk to his old friend at least once a month. It was cathartic… but no substitute for the real thing. He'd been wise, caring, full of humility and charity.

"I don't know what I'm doing wrong, Chris. I'm following what you taught me. But it's not going smoothly. We had a rally the other night and people came to blows. People fighting, over whether I should lead them. You'd have been ashamed. I couldn't get it under control."

He felt powerless, even as he vied for the most powerful job in the world. He'd known there would be compromises, that nothing was accomplished without give and take. But he hadn't foreseen a world of National Security Council warnings, and protests, and riots breaking out between his own supporters. It was like the nation was doused in outrage, and he was the match to set it all ablaze.

He felt a hand on his shoulder. Stu Chiasson had come over from the limousine, an umbrella opened to shelter them both. A few yards away, a Secret Service Agent stood looking slightly uncomfortable. "You know he wouldn't blame you for any of this, right?"

Stuart had known him almost as well. They'd both grown up down the street from one another, in Cave Creek. "I know he'd say that. Whether he really believed it…"

"He wasn't the type to say things he didn't believe," Chiasson said. "You know that, too."

Misner turned to face his old friend. "I guess I'm hoping if I can plead guilty to him, that act of taking responsibility for the shitshow this has become no longer falls to me. I've already admitted I can't handle it, so I don't have to fix it. I guess that's the internal, bullshit reason."

"So… now you've figured that out, you also know it's the cowardly, bullshit way out. And…"

"And we don't take the easy way out unless it's also the right way."

"He taught you that, too.'

"He did. He'd have said, 'there is no merit without decency.' He always liked that one."

Stuart rocked nervously on his heels. "I mean, you could just disavow the fringe groups: the white supremacists, the nationalists and militia types…"

Misner gave him a hard stare. "You know I can't do that. I've given you my reasons."

"Yeah… but…"

"That's not going to change."

"Yeah… but standing on principle by not acknowledging them is a mistake. I wouldn't say it if I didn't believe it. You know that."

"I know, Stu. But half the problem nowadays is that we give credence and credibility to everyone just by giving them a platform. If I acknowledge these people in any way, even to tell them to get lost, I suggest they matter. And they don't. Most people are repelled by them. It's better to ignore them and let them die from inattention."

Chiasson sighed a little. "I know Chris would've agreed with that…"

"He would.

"But most of Chris's life was before YouTube existed. Before social media. Before a news cycle every five minutes. Times have…"

Misner held up a hand. "Stu! Stu… I've made up my mind. I'm not going to dignify the fringe groups with any attention whatsoever."

Chiasson was silent for a few moments, an unfamiliar tension between them. It was a rare occasion when he could sense his old friend questioning his motives.

The wind picked up and the leaves billowed on the ground. "Have you visited…?" Chiasson nodded behind them, towards the other section of the cemetery, where Misner's parents, Joseph and Alice, were buried.

The candidate nodded. "I said a few words to mom."

His old friend bowed his head. "Not up to talking to the old man today, huh?"

Misner shook his head. "Lately, with everything that's been going on, I think a lot about how he was at the end, before…"

The official verdict had been an accidental prescription overdose. None of them believed it. Misner's father had slipped into paranoia and anti-social behavior when Misner was still a little boy, fueled by a bigoted, angry grandparent who prodded and programmed him. His mother had died suddenly of an accidental overdose when he was nine. By the time his father died three years later, it had almost seemed a mercy. If it hadn't been for Christopher Delph, he knew, he would have grown up alone, with no one guiding his direction.

"He'd be proud of you, if he could've been lucid enough to see how you turned out," Chiasson said. "Look: I told you when I followed you from Tucson that I'd stick this out with you to the end. Everyone expects us to lose this race. They have the nutbar on the opposite side of the aisle penciled in come November. But we've been here before."

"In Tucson. What was Diaz's lead when we jumped in? Fifteen points?"

"Please! It was still fifteen with a month to go. At the start? Try twenty-nine. You had zero shot, at least four more viable candidates ahead of you..."

"And yet somehow..."

"Diaz implodes with the sex scandal. O'Connor gets caught on tape disparaging Mexicans. Renteria had no personality to begin with..."

"Before we knew it, people were showing up at speeches, attending rallies..."

"And they got eight years of fantastic, humble leadership as a result. They'd have elected you for twelve more if..." Chiasson let it trail off, realizing at the last moment he'd raised the specter of his other political mentor, Jed Bryant.

"I wonder what he'd think of this."

"We're probably never going to know." They'd given Bryant little chance of recovery and it was a matter now of waiting for his family to agree to remove life support. "But he'd be proud of you for staying in the fight until the end. Until the last ballot is cast."

Misner nodded. "Yeah. Yeah, point taken. Come on." He clapped Chiasson on the back. "You're my best friend, Stu. And I'm glad you're here. Let's go meet the press, okay?"

57.

Oct. 26, 2020

VILLA CAMPANARIO, A village near Bariloche

The inn could've been straight from a Robert Louis Stevenson novel, right down to the pub sign, which featured half a Queen of Spades. Scrolling text underneath announced it as "La Reina de La Noche," *The Queen of the Night*.

From the front door, it had a view down the mountainside, tiny lights glimmering from homes along the way, over the tiny hamlet that carried on for a few miles, to the lake, where the late-evening moonlight reflected off the still surface.

Brennan pushed open the front door, greeted instantly by boisterous discussion, the pub's sound system straining to pump Argentine guitar folk over the din.

There was a prominent bar against the back wall, with the rest of the room filled by busy bench tables. A ruddy faced barkeep was polishing a beer mug as his customers laughed, joked and clinked mugs. He gave Brennan a confident and welcoming nod. The American made his way to the bar.

"You seem busy this evening," he said in Spanish.

The bartender recognized his accent immediately and answered in English. "It's like this most nights until the snow begins to fall. In truth, I wouldn't mind if it slowed down a little earlier this year. Anyway, what can I get you?"

"Looking for someone. He said he's got a room here. Last name is Steel?"

He nodded towards the back-left corner of the room where a short staircase led up to the next floor. "He said you'd be around. Room Four."

Brennan scanned the bar as he headed for the stairs. The only obvious exit was the front door; but local fire codes probably meant there was a secondary back exit. The patrons seemed oblivious to him, paying no attention. Everyone was in a group; no stragglers, no singletons sitting in a corner watching from behind a newspaper.

Peacock had arranged for a gun to be sent up from the Embassy in Buenos Aires, couriered as they travelled. He could feel the weight of the Glock in the small of his back. He'd preferred to keep things quiet; going in cold while expecting a firefight never ended well. They tended to be self-fulfilling, occurring because someone brought a gun to what could have been a discussion. But the handler had insisted.

He climbed the stairs. A long hallway led backwards, over the ceiling of the bar below, doors spaced evenly. At its far end, a tall window looked out at the mountain slope behind the inn.

Brennan checked his six as he approached Steel's room. He stopped outside the door and prepared to knock, apprehensive about moving ahead blind. The whole thing smelled bad. The meeting being so far from Bariloche; the Canadian demanding Brennan's presence; the lure of something 'really big' that he wouldn't elaborate.

He rapped on the door. "Steel! It's me. Open up."

There was no answer.

He knocked again. "Steel!"

Brennan's right hand found the butt of the pistol. His left hand tried the door handle. It turned freely and, as he felt the latch click away from the lock hasp, he pushed it open and stepped to one side, out of immediate blast range of any large-bore firearm. The door swung open and clunked against the interior wall.

He listened for a few moments for the telltale sounds of whispers or movement. When neither was apparent, Brennan peeked quickly around the corner and into the room, seeing no one.

He took a longer look, his gaze sweeping from the left wall and bureau, to the back window, to the bed on the other side of the room.

There was no sign of Steel. But he noticed a hissing sound, like an old tape recording. Brennan carefully pushed the door closed behind him and drew his weapon, training it ahead of himself, gun arm braced with his left hand. There was a short corridor just past the end of the bed, presumably to the bathroom.

Brennan made his way down the hall, the noise building. It was clearly the shower running, and it occurred to him his nerves might've been playing tricks on him; Steel was probably just showering – not that any amount of it could clean the stench of predator off him.

The bathroom door was a crack ajar. Brennan pushed it open slowly, the hinges creaking, the room lit brightly by a bare bulb dangling eight feet above. The shower curtain was half open. Steel was lying in the bathtub, which had begun to fill with crimson bathwater. His throat had been cut, and his body was blocking the drain. On the bathmat beside the tub lay a chef's carving knife, the blade smeared with the dead man's blood.

"Ah... shit," Brennan muttered.

Was it just a message? Or had they killed him not knowing he was planning to meet someone?

The blare of the police siren snapped Brennan back to attention.

That answers that question.

He ran back to the stairs and looked down, into the bar.

It was completely empty, the patrons and staff cleared out. That meant they'd known the police were coming, or had been quietly led out. Either way, it meant an imminent assault on his location... and going out the front unnoticed was out of the question.

He headed back up the corridor. There was a staircase at the other end. He jogged over to it but heard the footfalls immediately, boots clattering through the lower back door. Brennan sprinted to the window and looked through the smudged and dusty panes of glass.

Bars. But they looked rusty, perhaps vulnerable to a couple of good kicks. Beyond them...

A fire escape. He grabbed the twin metal handles on the window sash and pulled.

It stuck solid.

They'd nailed it shut.

He heard a thump as the door downstairs was flung open, the clatter of boot heels from men breaching the bar. "¡Policía! ¡Quédate donde estás!" a voice called out through a megaphone. Police! Stay where you are!"

Brennan yanked on the window with all his might, his biceps straining to budge the swollen, painted wood. It wouldn't give.

He heard the boots thump as they began to make their way up the two flights of stairs. They'd be on him in seconds, he knew. He pulled the slide on his pistol and ran back a few feet. A policeman's head poked around the corner of the stairs and Brennan opened up with the pistol, the burst of small explosions deafening, aiming wide but dissuading them from leaping into the fray.

At the back staircase, he took cover behind the door frame then checked around the corner, just in time to see a police flat cap coming up the stairwell. He aimed high, blasting two slugs into the concrete wall behind the officer. The policeman ducked on instinct, backing into the cover of the lower stairwell.

"Senor Kruger... Sir, you are surrounded," a heavily accented voice announced from the main stairs. "We do not wish anyone to come to harm sir. Surrender your weapon and lie down, face first, with your hands behind your back, please."

If nothing else, they were polite. "Si alguien mira por el pasillo, le disparare en la cabeza!" *Anyone even looks down the hall, I'll shoot them in the head*, Brennan announced in Spanish.

If he was lucky, they would want to negotiate, which would buy him a few minutes. Brennan studied the hall, the room doors. Perhaps there was something that could help him in one of the rooms. But if he gave up his position in the hallway, he knew, they would advance and pin him down.

The tear gas cannister arced lazily through the air from the main stairwell, fumes already streaming out of it, taking the decision of whether to act out of his hands. Before it could hit the floor, Brennan pulled up the bottom of his shirt, covering his nose and mouth. He pivoted on his left foot, sweeping out his right leg in a low, wide kick, his foot meeting the cannister at the exact moment it touched the floorboards, the improvised dropkick sending it flying towards the other stairwell doorway.

He was up in an instant and running after it. He looked back and fired two more shots towards the main stairs, anticipating the 'door check' from the lead tactical officer, forcing them back into cover.

At the back stairwell, the cannister had unloaded its contents, the landing thick with gassy fog. Brennan heard men coughing, the scrape and click of gas masks being dragged into place. His eyes began to tear up and he couldn't see how many there were, just dark shapes through the gassy fog. He fired another shot into the fog, aiming towards the ceiling joint to avoid accidentally hitting any of them.

He wiped the tears away with his sleeve and looked around frantically for another option. On the ceiling, a short, spring-held ladder was attached to the plaster, adjacent to a roof hatch. He jumped up and tripped the ladder release hook, the device dropping, a second row of steps sliding off the first, doubling the ladder's length.

Brennan pulled himself up, his eyes burning. He hadn't trained to handle tear gas in years. At the hatch, he used the butt end of his pistol to break the small, old padlock. From somewhere back in the corridor, he heard two more tear gas cannisters land. He pushed the hatch open and climbed up, onto the inn's broad, flat roof.

He sprinted to the front of the building and looked down. There were two officers standing by three squad cars. He figured on at least three or four on each of the stairwells. It likely accounted for most of the Bariloche police department. He ran back to the rear of the building. Two more officers stood by the back door.

They'll be reaching the top of the stairs by now. Need an exit. The roof had to be twenty-five feet up, at least. Jumping straight down wasn't an option, not without soft landing. He moved to the side of the building, looking north to an adjacent home's property. Brennan peered over the edge. *Too high to just...*

An old drainpipe was clamped to the wall. He stepped over the edge of the wall and lowered himself carefully. Ten yards away, the roof hatch slammed open once more. The officers' weapons clattered as they climbed up to his level.

Brennan grasped the old pipe and began to shimmy down. The screws holding its first bracket popped out immediately, the pipe pulling away from the masonry with a metallic creak. He let go for a split second, finding the pipe again at the second bracket, clinging on to the wall fixture. He kept his eyes on the pipe as he began to shimmy down. Above, an officer looked over the edge of the wall, then took aim with an Ingram submachinegun.

The American saw the officer's thumb flick off the safety. He acted on instinct, kicking hard off the wall with both feet, gripping the pipe with all his strength as it tore away from the wall and collapsed, sideways, like a tumbling pole. He let go five feet above the ground, taking the brunt of the momentum by rolling on his shoulder as it met the soft, damp ground.

On the roof, the officers lined up and opened fire, a rifle and pistol shots joining the quick, three-shot bursts from the Ingram. But it was dark, the hedges on the fenceline providing cover as he reached the barrier and vaulted over it, landing on all fours in a crouch.

There was a mansion about forty yards ahead, its back garden divided between shrubs and rock gardens, a few trees. He sprinted towards its cover. He needed to find a vehicle, he knew. They might have a description of him, possibly even his alias from the hotel. But finding somewhere to lay low and contact Peacock required mobility.

He could hear voices behind him now, officers approaching the fence, penlights carving arcs of light through the blackness.

Inside the large home, a dog began to bark frantically. He knew he didn't have time to wait and see if he was the cause; the police would be on him in moments. Brennan ran to the far corner of the house, past its rear windows, the interior dark, the owners either away or sleeping. He turned the corner and ran for the next tree, a tall evergreen. He crouched low, at its base, and surveyed the road.

The three police cars were unattended but there was still a man on the front door.

He cursed himself for having taken Steel's terms so cavalierly. They'd had the surname of his pseudonym, which meant they were well-prepared. The knife would be a setup, his prints lifted from something innocuous, like a glass he'd used at the hotel.

A car pulled up to the curb, twenty yards ahead of the police cruisers. The passenger window was rolled down. A man leaned over from the driver's side. He stared right at Brennan's position, as if he'd been spotted. "Mr. Brennan! No time for questions! Get in!"

Brennan sprinted the short distance to the road and climbed in. The man behind the wheel was elderly, perhaps in his seventies, broad shouldered but short, with a neatly trimmed grey beard. Before Brennan could even fasten his seatbelt, his rescuer stood on the gas pedal, the compact car squealing away from the curb.

58.

BARILOCHE

In her fifteen years as a newspaper and magazine reporter, Alex Malone had found success. But more often than not, she'd observed, success had found her. Maybe she'd made her own luck; maybe it had found her because she put herself in the right place at the right time.

Either way, she was having that familiar feeling of opportunity presenting itself once more.

Mrs. Schmidt had gone out with her husband for the evening to watch the local symphonic orchestra present a lineup of arrangements by Prokofiev. In her place, she'd left her fifteen-year-old niece, Eloise, a fact presented to Malone when she went downstairs to the bed-and-breakfast's cozy five-table dining room for the complimentary evening meal.

After asking her what she'd prefer from the handful of dishes their cook had produced and then disappearing to place her order of bratwurst and boiled potatoes, Eloise had reappeared and sidled up to her table. The room was otherwise empty. "Ms. Malone..." she'd said haltingly. "My English is not perfect... but I wanted to meet you."

Curious, Alex thought. No one was ever interested in the people who wrote the stories. "Miss..."

"Eloise!" she held out a dainty hand and Alex shook it. "I am hoping to become a reporter. My mother said you are a travel writer so I looked you up online." She blushed. "I hope you don't mind."

"Not at all." A fan? "Your mother?"

"Mrs. Schmidt. They are out for the evening, and... she told me not to bother you. I'm sorry..."

"No! No, please... sit." Alex gestured to the other chair.

The girl sat down quickly, as if Alex might change her mind. "You covered the North Korean attack in New York..."

"I did, yes."

"That... wow... that must've been so exciting. I mean... thinking so many people could have died..."

"It was scary as Hell, frankly. But that's not what most reporting is. I sort of stumbled into that one."

"So... you must know TV reporters and anchors and things? Do you watch CNN International? Do you know Christiane Amanpour? Have you met her, or even just talked with her? Is she as beautiful in real life as on TV?"

Alex held up both hands to beg for relief. "Hey! Slow down! I don't know her, no, but I've seen her at a few events. She's quite striking. Look, Eloise, most reporting..." And then she paused, and it occurred to her that one of those opportunities was about to go sailing by. "Hey." She turned side-on to face the girl. "I've got an idea: why don't I show you what a lot of reporting boils down to? Would that interest you?"

The girl's eyes widened and her mouth dropped open. "That would be so nice. Like, I mean, cool, you know?" She tried to rein in her enthusiasm, wary of looking too keen.

"Okay. Well... your mother runs the historical society, so she must have access to all sorts of local cultural items, memorabilia, documents...."

The girl nodded. "They have a huge store of it behind the museum in the offices. But... that stuff is mostly ancient... There are photos in black and white..."

In the era of the hi-resolution digital photo, it occurred to Alex that museums must've seemed like another world to teenage girls. The world had changed so much, so quickly. "Yes, but the best stories often start by rooting out something historical: a change in society, a government decision, a grudge between two parties. Real life takes time, and the kind of problems and challenges worth writing about take time, too."

The girl was frowning but nodding simultaneously in agreement – clearly with something she didn't quite understand. "Then... we will find a story in the archives?"

"Exactly!" Alex said. "How long are you expecting your parents to be gone for? We don't want you going out if you're going to get in trouble."

Eloise gestured towards the empty room. "We have no other guests right now. So... I do not expect they would mind too much. I mean, they will not be back until after eleven anyway..."

Alex smiled warmly. "That's the other thing you need: a little courage to paint outside the lines. Come on, let's go look for a story you can work on."

If she was lucky, Alex knew, she'd have the girl's attention for a couple of hours. She could pull a lot of local gossip out of her in that time, a lot of information about anything amiss in Bariloche, anything that would draw Brennan in. Combined with a deep dive into local history, something was sure to present itself.

59.

The sprightly senior drove them back toward the city, the road following the skinny, hooking shape of Lake Nahuel Huapi. Occasionally, he would shoot Brennan a mischievous glance. "You no doubt have many questions, not the least of which..."

"... Is how you know my name and who the Hell you are? Yeah, that's right at the top."

"My name is Simon Cortez, although my birth name was Simon Cohen," he said. "I was born in Buenos Aires, but I have lived in Bariloche for most of my life. We have a mutual associate in the United Kingdom who made me aware that you might need my help."

"This friend: would he be in the intelligence community, perchance? Maybe with..."

His rescuer cut him off. "Ah! As you're aware, these matters are delicate. But I believe I can give you some of the information you sought from the late Mr. Steel. Are you aware..."

"We knew what he was," Brennan said. "We needed an 'in' with the International Family."

"Ah!" the man nodded again then flicked on the left-turn indicator. "As they call themselves these days. They couch it as mostly supporting "individualism" and "religious freedom" contemporarily, but the same people are at the heart of it."

He turned the car down a darkened side road. "I'm going to show you something quite amazing tonight, Mr. Brennan. Very little of the truth of this is known publicly, though some has leaked out over the years. Do you swim?"

"If you're asking me to dive into a frigid lake at..." He checked his battered old Seiko wristwatch. "... ten to midnight in October? No, I don't swim, not in these conditions."

The old man chuckled. "It's not that, Mr. Brennan. I just want to make sure that if you fall out of the boat, you aren't going to drown."

"We're going fishing?"

"We're going trespassing," Cortez said.

He pulled the car up to a small pier, where three wooden skiffs were moored, tied up to the side of the dock. "More specifically we are going to Isla Huemul."

They descended a set of rickety wood steps to the end of the pier. Cortez led him to the third boat. "You mind rowing? I have arthritis in both shoulders..."

They boarded the skiff and Cortez cast off the line. "Point me in a direction," Brennan said.

The trip took twenty minutes, even though the island was practically adjacent to the town, the lake's choppiness slowing progress. Brennan did an occasional shoulder check, seeing the lantern that marked another small dock before Cortez's guidance was needed. "That it?"

"There are several private properties and docks on the island now, all but one owned by a tourism company. Yes, that's our spot."

They rowed up beside the pier and Brennan jumped out to tie the boat off. He helped the elderly man out of the boat and up onto the higher pier. At its far end, a rusted barrel served as a garbage can. Next to it, a sign had begun to corrode from age.

¡PELIGRO! MATERIAL RADIACTIVO PRESENTE. NO HAY ACCESO NO AUTORIZADO.

"Radioactive?" Brennan asked. "What have you dragged me into? Steel suggested the scientist, Gabriel Verde, was working with the IF. Is this his project?"

"No, this is much older. His compound at Nueva Esperanza is another matter. He has had… interesting visitors over the years, let me put it that way." Cortez nodded ahead to a distant light, where the outline of a large concrete structure hugged the shadows. "Come on, follow me. Let me show you the future some once envisioned for Bariloche. It may help explain why the International Family is here now."

"Look, before I go wandering into what might be some kind of government nuclear facility, I need a little more than that…"

"It is quite simple, really, Mr. Brennan." The old man removed his glasses to clean them with the front of his shirt. "When I was a young man, this island was considered the future of Adolf Hitler's Fourth Reich."

PART THREE

THEN

60.

December 3, 1948

MADRID, Spain

The Bishop of Hungary had been holding court on the hotel's sprawling dining patio, overlooking the foliage of Buen Retiro public park. He was an intense man in an ermine-and-velvet gown with matching skull cap. He had a pinched face that reminded Reinhard Gehlen of a rat.

A half-dozen young men sat with the religious leader at the circular glass table, listening intently as he described the evils of Judaism.

Gehlen observed quietly from a table nearby as the bishop gesticulated with both hands, ramping up the fervor. He was the most rabidly anti-Semitic man Gehlen had ever met, and he included Hitler on that list.

The former German intelligence officer had recruited a fair number of his Nazi colleagues into his new company, the Gehlen Organization. Few of them hated Jews with the sort of psychopathic zeal displayed by the bishop.

"He's quite insane, I think."

Gehlen looked to his left. Francois Genoud, the prominent Swiss fascist power broker, had sidled up to him. Genoud took a seat. He looked typically elegant in an off-white silk suit and dark tie, his hair slicked back. "Still… without his help, ODESSA wouldn't have been possible."

ODESSA was the official codename of the "Rat Line", the escape route used by Nazis to flee Europe. The church's role had been pivotal.

"And all of our efforts would have gone to waste. It's why we tolerate him," Gehlen offered.

"He's not without his financial benefits, either," said Genoud. "Some of his supporters in Rome have deep pockets."

Genoud had become the principal handler of finances for the Führungsring, the fledgling inner circle of Hitler supporters who had grouped together after the war, with Gehlen's assistance, to form the new fascist power base.

Some were members of the Knights of Malta, an ancient Catholic military sect that venerated nobility. Some, like Genoud, were merely financially powerful bigots. The Swiss man's contacts with anti-Semitic leaders in the Middle East guaranteed a steady flow of new funds and he had masterminded the mass theft of billions of dollars' worth of Jewish wealth and property during the war, using a maze of contacts within Swiss banking to help the Nazis hide it.

Gehlen didn't think much more of him than he did the Bishop, but politics made for strange bedfellows, sometimes. The former officer did not believe in white supremacy, merely that without a concerted effort to dominate the global political landscape, racial mixing would eventually wipe out Caucasians. That would mean the end of thousands of years of his family's history and culture. It wasn't a matter of anyone being inherently superior... merely that life always had to produce a winner and a loser. Gehlen preferred white Catholic nobility to win.

The route to winning had seemed to run through Hitler. That was no longer the case. Instead, Gehlen had come to realize that there were men as ruthless – and far less unstable – in all types of governments.

Those sharing both his religious views and his desire to dominate – whether or not racist and psychopathic – held pivotal roles in America, Argentina, Russia, Britain, even Germany. What was often mistaken by voters as assured confidence was, in his observance, often merely emotional immaturity wielded by ambitious men, men too arrogant to see their own limitations.

Gehlen did not doubt that even the reborn Jewish state of Israel would spawn men so ambitious they would always favor power over principle and, therefore, would work with former Nazis.

Creating a network of influence -- a decentralized political organization – that could control them was his new goal. If that eventually coalesced into a 'Fourth Reich', a new nation to stand at the network's head, all the better.

Genoud gestured for Gehlen to follow him. "The dining room is ready for us, I think."

The men went back inside the hotel and followed a short corridor to the private dining rooms. They had seating for eighteen at the long, narrow table but only a dozen were expected.

More guests filed in shortly after the two men. Gehlen took his place to the right of the head of the table, where they'd arranged for the Bishop to sit.

The other members understood how important it was to stroke the man's ego and keep their allies in the Vatican happy. It had helped provide, through the Red Cross and other affiliates, much of the forged paperwork that allowed former Nazis to proliferate across the globe, under assumed identities, often of Catholic children who died shortly after birth, their passing only recorded by their local parish.

Gehlen surveyed their turnout as everyone took a seat. The French designer, Coco Chanel, had been accompanied to the meeting by the right-wing political radical, Charles Lescat, with whom she'd recently visited Argentina. The former undersecretary of the Nazi Ministry of Jewish Affairs, Hans Globke, was seated across from them. There were representatives from Chile, Egypt and Argentina at the far end of the table.

He rose. "Ladies and gentlemen, if I may address you for a few moments. I wanted to introduce you to someone today who is pivotal to our efforts, a colleague who believes, as we do, that there are some favored by divine providence to lead. He is here to fill us in on our accomplishments overseas, and the steps that have occurred since the end of the war in Europe. May I introduce Otto Skorzeny."

He gestured to the door. The man who strode through it was tall, over six feet, with brown hair and a curving, vicious scar that ran from his nose to his left ear. He had the broad-shouldered, straight-backed confidence of a veteran officer.

Skorzeny gave a short, curt bow to each side of the table. "Ladies and gentlemen, Senoras y Senors…"

"Otto was one of our most successful intelligence officers with both the SS and the Wehrmacht. We have been working on ODESSA and 'Die Spinne' together since before the end of the war."

'Die Spinne' or The Spider, was Skorzeny's political strategy, based on Gehlen's observations about the nature of power. He had proposed that, just as fascism and dominance could exist within any political party, a supporting network could also be decentralized, held together not by a political party or body, but merely by mutual assurance – they would help one another, and damn the rest to servitude. Those who grasped for the largest brass ring would attract the others, like piranha on a swimming beast.

In that manner, any political organization could be subverted; any nation could be ruled.

The same principles of division that drove fascism's popularity could be recycled again and again – create simple, amorphous enemies for them to hate; brand them with detestable values and a single, recognizable name; exaggerate and exacerbate all potential threats; simplify the message; repeat each lie as much as possible; control the media and the breadth of the message; silence critics; encourage group acceptance of their new reality.

"Otto has just returned from his first trip to Argentina to check on progress. Otto?"

Skorzeny strode to the far end of the table and grasped the back of the chair with both hands, like a lectern. "We are making admirable progress, ladies and gentlemen, in sewing a new political reality, one which can stand as the vanguard against the communists. Our discussions with the governments of Paraguay, Chile and Argentina have been most fruitful and we have numerous former intelligence and science officers working in each government. Similar approaches have been made in the Middle East and North Africa and talks with those governments continue. As you are all well aware, the United States continues to be our most welcoming new home for the Reich's best and brightest. This... has caused some friction in South America."

Globke spoke up. "Our guest is unhappy with the arrangements?"

Skorzeny looked unsure how best to answer. "Not just Hitler, unfortunately. Many of the senior officers are wedded to the notion of a militaristic outcome, rather than amassing influence through propaganda and diplomacy. They have used their time in Argentina and Chile to build up arms networks, to influence military leaders. They do not like that so much attention is being paid to the scientists and the former residents of Eastern Europe, whom they consider lowly peasants."

A pair of waiters entered the room with bottles of wine and, with a wave to proceed from Gehlen, began to fill people's glasses.

"In a few minutes, we shall enjoy an excellent lunch. My apologies for the interruption, Otto, please continue."

"Of course, sir. As I said, the senior officers are not happy. They are content, however, that they are receiving substantial financial support for Richter's atomic experiment in Patagonia. He believes he can stabilize the reactor and produce heavy water elsewhere in Argentina, possibly the Tierra del Fuego region, using financial assistance from that nation's government."

"What about Hitler?" Genoud interrupted. "Is he still insisting you keep Mengele nearby?"

"He is. We believe he has developed a fantasy of immortal life, based on the nightmares he has about the bunker in Berlin. Mengele has convinced him that he can understand and manipulate human genetic material, that a newly discovered molecule called a "DNA" might allow him to create a new, stronger human body for the Fuhrer."

There were some chuckles around the table. "I did not claim it was a sound theory," Skorzeny said. "But we humor him. He is an important figurehead to the most loyal followers from the war.

"Bunker nightmares?" Chanel asked. "The suicides?"

"No. His dog, Blondi, was shot at the same time. It... plagues him, for some reason. He hasn't mentioned Eva Braun since we left Norway and I have no doubt that he does not bother to give her any thought. In any event, the men see a second Hitler and political control of the region, bolstered by nuclear weapons, as their glorious, inevitable future."

Gehlen rose again. "Thank you, Otto. It is, of course, just one of The Spider's many legs, our many opportunities. I understand you are flying out right away?"

"Yes, Colonel." Skorzeny clicked his heels obediently.

"Then we shall not keep you. Report back as soon as you are able."

Skorzeny left the room and continued down the hall, into the hotel's main lobby. His bags had already been brought down from his room and he just needed to check out. He handed the bellhop a tip. "Thank you, boy," he said, giving the young man a warm smile before heading towards the front desk.

The bellhop waited until he had turned away, then looked back towards the private dining rooms. His friend with the bottle of wine gave him a nod, his cue to find a telephone and report in what they'd learned.

61.

March 4, 1949

BUENOS AIRES, Argentina

Skorzeny slumped back in the heavy, throne-style wooden dining chair, a cigarette in hand, burning away. His head rested on his other hand, elbow propped on the other chair arm as he took in the latest dinner party with a growing sense of fatigue.

It had been like this for months, meeting politicians and gladhanding, stroking their egos to convince them that all they needed was as much German help as possible to handle the heavy lifting that came from being in power.

At the other end of the table, the President of Argentina, Juan Peron, was holding court, telling jokes to his coterie of hangers-on, the men cackling like hyenas at every punchline.

Peron was smarter and more able than most of the men in power with whom Skorzeny had dealt, but increasingly he saw signs the Argentine leader could be manipulated with flattery, that he was beginning to accept his own reputation as true.

Like Globke, Peron didn't really understand what they were doing, Skorzeny suspected. Peron believed in Social Democracy – strong nationalism and social intervention, while allowing capitalism to flourish. The Argentine leader did not understand – at least not yet – that eventually the leverage provided by unfettered capital would allow the totalitarian to take control, and that such a man required complete power to maintain that control.

Yes, they might be like Franco and insist on bringing in expertise to actually handle the heavy lifting. But they would have little time or see much priority, under such circumstances, in lifting up the weak. The weak would always be with them, Skorzeny believed, and should be left to their less fates.

Despite being an army man and enjoying the excesses of social privilege, Peron did not yet seem to understand that their purpose was to rule the world, not just petty fiefdoms in one region. He was arrogant, and he was egotistical. But he actually wanted to help his people, people without the wherewithal to help themselves.

It was pathetic, Skorzeny decided.

Peron pointed his way. "Skorzeny scowls, even as we enjoy the best side of beef he has ever eaten, eh?" the Argentine told his men. "Unless I am talking about how much money we can provide his friends…"

"Respectfully, Mr. President… it is not a one-way transaction. By the time we are done, you WILL be a nuclear power, the most powerful nation in the southwestern hemisphere. So… you'll forgive me if I'm all business sometimes."

"Forgiven! Forgiven, my friend, forgiven. But please… eat! Drink! Tomorrow, when you're in Patagonia, you can look back towards the city and wonder why we stupidly choke on exhaust fumes and factories when we could be enjoying the quiet of the country."

"Of course, Mr. President. My apologies if my dour mood…"

"It's nothing. You have your accommodations arranged, I take it?"

"I am staying with Maj. Helmut Schmidt, a former colleague. He has been most gracious about making all of the arrangements for me."

"And Richter?"

"He is already there, sir, and on the island, working with the Tokamak and the materials we brought over."

"Good, good! Then tonight, you must relax, eh? Like I said: have a drink, stop worrying so much."

A waiter leaned over Skorzeny. "Another mug of beer, sir?"

Skorzeny nodded. He didn't really feel like drinking heavily, but Peron was a key ally. Keeping him satisfied was paramount.

The waiter poured him another mug from a four-gallon jug. He waited until the German had taken an approving sip, then walked down one side of the table to the kitchen exit, halfway along the wall. The kitchen was busy with staff collected around stainless steel counters, prepping food.

He set the jug down on one and kept walking, through the kitchen backdoor, to the servants' quarters and the palatial home's back entrance. He checked his surroundings to ensure no one was listening, then picked up the telephone receiver from the small side table by the door and dialed a number.

"It's me. He's on his way tonight. Yes, Bariloche as you suspected. The target home belongs to a Helmut Schmidt, although he may be under another name, of course. Okay. Okay, bye."

He hung up the phone and went back to his duties.

62.

March 6, 1949

DINA HUAPI, A village northeast of Bariloche

It was chilly, the temperature having dropped near zero overnight in the foothills of the mountains. Skorzeny sat on the front porch of the tiny two-bedroom cabin and kept his eye on the large house a few hundred meters away, further back from the shoreline of the lake.

On the home's grand wrap-around balcony, Adolf Hitler was pacing back and forth. Even from a distance, Skorzeny could see that he had his hands clasped behind his back and that he had his official uniform on. He wasn't supposed to wear it but there was little harm. It was an open secret among the locals, particularly the former Germans, that Hitler was staying at the home until his own palatial accommodations could be finished, further up the lake.

It was a make-work project for the man, creating something similar to what he'd had in The Berchtesgaden.

Anything to keep him busy. He was driving his caregivers half mad, ranting and raving, demanding more drugs. The cocktail of amphetamines and strange toxins that the late Dr. Morell had prescribed him for several years had been toned down on the mutual agreement of his new physician, but was still enough to keep him bouncing between mania and depression.

Ronald Richter sat a few feet to Skorzeny's right, smoking a cigarette and nursing a mug of coffee. "I had the privilege to speak with him this afternoon and he seemed in... most energetic spirits," the physicist said. "Surely we are beyond fortunate to be in his presence."

Skorzeny stared at the scientist with unmasked contempt. Then he looked back towards the balcony and the pacing Hitler.

"He is a fool. He has always been a fool. His passion and self-confidence are products of narcissism, and once you realize that, you realize he is nothing but an empty vessel, to be filled with whatever distraction is required in the moment." Skorzeny turned his attention back to the scientist. "And you are a fool if you believe any of his nonsense for even a moment. I will grant you this one favor, Richter. I will tell you once and once only: all of this," he gestured around them, "is not an endeavor for weak-willed men. The purpose of this movement, this vision, is to no longer suffer fools gladly. To determine and chart our destinies as men of free will and vision, who take what we wish, and damn the rest. No one here will be on your side, Richter. No one will protect you. Each man may agree not to interfere or to speak ill of one another. But we are all in this for ourselves, as it should be."

Richter bowed his head slightly, his face flushed with embarrassment and perhaps some anger. He rose from his chair. "I am going inside. We... should not be discussing such things... such self-interested matters."

After he'd gone, Skorzeny allowed himself a small smirk. Richter was embarrassed by being called out, by the bigger man acknowledging who and what they were. But he knew it was true. The ultimate course of self-determination would always be to conquer the man across the table from you, not placate him or work with him. A man could not truly be free until he was entirely self-determined, and that would always come at the expense of others.

"He is a weakling, you know. He's not even a good physicist."

A colleague had sidled up to the chairs silently in the cool evening air. With his small, round head and piercing, narrow eyes, the man was among the few Hitler insiders who concerned Skorzeny. He wouldn't call it fear, as he'd never really felt fear in the way other people did. But he knew the man was utterly ruthless — a perfect exemplar of what he'd charitably tried to pass on to that idiot Richter.

"But Hitler believes he's a genius," Skorzeny said.

"Hitler believes a lot of insanely stupid things," his colleague replied. "He allowed me to vivisect an entire religious faith on the notion that they were biologically inferior. Think about that for a moment: he could not connect the basic lack of rationality using "inferior" subjects for biological experiments. He could not overcome the dissonant concept that they could be both "fiendishly clever financial overlords" and also "decadent weaklings." The man is as stupid as a wooden plank."

"What are you going to do with him?"

He received a hard look in return for the question. The man wasn't foolhardy enough to volunteer information this early into their exile, with nothing to be gained in return. "Why... I'll prolong his life, of course, for as long as possible, as promised. And I will find out how to extract and duplicate his genetic material."

"So his stupidity can continue for an eternity?"

The other man shrugged. "If he believes it to be so, that is what is important, is it not? After all, we want the Fuhrer of the Fourth Reich to be happy."

63.

Two hundred yards down the shoreline, Erud Cohen crouched behind the rotting frame of a wooden skiff and watched through a telephoto camera lens, the image blown up three hundred percent.

The man in the chair was definitely Otto Skorzeny, the former SS agent whom they'd identified as meeting three times with Juan Peron in Buenos Aires. He'd escaped from a camp in Europe a year earlier. The other man had been the nuclear physicist, Ronald Richter, who was still technically based in Germany but was spending all of his time in Argentina.

But he'd left, and another man had walked down the gentle slope from the mansion. The back of the house was illuminated by a row of globe lamps that ran along the patio balustrade. The third man too far away to identify.

A gazebo at one far end of the patio cast long slivers of shadow across an edge of the back lawn. And yet, the man had managed to hug those shadows all the way from the patio to the boat dock. Now, he was standing next to Skorzeny, close enough to the man's small pit fire to warm his hands, but far enough back that its glow did not identify him.

Cohen had been recruited a year earlier by Emri Barak, the Buenos Aires head of station for MOSSAD, the new Israeli secret service. Barak, who had a position within Peron's open household as a servant, had quickly developed a network of Jews based in South America to keep tabs on the Nazis, who had begun to flood out of Europe after the war.

So far, he'd identified a string of former SS officials who'd relocated at least temporarily to the Bariloche area, their movements funded by wealthy families sympathetic to the Knights of Malta, fascism and the church.

But the big names continued to elude them. There had been no sign of Martin Bormann, rumored to have escaped via Portugal to Paraguay or Argentina. There were rumors that Adolf Eichmann was living somewhere in Buenos Aires.

But the two big fish weren't even known to still be alive: Joseph Mengele, the so-called Angel of Death, who added grotesque tortures in the name of research to the menu at concentration camps; and Adolf Hitler, whom nobody in MOSSAD believed was really dead. His ego would not have allowed suicide, they were convinced, and such matters could be easily faked.

Cohen kept the telephoto lens trained on the second man, who was meticulously avoiding any ambient light. He was being so careful, it begged the question of his identity. The majority of Nazis in the region had held significant rank, but they were not decision makers. They were leaders of platoons, intelligence officials, camp commanders. But they were never in the Berlin inner circle or helping to decide the extermination policy.

The man in the shadows walked a few steps and took the chair to Skorzeny's left, the intelligence officer's head blocking Cohen's view of the other man's face.

Damn it, would you get out of the way?! It was infuriating. He'd been there for nearly twenty minutes and Cohen was beginning to believe the man would walk back to the house without ever exposing his face.

Skorzeny reached into his breast pocket and drew a cigarette case. He offered the other man one and Cohen felt himself holding his breath, waiting for the other man to reach over from his chair into the light. A bony white hand crossed the divide between the two chairs... and withdrew the cigarette without its owner leaning forward.

Damn it. This is turning into a waste of...

Skorzeny lit his own cigarette, then offered the flame to his associate. The man leaned over, cigarette to lips, his features coming into view for just a split second, illuminated by the glare of the naked flame.

Joseph Mengele.

He jammed his finger down onto the shutter release then wound the film to another frame with the thumb trigger. Hands shaking, he managed three shots, he believed, by the time the man dropped back into the shadows.

My God. He's here. He's here right now.

I have to tell Emri.

He felt his hip pocket and the lumpy shape of the twenty-two caliber Beretta. Mengele was only a few hundred yards away. If he could get close enough, he could kill the Angel of Death, mete out justice while it was at hand.

Cohen checked his surroundings. He'd snuck down to the shoreline from the road just past the village and walked a few kilometers to get there. There were guard posts at three of the homes directly adjacent to where Skorzeny was staying, along with unpainted, hastily erected cinder block walls topped by barbed wire. Any motion at all could invite investigation, and he'd considered himself lucky to have gotten that far to begin with. Any attempt at getting close was taking a massive risk.

But it would be a massive payoff, he told himself. *He is responsible for thousands of horrific deaths, and one of the evilest men who ever lived. He got away with it. But you can rectify that right now, Erud. You can get close and put a bullet in his head.*

Or... he could be discovered, caught. If he attempted a low-chance assassination and it failed, they would move Mengele again, be more careful the next time. And he had been ordered to not engage Skorzeny or any other Nazis he encountered; Emri had insisted on that.

The smart move, he knew, was to beat a retreat to his car, parked along the main road a few kilometers away. Cohen stored his camera in his shoulder duffel bag. He crouched low as he made his way back along the shoreline. He kept an eye on each home as he passed, looking for glints of moving metal or human motion.

At the road, he found the 1942 Ford and climbed behind the wheel. He opened the duffel bag and took out the camera. He wound the film in completely before opening it and removing the cartridge. He retrieved a small notepad and tore off the first blank page; he found a pencil in the sack and printed in small, neat letters "Mengele, Dina Huapi, March, 1949). He attached the note to the roll of film with a rubber band.

Cohen opened the glove box and took out a chrome flashlight. He undid one end and removed the batteries, before shoving the roll of film and note into the cavity in their place. He screwed the cap back on and returned the flashlight to the dash.

He started the Ford and pulled a U-turn onto the road, so that he was facing back towards Bariloche, then stepped on the gas. If he were lucky, the pictures would be clear evidence Mengele was still alive.

In the car's rear-view mirror, a set of bright headlights appeared. They were closing quickly and Cohen pulled the car slightly to the right so that the other driver could pass. The car leaped forward, as if its driver had stepped on the gas. A moment later it was parallel to his own and Cohen looked over, the darkness and glare from the moonlight making it hard to see who was in the cab. The passenger window rolled down, the barrel of the machine pistol extended before he could react.

Cohen swerved the car, off the road onto the verge, the other car pulling slightly ahead for just a split second, then slowing so that the passenger could unleash a volley of bullets from the oversized handgun. He felt the bullet's hot sting in the side of his neck and spasmed, yanking the car to the right, off the road.

It slammed into a tree with a sickening crunch of metal and the crashing of broken glass.

Cohen was slumped across the front seat but he could hear voices, the doors closing on another vehicle. He tried to pull himself up. He leaned against the door with his weight, his vision blurred from dizziness. It opened, and he tumbled out onto the ground.

He crawled away from the car, trying to get distance from his prize. Perhaps, if he was lucky, he thought, they would kill him and not find it.

He didn't hear the final pr-rap-rap of the machine pistol, spitting fire.

64.

CHESTER, Pennsylvania, a suburb of Philadelphia

June 2, 1949

Luigi de Cesare stood in the bedroom doorway and watched quietly as his friend prayed. Jacob Grech had been kneeling beside his wife's bed constantly for three days, barely taking time to sleep himself.

The former Maltese national worked with Luigi at the tire plant but had had to quit to look after Maria and their infant son, Mark. They wouldn't give him time off, even with Maria's condition worsening by the day.

Her doctors were baffled. They saw no signs of cancer but she grew weaker and weaker.

"I don't understand," Jacob said, without looking up. "I don't understand how God can let someone so loved suffer like this. I pray and I pray, but they still don't even know why."

"His tests are beyond us," Luigi offered. "If the Jews who owned the tire company would help with her medical bills…"

Jacob gave him a short, sharp stare. He'd heard enough anti-Semitism from his brother, who had also emigrated and lived in nearby Norristown. "It's not their fault that she is sick, or their responsibility to help. I know how you feel about them, but…"

"They are a cancer on this community, this town," Luigi said. Then he saw his friend's face further darken and added, "But… it is not a matter to discuss now."

"I need to put Mark to bed," Grech said, rising from his kneeling position. "Perhaps you should go home for the night."

Luigi nodded amiably and made his way out of the bedroom. As he passed Mark's room, the young boy was peeking, wide-eyed, around the door frame. Luigi gave him a wink and the boy disappeared into the room.

Outside, he made his way to the bus stop. His cover and role demanded an austere life, for which he'd been promised his family would be rewarded for generations. But the consequence was that his clothes were cheap and threadbare, and he rode the bus into Philadelphia rather than driving a car.

He got off in Center City and walked the two blocks to the Automat restaurant, where his contact was waiting, a former SS commander who'd been Ernst Muller in Germany but had been reborn as 'Palmer Stone' once in the U.S.

Normally, Stone met him alone. This time, an older man was with him. He wore an immaculate three-piece suit, his Fedora on his lap.

"My friend, good to see you!" Stone intoned, offering a hand to shake. Luigi checked their surroundings as they greeted one another, making sure none of the other diners were within earshot. Across the far wall, people lined up to remove pre-made trays of sandwiches and other light fare from windowed slots.

"This is Mr. Gehlen, with the Gehlen Security Organization. He was on the East Coast for another matter and decided to come and gauge our progress."

Luigi resisted the urge to salute and praise Hitler. It had been ingrained in him for so long that even now, four years after the end of the war, it was still near automatic. Instead, he gave a short, curt bow. "I have, of course, heard of you sir. May I say I am immensely proud to have this chance to meet you."

Gehlen maintained his pleasant demeanor, gesturing to the seat across from them. "Please... join us, won't you?"

Luigi sat down, feeling enervated. Reinhard Gehlen was the undisputed star of the movement, a former Intelligence Officer who had skillfully manipulated his way into a contract position with the Americans, advising the Central Intelligence Agency on whom they should recruit from the former Nazi ranks. Even the U.S Army in Europe allowed Gehlen leeway, turning a blind eye as he worked with the church and other sympathetic governments to smuggle his former comrades to safety.

"Tell us about Eternal Glory," Gehlen said. "Are we on schedule?"

Luigi nodded. "I've been slowly poisoning the wife for six months now. She'll be dead before the year is out."

"Good," Gehlen said. "It's unfortunate we had to take that approach, but she would not allow anyone near the boy. And he needs to be properly educated."

65.

NOW

Oct. 26, 2020

BARILOCHE

Simon Cortez sat on the rusting old guard rail as he finished the story. Brennan stood five feet away, arms crossed in guarded fashion as he waited to judge the old man's rationale.

"So... as interesting as that story was, none of it explains why we're here," Brennan said. "Or, for that matter, how any of this relates to you."

Cortez sighed deeply. "The man who left the note in the flashlight— the man murdered by the roadside that day — was my brother, Erud. He was working here on behalf of a MOSSAD agent, Emri Barak, who was based in Buenos Aires. And, I admit, some of what happened I have to draw from inference. We found the film and the note... but the photos were too blurry to have been of any value. The fact that Mengele's name was attached did not really mean anything as evidence..."

"But it did tell you he was here."

Cortez nodded. He rose to his feet and drew a pack of cigarettes from his breast pocket, lighting one. He offered Brennan the pack and shrugged at the refusal. "A terrible habit, but I am an octogenarian. At this age, I say we get a pass for bad health choices. It's good, though, that you do not."

"Occupational necessity," Brennan said. "I used to work in darkness a lot, and the light can affect your night vision. Plus, the smell is a giveaway."

Cortez nodded towards the building. "We didn't really know why both Mengele and Richter were here, initially. Even after we got into this place to take a look — after the Argentine government shut it down in Nineteen Fifty-Six — we weren't absolutely sure until later. But... come, I'll show you."

Cortez led him down the cracked concrete path. The tourism company that showed people around the site had kept it clear of overgrowth but the place was still completely rundown. Cortez took him almost to the backdoors, then veered off along one of the buildings until he reached a set of double trap doors.

He raised a foot over one side and brought it down hard in a stomp, the rusty old metal clanging. "The lock mechanism on these is already broken..." He brought his boot down one more time and the latched slipped open, the double doors caving in slightly. He reached down and pulled them open. "After you..."

Brennan climbed down the ladder. It was nearly black in the basement, but a red exit sign gave just enough light for him to know there was a large, open room ahead of them. Cortez followed him down the ladder then withdrew a penlight from his pocket. He shined it ahead of them and led Brennan to the far end of the large room.

Along the wall was a series of glass tanks, the top of each capped by a metal seal, electric wiring into them shorn clear by vandals over time. The tanks' glass was cracked but not shattered. "Tempered and bulletproof," Cortez explained before Brennan could ask.

Brennan had seen something similar somewhere before, but it took him a few seconds to make the connection. "They look like the tanks from one of the 'Alien' movies."

Cortez looked grim. "I have not seen this one. But... they must have done some research. Our belief — or, MOSSAD's, I should say, as I am long retired — is that they were medical storage tanks of some sort, for living matter. The most outlandish belief is that they were used to store Adolf Hitler as they attempted to restore their empire globally, with the dictator hoping they could create a new body for him using genetics."

Brennan saw where he was going. "The Mengele connection. Richter would give them the potential to make nuclear weapons, and Mengele would give Hitler long life. Or, perhaps, an heir."

"Precisely."

"But... as you said, this was all seventy years ago. How the heck did we get from them being here to me being set up by the IF for Brett Steel's murder?"

Cortez took a puff off his cigarette then flicked the ash with his thumb. "Because the IF are the Nazis, Mr. Brennan, put plainly. The same men and women, the same companies, the same religious orders, the same government agencies that affected the escape of so many Nazis to Argentina and America? They all exist still, and they are all infiltrated, to one degree or another, by these fanatics, these fascists. Many would not even classify themselves as such, due to fanaticism in one particular area or another — many are evangelical religious zealots, for example, rather than mere bullies. But they believe, ultimately, in the same thing: the right of ascension by force. Their delusional faith that any step they take must be acceptable, as they are chosen by God."

Brennan looked over the tanks. The idea that Adolf Hitler might have been stored in one of them for any period gave him a reflexive shiver. "And now you think they're back to finish what they started."

"Why else here — or, 'Nueva Esperanza', more precisely?" Cortez suggested. "And why else would they be funding the work of Dr. Gabriel Verde, a leading chemist and geneticist? The coincidence to their past endeavors is too great to ignore."

He might be right, Brennan thought. Peacock wasn't going to want to hear it; the official party line was that Nazis were passé.

Apparently, someone forgot to tell the Nazis.

66.

BRIGHTON, England

Rabbi Eli Barak watched the young man's fingers dance over the keyboard with smooth confidence, his eyes locked on the computer monitor as he checked a series of untrackable apps for messages.

"Anything interesting?" the Rabbi asked. Across the room, in a corner armchair, Martin watched them both with an air of inquisitive dread. He knew Eli well enough to realize he usually did not allow an opportunity to do some good pass.

"They found another IP address buried in some notes attached to the code," Charlie said. "It runs back to a server in Austria; they think it's Michael Wolf's company."

Martin raised a plaintive hand. "Is this really a good idea, Eli, given how many people are looking for Charlie right now?"

The theologian shrugged. "They killed your friend Ruby, which suggests they have no intention of handing Charlie over to the authorities or taking him alive. I would think any ammunition we can get..."

"You're forgetting that half of his problems are because he's wanted for legitimate reasons," Martin said. "Are we compounding those issues by letting him dig around online?"

The Rabbi shrugged. "I see nothing. I know nothing..."

"At least we should find out first if this is appreciated," Martin said.

"They prefer we maintain silence right now, for obvious reasons." The Rabbi nodded towards the young man.

Charlie had been half-listening and realized he'd just lost the thread. "Sorry... who's 'they', exactly?"

Rabbi Eli pulled up a nearby wooden chair to the side of the desk and sat down. "Charlie, have you ever heard of an agency called the MOSSAD?"

"So we're being direct, then," Martin offered caustically. "A little notice, perhaps."

Charlie stared at him, then at the Rabbi, then again at Martin Weiss.

He turned back to the Rabbi. "You... you're with Israeli intelligence." Martin's decision to head to the synagogue was beginning to make more sense. He turned his attention back to the Londoner. "Which means you're..."

Martin held up both palms, and his facial expression suggested mild embarrassment. "I didn't expect Joe Brennan to show up at my door with you, but... yes, to answer the question."

"And Brennan doesn't know, does he?"

Martin looked uncertain. "He suspects, I suppose. But I am legitimately retired; something like this requires my involvement? I get involved."

"Ultimately, we are on the same side, Charlie," the Rabbi offered. "We have our methods, the British government has its own."

Charlie stood up abruptly, his eyes darting across the room to the door.

"We're not going to hurt you or try to hold you here against your will," Martin chimed in. "I've saved your neck more than once already. But if you bolt out of here, I don't like your chances on your own."

"You lied to me."

"I omitted details..." Martin began.

"Which is the same thing as lying."

"Not exactly. But for arguments sake, I'm still the only person involved in this that you know who isn't trying to kill you."

"What else haven't either of you told me?"

The Rabbi gestured to the desk chair. "Please... I am an old man, Charlie. I do not have the energy to chase you. So please... sit."

The young coder grudgingly sat down again.

"I grew up the son of a policeman, in Buenos Aires, Argentina," Rabbi Eli said. "In Nineteen Forty-Eight, after the European conflict, Israel was fighting its own war with its Arab neighbors, over the partition. They needed new blood, new recruits. With veteran intelligence officers being dispersed across the Middle East, overseas stations were shorthanded. I was only a young boy of six. But my father, Emri, had served in the merchant marines between the wars and had some opportunity to work with codes, and coded transmissions. He was recruited to open MOSSAD's first South American field office."

"In Buenos Aires?" Charlie asked.

"Actually, no. Initially, he travelled to Osorno, Chile, as fledgling intelligence gathering by the new agency suggested that was where the Nazis had the most pre-existing sympathetic connections. But it became obvious very quickly that there were ideal local men to staff it; when he'd finished setting it up, he returned to Buenos Aires and obtained a position within the house of the country's president Juan Peron, as a servant."

"Peron? As in 'Evita'? As in 'Don't Cry for Me Argentina'"? Charlie looked flabbergasted. "This is just bizarre."

"It's not so strange," the Rabbi insisted. "Many South American leaders were devout Catholics who feared communism and believed it would end their way of life. Peron was no exception. He was not as ruthless as some of his peers, and he seemed to have a genuine love for his people. But he was also a great boon to the Nazis. He did not approve of their methods or of totalitarianism; but he was an anti-Semite and an anti-communist, and in those days, such sentiments led to strange bedfellows."

"So he allowed Nazis in to gain their expertise?"

"Exactly. So did the Americans, so did the British. For a short period, the same Nazi who tried to revive the Fourth Reich in South America — an SS officer named Otto Skorzeny — even consulted with my government, in Tel Aviv."

Charlie realized his mouth was hanging open. "The Israelis hired a Nazi!?!?"

"So did we," Martin chimed in. "Britain allowed an entire company of former German army officers to relocate here under assumed names. We allowed scientists to move here and work with our own men. We were trying to keep them out of the hands of the Soviets."

Martin could see the disbelief in Charlie's eyes, the disillusionment welling to the fore. "But you have to also know that some of us have done as much as possible to correct that. No one has worked harder than the MOSSAD to bring high-ranking Nazis to justice."

"You can help us," the Rabbi added. "At least, I believe you may be able to. Your skill as a..."

"...Coder," Martin jumped in. "Your skills as a coder could help us determine what Wolf is up to in South America. They could help protect Brennan, who is already there. They could help us convince our superiors that he needs assistance. All we need is for you to get into Wolf's server and see what you can find."

Charlie looked uneasy. "You must have a team of guys doing this back in Israel..."

The Rabbi shared his outward discomfort, at least for a moment. "We... are not officially involved in this matter. That is why Martin and I, who are both retired...."

The younger man caught on. "You're both retired. So neither of you is officially sanctioned by anyone..."

Martin shook his head. "No. No, we're not."

"Did you ever actually intend to help me? Or did you just see an opportunity?"

"I'd be lying if I didn't admit it was a little of both." Martin knew that wasn't what the boy wanted to hear; but it was high time they started treating him with complete honesty. He'd almost died at Ruby's. "That's what this business is, Charlie: A little give, a little take."

"And if I say no?"

"Then you say no," Martin replied. "We're not going to force you to do anything you don't think is acceptable. But consider what might be at stake. They suspect it's a bioweapon of some sort. If Wolf is tied to fascists and they acquire it, there's no telling the havoc they could wreak, the lives that could be lost."

Charlie felt empty inside. He'd trusted Martin completely but had been deceived. Even though it seemed to be for the right reasons, he knew he couldn't be sure about that, either. The alternative was to tell them to get stuffed and run. But whoever killed Ruby would be scouring the city for them, probably London as well.

All he'd wanted to do was impress the curvaceous bird from Bexley. He gave Martin a hard stare. "You realize I don't trust you now, of course."

Martin accepted it on face value. "Again... it's the nature of what we do."

Charlie let him stew in the discomfort of betrayal for a few more moments. He wanted to tell both the old men to fuck off. But his conscience was nagging at him, telling him that, for once, Sonya was right. For once, he really did have a chance to do something meaningful.

He sat down again behind the computer. "Fine. Let's see what Mr. Wolf's security is like, shall we?"

67.

BARILOCHE

The teenager was running from table to table in the back of the old museum like a debutante picking out dresses. "And this is all from the Nineteen Fifties! There are magazine articles — including one from *Life*! — there are all of these old black and white photos my grandparents took..."

The storage room was mostly shelves covered in sealed legal boxes. But each of the backlit glass-top tables was piled high with other material that had yet to be tagged or stored.

Alex opened one of the narrow white cardboard boxes of old prints. She began to flick through them. It was family stuff: people at the lake, leaning against a Nineteen Forties Packard, waterskiing, barbecuing with family. The same older man with a crew cut and rotund midsection was in most photos.

Nothing. She went through a few hundred prints. "Are all of these smaller boxes full of photos?"

"Uh huh, yes. My grandfather took them right up until the Nineteen Seventies."

"Does he have any from before they arrived here? From Germany?"

The girl frowned. "You mean from before the war..."

"Sure."

She shook her tousled brown curls. "They didn't like to talk about that, I'm told. He was very old and I was little when he died. He was a teacher for years and I think he was ashamed of the war. He taught us we should be proud of being from Germany and I think maybe he was worried we would think less because of... you know..."

"Hitler."

"The Nazis, sure."

"That must be a real pain, what with all the rumors around here."

The girl shrugged. "That was all before I was born. We don't talk about it too much. So... did you see anything interesting?"

"Not... that I can use immediately," Alex said tactfully. She was down to the last box of prints. "What about the rest of the museum?"

"Oh." The girl looked nervous. "The rest of the building is locked off. I only have a key to the family archives."

There wasn't a sign of anything remotely Nazi related and there were only a dozen of the prints left. Alex riffled through them: a ski weekend, some pictures from a wedding reception, a shot from a local school room from behind the kid's desks, the two men at the front of the room looking officious; a portrait of the rotund man and a middle-aged woman with curls.

"That is my grandparents," Eloise said proudly. "She was so kind."

Something the girl had said twigged Alex. "Wait a second... you said he was a teacher?"

"Uh huh, yeah..."

She flicked back to the shot from the classroom. There was the rotund man at the head of the class. Alex thought she recognized the man standing next to him, a tall, handsome individual with a broad nose. He was wearing a butcher's apron over his striped dress shirt and tie. She flipped the print over. On the back, in pencil handwritten Spanish, the inscription read, "Kurt with Erich, the new school, 1954."

She flipped it back over quickly.

"You know this man with him?"

The girl shook her head. "Not really. But he's in some of their older photos at the house. I think my mother said they were close friends. He ran the German community association or something."

It was Erich Priebke.

Malone remembered the interview, the ABC news piece, after he'd been arrested and extradited to Italy for war crimes. He helped co-ordinate the massacre of more than three hundred Italian civilians and deported thousands more to death camps.

"Sounds like an interesting guy. Plus, all of these are from a pretty neat era. Let's go look at those older photos."

The girl seemed hesitant. She looked up at the wall clock. "It's ... ten o'clock, nearly. My parents will be home soon and my mother really does not want me looking at that stuff. She said there are bad memories..."

Alex felt like kicking herself. But the reality was that sometimes a little deceit went a long way with sources. "Hey: don't let her intimidate you! My mother was tough, too. She didn't want me to be a journalist. But I know you won't let her stop you. Anyway... what harm are some old pictures going to do? It's like she doesn't trust your judgement, or something."

"Yeah..." The girl was frowning, but thinking about it.

"Come on," Alex suggested, gesturing towards the back door and placing the prints back in the box. She palmed the one picture with Priebke to slip into her purse. "We've got ninety minutes to have a quick peek. Cool old stuff from the Fifties? Are you kidding? We need to check this out!"

Eloise looked a little hesitant, but smiled, eager to please, then nodded energetically. "Okay!"

68.

Cortez drove Brennan back into town, stopping at a late-night pharmacy so that the American could buy a pay-as-you-go phone. They'd waited, the car parked at the curb, until he'd gotten through to his colleague.

"Peacock."

"I'm back. But my cover is blown and this line is probably hot. We need to reassess."

"Twenty minutes," Murray had replied before hanging up.

Cortez frowned. "That's it?"

"We have a pre-arranged muster point on the edge of the city, arranged in case communications are compromised. If they knew who I was from early on, the line at the hotel was almost certainly hot, which meant we couldn't discuss the locale."

The elderly man looked concerned. "Then... we must part company. I have maintained a cover here for five decades by changing my name and reinventing my past. Anyone who remembered my brother is long dead or gone from here. If I am identified as working with you... well... I have grandchildren now myself, Mr. Brennan."

"Okay, message understood." Brennan undid his safety belt and grasped the door handle. Then he had a thought. "One question: who from the UK tipped you off about me?"

The old man looked wary. "Please... you know I cannot..."

"Was it Martin Weiss?"

The man's expression barely flinched.... but it was enough. "As I said..."

"Uh huh. I'll tell Martin you said hello the next time I see him. After I sock him in the teeth."

The older man shrugged. "Not that I know who you are talking about... but someone such as this might have said something about expecting you to react this way. I'm supposed to pass along apologies."

"Duly noted." Brennan opened the car door and got out. "I can call a cab from here. Thank you, Simon."

"Good luck, Mr. Brennan. Don't trust anyone here. Most of the city is oblivious to all of this; but the roots of evil run deep."

69.

Alex stood nervously by the open pocket-door of the walk-in closet, casting furtive glances over her shoulder and listening for anyone coming. The girl was rummaging through a chest of drawers. She reached far into the back and pulled out an inch-thick photo album.

"Here it is! My mother takes it out sometimes when she's in here on her own. If I walk in, she hides it. Sometimes, she cries. I think it's because she misses my grandparents."

Alex took the book into the bedroom and laid it on the bed. She began to flick through the pages. The early photos were ancient; pre-war images of a child in toddler wear, blurry black and whites from the old country.

There was nothing from the war years, it seemed, the images abruptly skipping ahead to their house in Bariloche. Family gatherings, birthday parties, trips...

Priebke was in half of them, the same woman with him in each case.

They weren't just associates, Alex realized. Kurt Schmidt had been one of Priebke's closest friends, which meant he knew exactly who he was.

What he was.

Alex kept flicking through the pictures, looking for any landmarks that might stand out, anything that could connect them to the present day. There was nothing, just a seemingly endless supply of casual shots....

She turned the page. There was only one photo behind the protective plastic cover, a piece of land being excavated by equipment. It was surrounded by sandy foothills, the trees long gone.

"Where's this?"

The girl shrugged. "I don't know. I saw it once before, the first time I got a chance to sneak a look at the book."

Alex pulled back the sheet of clingy plastic film and removed the print. On the back, the same pencil hand had inscribed, "Nueva Esperanza, July, 1966."

"Huh. Ring any bells?"

The girl nodded. "With the name it does, of course! That is Dr. Verde's research community, south of the city."

"Dr... Gabriel Verde? The Nobel Prize nominee? That guy?"

The girl nodded, wide eyed and enthusiastic.

That had to be it, Alex thought. If it had just been the Nazi connection that might still have been coincidence, as unlikely as it seemed. But a leading researcher within spitting distance of Bariloche? It had to be why Brennan was there.

She flicked through the rest of the book but nothing else caught her eye. On the back page, Alex noticed the paper design on the back cover was peeling slightly at the corner. She tugged at it gently.

"Oh! I don't think you should do that..." The girl warned. "You might tear it, and my mother is..."

Downstairs, they heard the jingle of the front doorbell. The girl's eyes widened. She got up quickly and jogged to the upper landing to look over the bannister.

Alex quickly pulled back the adhesive sheet. Behind it, an eight-by-five inch black and white had been secreted away. The young man in the wedding photo was definitely an earlier version of the girl's grandfather. He was wearing a full Gestapo Officer's uniform, his peaked hat with death's head logo under his arm.

The girl ran back into the room. Alex pushed the sheet back down and handed her the book. "I wasn't here," she said. She walked out of the bedroom, hugging the wall so that she couldn't be seen from the landing below and slipping into her own room.

"Eloise!" Mrs. Schmidt called out. "We're home!"

Alex closed the door to her room and quickly packed her overnight case. Keeping the room at the hotel had proven a wise choice; it was eleven o'clock, too late to check out Verde's compound.

But she'd already decided that the second Mrs. Schmidt was out of her line-of-sight, she was heading for the front door.

70.

NUEVA ESPERANZA

Oct. 27, 2020

The two men Michael Wolf brought to the meeting were both large, thick-necked, with arms the size of a normal man's thighs and bulges in their jackets. The obvious intent was to look intimidating.

If Dr. Gabriel Verde was nervous, he wasn't sharing that fact with anyone. Instead, he sat on a wrought-iron bench in the back garden of his palatial home, amidst the wildflowers, a glass of mineral water held aloft in a champagne flute.

Wolf sat on the bench opposite him, his two guards hovering menacingly nearby, casting hard stares at staff who ventured near.

"I must admit, Gabriel, I expected you to receive me somewhat more formally than this. A conference room, perhaps. An office where the chairs fronting the desk are three inches lower than the host's."

Verde smiled genially. "You always have that way about you, Michael, as if you expect us to compete for something every time we meet. Can't I just schedule this somewhere comfortable precisely because I enjoy your company?"

Wolf wasn't sure what the researcher was up to. He'd always admired Verde, felt a genuine sense of jealousy towards his achievements. Wolf had more money, but Verde was rich and powerful in his own right and admired globally to boot. If people understood his true nature?

"You haven't been sending in regular reports for the last six months, now. I've sent intermediaries and we've asked politely for you to fill us in. But there's been next to nothing. And then, within spitting distance of our planned annual meeting, you announce you are closing your community's gates for an entire year. Naturally... we are intrigued. Perplexed, as the research you're performing for us should not require any such steps."

Verde sighed a little, as he might when talking to an impertinent child who doesn't know better. "Michael, Michael... you worry too much, my friend. The time lock is a dramatic move, I'll warrant, but it's the genetic research equivalent to what software companies — you have several, I believe — call a 'code crunch.' For a year, my people will be focused on nothing save the work. We are this close, I tell you..." He held his thumb and forefinger a centimeter apart.

"The code that was intercepted in London... Our intelligence sources indicate it may have been a bioweapon."

Verde scoffed at the notion. "Preposterous! The scientist who tried to steal it was trying to sell a method of genetic recombination that is essential to the project but has no real value outside of human cloning. As a weapon? Absurd."

Wolf studied the other man, his oversized valet, Manuel, standing dutifully behind his chair, a sworn protector. Verde seemed sincere; but, like many of Wolf's associates in the International Family, the scientist was supremely confident and always able to seem as such. It made lying convincingly second nature, and therefore his outward statements meant nothing.

They'd spent a great deal of money on Dr. Gabriel Verde, with the intent of rewriting history. The timing was critical, with the U.S. vote only days away and the global political stage set.

Wolf rose. "Two weeks, Gabriel."

Verde swept a hand in a wide arc. "You're not going to stay a while for the grand tour?"

"Two weeks," Wolf repeated as he rose. "We expect to see a functioning example in two weeks."

He didn't need to tell Verde what would happen if he failed them.

Wolf departed with his two guards.

A few moments later, Peter Bruner sidled up to the bench and sat down next to his friend. "They are going to be incensed when they discover what you've really been spending their money on after all these years. If it wasn't for your global reputation as a healer, they'd have been all over us long before now."

Verde smiled placidly. "It does not matter. In two weeks, the doors to Nueva Esperanza will already be closed. By then, it will be too late."

71.

Alex stared at the local street map. She'd parked the rental car by the side of the road just outside town, in the village of Dina Huapi.

Nueva Esperanza was another fifteen minutes to the south but the man at the gas station had suggested no one lived there except the compound residents, behind ten-foot walls.

As long as the drive was necessary, she'd decided, she had a chance to try and figure something out. *If I was a Nazi with money and I moved here,* she asked herself, *where would I live?*

The obvious answer had been by the lake. Google Earth had given her an overhead view of a string of large mansions, just outside Bariloche. A search at the local library hadn't produced current owners — that would take a title search of some kind — but it had produced some history, and the fact that several of the properties were once owned by a family from Northern Germany.

Stopping there on the way to Nueva Esperanza had just seemed sensible.

From the road, it appeared a second unmarked street diverged and ran in front of each house, a row of trees protecting them from view from the main highway.

Alex walked down the slope to the road and followed it. A wall appeared almost immediately, made of cinderblock and topped with barbed wire. It looked like something straight out of a POW camp in an old war movie. Above, an old telegraph line still ran next to the modern phone lines.

She tried to peer past the fence, but trees restricted her view of the main house, fifty yards away. She followed the barbed wire for ten feet until reaching a gate, secured with a padlock. Above it, in German and Spanish, a tin sign featured the silhouette of a German Shepherd. "Beware of the Dog. Trespassers will be shot."

Alex stood back a few feet from the fence and followed it with her eyes as it crossed the boundary line to the next property and continued. The entire row of mansions was similarly protected.

"You have got to be kidding me," she muttered. The visual effect of the telegraph line, the warning sign and the camp-style barbed wire fencing was undeniable. So was the age of it all, clearly dating back decades. Whoever lived there had made a show of their strength...

She heard the car before she saw it, dust blocking her view until it was near. The late-model Mercedes pulled up beside her and the passenger window rolled down. "Excuse me..."

Alex smiled back but ignored the man.

"Excuse me... miss," he said in accented English. "This is private property."

Alex gave him a small wave. "Not to worry. I'm on the road. The road's public, right? I mean, it has stop signs at either end of it, so..."

He leaned out of the window slightly. He was middle-aged with short grey-silver hair and spectacles. "You should know, madam, that the residents here prefer their privacy. Also, it is hunting season. You... may not be safe if you remain. Without an orange vest, well... you could be easily shot. Accidentally."

Alex felt her heart pounding. The man looked back and then forward, ahead of their car again, as if checking to see if anyone else was around. "I... I'll just be getting back to my car, then," she said.

"A very good idea."

"You have a lovely town," she offered as she walked back towards the slope.

The man smiled curtly. The Mercedes pulled away, dust and stones kicking up from the back tires.

Alex made her way back up the hill, keeping her eyes on the other vehicle until it was out of sight. At the top, she paused at the tree line to look back at the tops of the mansions, a sense of dread enveloping her.

72.

THEN

DINA HUAPI

April 5, 1955

Juan Peron, Argentina's undisputed President, paced across the expansive rear balcony of the lakeside mansion, his hands clasped behind his back. He leaned forward as he walked back and forth, his face a mask of irritation.

He strode over to Skorzeny, who sat beside the grand piano. He stopped and raised a finger, as if to say something, then thought better of it, perhaps figuring his anger would get the better of him, and continued pacing.

After another two minutes of watching the leader of the nation mutter and splutter to himself, Skorzeny asked, "Mr. President... perhaps I can put your mind at ease. Please... sit with me and have a drink."

Peron strode over to him. He leaned in until his nose was just a few inches from the German's. "Do you know what I was told yesterday? It was suggested to me that Adolf Hitler was in my country. That he lived, after the war, right here in Dina Huapi. That it might even have been this very house."

Skorzeny scoffed and waved a hand around them. "Please. The chandelier isn't even crystal. Hitler wouldn't have housed his dog in this place."

Peron looked sideways quickly, again tempering his own response. "I swear, Skorzeny, you treat this like it's a joke." He turned back to the man, red-faced. "But you and your people have caused me nothing but trouble."

"We helped you gain and maintain your power," Skorzeny said.

"You were not needed! And you threaten it daily with public ridicule. If it isn't over your mere presence and the international embarrassment, it is one of the many expensive projects. The worst is this... this ridiculous nuclear gambit. I have staked so much on your man Richter, and he has produced nothing!"

In reality, Skorzeny felt nothing for the man. He was a pawn, to be used. But he was an important one, protecting their back line via the largesse he and his fellow South American leaders had shown to the former leaders of the Third Reich. Peron still had major influence, even as his own mercurial nature led to increased speculation the military might overthrow him.

"Richter is working as hard as he can but the pressure you've put him under..."

"I'VE PUT HIM UNDER!" Peron thundered. "I'VE... The man promised to have a working Tokamak reactor on the island by Nineteen Fifty. That was five years and fifty million dollars ago. Where is my money, Skorzeny? What did he do with it if he didn't give us our reactor?"

Most of the money had been siphoned off to supply bribes to officials globally, Skorzeny knew, although some of it was going to the new "re-education" project in the Chilean jungle. That was expected to take several years to complete. The site included extensive weapons storage bunkers. "Nuclear technology is incredibly expensive, and your government's efforts to provide him with the heavy water facility..."

Peron leaned back in the wingback chair, looking deflated. It was rare, Skorzeny thought, to see him so downcast. "You are only guests here so long as I wish it," Peron finally muttered.

Skorzeny smiled back sweetly. "Of course, Mr. President."

73.

NOW

BRIGHTON, England
Oct. 27, 2020

Charlie worked into the wee hours of the early morning as Martin slept on one of two cots set up in Eli's study. The rabbi had, on Charlie's insistence that nothing would happen immediately, finally taken a break and gone home for the night.

In the quiet of their absence, he'd reached Tim via an encrypted app, then used a backdoor to the collective's FTP server to retrieve his tools: a handful of programs designed to test a server's defenses and probe for backdoors.

After two hours, he'd forced a denial-of-service attack on Wolf's server by flooding it with junk traffic. It had predictably switched to a secondary address which included an insecure admin backdoor account, which he'd discovered looking through the backup site's source code.

A third program had then auto filled the password identity and code string windows a thousand times per minute until the right admin combination — admin and $1234 — had been found.

It was a crude way to get in, but it was quick. After setting up a legitimate account using the admin back door, he ended the Denial of Service attack. Within a few minutes, the company's sites switched back to the main server.

He'd set up a streaming screen capture account on the dark web so that every page he visited was recorded down to the style sheets. But there was so much information it was difficult to figure out where to begin. He'd used the admin search function to try an "immigration" search and it had returned over a thousand files.

He sat back for a moment and thought about it. Charlie was accustomed to knowing his target: code for a game, industrial espionage. He had no idea what could be of any help to them.

"What are we looking at?" a voice asked.

He looked over his shoulder. In the glow of the desk lamp and screen, he hadn't seen Martin wake. "These are Wolf's corporate records, specifically everything they have on immigration. As you can see, the sheer number of files make it something of a 'forest for the trees' situation."

"Can you restrict the search to just files involving the United States?"

"It depends how they're tagged and how the search function works. But I can try." He tapped away at the keys. "All right, that cuts it to five hundred or so."

"What about by date? Anything involving the data hack would've been accessed more recently, I'd think..."

Charlie ran the search again, with the most recently amended and accessed files showing up first. "Okay, that made a big difference. Only ... twenty-three files have been accessed or updated in the last six months."

"Can you copy them without being detected?"

Charlie shrugged. "They're logging all of the server's activity, so there will be a record, without a doubt. It's just a matter of whether it's something they'll be able to notice any time in the near future. Probably not. It depends how much my little stunt to get in bothered them, I suppose."

"Then do it," Martin said. "Maybe once we've gone through this stuff, we'll have a better idea what on Earth Michael Wolf is up to."

74.

Oct. 28, 2020

LONDON

The SAS Tactical Unit was in single file, the men pressed up against the peeling paint of the apartment corridor wall, their numbers trailing down the stairs from the top floor.

On the second floor, Peter Chappell conferred briefly with the unit commander. Like his men, he was a veteran of numerous high-risk takedowns.

"The men are ready, sir." The CO was a short, stocky man with ginger hair and a moustache. "They're using rubber rounds, as you requested, and they've been instructed to take maximum care in securing the package."

The 'package' was Ken Loach. Chappell still couldn't believe the long-time systems analyst was a traitor. But he was the only man other than Grimes and Chappell himself who would've thought Charlie Rich was in Peacehaven, with Joe Brennan's friend Martin Weiss and his ex-partner.

It was the only explanation Chappell could see. But he wasn't about to let the matter sit at that. Loach was going to explain exactly how long he'd been on the IF's payroll, and what they were trying to achieve in South America and America.

And if he didn't talk willingly, they'd work on him until he did.

"I'm going to handle the door knock," Chappell said.

The CO looked worried. "That's... unwise sir, as you are aware. There is a higher risk of gunfire at that particular point than any other during an infiltration. I would be remiss if I didn't mention it."

"Yes, Sergeant Major, thank you for your concern. But I don't believe Ken is likely to harm anyone, except perhaps himself."

"It would serve you well to speak with him immediately after..."

"We're old friends, Sgt. Major. I'll not let the first notice he gets of any of this be a stunner chucked through his front door. All right? My mind is made up on the matter."

The major nodded once, perfunctorily. "Ay ay, sir."

Chappell climbed the staircase, one hand on the rail as he passed the crouched army men. At the door, he rapped on it three times firmly with a knuckle. "Ken! It's Peter."

He waited a few moments before hearing the faint sounds of movement through the door. Then Loach's voice rang through, nervous and tired. "Peter... thank God. Look... I haven't done anything. I promise you."

"We just need to clear a few things up, Ken. If you could come out, we can go back to the office and have a chat."

A pause. Chappell heard the door chain scraping the lock, but he couldn't tell if it was being secured or opened. "What do we have to talk about?" Loach asked. "I told you: I haven't done anything, Peter."

But you were obviously expecting trouble from the way you're reacting. That's not the reaction of an innocent man. "I understand that Ken, but there are procedures when we're concerned about information leaks. We're not accusing you of anything..."

"Then why here? Why didn't you just wait until I came in to work? I've been at MI6 for more than twenty years. We don't show up on someone's door unless they've been a bad boy. But I haven't done anything, I swear to you."

"As I said, we're not accusing....'

"Then you've already made up your mind."

Chappell kept his calm. "If you come out, at least we can talk about it. Or I can come in if you want."

"You'll be alone?"

The major tapped him on the shoulder. "Sir.... that's extremely high risk. He may be looking for a bargaining chip..."

Chappell instinct was to dismiss the man again, but he caught himself before doing so. He thought he knew Ken Loach as a gentle and decent man. But the prior twenty-four hours had put that into doubt.

He decided to trust his instinct. "Okay, I'll come in."

"Are you armed?"

"No."

The door opened a crack, Loach's face appearing, his expression gravely tense. "Who's out there with you."

"There's an SAS unit on the stairs," Chappell admitted. "There was some concern from the directors that you might resist."

The door opened another two inches and Loach grabbed Chappell by the collar, hauling him into the room before slamming the front door behind them. He had an old revolver, a Webley that looked like it dated to the Second World War. The hammer wasn't cocked.

"Christ... Ken, please... put that bloody thing down before you hurt yourself."

"I wasn't going out without a fight."

"Going out? What the bloody hell are you talking about, man? Look, you need to come in. We need to clear this up. Information only you were privy to has wound up with the other side..."

Loach staggered into the adjacent living room and slumped on the sofa, the pistol on his lap. "I know what happens now. I've been framed by somebody, or you wouldn't be here. You wouldn't be here without evidence; but there can't be evidence, because I haven't done anything. That means it's false, which means you won't believe me."

"Oh, pish!" Chappell insisted. "If there's an explanation...."

"Why all of the firepower, Peter? That doesn't look like you just wanted to talk. They came prepare to do me in..."

"You're being ridiculous. Any time there's a leak..."

"But there isn't. At least, not from me."

Chappell tried to phrase his concern carefully. "We've known each other a long time, Ken. If you got into trouble somehow — if you needed money... we can understand how things happen..."

Loach abandoned his blank stare and peered at his old colleague instead. "You don't believe me."

"We were very careful, Ken. The information I gave you on Martin Weiss's friend in Sussex..."

Loach frowned. "What about it?"

"Nobody else knew that but you. We knew that someone was talking to the International Family and had been for a long time. So we gave everyone on the Fifth Floor a different piece of information...."

"I haven't talked to anyone. You can check my mobile records, my phone records. You have complete access to my laptop already."

"Ken, Martin Weiss was in Peacehaven. When our men arrived at the scene we found an unknown male dead, along with a retired detective from the Met with her throat cut."

Loach's expression sank, his mouth dropping open slightly as he realized what Chappell was suggesting. He shook his head, his eyes seeming to bulge slightly behind the thick corrective lenses. "No. No. Peter, I swear to you..."

"Then you need to come down to the office with us right now..."

Loach's eyes darted from the front door back to Chappell, to the window on the far side of the room. His boss could sense him looking for an exit. "There's no alternative right now," he suggested gently. "This is going to happen, Ken, okay? I'm going to call the major in and he'll come in alone, and we'll..."

Loach thrust the barrel of the gun to his own temple. "I'm not going to jail, Peter. I'm sixty-one years old, and I haven't done anything."

Chappell held up both palms, "Ken! Jesus, mate... please... we can resolve this. Don't do anything silly..."

"No. You've already made up your mind. And I know the service; when they go after someone, that's it. That's it for them. That's... that's it for me."

"Just... go easy. Please. Put the gun down on the table."

Loach's hand trembled slightly. He began to draw the barrel away. "You'll get rid of the men in the hall?"

"I can't, but..."

Loach cocked the hammer on the gun.

The front door burst open, the first man through crouching low so that the two SAS officers behind him could get a line-of-sight on Loach.

Before Chappell could react, the older man pulled the trigger, the gunshot deafening, a light red spatter spraying the whitewashed apartment wall.

75.

In his Fifth-Floor office, Archie Grimes listened intently as Peter Chappell explained what had happened.

The deputy director sounded exhausted. "He looked ready to stand down and he was going to put the gun down. And then he cocked the hammer. The CO was listening at the door for any warning signs..."

"They heard the hammer go back and breached."

"And he shot himself."

"Christ."

"I was three feet away from him."

"Are you..."

"As well as can be expected. A forensics team is tearing his place and his online life apart as we speak. I'm going to take the rest of the day off."

"It's Thursday. You should take tomorrow, too, make a long weekend of it to decompress," Grimes suggested. "You'll talk to someone on Monday, of course..."

"I'm aware of the procedure..."

"Hang the procedure," Grimes said. "I'm worried about you, Peter. That's a horrific thing to have experienced, and it helps to speak with a professional."

"Yes. Yes, of course. And I will. Thank you, Archie. This has been a difficult day."

Chappell hung up the call.

Grimes went back to his files on Martin Weiss. He'd used Loach's login credentials a day earlier to retrieve the former policeman's extensive history, but so far none of it was suggesting where he might have fled to with the boy.

He thumbed through a Nineteen Ninety-Six tax return. Like everything else involving Weiss it was nondescript and normal. The man appeared to have no obvious vices, no money problems, nothing to indicate immediate vulnerability. His now-deceased partner at The Met, Ruby Downey, had records almost as immaculate.

Grimes flicked through a sheath of photocopied attachments to the tax document, receipts for donations to the Red Cross, Dr. Barnardo's, a synagogue, a...

He flicked back to the synagogue receipt.

Weiss.

Of course. He's Jewish.

Grimes was a student of history. Brighton had a large Jewish population and was the historical centre of the faith in the United Kingdom. He turned his office chair so that he could use an internet browser and began to search for synagogues and Rabbis in the southern city.

76.

BARILOCHE

The door to the remote cabin swung open, drawing Brennan's attention away from the file he'd been reading on Dr. Gabriel Verde.

Murray Peacock walked in, a shopping bag in one hand and a newspaper in the other. He closed the door, then walked over to the wooden bench in the kitchen and threw the paper onto the tabletop.

"Police Seek Tourist in gay love triangle slaying," the headline suggested. Underneath it were two pictures. The first was of Brett Steel, clipped from a family photo.

The second was Simon's driver's license photo. "They found your other friend last night just north of Bariloche. He'd been strung up from a tree with a rope."

Brennan felt a wave of anger. Cohen had stayed in the town, under threat, for five decades. One meeting with him had proven too dangerous.

He closed his eyes and drew in a slow, controlled breath. "He was an eighty-year-old man."

"You've evidently pissed off the wrong people."

Peacock didn't like Brennan's theory, based on Cortez's help, that the IF was merely an extension of the same fascists who'd underwritten the Second World War. It smacked to him of xenophobia or historical revision. But when he'd finally found them somewhere relatively anonymous to stay and they'd gotten word to Jonah Tarrant, the acting director's wish had been for Brennan to stay on it.

"At least they didn't get an image of you. You won't be able to go anywhere near the hotels though, and whatever description or artist's impression the local law enforcement work with will probably be pretty thorough. You haven't exactly been quiet since we got here."

Brennan knew he needed the logistical help, but the young handler's constant sparring was beginning to annoy him. He kept it to himself. "Did you make the arrangements for Nueva Esperanza?"

"You have press credentials for the event Thursday. Once the official media day is over, they're kicking everyone out who isn't government or on the project. So, whatever you need to find, you've got a window of a few hours. Word is that Verde has something big planned for the press conference, so there will be lots of eyes on the place."

"That's good. The more outsiders, the more crowds and noise, the easier it will be to operate."

"They'll be patting everyone down going in. We should talk about getting your pistol in..."

Brennan shook his head. "Too risky."

"What about my ceramic Sig Sauer?"

"That'll do. Easy to hide, won't set off any alarms."

"Once you're inside, you'll be on your own. I won't be able to help you."

"I'll just have to make do," Brennan said, allowing a touch of wry sarcasm to keep Peacock thinking.

77.

BRIGHTON

Martin was studying Charlie's work, trying to look quizzical and curious even though, in reality, he had no idea what the younger man was up to.

"So this series of charts is..."

"Spreadsheets. These are Excel documents," Charlie explained. "I used them to hunt for corollaries between the different files: matches for street addresses, surnames, cities, dates and so on. And this column here...." he pointed to the far right of the screen, "displays any matches."

Each of the little boxes in the column was divided down the middle, then filled in with details. It appeared to be a string of adult German emigrants on one side, and a list of Christian names, each followed by a number between zero and thirty.

"Okay," Martin said. "Let's suppose I can't see what you've obviously produced here, which is..." He let it hang there, waiting for an answer.

"All of the names on the left side belong to Germans who were placed in concentration camps and work camps between March 1943 and the end of the war. All of the names on the right belong to children, and their age in months, who were taken from those people and placed in an orphanage in Bonn. These two lists, in particular, were flagged by Wolf's people on the same day that Brennan recovered the immigration lists."

Martin frowned. "I don't see how it connects."

"I'm not sure I do either, except for one thing: the director of the orphanage in the files is listed as a "P. Shafer." In one of the other files, which includes a list of payments made by the German government to overseas corporations in 1945, there is a payment listed as going to "Gronau Foreign Aid Society." But there's an old carbon copy of a cheque attached to it, and guess who it's made out to?"

"Let me guess: P. Shafer, I presume?"

"It could be coincidence...except that we know Wolf's people accessed both files at the same time."

Martin sat down in the other wooded chair. "Why on Earth would the Nazis have been funding a foreign aid society? Could you find any record of Shafer after that?"

"I was stuck," Charlie said. "The Gronau Foreign Aid Society is referenced innocently enough in a couple of local history books from Osorno, Chile, in the Nineteen Fifties. Then it just disappears. No Shafer, no Society. No record in Chile, Argentina or Germany that I could find."

Martin shrugged. "Perhaps he died."

Charlie shook his head. He had a self-satisfied little smirk on his face. "In case of utter failure in all other areas... I 'Googled' it. Or, DuckDuckGo, in the case of this particular browser."

"You searched online... and found something?"

"Mr. Shafer, it turns out, was rather famous. He ran a 'religious colony' that ended out being a cult. He was also a notorious child molester, and there are suggestions he worked with the Pinochet government in Chile. They used his jungle camp to torture political dissidents."

Martin looked perplexed. "How would this information be of any use to Wolf now?"

Charlie shook his head. "I have no idea. The rest of this area of his archives is equally weird. It's file-on-file of emigration documents, for people from across Europe. Nearly all are Red Cross travel documents for refugees. Nearly all have the U.S. as the final destination."

"It probably related to ODESSA somehow..." Martin mused.

Charlie waited a moment but when no explanation came asked the question. "ODESSA?"

"An escape network for Nazi officers after the war. It received some help from the Americans because they wanted scientists to have access to travel and to choose them as their final destination. The Vatican was arse-deep in it as well."

"But... what's the connection?" Charlie asked.

"That's the big question. We need Rabbi Eli to make some calls..."

His timing was perfect. The phone on the desk rang and Martin answered it on the first. "Hello?"

"It's me," Rabbi Eli said. "I need you to come over to the house."

That struck Martin as strange. "You all right?"

"I'm fine. I just need you to come over to the house. Okay?"

"Yes, but..." Before Martin could finish the sentence, the Rabbi ended the call.

Martin stared at the receiver for a second. "That... felt off."

"What?"

"He wants us to come over to his house. But he lives on the other side of the city in Withdean."

"So...?"

"My car is probably hot, we know there's someone trying to kill you and we're hiding out at the synagogue for that very reason. Eli's too experienced to have us drive across Brighton."

"You think it's a trap?"

"I think it may be, yes. You'll stay here..."

"No way. If they come here, I'm on my own."

The young man was exasperating sometimes, Martin thought. But he couldn't come along; he was their real target, after all, not either of the older men. He reached into his jacket pocket and withdrew the .32 Colt pistol. "Here: it has seven in the magazine. That means you get seven shots. If you have to shoot someone, you point it directly at the center of their body and you pull the trigger until they stop moving. Understand? Try to be within ten feet if possible."

"Or..."

"Or you will miss. It's not the most accurate gun in the world, but it fits nicely in a coat pocket and has served me well for thirty-five years."

"But... what are you going to take with you? What if..."

"Wits," Martin said. "Well..." He removed the other pistol briefly from his pocket and flashed it to the younger man. "Wits and an abundance of caution." He headed for the door. "Don't worry. I'll be back soon."

78.

Oct. 29, 2020.

NUEVA ESPERANZA

The initial press briefing was being held in the parking lot outside the compound, four rows of metal folding chairs set up for the three-dozen media attending. There were reporters and photographers from around the Globe — but mostly from Argentina, Alex noted as she sat and took in the crowd.

The colony itself seemed about two or three football fields large, a ten-foot wall running around its perimeter with guard boxes at each corner. They weren't allowed in until the briefing was complete, at which point they would be given a short, guided tour, followed by a press conference with Dr. Verde.

She felt her anxiety building. It wasn't the first time she'd had to infiltrate someone else's turf. The last time she'd pursued one of Brennan's assignments, she'd wound up bugging an office in Las Vegas on behalf of a gangster.

But on that occasion, she'd had guidance from an expert computer hacker. This time, she was going in blind. She had her phone — they weren't being confiscated, at least, which gave her a high-res camera for images and a way to send files if necessary.... assuming she could connect somehow. What she didn't have was any idea of what she was specifically looking for.

Something to do with Nazis. Something to do with foreign governments, as Brennan had been in the UK most recently. Beyond that? I have no goddamned idea what I'm doing.

She felt a tap on her shoulder. Then a familiar voice whispered, "You have got to be kidding me."

Alex turned sharply. "Joe!"

"What are you doing here, Alex?" Brennan was wearing a photographer's vest and carrying a digital SLR camera. He already knew the answer, Alex figured, so asking was just professional courtesy. Or a chance to vent his annoyance.

"My guess is that I should be asking you the same thing. The last time we both wound up working the same story..."

"A North Korean spy almost blew up half of New York State. Yeah. But it's been years since I've seen you."

Alex looked unruffled. "Should I be calling ahead now when I work on something involving national security?" she asked. The theory was old-school journalism: throw out enough vague references to what you might know, and eventually someone takes them as knowledge and talks on the subject, confirming it.

But Joe wasn't biting. "Yeah... I know you too well to do the 'backwards confirmation' thing. I thought you were getting out of investigative stuff; didn't you have a TV gig lined up?"

She'd been tapped for a hosting job on a news panel show in D.C. "Yeah... the producer's wife, as it turned out, was working on the North Korean story..."

"You scooped her."

"And she got canned. I left a trail of pissed off colleagues and competitors in my wake on that one."

He shook his head gently. "You really do annoy people, don't you?"

A shrug. "Comes with the territory. Are you going to tell me now what we're looking for in there, or..."

"We? There is no 'we', Alex. You know how this works..."

She stared at him intently, her dark eyes burning a hole through him. "I know that when you were a deniable liability and multiple spy agencies were hunting you, I was the only person on the goddamned PLANET who would bail you out..."

A staff member in a skirt and grasping a clipboard wandered past their seats and Alex leaned back. They both remained quiet until she'd passed. "I know that I saved your life, more than once," she continued. "You owe me, goddamn it!"

He kept his voice calm and level. "Again: that's not how this works. I have an objective. I pursue that. I don't make the decisions. And even if I did, you're persona non grata with Jonah and the rest of the policy wonks at Langley, you know that."

"Yes, because you've always cared SO deeply about what management has to say. I have the same press access as you. The only difference is, I'm actually a member of the press. No amount of digging is going to suggest to them they should toss my ass out on my ear. You, on the other hand..."

"Alex..."

"We can work together or separately. But I guarantee you, it will go better if we work together," she said.

Before he could answer, a woman strode up to the lectern near the parking lot's perimeter, facing the press. "Ladies and gentlemen, thank you very much for coming today. As you're aware, the contents of today's tour are embargoed until Monday, four days from now. Please restrict any stories filed to the backgrounder and the press conference itself." She repeated the comments in Spanish.

A few of the photographers tested their equipment, snapping pictures as she spoke. "Of course, once we're inside all photography and video will be forbidden until the press conference. If you could concentrate on getting your images at the start of the address, Dr. Verde would be most grateful."

Joe turned back to Alex and whispered, "Do you have any idea why I'm here, or are you just trolling for an easy story."

"We're in Argentina. That takes it out of the realm of 'easy' right there. But... yeah, I've had a few hints." Alex checked their perimeter again for listeners. "For one, I wouldn't be completely surprised if a few of these people like to goose-step in their spare time."

He closed his eyes momentarily, his expression strained. "Alex.... Jesus Christ... who have you been talking to? These people... they're not play-acting 'fascist'. They've already killed one of their own and a senior citizen who made the mistake of helping me. If they have even a hint that you're here because you think some weird Nazi shit is going down, you will disappear. I don't mean they'll just kill you. I mean they'll make sure we never find you."

"Then... you'd better make sure you keep an eye on me, or who knows what I'm liable to say or do."

His eyes narrowed and he peered at her gravely. "You really are a piece of work sometimes."

"Takes one to know one."

"Do I at least get the privilege of knowing how you found me?"

She shrugged again. "Trade secret."

At the podium, the spokesperson was finishing up the lengthy list of rules. "Now, as soon as I conclude, we're going to have everyone line up at the gate. We will need to search any bags, of course, as there is a long prohibited contraband list for the community.... although we don't expect that to be an issue with members of the press."

"Ready?" Alex asked.

"You drive me crazy, you know that."

At the podium, the woman put her notes down and swung an arm wide towards the compound. "Then all that remains is for me to welcome you all to Nueva Esperanza: new hope, in a world that desperately needs it.

79.

DUBUQUE, Iowa

The debate had been back and forth for ninety minutes, two men in suits under the glare of television floodlights. Misner was known for his oratorical skills, his ability to cut through bafflegab and bull to get to the point.

But his competition, the President, was a showman, and no slouch at using the spotlight to denigrate his opponents. He'd left the matter of growing civil unrest to the end of the debate. In fact, he'd ignored it so completely that Misner had begun to think it might pass unremarked.

No such luck. The President gestured his way with an outstretched palm. "This young man would have you believe he's the best we can do in this country," he said. "He comes out, week after week, saying he wants Americans to 'get along', then takes a big dump all over our country with all the things he thinks we need to do better."

"Another gross mischaracterization," Misner interrupted. "Is that all you can do?"

"Quiet, sonny, you'll get your chance. He puts himself out there as this man of the people, the ex-military success story. But you go to his rallies, and it looks like the protests. It looks like the protests in Portland and Chicago and Wisconsin. It's people fighting, it's people trying to tear down our way of life. And for what? Why doesn't he just come out and condemn all of them. They're animals, and he likes that."

"Time, Mr. President," the moderator advised.

The president ignored the moderator and kept talking. "These people, they worship the guy. Nobody smart can figure out why. I sure can't and people, they think I'm pretty smart. But they – it's true! They worship the guy. And all he has to do is tell them all to get lost. All he has to do is say 'I disavow these violent criminals. But he doesn't. And that's the guy..."

"Mr. President... I'll have to ask..." The moderator began.

"That's the guy you want running the country?"

"Mr. President... please. Mr. Misner, you have three minutes for your rebuttal."

He'd prepared a response meticulously. He'd needed it to convince Stuart; if his best friend was worried, Misner knew, then the perception of him as endorsing or allowing the violence was serious, and potentially a problem at the polls. He'd been running for president in his own mind since he was eighteen, since deciding he could offer something more than the norm. He'd spent two decades examining politics, public policy and the administrative skills needed to get things done in Washington.

But when the question came, he decided it was better to speak from conviction. "My opponent is right to be concerned," he began. "Anytime Americans are physically clashing with other Americans, we need to step back and figure out why. But I've never believed that the answer to a problem is to ignore it or denigrate it, as he does. It's to address it. It's to figure out why this divide exists and to bridge it: not with rejection and mockery and condemnation, but with respect."

The hot lights were beating down upon them but for a few moments, Misner found himself enervated, his confidence making it seem as if they weren't even there.

"There will always be a small number of troubled, unhealthy individuals who cannot see past their emotional shortcomings, people who will cling to any belief or ideology then use it as an excuse for violence. But that's not what most of America's conflict is about. Over twenty years, bad actors – people with financial or power motives – have stirred up the divisions in this country.

"They've used the internet's massive reach to lie to each other, to deceive one another and to spread that sentiment to the rest of the public. They have turned us against one another. And that has to end. We don't do that by rejecting people; we don't do that by "disavowing" them. We do it by showing we actually care. By sitting down with them and hearing their stories. By reaching across the aisle…"

"Time, Mr. Misner."

"… and showing that even when someone is wrong, we don't' have to hold our all-too-human fallibility against one another. By working together, not dividing. So no: I won't disavow any of my fellow Americans. But I will listen to them and, with their help, fix what this country has become."

A smattering of applause broke out in the TV audience. The moderator pivoted sharply. "Quiet, please!" They'd agreed to remain neutral and it probably breached that rule.

Misner didn't plan to hold it against them.

80.

BRIGHTON

Rabbi Eli's four-bedroom house in Withdean was behind an old pale brick wall, wisteria creeping over the arched gate that led into his front yard. Martin hadn't been there in ages, not since before both men lost their wives. How long had it been? Ten years, at least.

He parked half a block away and walked up the hilly sidewalk, keeping an eye on the neighbouring homes for signs of activity, for anyone who might be in harm's way or able to alert police if things went sideways.

After making sure the road was clear, he pulled the pistol from his pocket and chambered a round, then secured it in the same spot. With hands in both coat pockets he was just another pedestrian; but he was ready for what he expected would be trouble.

Eli's call had been all wrong. Even his tone had been off, probably deliberately. It wouldn't be MI5 or MI6, of that he was certain. The latter shied away from domestic operations even when a larger international target was involved and the former would have brought multiple teams, multiple men, sent people directly to the synagogue.

No, this was a trap, an attempt to bait him out of cover and remove him from the equation. He wondered how they'd connected him with Eli; the Rabbi had worked for the MOSSAD for nearly sixty years, so it was possible they'd had him under surveillance all along.

But why not just take all three of them at the synagogue? That seemed a tactical decision.

A car passed but paid him no attention. The neighbourhood road wasn't busy, with most people at work on a Thursday afternoon. He stopped at the gate to the house next to Eli's. There were no cars visible outside although he supposed they might be retirees. Martin checked both directions for curious eyes again; then, once sure it was clear, he opened the gate and walked into the gravel parking area.

He went directly to the front of the house and followed the path that led to the front door. It kept going to the other side of the house and Martin followed it until it reached the gate to the back garden. He unlatched it, entered, then latched it behind him.

At the backdoor to the kitchen, he peered in through the window, checking for signs of life again. Seeing none, he made his way across the back of the house. At the French doors to the living room, he paused and checked inside once more, continuing once satisfied to the far hedge.

Martin pulled the hedge branches aside just enough to create a small hole, allowing him an angled view of the back of Eli's house. There were no signs of intruders or motion, no guards making it obvious something was wrong.

They would be cautious, he knew. They would have Eli answer the front door as if everything was fine and get him quietly inside before they executed both men. Guards outside would frighten him off. If Peacehaven was an example to go by, the IF didn't have scores of local operatives at their disposal, which likely meant a limited team of two or three men.

He needed a distraction: something to draw them out and separate them. His eyes flitted back to the yard and scanned it for anything useful. There was an old apple tree, a cherry tree with a rotting old treehouse in it, and Eli's rock garden.

Martin followed the hedge line until he was between the two houses. He pushed his way through the thick foliage, hoping the noise wasn't enough to penetrate the home's walls and alert anyone.

He scurried to the base of Eli's house, on the back-right corner, adjacent to the kitchen side door. He looked down the line of the building; it had the same French doors and steps halfway along as the home next door. He stayed low, slipping beneath the kitchen window, his aging knees aching from the awkward position.

At the edge of the French doors, he used the visible angle into the room to look for something reflective. But there was nothing, no way to check who was on the other side of the room from his hidden position. He poked his head slowly and gradually around the corner.

The place was a mess, as if turned over in a search. There were two men, both dressed casually. One was standing at the end of the narrow wall that divided the kitchen from the front hallway, holding a gun on Eli, who had eyes on the front door.

The other man sat on the sofa, pistol on the coffee table in front of him.

He's watching his friend when he should be watching their six.

Martin crept backwards a few feet until he was on the lawn, next to the rock garden. Keeping his eyes on the French doors throughout, he reached down and felt around in the dirt until he found a roundish rock, slightly bigger than a golf ball. He pocketed it, then snuck back to his spot by the edge of the window and made sure the man's attention remained diverted. Martin scurried across the patio to the other side of the house.

If his memory of the layout was correct....

Halfway along the north-side wall was a small window to the main floor half-bathroom. Ten feet above it was the window to the upstairs guest bedroom. The bathroom window was already open a crack, and Martin pushed it up gently.

The window frame creaked from warping, the noise short and sharp like nails on a chalkboard. He stopped, drawing in his breath sharply and holding it, waiting for the sound of anyone checking it out.

He let five seconds pass, then ten more.

Martin reached up again, pushing more gently this time, the window sliding up.

He left it open and moved to the front corner of the house. They'd be expecting him to ring the bell, come to the front door. He intended on obliging. But the timing had to be perfect.

He walked to the front door and rang the bell, then ran back around the corner of the house to the bathroom window. He waited for the sound of the front door being opened, then heaved the round stone at the upper bedroom window, shattering the pane.

Martin reached up and pulled himself through the bathroom window, his joints aching. He got up off the floor, pistol in hand, and made his way to the bathroom door.

81.

The back doorbell to the synagogue rang five minutes after Martin had left.

Charlie wasn't sure what to do at first. There was no way of checking who it was without opening the door. Instead, he stood there for a minute and stared at it, waiting for someone to ring the bell once more. He knew it wouldn't change his options, but thought perhaps the extra time required would give him an idea.

Instead, the phone rang in the office, twenty yards away. He backtracked to the entrance, just inside the main door to the synagogue proper. On top of the desk, the first clear button on the multi-line office phone was flashing. He gave the back door one more look to make sure the bar across it was lowered and the large deadbolt was in place, then headed over to the desk.

"Hello?"

"Charlie? Archibald Grimes. I'm a friend of Rabbi Eli and Martin. He wanted me to come and keep an eye on you. He said something about going over to Eli's and he knows I live down the road..."

He sounded bored, almost put out. "How do you know Martin?"

"I used to be a policeman with him, in London, years ago. I'm retired now. But a friend in need is a friend indeed... even when he hasn't called you in three years."

It was the same refrain he'd heard from Ruby. But... "I don't think he'd want me talking to anyone until I see him again," Charlie said. "Can you come back later?"

"He specifically said he needed me to look after you, so... no. I can't. I'm at the back door, actually..."

"I'm not certain..."

"Charlie, I'm eighty-two years old. I am tired. I'm supposed to be at my bridge club now having lunch and losing to the Mendelbaums at Majeure Cinquieme ... would you please open the bloody door?"

"Hang on." He put the phone down beside the cradle.

Charlie walked back over to the door and stared at the heavy bar and deadbolt. He felt frustrated, obtuse. A third option wasn't presenting itself. The man seemed utterly irritated by the fact that there was even a debate, and he sounded old; it wasn't as if anyone was going to send an eighty-year-old hitman after him.

He lifted the bar to one side and unlocked the deadbolt.

82.

The men had been waiting for Eli when he'd arrived home that morning.

He hadn't wanted to leave the synagogue, but he had a cat to feed and a household of chores and responsibilities to take care of.

True, it was just him now; his wife Chandra had died a decade earlier and the boys were in America. But he took pride in being self-sufficient even as he reached his eighty-fourth year. And there had been no reason to suspect his cover was compromised or his guests followed.

They'd hit him with a blackjack. When he'd awoken, his hands bound together as he lay sideways on the sofa, he realized they'd tossed the house. Furnishings and fixtures were turned over, cushions torn open, books knocked off the wall shelves into piles on the carpet below. One of the men had handed him a phone and told him to call the synagogue, to get Martin over to the house. They hadn't asked about Charlie.

Eli had a pistol in his bedroom, but he knew it would do him no good. The plastic restraint on his wrists was likely steel-reinforced and unbreakable. After he'd made the call, they'd hurried him to the end of the front hallway, to bait the trap.

And then the doorbell rang.

The man behind him was tall and thin, with a sharp, narrow face and unruly brown hair. He poked him in the back with the pistol barrel. "Answer it. Get him inside and into the living room."

They were clearly planning on ambushing his friend. Martin would follow Eli into the other room and the man in the kitchen doorway would step behind him and put a bullet into the back of the former policeman's head before he knew what had hit him.

Eli couldn't allow that to happen. He intended on opening the door and warning Martin right away. He knew the man would probably shoot him in the back of the head. But he had lived a long life, one in which he was content.

He walked down the hall and opened the door.

There was no one there.

From somewhere upstairs, he heard a crashing sound, like glass breaking.

The other man stepped out of the living room and came to investigate. His watery, pale blue eyes danced around as he searched for a sign of trouble. He nodded to his friend. "Go. I'll keep an eye on him."

His partner went up the stairs, pistol at the ready.

"The easier your friend is to deal with, the better this will go for..." He didn't get a chance to finish the sentence. Martin came up behind him silently, emerging from the hallway near the bathroom door. He looped one arm around his captor's neck, the man's carotid wedged tight by the crook of his elbow, his right hand grasping the man's wrist in the same precise movement and slapping it backwards, against his own knee, the gun bouncing off the hall carpet.

The man gasped for air and threw his weight backwards, shoving them both into the wall as Martin tried to choke the air out of him. Martin kept his grip and composure, slipping his free hand under and around the man's right shoulder, locking the choke hold in place and restricting his motion.

The gunman struggled frantically, throwing them both sideways onto the ground. Martin held on tight, ignoring the pain in his joints from the fall. The man was pushing hard, trying desperately to get out of the hold. His strength began to ebb, the color of his face turning a deep purple as he asphyxiated. He relaxed, lost consciousness and stopped fighting.

Martin held the choke hold for several more seconds, ensuring the man was out. He reached into his pocket for the Colt .32. But the pocket was empty.

I've dropped it somewhere. Probably when climbing through the window.

He looked around the prone man's body for his gun. The second gunman's footsteps came pounding down the stairs, his gun hand extended, Martin caught cold.

The gunshot was an explosive crack, the tight confines accentuating the booming recoil. Martin looked down at his own chest instinctively in the split second before realizing that he was fine. He looked over at Eli, lying on his side, where he'd scrambled to grab the other gun.

On the stairs, the second gunman was pawing at his mouth with one hand, his gun hand having dropped limply to his side. The bullet had gone directly through the man's open mouth, blowing a hole through the back of his skull. He pawed at it for a second more before dropping to his knees and sliding, lifeless, to the bottom of the stairs.

Eli dropped his head and breathed a deep sigh of relief.

The first man began to stir. Martin reached down and grasped him around the head, using the man's chin for a grip. He yanked and twisted with all his strength, the man's neck breaking.

Martin staggered to his feet, drained. He moved to his friends' side and helped the octogenarian get up.

"I'm sorry," Martin said. "I'm so sorry we brought this to your door."

Eli hugged him, just for a moment. He lingered with one arm around his friend's shoulder. "This is on no one but those fascist bastards. And don't you ever forget it."

Martin frowned. "I don't understand. Why just two men and why here? Why not back..." He realized the implication immediately. "Charlie. They weren't coming after me. They were getting me out of the way."

"We have to hurry," Eli said. "You drive."

"You stay here and call the police," Martin insisted. "You stopped two burglars in a tragic home invasion."

"Don't be foolish! You need all the help..."

"I've asked too much already," Martin said, heading out the ajar front door. "Call the police, lock the doors and keep your head down.

83.

BRIGHTON

The man at the door had been, as he'd suggested, extremely old.

Charlie felt a comforting warmth when he invited Archie Grimes inside; he'd never been a fighter, but he was quite sure that if the need arose, he could beat up an octogenarian.

And the man seemed so amiable, reminding him immediately of someone's grandfather.

"Thank you, I suppose," Charlie said. "That's the least I can offer. Oh..." He looked back over his shoulder. "That and a cup of tea, perhaps? There's a kettle in the office."

Grimes nodded politely. "That would be rather nice, thank you."

The boy was older than he'd expected. They'd made him sound like a juvenile delinquent, but he was clearly in his twenties, stubble from two days without a shave beginning to illustrate the fact. That would make things easier.

But first, he needed to find out what the boy had uncovered and what the Americans knew about the International Family. The code itself wouldn't have been enough; even Michael Wolf, whose father had recruited Grimes decades earlier and who was funding Verde's research, had been puzzled by its content. But Grimes had helped plan and institute operations for MI6 for four decades; he knew the Americans would go to the source. Their South American contacts had already flushed out one fly in the ointment, albeit without squashing him in the process.

He followed Charlie to the office. "I'll just get the kettle boiling," the young man suggested. He went over to a sideboard and plugged the pot in. "I've been trying to kill time while Martin's gone by..." Charlie stopped himself. "Never mind. I probably shouldn't get into the details."

Grimes gave him a perfunctory wave. "Not to worry. I'm old enough that it's all largely irrelevant to me. Besides, he gave me the gist..."

"Oh! All right then." The kettle began to rattle and Charlie unplugged it, then poured the boiling water into the adjacent teapot. "I'll just give it a minute."

"Three, at least," Grimes said. "One can't steep tea in under three minutes."

Charlie smiled and nodded politely. "Fine."

"You must let me in on what he's got you doing now; knowing Martin, it's something nefarious."

Charlie nodded. "Yeah...well... nefarious might be stretching it. I mean, I'm just poking around. I'm not stealing anything."

Grimes peered at him. *Where would he be...* "Wolf's company, would be my guess?"

"Exactly. And so far, it's just a bunch of archive material they've been collecting and accessing. Old files from the Red Cross, from U.S immigration, army documents from the post-Second World War period."

"The wee days of my youth," Grimes said. "I was born before the war ended, you know!"

Charlie's eyebrows rose in surprise. "I suppose... now that you mention it the math adds up. You have lived a long time, haven't you, Mr. Grimes!" He lifted the tea pot and filled one of the two cups. "Milk?"

"Just a spot..."

Charlie handed him the cup and saucer. "There you are."

"I must say, now that you mention the war, you've gone and made me all nostalgic. Can you show me some of them?"

The young man brightened up. *He likes to show off what he can do,* Grimes thought.

"Certainly!" Charlie rounded the desk. Grimes checked its contents quickly for anything that could be used as a weapon. Letter openers could be particularly dangerous. But it was just a PC, a desk calendar, a Newton's Cradle desk toy, some photos, probably the Rabbi's grandchildren.

Charlie sat down in front of the computer. "Here: come look at this."

Grimes walked over and stood behind the seated lad. "That looks like U.S. Army, if I'm not mistaken..." It was a ration card issued to a Polish man living in Vienna, with a U.S. army stamp. "And it's all this sort of thing? Is there any rhyme or reason to it?"

"We think so, yes." Charlie pulled up the spreadsheets. "All of the names in the first column are resettlements from countries liberated by Soviet forces and that had existing puppet Fascist governments. All of the locations in the second column are where they ended up living, in America.

"And all of the locations in America match up with sites most heavily targeted for rioting or protests in the troubles they've been having before the election."

"I see," Grimes said, leaning over the young man's shoulder to study the screen. "And... the code. Did they get any further in figuring that out? Martin sounded quite perplexed." Grimes leaned back so that he was out of Charlie's line of sight once more. He reached into his pocket and silently drew the Smith & Wesson pistol, screwing the suppressor onto its threaded barrel.

"I don't think so," Charlie said. "If I'm honest, Martin hasn't been keeping me updated. I don't really blame him. I kind of bolloxed all of this up for everyone to begin with..."

"Oh, don't blame yourself," Grimes said, raising the pistol and pointing it at the back of the boy's skull. "In the end, I'm sure you didn't mean any harm. "

84.

NUEVA ESPERANZA

They led the throng of forty or so media through the steel main gate, down a short road. Malone studied their surroundings, peering between the other bodies in the walking group.

The place was entirely surrounded by ten-foot walls, guard towers at each corner. The distance to the far corner suggested it was the size of a pair of football pitches square. Fifty feet past the gate, a portico led them through a second interior wall, frontage to a series of offices and other rooms.

As they passed into the square beyond, Malone realized the property was divided into increasingly smaller squares within one another, although the main office block featured a pair of wide openings to the north and east, creating a mazy street system.

Past the main block, the interior central square was slightly raised, reached by five broad, flat marble steps, a five-thousand-square-foot rectangle. On its north and south sides, the lower floor of offices had been replaced by Romanesque pillars, allowing people in the main complex to see into the area.

At the front of the tour, the public relations flak was walking and talking. "Dr. Verde designed Nueva Esperanza to be pragmatic and functional, maximizing indoor working space whilst also maintaining as many outdoor common areas as possible. With more than four hundred volunteers working on his latest project and nearly six hundred staff, free time is at a premium. Therefore, it was important that the compound become a true community. And, I'd say that if you look around at the smiling faces of our wonderful staff, you'd agree he made the right choice."

The press crew looked ragged and experienced, Alex thought. These weren't kids right out of j-school or college, naively taking what they were being told on face value; everyone knew the tour guide's job was to paint the place in an impeccable light while keeping them moving, so that questions were held until later and minimized. From there, they would doubtless go directly to a press conference – given some time to mingle, perhaps, with the obligatory spread of free food to continue the process of putting the reporters at ease. As soon as most had eaten something and before they could begin fomenting conspiracy theories amongst one another, she would roll out the main event, the legendary geneticist.

Under any other circumstance, Malone would have tuned most of it out, actively listening only for snippets that were out of place, that indicated an angle of concern for readers even as she took her own notes on the place and studied it. But these weren't normal circumstances; she let her digital recorder run and stayed close to the front of the pack, picking up every word the woman said to go over later. Brennan was three feet to her right, and when she glanced his way it was obvious he was also assessing the place: the purpose to the office layout, where the security might indicate higher importance; the number of workers who weren't smiling but were, instead, studying them, even as they pretended to take part in non-security related activities. Exits, and places where it might be easier to get out of the compound than via the front gate.

"… has been responsible for some of the most groundbreaking research into hereditary illness in human history, leading to his nomination in 2018 for the Nobel Prize. He has dedicated his life to lengthening the life expectancy of others. We're entering the central square now. Unlike the perimeter walls, which contain administrative offices, here they contain the living quarters for our extended family, as well as recreation facilities, a conference hall and a dining room. As we walk to the central square, you'll notice immediately the central tower, where our safety consultants have their offices and have a three-hundred-and-sixty-degree view of the property…"

"Yeah, and some dude with a sniper rifle, I'm betting," Malone muttered to Brennan.

"Shhh."

The guide turned and walked backwards for a few steps. "As we enter the central community square, you'll see we've set up folding chairs for everyone and there is a buffet table with a full lunch selection for you, so that everyone can enjoy the news conference on a full stomach."

A murmur of appreciation went through the group. Malone sighed inwardly. Her media colleagues were so predictable it made her head hurt.

The group walked up the broad, flat marble steps. "You are welcome to speak with any of the staff attending the press conference but we would ask that you limit your questions to those individuals and not interfere or otherwise bother the other residents. We've invited thirty-six workers from a selection of backgrounds and ages..."

They were laying on the "normalization" routine pretty thickly given Verde's impeccable record. She'd called her editor at the magazine and, after giving him five minutes to remind her what an ungrateful, unethical shrew she was, she'd had him send her as much intel on the good doctor as possible.

An evening poring over it had revealed very little that wasn't obvious; he was an orphan, adopted from a group home in Bahia Blanca. He'd been accepted on a poverty relief scholarship to university at the age of fifteen, received his master's in human biology by eighteen and his doctorate by twenty. Fifty years later, he was rich, beloved for his role in saving lives, and otherwise a mystery.

Brennan stopped walking. They were standing behind the last row of folding chairs as the other media streamed over to the buffet. He looked around at the impressive surroundings. "Not what I was expecting."

"Which was?" Malone asked.

"Something more... I don't know... temporary? This is decades of building a community, a small town, in effect. They can call it a compound, but this isn't some temporary workspace. He could be hiding a small army in this place..."

Malone nodded towards one of the burly plainclothes security standing at the perimeter of the square. "They might, at that."

"Yeah… just because he could, that doesn't mean he is," Brennan said. "This place looks professional. It looks like he's exactly who he says he is. I don't see any stormtrooper types, or glaze-eyed cult members. The staff all look young, and cheerful…"

Malone looked around. It was true; the workers were milling about with the media as they chowed down, answering questions and being casually social. "It doesn't square much with the whole notion of militaristic Nazis."

At the podium, their guide was talking with a silver-templed man in a dark grey suit and open collar. He shook her hand with a proffered palm and a grip of her forearm. He smiled rows of gleaming teeth. He ambled to the microphone with laconic ease. "Ladies and gents… good to have you all here today."

American, Malone thought. Makes sense. Most of the Latin American reporters she'd met spoke English and a third of the contingent was foreign.

"I'm Blake Dennis, director of communications for Nueva Esperanza's International Relations Division, and I'd like to welcome everyone to this very special day. In a half-hour's time, Dr. Gabriel Verde will address all of you and fill you in on just what he's been preparing. After that, we'll have a tour of the facility, followed by a question and answer with me and one of our specialists. In the meantime, please do chat with our staff and they'll answer whatever questions they can."

Brennan tapped her on the arm then gestured to the far steps, out of the north side of the square. "If ever there was a candidate…" The girl he pointed out was ten yards from the nearest other person, at least. She wore a tank top and shorts, but she'd crossed her arms over herself as if cold. "She looks gun shy."

One of Alex's developed skills as a reporter was reading body language, tone of voice, and reacting appropriately. The girl looked nervous; not terrified in the way a reluctant cult member or prisoner might be, but simply socially awkward about talking to members of the media. It was charming in a very Nineteen Nineties kind of way.

"Come on, let's take advantage before one of the other hyenas notices her." She walked over briskly, searching through her lap top bag as she approached, like the girl was an afterthought. Brennan followed at a discreet distance, hovering six feet behind her.

"Oh, hi!" she said as they reached the girl.

She flashed a quick, anxious smile. A half wave. "Hi." She faltered slightly, as if realizing she'd forgotten something. "Oh!" She reached out a hand to shake. "Sorry. I'm Allie."

"Nice to meet you. I'm Alex." Alex looked back over her shoulder at Brennan. "He's with me." She glanced around at the nearly hundred people in the square. "Pretty weird, huh?"

The girl blushed and grinned, clasping her fingers with her other hand ahead of her like a nervous fan. "Uh... yeah. I'm not really used to talking to media and stuff..."

"You're American?"

She nodded. "Uh huh."

"I'm from D.C.," Alex said. "It's actually warmer there today than it is here, can you believe that?"

The girl nodded. "Yeah... it... gets pretty cold." She was awkward, to say the least.

"Where are you from, Allie?"

"Vermont. Newport. It's this little town on a lake near Stowe. I mean, near the ski hill. I mean... it's like, right near the Canadian border."

"Wow! Long way from home, huh? How did you end up down here?"

"My folks, mainly. They wanted me to get into a good school, mainly. My high school... it was real good for sports and stuff. Like, the football team produces guys who get scholarships. The hockey team, too. But for me, it didn't have the extra-curricular options..."

"So, your parents volunteered you?"

The girl nodded. "Dr. Verde has connections at top Ivy League schools and the amount of money he was offering... well, we're not supposed to talk about that kind of stuff. But it was enough to pay for school. He's a great man."

"No doubt!" Alex said. "A Nobel nominee and all." She let it hang there for a second, then looked back at the crowd and crossed her own arms uncomfortably. "Still... you must have been worried, at least a little? When I was a kid and I had to get a simple shot, I'd get so nervous I couldn't sleep the night before..."

"I guess," she said. "But it's..." The girl frowned and stopped herself. "I shouldn't talk about the treatment. We're supposed to leave that to Dr. Verde."

Alex changed tack. "Oh, sure. It's only a half hour or so anyway, I can wait." She turned on her heels slightly as if her attention was diverted from the girl. She watched the other media milling about, chatting with staff, scribbling shorthand, recorders held aloft. "So... you like this place? Do you get into town much?"

"They let us go in sometimes. Not often. But for the first year..."

"Year? How long have you been here?"

"Four years," the girl nodded as she said it, as if she figured Alex already knew. The reporter's easy manner was relaxing her. "I mean, we got here ... I guess, just over three-and-a-half years now..."

"We?"

"Oh..." She looked nervous. "I'm not sure..."

Malone laughed. "It's okay... like I said, they're going to fill us in soon anyway."

The girl looked relieved. "My brother, John... some of the volunteers were already sent on their assignment..."

Malone looked about the square. "Not many, though, from the looks of things." It was an oblique statement, based on nothing and sounding innocuous, but designed to elicit more information.

"Only a hundred. But..." The girl frowned. "I shouldn't be talking about the details."

The reporter gave her best look of concern. "Are you okay? You're not going to get into trouble for talking to me, are you? I don't want you punished..."

She looked wide-eyed and innocent. "Oh... they don't really discipline us. They're really good to us... really! I know in town they talk about us like we're some weird cult or something. But it's just a research commune..."

Malone gave her a small tug on the arm. "It's okay. I believe you. I went to an all-girls' Christian academy. Everybody assumes it's like something out of *American Horror Story* or something..."

"Right?" the girl said. She sounded happy to have a friendly, sympathetic ear.

Ten yards away, a woman in an austere brown skirt had been watching them talk. She tapped her ear and said something to someone via an earpiece then strode over. "That's enough for now, Allie," she said gently. "Let's make sure that we mix and mingle, talk to everyone." The woman gave Malone and Brennan a cheerful smile before shepherding the girl away.

"They don't want anyone getting too close to the test subjects," Brennan said. "They're limiting their time but only if someone looks too interested. They'll be checking on us. I'm going to see just how cautious they are. Stay here."

He strode off towards the steps, following them out of the central square to the larger courtyard. Brennan crossed it to the interior housing that surrounded the giant rectangular common area, creating its four walls. Each unit had a giant front window and Brennan followed the frontage, looking through each window in turn. He received surprised glances and stares back from the residents inside. He used the glass to keep an eye on the area behind him. He wanted to know how quickly he'd pick up a tail if he wandered.

After forty yards, a pair of men in suits strode into the courtyard from the outer perimeter by the gates, directly behind him. He caught their image for a split second in the glass as they swung wide to pick up his trail. He walked another ten yards before another guard in plainclothes appeared in the fifteen-foot gap between buildings directly north.

Brennan stopped for a moment, as if slightly confused, then turned in a circle as if orienting himself. He strode back across the courtyard to the brief flight of steps into the central square. Malone was waiting for him in a back-row seat. "So?"

"They're being very careful. If we're going to get a look at this place, it's going to be during the tour."

At the podium, the PR man flicked the mike switch to 'on'. "Testing… Okay, ladies and gentlemen, without further ado, I'd like to introduce you to your host here at Nueva Esperanza, a man of whom much has been said and yet still not nearly enough. A scientist, a humanitarian, a philanthropist. He's here to tell you about an exciting new discovery, a genetic treatment that will write a brighter story for humanity's future. I give you… Dr. Gabriel Verde!"

The entourage near the podium cleared a path and Verde appeared, elegant in blue blazer and light slacks. He was handsome in an old, leathery guy sort of way, Malone thought. Although he was smiling, his dark eyes seemed penetrating even from twenty yards away.

Verde waited for the applause led by his PR team to die down. He took a calming breath. "Ladies and gentlemen, I thank you for travelling so far – thousands of miles for some of you – to join me today in this momentous occasion. It is the beginning of a new era for humanity. A brighter future, free of many diseases that now plague our populations. And you are here today to witness it. From today, everything changes."

85.

CEDAR RAPIDS, Iowa

Jonah Tarrant had never been fond of the spotlight. Now he found himself in a sidewalk greeting retinue, on the street side of the barricades, a foot behind Matthew Misner as the presidential candidate shook hands with the throng of well-wishing voters, cameras recording everything.

But that had been Misner's request. He'd made it clear he'd had enough of flying to Washington to be lectured, so if Jonah wanted to speak with him in person, he needed to visit the campaign trail.

"This really isn't the ideal place or time to talk about this kind of thing." Jonah had to raise his voice to be heard over the crowd and occasional police siren. "Are you sure we can't step aside for just a few minutes...?"

"My time is not my own right now, Acting Director," Misner responded, before shaking an elderly supporter's hand. "Thank you, ma'am, sir, your support is so appreciated.

"This is getting more serious by the day and we only have five of them left before..."

"I'm well aware of the date and the situation, Acting Director..."

"Then you must know that the more militant side at these appearances…"

"The hard right. The white supremacists and fascists…"

"Yes. They're talking about disrupting polls on election day. They're using the pretense of stopping voter fraud, even though audit after audit shows it's not a real issue and never has been. People can't be afraid to go to the polls…"

"Agreed… but hardly an issue for the next director of the CIA, now is it? Thank you, sir! Thank you for your vote…" Misner kept his attention glued to the voters.

"This is a real concern, sir, one you could've helped allay at the debates if you'd disavowed…

Misner stopped walking for a split second. He didn't bother to lower his voice; if anything, he wanted voters to know exactly how he felt. "I've made it clear why. You can continue to doubt my motivations all you want, Mr. Tarrant. But I will not play that game. I will not play Americans off against one another. And if you ask me to, you're letting whoever is responsible for all of this division and hate win."

He resumed the greeting line.

Jonah followed behind. The man was being obtuse, as far as he was concerned. He understood the man's principle, or at least his statements of such. But that didn't change the pragmatic reality that all of the issues were at his events, and all of them involved groups who didn't really deserve a broader hearing.

It left him wondering whether Misner was closer to the root of the problem than he was letting on. So far, there was no evidence of it, just that foreign actors were spending a fortune on social media advertising and fake online outrage.

But Misner knew that, too. And still, he wasn't budging.

"You understand, I hope, that there are people who are beginning to doubt whether you really want the protests and rioting to end."

Misner stopped once more, for just a moment. "Like I said in the debate: there will always be idiots out there who want everything to just burn. But I'm not giving them the matches."

He resumed walking.

Jonah watched him for a few moments, his outward confidence and charm with the people waving and reaching for him. Was the empathy he projected just as genuine?

Or had they underestimated Matthew Misner?

86.

BRIGHTON

The old man was being generous with his compliments, Charlie knew.

The young coder stared blankly through the computer screen, his memory drifting back to two days earlier, and Ruby's smiling face. If he hadn't selfishly tried to impress a girl by breaking into the ministry, she'd probably still be alive, he told himself.

His gaze drifted to the Newton's Cradle, five silver balls hanging from threads and a frame, placidly still on the desktop. He saw his reflection cast back from them, warped like a funhouse mirror from the curves of their surfaces. He saw Grimes' arm raised...

Charlie threw himself sideways, the gunfire a deafening bang even with suppressor attached, the computer monitor blown off its stand by the bullet. He scrambled around the side of the desk on his hands and knees as Grimes coolly walked out from behind the desk and took aim a second time.

He crawled past the other chair then kicked it backwards, hard. It bounced off Grimes' legs and he stumbled, catching his balance with one palm on the desktop. Charlie found his feet and sprinted out of the room. Another shot sounded, a supersonic whine from the bullet as it whizzed past his head and buried itself in the hallway wall.

He turned toward the back door, then realized they'd dropped the bar. By the time he raised it and unlocked the deadbolt, he'd be a sitting duck.

He sprinted the other way, into the synagogue proper, hoping the front door was unlocked. Charlie's heels echoed on the wood floor, ringing through the cavernous structure. He darted down the aisle, past the congregation seating to the...

He stopped dead. A grand piano and a pile of other pieces of furniture were stacked against the front wall, blocking the main doors.

What had the Rabbi said? That they'd been closed for renovations.

He crouched down behind the last aisle of pews.

Then he remembered.

The pistol. Martin had left him the little pistol...

And it was in the desk drawer of the room he'd just left.

Charlie closed his eyes and tipped his head back, the anxiety of the moment washing over him, feeling like an idiot.

"You won't get out that way." Grimes' voice echoed from the other end of the vast building. At least his age was slowing him down somewhat, Charlie thought. That had to be worth something. "I took a look when we were coming in and the main doors are blocked. Rather bad timing for you, I'm afraid..."

Charlie crawled to the far end of the pew, near the wall. Along the wall, under the first row of elevated private boxes, was a series of framed old prints. He could see the room reflected in their glass; Grimes was pin-sized, which meant he was still near the office, probably trying to figure out where Charlie had concealed himself before flushing him out.

"There's no point hiding from me, Charlie. Your friends are both dead already."

Charlie's heart was pounding in his chest. He needed to get to that pistol. That meant waiting for Grimes to begin methodically searching the pews. He tried to calm his breathing, stop hyperventilating.

He'll go down the middle so that he can see both sides. But he's old and slow…

As he'd expected, Grimes began to make his way down the center aisle, glancing in each direction as he passed row on row.

Just wait, Charlie my son. Just wait until he's past halfway…

Grimes ambled forward, his gait stiff from the passing of years. "Charlie, this will be much easier if you give yourself up. Then I won't have to kill you. I promise."

Just a few more steps…

Grimes stopped walking halfway across the congregation hall. "You've nowhere to go, Charlie, and I have all the time I need. No one is coming to help you. Wouldn't it be better if we just worked together? Your friends Martin and Joe haven't done anything but make things worse. Come out, and we can talk this through."

He was still too close to the back of the building, Charlie knew. If he ran for it, Grimes would be close enough to shoot him in the back and wouldn't have to worry about catching him. *Just a dozen feet more. Come on, you old bastard…*

"If you're thinking of getting past me, Charlie, then I think it's only fair to mention that after four decades, I could knock ten pence off a shelf with a bullet at twenty yards. You wouldn't have a chance, my boy. Now show yourself, before I become irritated and decide to rescind the offer."

It was time to try something. Charlie crept forward along the left side of the pews, just far enough to be level with the last row of seats. As he'd expected, there were Torahs in a small shelf in the back of each pew. He took one of the two-inch-thick pocketbooks and tossed it a few feet to his right, the heavy book slapping the ground as it landed.

Grimes heard the book and pinpointed its location instantly.

He shuffled towards it and Charlie backed up, to the left aisle.

Grimes was almost parallel, nearly at the point where he'd be visible. Charlie dropped into a sudden sprint, running for his life towards the back of the room. Grimes wheeled around and got a shot off, but at a moving side profile now more than twenty feet away.

Charlie rounded the corner to the hallway, hearing the 'thwip' of the bullet as it passed his ear before he heard the third shot. He barreled into the office, half-tripping over the overturned second office chair, The floor and desk were covered in shards of computer monitor and chunks of plastic.

He'd never fired a gun before and Charlie was terrified but he knew without it, he had no chance. He grabbed at the desk drawer handle and yanked it open.

Charlie stared down, agog, at the empty desk drawer.

"You're probably looking for this." He looked up. Grimes's lanky frame filled the office doorway. He had his own silenced pistol in one hand and a two-finger grip on the butt of the other gun. "As I said, I've been doing this for a while, Charlie." Grimes approached the desk. "Sit."

Charlie obeyed, sitting down on the computer chair. Grimes reached forward and took the phone off the hook. Then he raised the barrel to point it at Charlie's head once again.

They both heard the 'thump' at the same time, a bass-heavy thud, like someone dropping a bucket of wet sand. Grimes turned his head towards the door for a split second.

Charlie reacted, grabbing the hot cup of tea from the desktop and hurling it into the other man's face.

"Gahh!' Grimes squealed, the liquid not hot enough to do serious damage but uncomfortable nonetheless. He squeezed off a gunshot wildly, the bullet thudding into the ceiling as he stumbled sideways into the sideboard. Charlie bolted, around the desk and out the door to the hall, Grimes recovering quickly.

Charlie ran for the back door. He heard another loud thud coming from that direction. He knew he didn't have time but he had no other options. It was only a few feet…

His toe caught a corner of the old, curling linoleum tile, his momentum still pushing him forward even as it tripped his feet. He slammed to the atrium floor. Ahead of him the door thudded again, louder, like it might splinter. He rolled onto his side and to a crouch just in time to see Grimes arrive, a few feet away, raising the pistol one last time. "I'm sorry Charlie. You've run out of…"

The door burst inwards, the wooden bar cracking in two, splinters and debris flying into the atrium beyond. Grimes raised the gun and opened fire. Charlie covered his head and tucked into a ball, two more gunshots sounding, then another, both men shooting at one another, the string of small explosions deadening his hearing to a whine.

And then the gunfire stopped.

87.

Martin broke every limit getting back to the synagogue, Eli's little BMW zipping nimbly in and out of traffic. He'd tried to call from Eli's mobile but the phone had come back busy repeatedly, which wasn't a good sign. The lad wasn't supposed to be talking to anyone.

The other possibility was that someone was there and had taken the phone off the hook. That would be more problematic, but it made sense. Charlie wasn't a professional; they would expect him to be easy pickings once isolated.

He cursed himself for being so stupid as to leave the boy alone. He remembered how he'd been at that age, right before joining the military, full of ambitions and practically fearless. Would he have handled himself any better than Charlie had? Probably not.

The BMW squealed to a halt at the curb. Martin jumped out and ran through the back gate, to the synagogue's rear entrance. Eli had given him the deadbolt key, so as long as the boy hadn't...

He tried the door. It opened a quarter-inch before being blocked by the restraining bar.

He barred the door.

He barred the door because I told him to.

Martin cursed internally again, then put his shoulder to it, the door buckling slightly but not giving. He heard a gunshot from inside. "Damn. Damn, damn, damn..." He backed up fifteen feet and ran at it, lowering his shoulder at the last moment, hitting the door full force right at the level of the bar. The door buckled inwards but didn't break. He ran back again, taking a few more feet, until he was almost to the storage building behind the synagogue. He hurtled ahead then slammed his shoulder into the door once more, this time hearing slight splintering as the old wooden barrier bent without breaking.

You have to do this, Martin. You have to do this or Charlie's a dead man. Come on, old man, show them what you've got...

Martin charged at the door and slammed into it with his shoulder and hip simultaneously, a furious body check right out of a hockey arena. The bar snapped, the pressure giving instantly, the back door flying open and slamming into the wall. Martin leaned to his right, allowing his natural momentum to carry him past the doorway but then pitching sideways, towards the wall. As he'd anticipated, a hail of gunfire erupted towards the doorway. He raised his pistol and fired directly at the source of the explosions, three shots, letting his aim drift down by an inch with each, trying to account for center mass and different heights.

The smoke cleared and he watched as Archie Grimes dropped first to his knees, his gun beside him, before pitching face first onto the tile floor. A pool of dark crimson blood began to form around his body.

Charlie was sitting on the floor just ahead of the corpse, panting wildly, a look of absolute shock on his face, his arm and one leg drawn in towards his body, like a child trying to shield himself from a beating.

88.

BARILOCHE

Oct. 29, 2020

Peter Bruner sat in the second row of the Cathedral of Our Lady of Nahuel Huapi and prayed quietly to God to forgive him.

"Holy Father, I know what we are about to do must be the most mortal of sins. But I have given a vow to help the man who saved my child. I am bound to his decisions and he in turn to his beliefs."

The truth was Bruner had convinced himself that Verde would fail. That the virus would perhaps cause suffering and death, but that it would be unable to achieve his employer's ultimate goal.

Verde had been working on it for three decades, his life's achievement and the consequence of his bizarre upbringing. But in the meantime, he had authored drugs and treatments that had bettered mankind, Bruner told himself. He had already saved countless millions... even as he planned to murder millions more.

And among those saved had been his son, Hans, the only remainder of his late wife, Gretta. He'd been destitute after spending his small fortune trying to find novel treatments for the boy's spinal condition. It had been Verde who had saved him, at the cost of his utter loyalty. He had been able to rebuild his life as a banker in Switzerland, he had been able to advance his position within the organization that sheltered his fascist father after the war.

That he believed in neither fascism nor Dr. Gabriel Verde's good intentions was no longer of any consequence. Whatever was to come, he knew he would be partly responsible. So he prayed, because although he did not expect forgiveness, if it was to be offered, it would only be from on high. He was not forcing Verde to go ahead with what he termed his "day of ascension." But he would not lift a finger to stop him, either.

He felt a tap on his right shoulder. Bruner turned and looked up. The two men both wore black leather coats and dark shirts, along with driving gloves. One jerked his head towards the church door. Bruner knew it wasn't a request.

They led him outside to a limousine. The back door opened and one pushed him forward. Bruner climbed in. One of the guards climbed in after him and sat on the jump seat. The other slammed the door behind them, and the limo began to roll.

"Hello, Peter." Michael Wolf looked relaxed, his legs crossed, a glass of brandy in his left hand. "Drink?"

"I'm fine. Look, you could have…"

"What's he doing with my money, Peter?"

"Michael, I'm sure if we can sit down on Monday…"

"Let me rephrase that," Wolf said, reaching down to the seat beside him and coming up with a pistol. He leaned across the divide and rested the muzzle against Bruner's forehead.

"What's he doing with my fucking money, Peter? And if I hear anything other than the truth – any delay, any obfuscation, any demand for civility, even, I'm going to paint that driver's shield with your brain."

There was loyalty, Bruner knew, and there was suicide. "He… has been working on a project for many years. Many years. You must understand: it is all he believes in, this plan."

"I know. I know what it's supposed to be. I'm asking you…"

"With all due respect, Michael, you do not. You do not know what he plans, and you do not know who he really is."

"Then tell me, Peter, and you might actually get another chance to fly home to Geneva in one piece."

Bruner sighed. "In a sense, you created him. Well… not you personally, of course. But the movement. He was born to it, you see."

89.

THEN

COLONIA DIGNIDAD, Chile
A religious colony deep in the jungle

April 3, 1967

It had been a long trip from his vacation home in Ireland and Otto Skorzeny was tired. They'd driven directly from Osorno, it was twenty-seven Celsius and there was so little wind that even being in an open-top jeep had not helped.

Still, he was finally there. He hadn't been to the colony in five years – five busy years, spent playing the MOSSAD off against the Egyptian State Security Investigation Service, founding a fascist lobby and fundraising group in Spain, as well as ensuring his own Paladin security group based in Spain was profitable.

He wasn't expecting great results. Mengele had been sporadic in his reports, at best, and the man was clearly insane. But his knowledge of genetics and ideas had been reconfirmed and studied by their other scientists, in other countries.

Peron and the nuclear option were long gone. Skorzeny doubted now that South America would ever be home to the new Reich. It had been too unstable, the dictators and politicians too self-absorbed to last before their public or opponents or military tired of them. Many of the upper rank Nazis had died from poor health, a few from age. Some, like Bormann, had simply disappeared. Others had begged off involvement to take their chances alone in old age, terrified of what had happened to Adolf Eichmann – and, they suspected, others – at the hands of vengeful Israel.

But he still had influence across the region, they still had financial support. The beauty of Die Spinne was not merely the escape network; it was the tendrils of influence that touched every area of western society.

Still, Mengele continued to work on the esoteric. If nothing else, the colony provided them with a staging base for paramilitary training and weapons storage, issues that could prove important whenever a government became unstable enough for opportunity to present itself. They'd moved most of the secret weapons caches from private homes in Argentina, Colombia and Paraguay to the bunkers below the colony, even as the land above extended for miles, offering housing, agriculture and a sect of cult members who would defend it to the death... fearing much worse at the hands of its Nazi administrators.

The jeep pulled to a halt outside the main hall, a German hotel-style two-story building. They'd cleared acres of jungle to develop the place, with help from their many friends in Chilean politics and the military. In exchange, they'd used it to teach the Chilean government how to effectively torture their political enemies.

A side door to the building opened and Mengele emerged. He was dressed casually in a short-sleeved aertex shirt and slacks. He was in his late fifties now but still spry, grinning toothily, his greying brown hair slicked back.

Skorzeny hated the man. For the former intelligence officer, fascism was about the right of the champion to conquer and lead, the need to win at any cost. But Mengele was a psychopath.

"Otto, my old friend!" Mengele reached out to hug him but Skorzeny backed away and took his hand quickly in a firm shake, instead. "Yes, yes, of course! Always so formal! Come, let me show you my work."

He led them to the rear of the main building, where a door led them down a flight of stairs to the building's expansive basement. "Of course, I imagine you have not seen the Fuhrer for a great many years! He has changed quite a bit, as you might expect."

At the bottom of the stairs he punched an alphanumeric code into a keypad and a steel door unlocked. Mengele slid it backwards. Beyond it, Skorzeny could see the enormity of Mengele's operation, a half-acre of tables, tanks, burners, oscilloscopes. It was like something out of a horror movie. Along the left wall were three tanks filled with a pale green fluid. It was at least twice the size and scope of the old lab they'd set up for him on the island, beneath Richter's failed reactor.

Skorzeny had a sharp intake of breath, shocked at the sight. In the middle tank, Adolf Hitler stood suspended. He had a clear plexiglass oxygen mask over his nose and mouth and his eyes were open, albeit docile and staring straight ahead, unblinking. His head had been shaved but they had allowed him his moustache, an affectation Mengele doubtless found amusing. His emaciated body had been cut away for samples, hunks of flesh missing in a patchwork of scars and exposed red flesh, from neck to toe, ribs protruding through near-translucent pale skin, stitches and scars covering him like a patchwork quilt.

"He is barely conscious at his most lucid and when that happens the pain is likely so agonizing as to have driven him delusional and psychotic years ago. Ninety percent of the time, he is unconscious, which suits the purposes of harvesting his DNA. He is fed via an intravenous drip."

"But... you haven't managed an actual clone of him, still, after all this time?"

Mengele frowned. "Don't speak to me like one of your lickspittle underlings, Skorzeny! Let me remind you that I am the one who has managed to keep him alive. And... we have had one success, as you are aware."

"Yes... the boy."

"He's in the incubator room right now, I believe." Mengele nodded towards the back wall, where two rooms were enclosed by half walls and tall glass windows. "Follow me."

They crossed the vast work area. Mengele knocked on the door gently, then opened it. "Otto, would you come here, please?"

Skorzeny shot him a foul look. "Really?"

"I thought you'd find it quite funny, given that you're the only senior man in the movement who doesn't have DNA in the lad. If you prefer, call him by his middle name: Gabriel."

The boy turned from the petri dish he was studying and walked over. "Sir...?"

"He's only twelve, but he is already assisting me and working at university level," Mengele said. "He has a natural affinity for science."

The boy had a blank, emotionless expression, as if no thought at all crossed his mind. His eyes were small and dark and seemed to peer right through the former SS colonel. "He is... special, is he not?"

"Oh, most certainly. If he harboured any weak sentiment, we ensured it was removed."

"How so?"

Mengele sighed, as if bored by old memories. "Mostly just by giving him to Shafer for punishment, like the local children."

"He disciplines them?"

Mengele nodded his head slightly from side to side as if weighing definitions. "Discipline. Punishment. It's two sides of the same coin, really. For the most part, I believe he rapes them repeatedly. With the German children, he typically has their parents watch, then destroys the parents mentally and physically in front of the children until they are so emotionally numb they will do anything he says, just to go back to their little pens."

Skorzeny didn't really care about the orphans, or the strange amalgam of test-tube generated Nazi genetic material that stood ten feet away, studying him like he was an insect. But even he felt a shudder of revulsion at how Mengele casually discussed destroying children's lives.

The upper ranks of both the Knights and the International Family were as crawling with pedophiles as the Nazi hierarchy had been – one of the reasons they'd been so vociferous in accusing their enemies of it, as Goebel's propaganda classes had taught. "Will the boy ever leave here?"

Mengele shrugged. "Probably not. I am curious to see how far we can push him before he becomes psychotic. He harbors a grand desire, to develop a perfect race genetically and to wipe out most of humanity in the process. He's quite mad, already, which is wonderful to watch. I've wondered whether I can make him so immune to feelings that he would eat another person."

Skorzeny took another deep breath. Mengele's reputation as the "Angel of Death" in the camps had evidently been well-earned. He was truly deranged.

He needed to get out of there, get some fresh air and clear his head of Mengele's horror show. "A clone of the Fuhrer... How close are you?"

The former concentration camp murderer held both palms wide. "If you wish me to lie to our financial backers in Europe and America, I can certainly do that. But the truth is I don't know. We get closer each year."

It was not the answer they were going to like, Skorzeny knew. He would count on Francois Genoud to placate them. In the meantime, he needed to get back to Osorno. There was yet more work to be done.

90.

April 5, 1967

OSORNO, Chile

At a large circular table covered in a white tablecloth, Francois Genoud was holding court. The Swiss fascist and banker wore a white linen suit with black tie. He shared the table with a half-dozen members of the German Officers' Club, a local institution that predated the war.

Genoud was telling humorous anecdotes, the officers laughing heartily in unison. It would be nice, Skorzeny decided as he approached the table, to be around reasonably sane people for a few hours. A day with Mengele had been almost too much.

"Skorzeny, my good man!" Genoud didn't rise, instead gesturing with a wide sweep of his arm to the empty seat on the other side of the table. "Join us, won't you?"

Skorzeny pulled out the chair and sat down.

"Gentlemen," Genoud said, raising his glass, "to the Colonel."

The men raised their glasses in a toast, their voices in unison. "The COLONEL!'

Skorzeny gave them a perfunctory wave. "Yah, yah... thank you, of course. But I need a bloody drink."

Genoud frowned. Skorzeny was famously sober most of the time, preferring to get his thrills from competition. He'd been working for twenty years on the plan that had been called Die Spinne, then renamed the Fascist International. It was about to be reborn once more as the International Family, the pseudo-religious global arm of dozens of powerful lobby groups they controlled.

It showed in how much he'd aged. For the past five years, Skorzeny had been an agent of chaos in intelligence circles, working for both the MOSSAD and the Egyptians whilst still advising Franco's fascist government in Spain and dictators globally. The dual roles seemed to have almost shrunk his towering figure.

"The struggle goes well, Francois?" Skorzeny asked.

"It does. The older German families in Osorno, Santiago and Bariloche have all agreed to contribute more money in the coming year. I will be speaking with our supporters in Paraguay, Bolivia and the United States over the next few days."

"About that..." Skorzeny asked as the waiter poured him a glass of red wine. "I looked at the data Gehlen's people provided and noticed you have almost as many American radical groups that you are supporting on the political left there as you do on the right. That seemed incredibly careless..."

Genoud smiled genially. "Not at all, my old friend, not at all. In this matter we must always consider the long-term consequences, the typically unforeseen outcomes. None of these groups have the agency or leadership to make a real political impact. But they will damage the reputation of their own side; they will sow dissent and chaos on occasion. And, when we finally succeed and place our preferred men in the White House and 10 Downing Street, they will provide a perfect villain to rally against. In the meantime, they will serve to fracture the attention and resources of those on the left. So, you see, it is very much like your own campaign, towards the end of the war."

Before Germany's surrender, Skorzeny had himself looked to the future, gathering as many English-speaking German SS and Wehrmacht officers as possible and disguising them in prisoner groups likely to soon be 'liberated' to the west. Long before Gehlen had used his bartering power with his fellow Knights of Malta and with the American OSS, hundreds of intelligence officers had already infiltrated Britain, in particular.

It was how they would eventually win, Skorzeny knew: by playing the long game, as Genoud suggested. By charting a future course and anticipating the results, then adjusting based on reactions – a chess match, with global stakes.

"Very clever," he said. "And thanks to ODESSA and Gehlen's political lobbying, the Americans import thousands of Eastern Bloc refugees who fear nothing more than the mere mention of the word 'communist'. It will not take long to convince them that it is synonymous with social democracy and for them to teach their children… even as our associates in West Germany muddy the use of the term in building a laissez-faire economy."

"De Gaulle must be going mad watching them." Genoud almost snickered as he said it.

Charles De Gaulle governed France on a distinct mix of Republican conservatism and social justice. It was clear to Skorzeny that driving the pragmatic French president to distraction was important to Genoud, a hated figure in the neighboring country. Such was the predatory nature of the pure competitor.

"What about Robert Kennedy?"

Genoud took a deep breath. "We're taking care of that. In the meantime, even though 85% of the issues they face as a nation are agreed upon by the vast majority of Americans, we manage to focus them on the remaining 15%. Within a generation, they will distrust each other. Within two, it will be hatred. Within three, they will be begging for strong leaders to crush their enemies."

91.

April 18, 1967

PHILADELPHIA

The man who entered Francois Genoud's room at the Hilton wore a simple raincoat and flat cap, which he removed immediately, clasping it with both hands in front of him like a nervous arrival at Ellis Island.

Genoud's valet, Marcel, announced him. "Mr. Luigi de Cesare, sir."

"Luigi," Genoud offered, without rising from his armchair. "You appear nervous. There's nothing for you to worry about."

Luigi gave a quick nod of appreciation. "Thank you, sir. I... I am sorry for the state of the program and the troubles we have had. It is my responsibility, of course..."

"Don't be foolish, my good man. Please! Sit!" Genoud gestured to the opposite armchair.

De Cesare sheepishly joined him, looking uncomfortable, his body language stiff as he perched on the edge of the seat cushion.

"Now... let's talk about the boy, shall we?"

Luigi nodded enthusiastically, overselling it. "Of course, of course. As you know, sir, his father died prematurely. We had invested many thousands of hours into challenging Jacob - we poisoned his wife, we had him fired repeatedly. We broke him down and then gave him targets for his hatred..."

"But that doesn't stop cancer."

"Before he could fully indoctrinate his son, Mark, he passed away. He had spent more time with his nephew, Joseph, who is slightly older, and we decided to refocus our efforts there. It was going well; he received his diploma from high school and was accepted into Yale where he is about to graduate. But… he seems unbalanced."

"How so?"

"He is emotionally unstable, prone to both manic depression and grandiosity. His father, who died shortly after the war from influenza, seemed more stable, so we did not expect it…"

Genoud frowned. "That won't do at all. Even if you manage to use his derangement to indoctrinate him, he'll never be able to hold up the public face we require. He'll never be able to run for office."

"Yes sir…"

"This may prove disastrous," Genoud said. He frowned and peered at the man. "Why didn't you alert us to this earlier?"

"I…"

He could see the terror in the man's eyes. "Never mind. What's done is done. The most troubling part is the time and expense; two generations of building up family friends and associates to seed them with misinformation and ideology!"

Luigi meekly held up one hand like a nervous school child. "If I may, sir… there is one avenue we might yet pursue in this regard."

"Go on."

"Joseph's girlfriend, Alice, is pregnant. I would propose focusing on ensuring he is successful, so that he has the financial means to send his son to a good school. In the meantime, we will ensure that from the earliest age, he knows who and what to believe."

"A third generation?" Genoud pondered the possibility. "Why not? The original plan was ambitious but unrealistic. Extending our reach globally absent any structure or public face was always going to be difficult. But eventually, we will have near-unstoppable influence. Could that take another twenty or thirty years? I think we should assume so." He smiled at the man. "Thank you, Luigi De Cesare, for your many years of tireless sacrifice and loyalty. You may go now. We shall be in touch with instructions."

Luigi nodded once more, flat cap still grasped in two hands as he made his way to the door and out of the room.

Genoud waited until the door had closed before gesturing towards his assistant. "Have him shot and disposed of," he said. "Incompetent fool. And get in touch with Gehlen, see if he approves of using Joseph's son. At this rate, I'll be dead before any of this comes to fruition. But by then, we may have our perfect candidate, and our genetically perfect young man to be his protégé. And we will have won the war after a half century of waiting, without having to fire another shot."

92.

NOW

Oct. 29, 2020

BARILOCHE

Wolf waited until Bruner had finished his story. "So this lifelong ambition that he harbored as a child..."

"A true master race," Bruner said, sighing from the weight of it all. "As I said, it has been his belief all along, that in order to create a better human, we had to purge the ranks, as it were."

"And how does he plan on doing that, exactly? A virus? A bioweapon?"

Bruner shook his head gently. "I do not know the scientific details, just that he intends to lock the doors to the compound at noon tomorrow and, I must presume, somehow unleash his devastation upon the world. He claims it will wipe out half of mankind within twenty years, during which time his commune will be busy creating a better, true Aryan race. And when the dust settles…"

"When the dust settles!?" Wolf made no attempt to hide his alarm. "It sounds as if he intends to wipe out his own benefactors. He has made no provision to protect any of us…"

"This is true, yes. He claims that members of the Family who are of superior genetic stock will survive, thus the claim that only half the world's population will be decimated."

"And… you don't sound as if you believe him."

"The manner in which he discusses the outcome leads me to believe he is unsure of whether it will work and, if it does, whether it will spare anyone."

Wolf's gaze narrowed as he pondered the scenario. "How many couples are there in the compound?"

"About four hundred who are viable, I believe."

"But… unless my basic knowledge of natural selection is far off, that might not be enough to keep the species alive until there are enough people left to stave off disease, genetic drift, environmental factors…

"He is confident otherwise, based on his belief that they are superior humans. We have taught him, from the earliest age, that those of noble bloodlines, those of ancient character and ruthless ambition, are to be elevated. He merely sees this as the first and best opportunity to do so. In that, he is no different from religious zealots who believe a better world awaits if they end this one first – except he thinks Heaven should be here, on Earth."

Wolf slumped back in the limo passenger seat. He was unaccustomed to being shocked. If what he was being told was true, Verde had hoodwinked them for decades. He'd tricked the IF into thinking they had recruited him to create a clone of the Fuhrer, when in fact he had been manipulating them all along.

And now, it was probably too late to stop him.

NUEVA ESPERANZA

Gabriel Verde had been waiting for thirty years to make the announcement. In that time, it had been written and it had been rewritten. It had been massaged into a soft-sell and hammered into a hardline proclamation.

In the end, he had settled on a version of the truth, something that bore the earmarks of reality but kept the outcome firmly divorced from it.

"Ladies and gentlemen of the press, what I offer the world over the next year is a dramatic change in how we view and treat infectious disease. Tonight, at midnight, a time lock will seal Nueva Esperanza off from the rest of the world so that we can spend one full year producing, in volume, a new immunity boosting agent, a series of vaccines that function at the genetic level, offering nothing less than freedom from hundreds of fatal diseases that have plagued mankind."

A murmur rippled around the press area.

"I am aware, of course, of the magnitude of this statement. As evidence, we have sent out into the world one hundred young people who have already received the treatment and have lived with it for two years. In that time, they have not only been exposed, with no signs of contamination, to some of the deadliest viruses known to mankind, they have also developed a new type of internal antibody, one that can be passed between generations, which continues to defeat disease handily long after a single treatment.

"We have asked these young people to be our global ambassadors. To visit countries across the Globe inviting world leaders and physicians to inspect them for any sign of cancer, of malaria, of smallpox, of influenza, of coronavirus, of H1N1. All are easily defeated by a properly treated individual."

A group of daily media were leaving their seats, drifting to the back of the square to use their phones and contact their editors. They all wanted to get to air or online first with the claim. Verde watched them shuffle off, as they'd expected.

A stream of hands shot into the air, reporters wanting to ask him questions. Verde held up both palms in supplication. "Please! Please, ladies and gentlemen, as Blake mentioned, we will have some staff available for a question-and-answer after the tour. But let me reassure you, this is very much a reality. I have spent thirty years and hundreds of millions of dollars, much of it supplied by generous benefactors, to develop this protocol. And I am aware that, in terms of illness and death around the globe, it will change everything."

The press was fully fomented. Verde felt a moment of sublime power, knowing that years of playing to their sentiments had cast him in the role of the hero benefactor. They wouldn't question any of it.

They would restrict the carriers from being poked and prodded too much, but he was certain the virus was so slow in its progress and dormant that, barring something unforeseen, they would not recognize it.

At least not for months, not until it was too late. By then, the hundred chosen would have spread it to millions.

Those with the strongest natural immune systems would survive, laying the groundwork for the ascendance of a new master race. And he had not been completely dishonest about the process, either: the virus could be spread from mother to infant, as it would take nine to twelve months before symptoms began to show, before their internal organs began to fail and their immune system was overwhelmed and co-opted to replicate the virus.

He thought back to the Colony, and Mengele, his torturer and his mentor. He would have been amused as well, Verde thought. He was so small-minded, taking such joy in torturing children and aging Nazis. People called him the Angel of Death, a title Verde had come to crave for himself. He had promised Mengele at the age of twelve that one day, he would destroy mankind and bury them in a blackness as deep and dark as his own soul, only to see humanity reborn in glorious purity.

That day was finally here.

93.

The tour of the compound was as barebones as Brennan had expected. After showing them a pair of typical staff residences, they'd been led through a series of offices surrounding the main courtyard, followed by a large laboratory where they claimed most of the work was being done.

At the front of the lab, the guide gestured to a pair of white-coated lab techs who appeared to be operating a high-speed centrifuge. "Drs. Lindsay and Chan are separating these samples, which will then go to the testing stage, to see how their components react to the vaccines..."

Brennan tapped Malone on the arm. "Look around," he whispered. "What don't you see?"

She studied the large room, the six rows of long tables, the hi-tech gadgets placed around the periphery. "An obvious answer to whatever you're getting at?"

"No security," Brennan said. "Think about it: this is where they allegedly cook these miracle drugs up. But they don't even have a man on the back door."

He was right. Malone frowned. "So you figure this is..."

"All for show, yeah," he whispered back. And did you count the beds in the dormitories?"

"It hadn't occurred to me, no," she said. "Why? Why would I have done that, Joe?"

"Because they already told us they have four hundred volunteers and a total population of over a thousand. So... why are there only sleeping arrangements for two-hundred and fifty? And yeah, I double checked the math."

"More razzle dazzle," she said. "Don't look at the man behind the curtain?"

"Yeah. We ain't in Oz, Dorothy, but this whole thing smells like a yellow-brick load. They have to be hiding the rest of them somewhere. We've seen enough people so far today to know there's no way those apartments are sufficient, any more than this lab is working on the biggest development in the history of medicine. We need to find out what's really going on here."

"So what's the plan?"

"We haven't seen inside the main office complex, off the central square. There are still people milling about and journalists interviewing them. I should be able to slip in."

"And if they catch you..."

He shrugged. "The media are getting tossed out in four hours anyway. Besides... you know I can handle myself. The thing is..."

"What?"

"That building isn't big enough, either, for the scope of operation Verde was talking about. So... what are we missing?"

Brennan saw the idea flit across her face, Malone suddenly delighted with herself. "Hah!" she said.

"You've figured something out."

"Yeah... and as these things usually are, the most obvious answer is probably the right one. Let me repeat your question back to you..." she said, as the tour guide led them, en masse, to the door back outside, "what haven't you seen since we've been here?"

"Shoot."

"Telephone lines. Or infrastructure of any sort. We're fifteen miles from the city, but there are no connections to the outside world. At least, not that we can easily see."

Brennan looked down at the cement floor passing beneath them. "We're standing on top of it."

They followed the press group back outside. As he'd predicted, the courtyard was still buzzing with activity, reporters holding digital recorders up to residents' mouths, cameras snapping pictures and shooting video. "When we get back to the press area, see if you can get the PR types looking south, toward the front gates. Maybe stray that way and ask a loud question from ten yards away or so."

"Will do. Then I'll join you."

"The Hell you will. We have no idea what's in there..."

"Joe, for crying out..."

"NO." He emphasized it. "Are you nuts? Just... stay out here until I'm done, or you're a liability."

They separated, Brennan strolling over to the buffet table and grabbing a paper cup of juice while Malone went over to the agreed spot. The PR director, Blake, was answering a handful of queries close-up from eager young reporters. From twenty feet behind them, Malone asked loudly, "Blake! Blake, what if this doesn't work?"

Brennan put down the cup and walked over to the side door into the offices, without looking back. He entered, then closed it behind him. A short stairwell led both up and down. He looked down to the next landing. A grey steel door was protected by a punch pad.

He crept up the stairs to the side entrance into the public office, a broad, tall-ceilinged space that served as both an atrium and a service location. A long counter ran the length of the left side of the room. Clerical staff were helping a man with a request. Along the back wall, a set of grey concrete steps led up to the second floor.

Two men were standing at the bottom step. The taller, thinner man was slightly older, well into his senior years. He was vaguely familiar, but Brennan couldn't place him, which was concerning. The other man was Verde; he seemed less imposing next to the bigger man, and his tan and flecks of remaining dark hair made him look younger as well.

"... have had enough. This cannot end well," the older man said. "They made the point quite forcibly."

"Peter, please... this is not the place or time," Verde said, snapping a quick look at the counter to see if the staff were paying attention. "When everything is settled tomorrow, we can worry about such matters, okay? Now... I need to see to preparations." Verde grasped his friend by the hand and forearm and gave him a passionate shake. "You are my oldest friend. Don't make me worry about you, okay?"

Then he turned and began to cross the atrium, walking right towards Brennan.

Shit. He couldn't see a reason why he'd be recognized, but he also knew he'd look strange standing on the steps, staring at Verde, wearing only a press tag. He composed himself and walked up the steps, right by Verde as the man went in the opposite direction. Brennan walked over to the counter. "Bathroom?" he asked the clerk.

The clerk pointed to a set of double doors under the stairs.

"Never mind, false alarm." Brennan turned and went back down the steps. He turned the corner and saw the coded door swinging shut. He leaped down the five stairs and thrust his arm out, blocking it at the last second from closing.

Brennan leaned around the door frame. A long corridor lit by tube lights ran a hundred feet from the entryway across the compound. Verde was walking near the middle of it, a shorter man in a white coat next to him, telling him something Brennan couldn't make out. At the end of the corridor, they turned right and disappeared.

He didn't see a guard station but there was probably one somewhere near, he knew.

An electric cart with two staff in the front seats crossed the halfway point of the hall and Brennan ducked back, out of the way. He knew he couldn't stay there; eventually, someone else would come in through the basement door, and there would be nowhere to hide. He entered the corridor and walked cautiously until he reached the first door, in the left wall. It was wide open, and he peeked around its corner quickly to see what he was dealing with.

The entire left half of the ground floor appeared to be a vast auditorium. Stairs from the hall led down to floor level twenty feet below. Its far wall stretched sixty feet, at least, and was lined with glass-fronted smaller rooms, perhaps for observation or isolated testing. At the far end of the hall, under the same catwalk that ran back to the stairs, sat a line of tanks similar to those on the island – but sleeker, newer, the wires and cables hidden. Ahead of it, a dozen treadmills were in use, people tied up to EKGs and other monitors. A small forest of tables filled the middle of the room, most occupied by people either taking or giving medical doses. The right side of the room was a mix of white plastic technology, robot arms and centrifuges, monitors and touchscreens. In the corner was a room that, from a sharp angle through the side window, appeared to contain an MRI.

There must have been eighty people working and being tested. He ducked back around the corner. Wading into that was suicide. Besides, he knew he needed access to a computer terminal, something that might give him some idea of the project the IF was funding, maybe its scope.

The next two doors left exited onto the catwalk. But halfway down the hall on the right wall was another, closed. The door read "Systems and Technical Support." He knocked gently.

"Come in!"

Brennan opened the door cautiously. It was a big room, once again, but a fraction of the gallery across the hall, and on the same level as the corridor. It was probably directly under the administrative offices, he realized, on the other side of the customer counter. The room was dimly lit by more fluorescent tubes, the walls and floor grey concrete. It was split down the middle by three rows of server towers, eight-foot-tall racks carrying the complex array of operations required to keep the place going.

From the other side of the towers, a testy man's voice said, "Whatever it is, I can't help you right this second. We've got enough crap to deal with already from the big show." Brennan drew the pistol from the back of his waistband and crept along the gap between the servers. As he passed through, he caught sight of the man. He was sitting at a circular desk, a curved twenty-seven-inch monitor ahead of him. It appeared linked to four others. He controlled it all from a mechanical keyboard and trackball, both hands garbed in the kind of wrist supports favored by carpal tunnel sufferers.

Brennan walked towards him briskly. The man's glasses slipped down his nose at the sudden intrusion and he rolled his chair backwards, aware Brennan wasn't wearing a company pass around his collar. "Hey! This area is off limits!" he said in Spanish.

The American leaned down, flipping the pistol a half-turn in his right hand and using the butt end to strike the man squarely in the forehead. He fell backwards off his chair.

"AIIGGH! Fuck!" He tried to scramble to his feet, but Brennan took a half-step forward and trod on the man's left hand, pinning it down. He held the muzzle of the pistol to the tech guy's temple. The man took on a panicked look, his eyes darting around.

"Calm down!" Brennan advised. "If you want to survive this encounter, it's important that you remain completely calm. You get me?" The man nodded too quickly to be calm, but kept his mouth shut, which had been the point. "Okay. You have access to everything in the system, right?"

The man nodded.

"Good. You're doing really well… what's your name?"

"Emilio."

"You're doing really well, Emilio. Now, here's the thing. I need you to do something for me. If you don't, I'm going to give you one warning, and by that I mean I'm going to break bones, not kill you. The second time, I'll decide you're no use to me, and I'll kill you. Do you understand?"

The man's eyes narrowed and he appeared about to weep. Brennan gave him a gentle slap with his left hand. "Hey! Calm down. I told you you're doing good. That's good, right?"

The man nodded.

"Then let's keep things positive. Get up and sit down."

The technician followed the instruction.

"Now, you're going to log in as Dr. Verde..."

"I can't. He is always logged in. It won't accept..."

"You can override it?"

"I... I mean, I can access anything with admin logon but..."

"Then do it."

"But..."

"Are you more scared of losing your job, or me killing you?" Brennan asked bluntly.

The man began typing. "Okay, I'm in."

Brennan gestured with the gun. "Move your chair to one side."

The man did as ordered. Brennan took off his belt. He turned the man's chair around. "Put your hands behind your back." He tied the man to the chair, then took off the worker's tie and stuffed it into his mouth.

Verde's desktop was organized into a string of folders. He began to sift through them. Most were unintelligible, notes about hard science that Brennan didn't understand. There was a file that was nearly twenty years old, however. A wide search brought up its folder, which hadn't been updated in more than a decade. It was labelled "Angel's Wings."

Brennan opened it. He withdrew the USB drive from his pocket and inserted it into the terminal under the desk. He copied all of the folders, then pasted them to the memory stick, thousands of files beginning the copy process.

He studied the room while they copied over. On the far wall was an overhead map of the hidden basement. It was enormous, seemingly covering the entire square footage of the compound above it. The hallway seemed to end at a t-junction, with more corridors leading to other sections, including housing, a detention center and a large mess hall. There appeared to be another exit past the mess hall, and he wondered where it came out. Outside the walls? It seemed possible from the scope.

He turned his attention back to the monitor and opened the oldest file. It was a series of steps, an iterative test process involving a young woman. Her black-and-white photos were initially dated from Nineteen Sixty-Five, but got older in sequence. Her appearance seemed to worsen in each photo, growing tired, haggard, then emaciated, then scabrous.

"Subject died after prolonged forty milligram dose of compound number one hundred and thirty seven," it read. "Elapsed time, three years, four months, eleven days."

He kept flicking through the notes, each test subject more dire than the one before. Brennan went back into the folder. The most recent note was nearly five years old. "Despite near-perfect stability, a more rigorous testing procedure may reveal ways to speed the process without compromising the low detectability level for the virus," Verde wrote. "In its current form, mass transmission and infection could take three to five years, potentially allowing time for a vaccine or other solution to be found. The ideal transmission rate would take one year to fully compromise the patient but be spreadable within ten days of injection by the carrier."

At the bottom of the page was a chart. At first, Brennan wasn't sure what he was reading. Then he interpreted it. The horizontal bar was years passed. The vertical was the global infection rate. By thirty-six months, it had topped four billion people.

In a side margin, Verde had added, "By keeping the cure to a minimal available dosage, secured by the time lock, one year could temper any response to zero?"

Brennan turned away from the screen. The volunteers who had already left were infected. If Verde felt comfortable proceeding, it meant he'd probably reached the point where they became contagious within ten days, as he'd planned. That meant they had, perhaps, a week to round up all one hundred, before Verde's virus unleashed death across the globe.

He walked behind the tied-up technician and removed his shoe, securing the USB stick in the heel while out of the man's line of sight, before putting it back on. He moved back to the desktop, but noticed his captive's wide-eyed stare, his own gaze flitting over to a small monitor in the upper corner of the room, near the door.

It showed a view of the hallway. A group was walking down it.

Brennan ducked low behind the desk and chambered a shell in the pistol.

There was a knock on the door. "Mr. Brennan! We do not wish any unnecessary violence. We have your friend. It would be wise for you to give yourself up."

Brennan's gaze shot back to the monitor. Sure enough, standing between two of the blurry figures was a shorter woman roughly Malone's shape. He closed his eyes, caught by a moment of stress and irritation.

"We are coming in, Mr. Brennan. We would be most grateful to not have to shoot her."

94.

Malone had been dreaming, but the images faded as she gradually regained consciousness. She blinked hard, blinding surgical lights above stabbing at her vision. She tried to move, but she'd been restrained with leather straps, tied to a gurney.

She'd given Brennan ten minutes before following him into the main office. Getting into the secure area had been easy enough; then she'd taken a wrong turn and bumped directly into a security guard. They'd injected her with the hypodermic right before Brennan had surrendered.

He'd been struggling as they followed suit, a man restraining him on either side as everything faded to black. Then she'd come to, immobilized.

The gurney began to tilt forward, a motor whirring and vibrating its steel frame. After a few seconds, she was three-quarters upright, like an Egyptian mummy on display, minus the wrap.

"Ah, Ms. Malone! You're awake. Marvelous!" Verde stood on the other side of the small room, near a glass window that looked out onto the broad auditorium.

Five feet to his right, a short southeast Asian man in a checkered short-sleeve dress shirt was setting up a digital camera and tripod. To the diminutive technician's left, a table was covered by a white cloth, steel surgical instruments set up atop it.

"Mr. Dap was what you Americans would call… I think this is right… a real 'up and comer' in Kampuchea, under the Khmer Rouge. Unfortunately, the locals got rather tired of being vivisected by him, and he required new employment. I was going to interrogate you myself, as I have a … history in the area. But on reflection, it seemed somewhat beneath me. In the scope of the number of people I'm going to kill, you're not even a rounding error's rounding error."

Verde took off the lab coat he'd been wearing all day. He had a purple silk shirt and tie under it, and he rolled up the cuffs on the shirt sleeves. "Still, it's rather warm down here today. I must talk to the maintenance staff about that…"

Malone tried to talk but her throat muscles seemed paralyzed, the barest squeak emitting.

"Oh, that's the paralytic, unfortunately," Verde said. "It's quite powerful, a curare derivative I picked up from a local shaman many years ago. Your friend Mr. Brennan is watching you in the interrogation room next door, through the one-way glass, right now."

The smaller man had begun to disinfect the surgical tools with isopropyl alcohol. Malone felt a surge of panic, her heart racing.

She flashed back for the barest of moments to the night, five years earlier, when a North Korean spy had stood above her prone figure, about to end her life. It had been terrifying, but this was no less so, the notion of being agonizingly tortured somehow worse than death.

"I thought about working on Mr. Brennan and we actually got started, but after a few minutes it was apparent that he has been thoroughly trained to withstand typical methods involving intense neuropathic pain. My lieutenants found some information about him via a Dark Web broker; he's been in some impressive situations. And on at least one occasion… you alongside him."

She tried to call out, but the barest dry cackle emerged.

"My mentor was a man utterly bereft of any real human sentiment, addicted to the adrenaline from causing pain. He observed, when we lived in the jungle together, that it was much more effective to gain compliance by torturing or assaulting a child than it was to do the same to their parent. The parent cared more about the other person than themselves. I imagine Mr. Brennan has a similar degree of self-sacrifice to him, based on his track record. I think it would be unbearable for him to watch and listen as Mr. Dap flays the skin from your body."

She could picture Brennan at an interview table, his wrists chained to a tether, watching her on a flatscreen as Mr. Dap approached with the scalpel. Malone had spent the most harrowing days of her life with Joe Brennan and she knew what a good man he was. But she had no idea what he might have found before she was caught; she had no idea how high the stakes were.

And that meant she had no idea whether he would intercede when the little man started to slice her to pieces.

"I—I don't know anything..." she managed to scratchily whisper.

Verde smiled warmly. "I don't care."

The torturer stood next to the tilted gurney, his eyes curious and wide as he studied her from head to toe, like an auctioneer assessing a piece of furniture.

"Now, Mr. Dap... did we agree on a place to begin? I believe you'd brought me around to the notion that Ms. Malone might be more interesting in appearance without her nose..."

Verde's assistant grinned widely and chuckled, like a bully with a birthday cake. He raised the scalpel, holding it like a fine fountain pen, the flat of the razor-sharp blade brushing the side of her nose. He burbled like a happy child, then blurted out something in a language Malone didn't understand.

"Yes! Yes, yes, as you wish," Verde said. "I imagine it will be quite painful. Now… Ms. Malone, I have a ceremony to attend in fifteen minutes…"

"The… timelock," Malone managed. Even debilitated, she pushed for more information.

"Quite so. Once engaged, titanium blast doors will engage on both sides of the facility, closing us off absolutely to the world above. The exterior entrances will be concealed and we are thirty feet underground. Nobody will ever hear from you again, Ms. Malone. You've written your last story."

The tiny torturer leaned over her, using the surgically gloved thumb-and-forefinger on his left hand to hold her eyelid open. He reached down with his other hand, the blade glinting under the surgical lights.

95.

WASHINGTON

Jonah Tarrant stared out of the office window at the trees adjacent to the Langley Headquarters' parking lot. The leaves were falling, the branches nearly all stripped of foliage for the Fall.

He was always morose at this time of year, as they approached the anniversary of the moment he'd shot and killed his treacherous former boss, David Fenton-Wright, saving reporter Alex Malone's life, but opening a rift in his own soul, the weight of killing a burden no man should have to bear.

They needed some good news. There were just days left, and they still had no idea what the International Family was up to in Argentina, or in the United States. He felt the gravity of his responsibility, the knowledge that the entire nation could pay for his decisions. It was more than a man in his forties should have to take, he thought.

It was the kind of responsibility that required a wiser man, probably an older man. Perhaps that was why so many of his predecessors had been in their sixties, Tarrant supposed. They'd made that many more mistakes, survived those extra near misses. At the least, their calluses were thicker, their skin tougher to penetrate.

There was a knock on his door. "Come in," he yelled, pausing for one last look outdoors before turning.

It was Adrienne Hayes. "We might have something."

But she didn't look like they had something, Tarrant thought. She looked as though she was as gravely worried as him. "Why do I not feel convinced this is big?"

"I'm not sure we have time to do anything with it. Or what it means, if I'm being frank, Jonah."

"Nevertheless, you're here, which means you think I need to know about it." For all of her faults and her caustic ambition, his number two understood how busy he was and when to stay away.

"One of the analysts found an unsolved homicide from Nineteen Sixty-Seven, in Chester, Pennsylvania."

That twigged his ear. He'd been over Matthew Misner's book-thick biographical folder. There was something in there about Chester. "What's the connection?" he said. "Grandfather?"

"Great uncle. The victim, Luigi De Cesare of Chester, was shot with a Luger and dumped with weights into the Delaware River. He didn't lose enough flesh to rot or predation until the ice was out the next spring, at which point he popped up but was unidentified."

"So…"

"So a Philly cop with a habit of digging into cold cases got a private lab to run a cheap DNA screen on some of the recovered clothing and they got a match with a family still living in Philly. It seems Grandpa Luigi disappeared in the late Sixties. He had a membership in what the family describes as "a secret men's club, a society of some sort." They figured it a cover for compulsive gambling, as he never seemed able to get ahead, and that maybe the Philly mob wacked him."

"They had that tough reputation… but I'm guessing that's not the important part."

"The important part is that for fifteen years, after moving here from Italy, his neighbor was one Jacob Grech, the great uncle of Matthew Misner. And get this: according to their emigration and resettlement records, they came over on the same ship."

"And…"

"And the family admits that grandma did not speak highly of Luigi. In fact, she called him "Quel bastardo fascista!", or…"

"That fascist bastard. Yeah, I get the gist."

"He was a Mussolini sympathizer and brown shirt in Italy. The grandmother also remembers that he was at Jacob's house a lot, and she worried about him teaching fascist views to the two boys, Mark and Joseph."

"Joseph Misner? Matthew's father was Jacob Grech's nephew?"

"He helped raise the boy."

Jonah turned back to the window and looked back out at the fallen leaves. They could throw a team on a lead like that and it would still take months to get anything useful, if it even existed so many years after the fact. He could try to grill the candidate about it, but he'd become annoyed by the constant inferences that he was up to something no good.

"Jonah…"

"Yeah… Yeah, just thinking. Have we talked to the cold case cop?"

"We have. He has a theory that De Cesare met regularly at an old automat restaurant…"

He turned back to her. "A what?"

"An automat. Did you ever see those old Doris Day movies? They had them in those. They were self-serve restaurants where all the stuff was in wall slots…"

"Oh. Oh yeah, those. So…"

"So… it closed decades ago. But he's still working the case…"

"Okay."

"Jonah… If you don't mind my saying, you don't seem yourself. Do you want to get someone going on this or…"

He nodded absently. "Yeah. Yeah, sure. See who you can get free, okay? Handle it."

"Are you…?"

"I'm okay. Just tired. I haven't had a day off since New York, two years ago. When this is done, no matter what happens…"

"Yes?" She looked momentarily fascinated, like a kid who's waiting to find out if they've been singled out. He had to remember how much she wanted his job.

"I'm going fishing."

He turned back to the window. It was cold outside. He hated it being down to Brennan again, like their fates were constantly tied. He'd given the man what he wanted, a way out. Then he'd foolishly brought him back in, used him for a job as a favor to Carolyn and put him back into the mix as a consequence.

On the whole, he liked their chances better with Brennan than without, which he also hated. Whatever the spy was doing, Jonah was certain, he'd be on top of things.

96.

NUEVA ESPERANZA

Brennan watched helplessly through the two-way glass as Verde and his assistant next door prepared to torture Alex. The torturer walked over to a steel table draped in a white cloth and selected a scalpel.

The agent yanked at his restraints; his wrists were shackled together by a chain that in turn was secured through an anchoring iron loop attached to the table.

A middle-aged, white-coated scientist with a balding crown of hair and a stubby moustache had been asking Brennan questions, sitting on the side of the rectangular table, near enough to be personal but just out of reach. When the American yanked at the chain, he scribbled a notation.

The sound of the pencil scratching on paper continued for a few seconds. Brennan eyed him contemptuously. "What possible purpose could you have for taking notes?" he asked.

His captor shrugged. "Dr. Verde keeps precise records of every change we make in the facility, for the purposes of iterative improvement. How do you feel, Mr. Brennan? Does the threat of your friend's imminent pain and suffering anger you?"

"I prefer to think of it as extra motivation for that special moment."

The man appeared puzzled. "That… special moment?"

"When I snap your neck and end your life."

The man looked genuinely taken aback. "I … I am just doing my job, Mr. Brennan, following orders…"

"Yeah, you fascist types are good at that, aren't you? It won't help you. And if she dies, I'll make sure you die a lot slower."

He knew the threats weren't likely to produce any helpful action, but they seemed to unnerve the smaller man, and that could only help. He'd been slowly moving the chain one link to each side, then two, then three, probing for a weakness. Finding none, he'd begun assessing how he'd get out of the room once unchained. Even if he could disarm his interrogator, Brennan knew there were still two guards on the other side of the door who would likely hear it and intervene.

In the other room, the torturer had picked up one of the scalpels and approached Malone. Verde said something, then left the room. The man leaned over her.

You're out of time. Screw subtlety.

"Now, Mr. Brennan, I'd like you to watch as Mr. Dap works on your friend and be sure to let me know when you're ready to discuss your plans with ---" Before he could finish the sentence, Brennan stood and leaned forward, placing both hands on the iron hoop like a gymnast on a pommel horse. He swung his legs out wide, the chained chair coming with them as he smashed it into the interrogator, four feet away.

The chair splintered as the tiny man went down, stunned. Brennan leaped to his feet, pushing off them and flying through the air, coming down knees first on the man's head. He felt a sickening crunch of breaking bones but didn't bother checking, certain the man was either dead or incapacitated. He reached down and fumbled through the other man's pocket for the keys, knowing he had just seconds until...

The door swung wide open, the two guards rushing in, both carrying automatic weapons. They trained them on the prone American. Brennan raised his arms.

They approached him. The American glanced at the one-way window on the wall. The noise had given Mr. Dap pause and he stood a foot clear of Malone, waiting to find out what had just happened.

"We have instructions that should you attempt to escape we are supposed to kill you on sight." The guard smiled as he said it, raising the rifle to shoulder height and aiming down its sightline. "Adios, you dirty mother —"

The man stopped talking and his face contorted into a look of pure shock. His partner, two feet away, did the same.

Both men tried to reach behind them for the split-second it took the two stilettos to slide into their basal ganglias, the clumps of nerves connecting the spine and the brain. Both slumped to the ground, dead.

Peter Bruner stood there for a few seconds, the two knives dripping blood onto the tile. He moved over to Brennan, taking the key from the dead interrogator's pocket and unbinding their captive.

"I don't get it," Brennan said. "You're his right-hand man."

"I owed him a life debt," Bruner said. "He saved my child…my boy. I never believed he would actually go ahead with this insane plan. And besides, if he succeeds, the International Family will put a price on my head that guarantees I won't survive a year."

Brennan finally understood. "He wasn't working for them at all. He was just using their money."

Bruner nodded. "They wanted him to create a master race. But Gabriel did not want them to be part of it, only his own genetically superior subjects. I … believed they would have a contingency, a loyal believer close to him who would end this before it got out of hand. But that did not happen."

"Let me guess: you figured the Nazis would be competent this time, right? Good call, genius." The American's attention shot to the window as he rose to his feet. "Alex…!

"You don't have time to save her," Bruner insisted. "There are two guards on that room, also, and Verde will trip the time lock in a matter of minutes.

350

Brennan grabbed the elderly man by the collar and shoved him into the wall. "If she dies, you die."

"Please... Mr. Brennan, be practical. She has no time left..." Bruner turned his head towards the one-way glass and Brennan's eyeline followed. Mr. Dap had walked back to the gurney and was once more leaning over her, the scalpel hovering over her left eye.

The American ran towards the one-way glass and threw his shoulder into it. It buckled slightly but didn't crack.

"It's safety glass, bulletproof," Bruner insisted.

In the other room, the shaking of the glass gave the torturer pause once more. He stood up straight and looked back over his shoulder.

Brennan knew if they were going to save her it had to be right then. He glanced around the room, a growing sense of helplessness gnawing at him. Then he fixed Bruner with a hard glare. "I have an idea but I need your help. And if this doesn't work...we're not even yet."

They had just one shot, he knew, before Mr. Dap began to cut Malone to pieces.

97.

Mr. Dap had been chattering for a minute straight. The tone suggested he was talking to himself, but Malone couldn't be sure. Then he leaned over the gurney and looked directly at her as he chattered once more.

"I don't understand," she offered feebly. She tugged with her fingers at the leather restraints but they hadn't given a millimeter.

"I say in Vietnamese, 'you have lovely eyes'. And now I cut one out to keep it, for souvenir." He grinned maniacally and laughed slightly, a loopy, crazed giggle. The point of the scalpel rested ever-so-briefly on the soft skin of her eyelid. Alex began to tremble uncontrollably, every muscle trying to pull away from him, her shackles making it impossible.

The ceiling caved in, tiles crashing to the ground as Brennan plunged out of the crawl space, falling to the concrete floor ten feet below. Mr. Dap did not flinch, turning and charging at the crouching figure, swinging the scalpel in rapid arcs, slashing at the American spy with abandon.

Brennan rolled backwards and came to his feet, but the smaller man was fast and was on him immediately. He blocked the first two swipes with his forearms, the scalpel slicing through his shirt and skin cleanly, warm blood beginning to flow over his arms. The torturer leaned in abruptly and stabbed at his torso, the scalpel sliding into Brennan's stomach... but only as far as the one-inch blade could carry it.

Mr. Dap looked up, alarmed, realizing his mistake just as Brennan's left fist came down on his wrist, shattering the small bones, the scalpel still lodged in his stomach muscles.

The smaller man screamed at the pain, just as Brennan's right hand caught him flush on the chin, knocking the man unconscious. The doors to the chamber burst open, the two guards charging in.

They raised their weapons... and once again, a look of open-mouthed shock struck both of them. They collapsed, Bruner standing behind them as he had in the interrogation room, the stiletto knives finding their target efficiently.

Brennan rushed over to Alex. "Are you..."

"I'm... I'm okay," she said. "Just groggy."

Bruner joined him and began to untie her. "Go! We do not have time..."

Brennan sprinted across the cell to the door.

"Where are you going?!" she demanded. "Wait for me, already!"

"He's right, we don't have time," he said. "Remember what he said outside: at midnight, a time lock will shut this compound tight, and the cure to his deadly virus with it."

"There's a cart in the hall," Bruner said. "Go! Now!"

Brennan found the golf cart and stepped on the accelerator, the electric vehicle shooting forward down the long corridor, towards the main auditorium.

On the wall near the detention center doors, an analog clock read 11:57.

He prayed it was slow.

He didn't see the two men; they waited until the last moment to step out of the Systems office, both with pistols extended. "Halt or we open fire!" one yelled.

Brennan ducked low to the steering wheel and floored the cart, the tiny needle on the dash gauge hitting thirty-five kilometers per hour as it slammed into both, their gunfire high and wide of their target.

A body flew sideways, into the wall, skull cracking against the stone. The cart swerved from the impact and crashed into the wall opposite. The second man was scrambling for his pistol, his fingers finding the butt of the gun. He began to turn back to Brennan.

The American yanked hard on the steering wheel, the semi-circle of plastic and rubber coming free in his hand. He lashed out with a mighty cut, the wheel slamming into the man's temple, knocking him cold.

He climbed out of the damaged cart, grabbing the man's pistol from the floor. On the man's wrist a few feet away, a watch dial ticked down, the two hands nearly converging at twelve.

He sprinted down the hall, reaching the third concourse door a moment later. Brennan ripped it open. At the back of the auditorium a vast computer workstation fronted the enclosed examination rooms. A handful of men were standing in front of it, including Verde, his ever-present bodyguard Manuel and the public relations man, Blake.

In front of Verde, projecting slightly from the console, was a large red button.

The sound of the door slamming open caught their attention, everyone turning to the exit. Verde's face contorted with rage. "Stop him!" he screamed at the half-dozen guards standing ten feet away.

They turned in unison, machine pistols that had been slung over their shoulders brought to bear. Brennan dove head-first down the steps, sliding on his chest along the smooth metal edges to the bottom as gunfire riddled the concourse, bullets tearing holes in the hallway wall. He rolled into a crouch behind a centrifuge.

It could've been worse, he told himself. *If he'd done this earlier, you'd have eighty scientists in here as well.*

The guards peppered the technology with gunfire. Brennan looked up at the wall. The clock stood at 11:59.

"KILL HIM, YOU IDIOTS!" Verde screamed, apoplectic with rage.

Brennan knew he was out of time. He peeked around the end of the block of machinery. A volley sent him back into cover, but he'd seen enough, a digital readout above the key counting down from 30 seconds...

29...

28...

He sprinted to his right, behind the open lab tables, emptying half the pistol's clip in the guards' direction and forcing them to scatter for a few seconds. Brennan made it halfway to the back wall before they had an unprotected bead on him again. He ducked low, beneath the tabletops, creeping on his haunches.

21...

20..

19...

18...

He rounded the end of the row of tables. They were just twenty yards away, closing on both sides. He stayed low, out of the guards' line of sight. They'd find him soon, he knew, but the row of furniture would provide cover almost to...

A guard stepped out in front of him, spotting him at the last second and raising the machine pistol. Brennan aimed center mass and squeezed the trigger, jerking it with atypical panic, the bullets striking the man in the middle of his chest.

12...

11...

10...

9...

"You're too late, Mr. Brennan," Verde said loudly. "I made a promise to the world to deliver change, and I intend to keep it." He reached for the button.

Brennan rose to his feet and sprinted, ignoring the other guards, gunfire crashing through the "bulletproof" safety glass along the back wall, pieces shattering to the ground. He saw Verde's hand rest atop the button and he raised the pistol, squeezing the trigger one more time.

It clicked and the slide drew back, the chamber and magazine both empty. Brennan stared, slack-jawed, at the useless weapon, realizing he was out of time and options.

Verde was right. He was too late.

"To a new and better world," Verde said.

The hand came out of nowhere, reaching up beside the scientist, the gun at Verde's temple before he could react, the concussive blast knocking him over sideways before he could push the button. The bullet blew a hole through the right side of his skull, bone and brain matter smattering the console.

Verde dropped prone to the ground, dead before he reached it.

Brennan stood and stared in shock. The remaining guards had turned that way but had not opened fire, obviously as stunned.

Verde's bodyguard, Manuel, stood with his pistol extended, smoke still drifting from the muzzle. He saw Brennan staring at him, then looked down at the body of his long-time employer.

He gave Brennan a half-smirk, half-grimace. "Heil Hitler," he said. He placed the muzzle under his own chin and pulled the trigger.

98.

Nov. 1, 2020

LONDON

Peter Chappell stared at the extensive file folder on top of his desk. He still liked things on paper. Atop the sheath of pages were candid photos of Verde and the compound, along with an older service headshot of Archie Grimes.

He closed the cover of the folder. "Right then, I expect that covers most of it," he said. "What isn't in the file we'll get out of Peter Bruner. Our Argentine colleagues are quite rightly rather embarrassed by all of this. They're somewhat sick of being seen as a haven for Nazis."

On the other side of the desk, Brennan sat with Jonah Tarrant, Martin Weiss and Charlie Rich. They'd spent three hours going over the details of Verde's plan. The hundred youth he'd recruited to spread the virus had been discretely picked up by authorities in forty-six different countries.

"There is still, of course, the matter of young Mr. Rich..." Chappell leaned back in his chair and arched his fingers together, resting them above his belly as he gave Charlie a withering stare. "Regardless of his help in tracking down the data the International Family found so important..."

"A not-inconsiderable effort on his part..." Weiss reminded him.

"And it's apparent importance to our American colleagues..."

"The IF has a bigger goal," The CIA acting director interjected. "Verde was threatening that, so they got rid of him. But that means it's still a significant issue, whatever it turns out to be."

Brennan hated the doubletalk. They both knew the IF was targeting the election, trying to get Matthew Misner elected. They just didn't know why. "If it wasn't for Charlie, we wouldn't have known the virus existed in the first place," he interrupted. "Maybe we quit the officious limey bullshit and give the kid a break. Okay?"

Chappell sighed and leaned forward. "It most certainly is not okay, Mr. Brennan. What message would it send if we allowed any young person with a laptop to get off scot-free for breaking into a government institution?"

Charlie hung his head.

"However," Chappell continued, "given the fact that he placed his own life at considerable peril to help unmask Archibald Grimes as a double agent... the consensus is that a non-felonious charge with a sentence of community service might be in order. We've unfortunately lost our lead systems analyst, thanks to Archie Grimes' misinformation. We could use someone who's less management inclined and more technically up to date to come in and work with us. If such an agreement were reached with young Mr. Rich, perhaps the charges could be waived."

Charlie perked up. "Really?"

Chappell tried his best at a reassuring smile. "Really."

After the meeting, the four took the creaky, slow elevator down to the lobby of the SIS building. "This is where I leave you," Weiss said. It had occurred to him that Joe still didn't know he was with the MOSSAD. The quicker they separated, the less likely it was that Charlie would raise the point. "Can I give you a lift somewhere, Charlie?"

The young coder nodded. "Yeah. Yeah, there's a pub in Highgate that has a large pint of Smithwicks with my name on in. You should join me. I'm buying."

"Bloody right, you are."

"I owe you --" He turned so he was facing both Martin and Joe. "I owe both of you my life. I don't know how to..."

Brennan raised a palm. "It's what we do. And you're welcome. Just... stay out of trouble, okay, kid?"

Charlie smiled devilishly. "Oh... I'll try." Then he frowned and turned back to Martin. "I'm sorry about Ruby, I truly am."

Weiss clapped the young man on the back. "That was on Archibald Grimes, not you. Ruby... Ruby was wonderful. But knowing her as a copper, she'd have been proud that her death helped save your life. It won't bring her back but at least she mattered, right to the end. That's more honor than most people find in the end, I'd say. All right?"

Charlie shrugged reluctantly. "All right is the best we can hope for, I suppose."

Weiss pointed them towards the front doors. "Let's go get that beer."

"My friend Aubrey will be there. Be warned: he thinks he's incredibly funny."

The former policeman sighed a little as they walked off together. "In for a penny, in for a pound, I suppose."

Once they were gone, Brennan nodded Jonah Tarrant's way. "And us? I take it once your people have paid me for all of this, we're back to keeping a respectful distance."

"If that's what you want, Joe…"

"Yeah. Yeah, that's what I want, Jonah."

The other man took out his phone. "I'll call for a car. It's time we went home."

THEN

May 30, 1996

GENEVA, Switzerland

His bones ached.

Francois Genoud leaned on the mahogany cane and sorted through the book-sized jewelry box on his study bookshelf. He was eighty-one years old, and he no longer slept for more than a few hours at a time. He knew his life's work, to see Fascism restored to power globally, would go unfulfilled while he still lived, and it ate at him more thoroughly than the cancer destroying his digestive system.

He withdrew a pile of old letters, the pages turned faint brown with age. He saw his address on the first envelope and the return address in the corner and smiled.

Genoud turned awkwardly and paced back to his Louis XV rolltop desk. On one corner, a silver tray held the remainder of the pot of coffee his nurse, Martina, had brought for him.

Genoud sat down behind the desk. He placed the small pile of letters on top of it. Had it really been so long?

He opened the first. It was dated June 18, 1975.

Francois,

By the time you receive this, I may already be dead.

The Jews could not kill me, nor the Godless Russians, nor the fatuous Americans. Tobacco, however, has had no such hesitation.

I prefer to think all we smokers have always known that inhaling a burning leaf cannot be good for the constitution; but I found it to be a salve for the soul.

Nonetheless, it was deadly, and it has killed me.

I have lung cancer and am not expected to survive the summer.

I am at my Madrid home, where people fuss over me and leave me feeling, in general, like a bloody invalid. I have tried to keep myself busy by writing to my colleagues in intelligence from around the world and receiving the odd phone call. I considered writing my memoirs but decided that most would not believe them, and those that did might condemn me to Hell.

But I would not change a minute of it. Oh, if I could, I would have shot that idiot Hitler in the head myself, back when Canaris and his mates were plotting. But once the fate of fascism was tied to him, that was no longer an option.

He was such a powerful figurehead, even in his insane days of delusion, that I regret we failed in our bid to clone him. Mengele, as you know, fled and disappeared. The old guard in Argentina, Egypt and Syria is tired, dying off. They are in hiding, hounded by Wiesenthal and his people.

But we still have Eternal Glory. When the time is right, the groundwork will be in place. I can go to my grave knowing that although my time comes, the struggle is not yet over.

When I am judged by God, at least he will know that, whether condemned for eternity for my blood lust and pursuit of power, I was true to my beliefs and convictions: in the legacy of Charlemagne, of the Knights of Malta, the Junkers and the warrior nobility that raised our species from the mud.

We have long been friends though I confess I had few soft spots for anyone in this life. I wish you the best in the continued struggle. Go with God,

Otto Skorzeny,

Madrid, Spain

P.S. – Our IF contact in Russia is optimistic, I'm told. He has managed to recruit a young lawyer, a recent graduate from Leningrad State University, who we believe will have a bright future in politics. If not America, perhaps…?

Genoud folded the letter back up and placed it back on top of the pile.

Skorzeny had died a month after its arrival.

Eternal Glory? It seemed to have faded into the realm of hope, at best. The boy had become a man, guided by the last of their appointed mentors. He joined the military, served with distinction in Iraq, and now was a wealthy stockbroker.

But the mentor, a physicist named Christopher Delph, had cut off contact; their international ranks had thinned. The hard right was out of vogue, and there was no longer an infrastructure in America to monitor their project properly, to pressure the man.

Genoud's age and poor health restricted how much time he could spend recruiting and lobbying. Fascism had no public face anymore. Skorzeny's dream of a spider-web, a movement without structure, had kept them alive. But it had also robbed any vitality from recruitment.

Genoud had high hopes that the new leader of the International Family, Michael Wolf, would turn it around. He was young; just thirty and newly appointed as CEO of his father's companies in Vienna.

Until that happened, however, the project seemed stalled. He knew the reality: that three generations of political groups had been seeded with IF money, used to sow social discord; that the quality of life in the United States would go into sharp decline as more money moved to overseas manufacturing on third-world wages. Within twenty or so years, by early in the new millennium, Genoud guessed, the stage would be set. Only then would they learn if their ultimate gambit paid dividends.

But he knew he would not be around to see it. The cancer could perhaps be beaten, but Genoud was tired of the fight. On the table next to the jewelry box sat that morning's issue of Paris' *Le Figaro* newspaper. It was turned over to the lower-half fold. A headline in bold type in French read, "Swiss financier probed in terror, holocaust theft cases." A fifteen-year-old head-and-shoulders photo of Genoud sat underneath it in black and white.

The single gunshot echoed through the old townhouse, Genoud's blood spattering the front page as his body slumped over the desktop.

99.

NOW

LANGLEY, Virginia

Nov. 3, 2020

The conference room on the fourth floor of the Central Intelligence Agency was having its most casual night in a decade.

Most attending were officially off work but had had some role in ensuring the election's safety or investigating foreign influence. They'd been allowed to expense pizzas and Jonah Tarrant had even okayed a couple of beers each.

Analysts who rarely got to see the inside of the conference room had taken most of the soft, leather-bound chairs that surrounded the enormous oblong table. On the wall, the eighty-inch projector had on CNN's coverage of the results.

"You look nervous."

Tarrant turned, hands in pocket. He hadn't expected to see Joe Brennan again any time soon. They'd deposited his check for both assignments. "I thought you'd be staying away and spending tonight with Carolyn and the kids."

"She understood. I couldn't shake the feeling after London that there was something you weren't telling me. That it wasn't just the coincidence of skinheads and militia showing up at his rallies."

Tarrant studied his own shoelaces. "This might be one you should just drop, Joe," he said gently.

"I hear you called Malone's editor, convinced him to spike her story."

He looked circumspect about that, like he wasn't happy to have made the decision. "I don't like interfering with the press. But he agreed a lot of what she had was speculative, without her getting to see Verde's files."

"You could have just given her this one."

"And terrified half the world's population into thinking there are mad men around the corner trying to poison them? I don't think so. Besides, she got the scoop on his "suicide". She'll still get paid. She'll still get credit."

"She just won't get the real story, which is what she values."

"I can live with that."

"So? What is the whole story, Jonah? What haven't you told me, as usual?"

He clearly didn't want to discuss it, his discomfort etched across his face. "A lot depends on..."

He was interrupted by a cheer from the other end of the room. On the giant television screen, an anchor was announcing results. "... of the vote counted, we are confident in projecting that, even with absentee ballots still to come, Matthew Misner has been elected the next President of the United States."

The camera cut to a remote at Misner's headquarters, the crowd going insane with joy, champagne corks popping, volunteers hugging one another. Then it cut to a podium. "It appears we're about to hear from the President-elect now..."

At the campaign office, speakers began blaring "Celebration" by Kool and the Gang. As Misner walked onto the stage, his wife and young sons in tow, streams and confetti rained down.

He was smiling confidently at the podium, waving to sections of the crowd. A few feet to his right, his campaign manager, Stuart Chiasson, stood proudly applauding.

The crowd quieted on command as he prepared to speak.

Misner nodded a few times, as if too impressed with them to begin.

"WE LOVE YOU MATTHEW!" someone screamed at the back of the room.

"And I love each and every one of you! And I thank you, Ginny and the kids thank you... Tonight, you've made me so proud to be your candidate, and so proud to be an American."

The crowd broke into more cheers, a frenzied celebration. "MATTHEW! MATTHEW! MATTHEW!"

He used both hands to quiet them. "I also have to thank my best friend of forty years, Stu Chiasson, for once again running the campaign and doing all the real work!"

The crowd interrupted again, chanting Stuart's name. A few feet away, he began to blush furiously.

"We're going to Washington to make changes," Misner said. "We're going to Washington to help this nation heal. To end the division, the petty squabbling and the overwhelming influence of greed..."

As the crowd drowned him out again, he appealed for silence. Brennan tapped Tarrant's shoe with his own to draw his attention. "Is he on those lists we got from Wolf's company, Jonah? Or maybe his parents?"

The acting director looked bleak. "That's on a need-to-know basis..."

"And."

"And you don't."

"He's just been elected President of the United States..."

Tarrant nodded. "He has."

"Yet you don't seem worried."

But Tarrant was terrified. He had no idea whether the International Family had gotten to Matthew Misner somehow. He also had no doubt it had targeted and supported his campaign, as had dozens of known members.

He'd been screened back to childhood, to his twelfth birthday, his father's suicide and his adoption by Professor Christopher Delph.

Delph's family was on the list, too, having fled East Germany at the end of the war and Berlin's partition. But three decades had passed since then, three decades in which neither man had given any sign of disloyalty to America or of radical beliefs. Delph had been dead for six years.

"You don't know, do you?" Brennan asked. "That's why you couldn't stop tonight. You have no idea where his allegiance lies."

"No. No, we don't. Despite the fringe support, he didn't encourage them. He said all of the right things while running. And ultimately?" Tarrant took a deep, anxious breath of air. "Ultimately it's not up to us whether the world sets itself ablaze."

Misner had quieted the crowd again. "My Fellow Americans, the last year has been one of continual challenge and pain. We have been pitted against one another too often. We have judged one another from afar, relying on the half-truths and exaggerations of Internet culture to guide us, rather than common sense and decency. And it has to stop. This... fear, this rank distrust. This belief in conspiracy, that there are easy villains to blame for every problem, that everyone who disagrees with us is somehow wrong or evil. It has to end for this great nation to not only thrive, but to merely survive.

"In my term I pledge this: I shall work to make the greatest country in the world even better. I shall reach across the aisle to our ideological adversaries, in the recognition that no one side can lay claim to all the right answers. More than anything, I pledge to continue to do what I've tried to do my entire adult life, which is to fight for you, to fight for a better tomorrow. To fight for the things that I believe in and to represent the values you cherish. Together, we can accomplish anything. Of that I have no doubt."

"You have evidence," Brennan insisted, the room's attention glued to the big screen. "You have a paper trail; you have the data Charlie Rich recovered..."

"We have nothing," Tarrant replied. "We have patterns, we have fifty-year-old lists. We have donations from some of the wrong people. And we know, roughly, what the IF has been up to since the Second World War. But none of that is proof of anything concerning Matthew Misner. And you know that, Joe. You've been doing this too long not to."

"So... in the end, nothing changes? All we can do is hope?"

"Hope can be a powerful thing," Tarrant suggested. "Don't knock it until you've tried it."

100.

THEN

September 4, 1980

TUCSON, Arizona

It was just after four in the afternoon and twelve-year-old Matthew Misner sat on the empty bench at a playground, watching older boys play pick-up basketball.

It was nearly ninety degrees, despite being early fall. He was depressed and angry.

They'd expected him to go straight to the house from school. It was his last day there, the last chance to spend any time in the home he'd been raised in. Since his mother's death that June and his father's suicide a year prior, he'd been living with Stuart's family while a guardian was arranged. Strings had been pulled, he'd been told, to have him taken in by one of his father's closest friends from college.

He was supposed to be meeting the man at their house, down the street. Then he was supposed to leave it forever, to go live in Cave Creek, just outside Phoenix, with the man and his wife.

But Matthew didn't know him, and he didn't want to go. He didn't want to leave his school friends; they were the only constant in his traumatic childhood, one that had seen his father go slowly insane, ranting about global conspiracies, going on anti-Semitic screeds about bankers running the government and Israel running the bankers.

He wondered what the new guardian was like. There had been an older man, when he was just eight, whom his father had introduced to him and used as a babysitter. It had been presented as a chance for him to help the old man, a neighbor, but Matthew had stopped going to see him, uncomfortable at the man's brazen malice towards his caregiver and adult daughter.

If this man was as unpleasant, it would not be good. Not that it seemed life ever really could be now that his family was dead.

"Matthew?"

He turned his head quickly. The man standing at the end of the bench had a light, round-collared jacket on that said "Club International" on the lapel. He seemed ancient, though not as old as Matthew's own father or the neighbor.

"Matthew, my name is Christopher. I'm a friend of your father; I guess they told you about me. We went to University together at Yale."

The boy hung his head, breaking eye contact.

"Matthew, I understand this has got to be really hard for you…"

"Did your father kill himself?"

"Well… no."

"Then you don't understand."

Delph nodded without immediately replying. Instead, he sat down on the other end of the bench. "Do you mind if I ask you a question, since I've told you a little about me?"

"Whatever."

"Do you like yourself?"

That was odd. No one had ever asked him that before. "What?"

"You know… are you happy with who you are as a person?"

"I don't know." Matthew felt perplexed. "I'm twelve."

"Yes, but you're also gifted, a very bright person. Let's say you could; let's say you looked inward a little, at who you are and how you behave and think. Are you happy with who you are?"

Matthew frowned, and this time the other man paid attention, the look one of profound sadness, a little boy who felt overwhelmed by the world. "No. I feel stupid. I feel like I'm treading water all the time, like if I can't figure out what everyone wants from me, I'll sink."

The man turned his way slightly. "That's pretty normal at your age. But… what if I told you that you didn't have to feel that way, that you didn't need to be so confused by how to make everyone happy? What if you knew what was expected of you and were okay with it? Would you like that?"

He shrugged. "Yeah. Yeah, I guess. But…"

The man reached into his coat pocket and removed a small black book. "This is for you. It's something very special, handed down through four generations of my family. There's an inscription for you in the front."

Matthew took the proffered book. The gold gilt type on the front cover had been worn away by time and he could just barely make out the words "Book of Common Prayer."

He opened it and began to read.

Aug. 29, 1980

Dear Matthew,

This book was handed down across four generations and travelled thousands of miles to reach you.

But first, it was given to my grandfather, Wilhelm Canaris, by your great-grandfather, Hassan Al Saad.

Without Hassan's intervention to save my grandfather from certain death, I would not stand here today. My children would not be alive. My wife would not be the woman I have loved and yearned to be with for forty-two years.

I was born into privilege and money, Matthew.

For many years, in order to accept how much more comfort I had than others, I chose to delude myself. I allowed myself to see others as lesser and myself as somehow deserving of God's favor.

I was surrounded by familiar people and families from the old country, people who reinforced this selfish message.

But my grandfather knew better. He died during the Second World War, executed for plotting to assassinate Adolf Hitler, an evil man. He felt great guilt, he told my father, for failing to recognize prior to 1937 what Hitler was. He attempted to rectify that error, unsuccessfully.

He kept his family secret to protect them. He knew what his nation had become. He would tell my father that "there is no true merit without decency. As long as we never forget that, we will be fine."

So: we will take a journey together as you come to live with us, and as we both learn how to be more decent.

Much of what I tell you will run contrary to what you have been taught. I know your father was a good man at heart, before evil interests interceded and drove him to his end.

But I believe in you, and I believe you can open your mind to new ideas. To difference and change. To accepting the differences in others not as weaknesses but as gifts.

There will always be people who want to control you, Matthew, powerful people with big ideas for how the world should be. People who tried to drive your father to hate others and will do the same with you. And I know this, because they wanted me to do it also, you see.

They have a lot of money and power, but also a lot of bad, selfish ideas. Ideas that don't include most people being free. We'll have to be careful. But if you work with me, we can make sure they don't succeed.

We can do it just by being more decent. By helping others.

And I can repay to you the debt my grandfather owed a fisherman, a simple man who took great risks nonetheless. The man who saved his life.

And mine.

Sincerely,

Christopher Gunther Delph

Matthew finished reading and closed the cover. He wasn't sure what to make of it. But he felt... better. For the first time since he was very small, he did not feel quite so alone.

Delph rose and held out his hand. "Yes?"

Perhaps it was emotional dissonance, born of years listening to conflicting messages. But it only took a moment for the boy to accept it and shake.

It was the first time Matthew had smiled in months.

The professor saw the steely determination in the boy's eyes and felt a swell of relief. Ultimately, he knew, all that it took to stand up to evil was a person having the strength of will to do so.

And he knew he was not too late.

THE END

ABOUT THE AUTHOR

Ian Loome is an Anglo-Canadian author and journalist. He lives in Alberta with his partner, Lori, and many pets, who shed joyfully.

Made in the USA
Las Vegas, NV
06 January 2023

65063057R00205